SAVAGES

Clemens Lucke

Cover designed by Sarah Jane Bennison

First published in the United Kingdom in 2017 by CompletelyNovel.com

ISBN: 9781787231795

For Sarah Jane

"How we see the world changes what we find there."

Iain McGilchrist

LUCKE FAMILY TREE 1640~1753

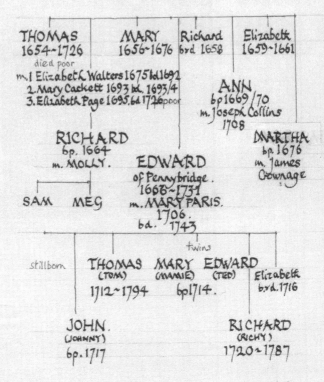

Thomas of Lamberhurst Slade
bp. 1633~bd.1705 will proved 29 Sept 1705
m. Mary (Dorcas)

THOMAS
1654~1726
died poor
m.1 Elizabeth Walters 1675 bd 1692
2. Mary Cackett 1693 bd. 1693/4
3. Elizabeth Page 1695. bd 1726 poor

MARY
1656~1676

Richard
b x d 1658

Elizabeth
1659~1661

ANN
bp 1669/70
m. Joseph Collins
1708

RICHARD
bp. 1664
m. MOLLY.

SAM   MEG

EDWARD
of Pennybridge.
1668~1731
m. MARY PARIS.
1706.
bd. 1743

MARTHA
bp. 1676
m. James
Crownage

stillborn

THOMAS
(TOM)
1712~1794

MARY
(MAMIE)
bp 1714.

twins
EDWARD
(TED)

Elizabeth
b x d. 1716

JOHN.
(JOHNNY)
bp. 1717

RICHARD
(RICHY)
1720~1787

Names in brackets for the purposes of the story

4

Prologue   1666
Slade Farm, Lamberhurst, East Sussex

While the destructive forces of plague and fire raged through the City of London, new life was quickening in the quiet rural village of Lamberhurst. In The Slade, overlooking the village was Slade Farm, where the Lucke family awaited the birth of a child.

Old William sat dozing in the warmth of the parlour fire. Sounds of laughter floated to him from the kitchen where the women were gossiping over their work.

Dorcas, a well-built, capable woman, appeared in the doorway and came to William's side. "Be you comfortable, Farder?" she asked. "I'll be agwain to me chamber prensley. Tell Tamsen if there be aught you needs."

William patted the pregnant belly of his daughter-in-law. "Be this un on 'is way, then? Shall I see un afore I passes?" he asked.

"Behopes 'twill not be long. 'E be kickin' me all-on!" She laughed and planted a kiss on William's forehead before going upstairs.

The old man gazed into the fire and mused on the number of children Dorcas had produced. Would this one be the third or fourth (not counting those that had died)? His son, Thomas, was a lucky man. He would have plenty of help on the farm when they all grew up. William sighed. His thoughts were often in the past nowadays, but all his thinking would never change what had happened.

It was time he sought some fresh air. His limbs were stiffening. He heaved himself out of his chair.

Tamsen came out of the kitchen. Her dark hair was greying and her face had lost its youth. The wife of William's deceased brother Michael, she remained part of the family, coming over to Slade Farm whenever she could. She'd been here more frequently lately as the birth of Dorcas' child became imminent.

She looked at William and said, "Where be you minded ter go, Brudder?"

"I be agwain ter take a walk down the whapple way, Tamsen." William found his stick by the chair and walked across the room.

"Be sure en not ter go too far," she said, "I'll get young Mary ter come along of you."

But William had already left the house. He wanted to be on his own, to sit in his copse for what might be the last time.

On the way he met his son Thomas, with Junior, bringing the tools back to the skillon after the day's coppicing. William gave up any hope of being alone. Junior was told to accompany his gaffer. Then Mary caught up with them. William found himself walking down the grassy path with a grandchild on each side.They reached the copse and found an old tree trunk, lying recumbent on the leaf mould. Moss was growing on the rotting wood. Mary rubbed the soft cushions with the tips of her fingers. She looked up at her gaffer, her nose wrinkled.

"This tree were fallen by last winter's storms," said William as they sat down.

"There's things a-growen on it," said ten-year-old Mary. She stroked the moss again then looked round her at the hazel coppice.

William said, "I helped ter plant these trees when I were your age en I larned how ter coppice them when they were growed. Today, Junior's been helping yer farder ter do the same."

"They've been a-growen all that time," remarked Junior, who was already twelve-years-old.

William was quiet for a few moments, then he started to tell the children stories about the copse. He told them about the storm when the cows breached the hedge and how he was taught to mend it with layering. He talked of Jane, the love of his life; the birth of his son Thomas, their father and of Jane's death. They heard about the bluebells in the spring and how precious this place was to him.

He took a hand of each of his grandchildren and said, "Junior, as you be yer farder's eldest son, this woodland will be yourn one day. You mun promise ter care fer un fer ever en larn yer children ter care fer un too."

Junior nodded. The children left their hands in William's old work-worn ones. They were moved by the sound of his voice in the stillness of the copse. The memory of this evening would echo in their minds for a long time.

After their dinner and later that evening, back in his chair in the parlour, William was conscious of an aura of expectation.

Thomas came in with two mugs of beer and stood them on the hearth to warm up. He sat opposite his father by the fire and said, "Dorcas' birthen pains have started, Farder."

Tamsen came through the parlour to lift the kettle from its hook over the fire saying, "Will you come after me en bring un down betimes I've emptied un, Thomas? Us'll need more water hotted up."

When Thomas had settled himself in his chair again the newly-filled kettle was beginning to sing over the fire. Both men became pensively silent for a while.

William lifted his beer from the hearth and took a long draft. Then he said, "Thomas, I needs ter tell you this afore I passes on. Me Uncle Thomas, on his deathbed, told me about a sum of money that 'e'd put in a safe place fer me, intendin' ter tell me. But I were managing fine without en 'e grew fergetful in 'is old age. I think 'e said, '*Its in the cl...*' en started coughing. 'E died afore 'e could get the words out. I never knew where 'e'd put un. It be in this house somewhere but I've searched all over. If you can find un, it be yourn. Mebbe 'twill turn up when the need arises."

Thomas said, "I'll look fer un, Farder, but I racken you would have found un if 'twere true. 'Twere more likely ter be yer uncle's mind a-wanderin' afore 'e died."

William gazed into the flames as he recalled his dear Uncle who was more like a father to him. He had named his only son after Uncle Thomas. The clock in the hall was a wedding present from him. William remembered the day of his wedding to Jane and his mind turned to his brother Edward, who caused the family so much concern that day and whose life had gone so horribly wrong. William still grieved over the way he had misjudged his brother. How could he have thought that Ed had set fire to the hay? When they were children, they were bre'ncheese friends.

The lusty cries of the newborn roused William from his musing. Thomas jumped out of his chair and ran upstairs. Presently, he came down carrying a bundle.

"Farder, meet my new son," he said. William took the child, cradling him. He was a fine, sturdy baby. He looked at his grandfather with deep black eyes and sighed.

"Ye shall call un Edward," said William.

Part One

Chapter One 1698   Slade Farm

In which Edward starts keeping accounts

Alone in the hall, he unwrapped the book and laid it on the table. The shiny brown leather cover winked at him in the flickering candlelight. He picked it up, stroking its smooth surface, the tooled pattern on both sides. He held it to his face and sniffed the leathery fragrance, then opened it carefully. The white pages stared at him blankly.

Edward Lucke had learned to read and write with the aid of the family Bible but had never had a book of his own. This book had cost him his first wages. It was for writing in. Now that he was working for a master as well as for his elder brother he needed to keep an account of all the money which was owed to him and when it was paid. On the table was a bottle of ink, a freshly-sharpened goose quill and a pot of sand.

Edward opened a drawer in the dresser. He took from it scraps of hide, parchment, paper and cloth. Written on these were the accounts which had accumulated over the six years he'd been working for his brother Thomas Junior. He sifted through them. Some had a big cross over them as paid. These he discarded. When he'd arranged them in date sequence he took the quill and dipped it in the ink. He stared at the blank pages in the book. He didn't want to spoil them. As his hand shook, a drop of ink fell onto the table. In order not to waste any space in the book, he started on the inside of the cover. Taking a deep breath, he began to write down what his brother owed to him:

Thomas Lucke's account.
In the year of 1692 for going to Medston 6 times
    0 – 12 – 0

That year he'd made a number of journeys to Maidstone for Thomas. He'd also worked on the farm for him. As he added up all the money owing, Edward felt anger rising in his chest. He had to put the quill down. Now their father was retired, Thomas Junior was Master of Slade Farm and also head of the household. It was Edward who did most of the work. Thomas spent his time riding round on his horse, flirting with the girls in the village. He had little idea of what was going on on the farm.

The clock on the dresser chimed midday.

Edward heard shouting in the next room. Ann's voice rang out, followed by Thomas' gruff reply. Edward sighed, his sister and brother frequently argued. There was no point in trying to do any more work with that row going on. He sanded the page he'd been writing on, packed up the writing tools and scraps of accounts, shut the book and put everything away in the drawer, making sure that he remembered the sum his brother owed him. He recalled watching his father put his account book in this drawer, years ago. Thomas never kept accounts.

At forty-four years of age, Thomas Lucke Junior had grown from a lithe, handsome youth into a large, ungainly man who was fond of his beer. His third wife, Eliza was patient and faithful. She didn't attempt to admonish him for his misbehaviour, though there was often pain in her eyes. As Edward entered the parlour, his brother's bulk seemed to fill the room, in contrast to his sister Ann, who was a tall, slim woman with dark hair. She stood by the door to the kitchen, red spots of anger on her usually sallow cheeks.

Thomas swung round to face him, knocking his half-empty mug of ale onto the floor. He said, "Edward, will you get this woman out of me hair? I can't abide she naggin'." He bent down to pick up his mug from the pool it had left, peered into it and banged it down on the table.

Edward looked at his younger sister. "What's 'e been at now?" he enquired wearily.

"It's what 'e ain't been at, the lapsy addle-head. But 'tis none of thy concern, Ed. Too late now to make amends. I'll be bodgen, I've got work to do. I'll pay Muvver fer the butter on the way out." Ann left by the back door.

Thomas Senior sat quietly in his chair by the fire, sucking his pipe. "Thanks be 'er be gone, stirrin' us all up. This room be too small fer argifying. Thomas, go en do some work for a change. You be blocking the fire with yer great body en I be minded ter talk to Edward."

As his eldest son left the room singing a bawdy song, Thomas Senior shook his head. He said to Edward, "There beant ever any peace in this house. Get yerself a beer, Son en come en sit down. Now, I be avised you be abouten leave us, like the others."

Edward brought his beer to the fire and placed it on the hearth. He sat in the chair opposite his father. Fondness for the old man conflicted with his need to leave the family home. "You knows I can't work fer Thomas, Farder, I've tried, but 'e be no master. 'E don't care about the farm. En when 'e does work 'tis shoddy en I have ter finish it fer un. 'Tis time I earned a praper living en got meself a wife. 'Tis no good bidin' 'ere." He took a sip of beer.

Thomas Senior took the pipe from his mouth, knocked it on the hearth, then tucked it into his pocket. "When I were thy age, I were minded ter raise a gurt family so's ye could all work on the farm. I weren't a good farmer, but me farder built up this place from naught en I didn't want ter disappoint un." He paused, sighed deeply and continued. "Junior were a rebellious young varmint right from the start. Dorcas let un run rings round the liddle uns.

They all died, bless 'em." He paused. "Then Richard were birthed en you soon after. Ann en Martha came later. I beleft I had a fambly again en us would all labour tergether ter keep Slade Farm a-worken. Me dreams was fulfilled en me farder would rest in peace. But Junior ain't turned out like I hoped. Richard en he was allus at two en you did yer best ter keep the peace. Junior were jealous of thee. 'E rackoned I favoured thee above the others… En I s'pose I do. Ann has never tolerated Junior en Martha, bless she, she be the bly of thy muvver. She just gets on wiv it.

"Richard left home as soon as 'e could; just now Ann's moved out to the cottage and is busy with 'er own business en you can't wait ter get away; that leaves yer sister Martha. She do's what she can en so does Eliza, but they beant farm labourers. Slade Farm's going to ruin, Edward and there's naught I can do about it." He leaned forward and put his head in his hands.

Edward attempted to comfort his father. "You have James. 'E be a good manager. 'E minds what ter be at. Thomas should find a couple of good labourers."

His father raised his head. "James en Moses have held the farm together, but they be gettin' in years en I don't know how long they can carry on. There be no-one ter manage the hop gardens en the oast."

15

"'Tis time ye slaughtered some cattle fer meat. They'll be past it anon and come winter there'll be little fother fer 'em," said Edward.

"Mmm." Thomas nodded. "Us could keep a small milking herd, let some of the pastures lie fallow en slaughter some of the sheep, dappen they be sheared."

The door opened. Martha came in, carrying bread and cheese. She was small and plump, like her mother, with a healthy complexion and bright eyes. Her brown hair was tied back under her cap.

"Be you bidin' fer coager, Ed?" she asked.

Edward looked up. "Yus," he said.

His father pleaded, "Why can't you bide 'ere, Son?" See that Thomas pays thee a praper wage. When 'e be gone, the farm 'll be thine."

Edward was growing impatient. He had to break away from Slade Farm to manage his own life. It was futile staying here being his brother's victim. Why couldn't his father see that?

He raised his voice. "Thomas agreed ter pay me fer work five or six year gone. I've rackoned 'e owes me up'ards of seventeen pounds. How can 'e ever be able ter pay me? The farm beant raisin' any money. There be barely enough fer ye ter eat en there be debts ter pay. The farm'll be worth naught dappen 'e be put in." He got up. He was angry now. "Can't afford ter bide 'ere. I be thirty two years of age. If I'm ter find a wife I needs money ter live on. 'Er won't want ter marry a pauper. There be a cottage at Bat'urst's place where I can bide. He went to the door. "I'll call back fer me things." As he went out past the kitchen he called, "Ferget me coager, Martha. I be bodgen."

Chapter Two   1698 Autumn

In which Edward calls on Mr Dewe

The late afternoon sun cast a warm glow on the buildings on the east side of the yard. Long shadows stretched across the cobbled ground under their feet. The evenings were drawing in.

George Bathurst was tall, handsome and only a little older than Edward. A bachelor, he had recently inherited Finchcocks Estate near Goudhurst. He practiced as a lawyer in London and dressed elegantly in a long jacket, knee-length breeches, hose and heeled shoes. His shoulder-length wig was topped with a wide-brimmed hat. He towered over Edward as they stood and talked. Edward could imagine him in his lawyer's wig and gown. His quiet voice and gentle nature belied his appearance. Edward had no fear of his master, only respect.

"Tomorrow, I wish you to take a letter to Mr Dewe at The Parsonage in Lamberhurst," he said to Edward. "You can take one of my horses this time, but there will be occasions when you'll need your own horse. Bring the spaniel to me in the parlour when you come to collect the letter."

"Yus, Sir," said Edward. "Shall you be needin' me fer the rest of the day? I've business in Lamb'rurst."

"I'll need you in the evening. I'm going out to dinner and will want you to come with me and look after the horses. Be back here before five o' the clock."

"Yus, Sir."

Early the next morning Edward put on his breeches and took his shirt to the yard where he washed himself at the well. He pulled his shirt over his head, ruffled his wet hair with his fingers, then walked over to the stables where Ming waited to be let out. She was of the breed made popular by King Charles. She couldn't be trusted outdoors without a leash. If she'd belonged to Edward, he would have trained her to do as she was bid. But in the house she was a lap dog and was fed on sweetmeats.

When Edward opened the top of the stable door he said, "Sit." The dog knew she wouldn't be allowed out until she sat. Edward opened the lower door then said, "Stay." He reached for the leash which was hanging on the wall and attached it to the dog's collar saying, "Good dog." He felt in his pocket for a piece of cheese to offer to the dog. Ming remained sitting as she took the cheese. Edward said, "Come now," and led the brown and white spaniel out into the yard, her tail waving with pleasure.

In the parlour, Ming was released from the leash. She ran to leap onto her master's knee, snuffling around his face and wagging her tail. After their greeting, Bathurst picked her up to put her on the floor. He got out of his chair to give Edward the letter which was lying on the sideboard.

"Make sure you hand this directly to Mr William Dewe, no-one else. If he's not at home, call back later."

"Yus, Sir," said Edward taking the letter. He went back to the stables to choose a horse. It would take too long to walk to The Slade and back.

William Dewe was at home when Edward called. A short, robust man, he wore a tightly curled white wig which framed a florid complexion and a clean-shaven chin. He took the letter then ushered Edward into the parlour, puffing with the exertion.

"I'm glad you called, Lucke. You lived in Lamberhurst before you went to work for Mr Bathurst, did you not?" he asked.

"Yus, Sir. Me fambly bide at Slade Farm."

"Just as I thought. I need to find a new supplier of meat," said Dewe. "I do a good deal of entertaining and will need it delivering here every two or three days. D'you know of a farmer who could do that?"

Edward was interested. He said, "Me brudder has a fair number of cattle en sheep. I believe 'e were consideren slaughteren some of 'em. I can ax un."

Dewe was pleased. "Would you do that? Could you let me know today?" he asked.

"If 'e be agreeable, Sir, what meat will you be wantin' termorrer?" asked Edward.

"I'll have beef; two good-sized pieces for spit-roasting. My cook can make pies with what's left over… and one tongue," Dewe replied.

"Very good, Sir. I'll be back afore noon with the answer." Edward left the house, humming to himself. He rode up the hill to The Slade in good spirits. This could be the answer to his brother's debts.

He found Thomas in the hog pound. A litter of piglets had been delivered. Thomas had pieces of straw stuck to him. Edward couldn't help laughing.

Thomas grimaced. "You may larf. You've slid out of real farmer's work en gone to be a manservant." He said the last few words in a squeaky voice wobbling his head.

"I've come ter make a proposition, Brudder," said Edward, ignoring the goad. "You owes me a good sum of money fer all the work I've done fer you over the last few years." They started walking towards the well. "I knows a man who will buy meat reg'lar. If you supplies the meat en 'e pays me, I'll knock it off what you owes. What d'you say?"

Thomas stopped walking, looked down at his muddy boots, then at Edward and said, "What makes you think I be minded ter slaughter me stock?" He walked on.

Edward followed, saying, "If you had less cattle en sheep, you'd have less need fer fodder over winter. That'd mean less work."

"Who's going ter do the slaughteren en butcheren?"whined Thomas.

"James knows what ter be at," said Edward, "en Esland be strong enough."

They reached the well. Thomas removed his round frock and drew the full bucket up. He cleaned the slime off his hands, splashed his face, turned his frock inside out and dried himself on it before throwing it to one side.

"This be yer chance ter get yerself out of debt," said Edward.

"'S'pose." Thomas went to the back door, kicking his boots off before he walked into the house. As the brothers passed the milkhouse, buttery and kitchen, Edward realised how much he was missing the familiar smells of cheese and butter making, brewing and cooking. When they entered the parlour their father was in the usual place in his chair by the fire. Their mother, Dorcas, had just put a batch of bread into the oven to bake. Edward went to embrace her then took a seat on the bench by the table. Dorcas stood by the door, hand on hip, not wanting to miss the ensuing conversation.

"Farder, I've found a buyer fer meat," said Edward.

Thomas Senior looked up. "That be good news, Son. Who might that be?" he asked.

"Mr Dewe at The Parsonage. 'E entertains re'glar, like en 'e wants gurt pieces of meat delivered a'most every day," said Edward.

Thomas Junior went to sit in the chair opposite his father, who said to him, "You could reduce yer stock over the next year en get enough ter pay another labourer, Thomas."

There was a long pause. Edward knew Thomas could be stubborn, but the proposals made good sense.

Dorcas said kindly, "'Twould mean less work fer thee, Son."

"Orright, I be agreeable," said Thomas, irritation distorting his voice. "There be beef hanging in the oast, ready fer market."

Edward went to stand at his side and said, "Meck certain sure you write down all the meat you send to The Parsonage en find out what Mr Dewe needs fer the follerin' order, each time."

Their father nodded in agreement. "I can help with the slaughteren en butcheren if need be. 'Twill give me summat ter be at."

Edward continued, "Fer termorrer 'e wants two big pieces of beef fer spit-roastin' en one tongue. I'll see that 'e pays me fer what 'e's had. Now, you'd best get butcheren en meck sure 'tis good meat. I'll tell Mr Dewe." He turned to face his father. "Can I buy a peck of oats off you, Farder?" he asked.

"Surely, Son. Go en help yerself." Thomas Senior looked up through watery eyes. "You be a good son, Edward."

Edward took six pence from his purse and gave them to his father. On his way out he called farewell to the women in the kitchen, then collected a bag of oats for Ming from the grain store before riding down the hill into the village. As he passed The Parsonage he stopped to give Mr Dewe the good news then made his way back to Goudhurst.

Gerald Paris was a friend of George Bathurst. Edward had been buying hay and straw from him at The Butts farm on the other side of Goudhurst. Now he needed to find a supplier of oats. He just had time to ride over there and back before his master needed him.

As he rode along the lane leading to the farm he came up behind a girl going in the same direction. Her blue skirts swung from her hips as she walked. He couldn't see her face as she had her back to him. She wore a straw bonnet and carried a trug full of fresh flowers. She did not look up at him as he passed. He was sure it was the same girl he'd seen in the village.

Edward found John Paris, the son, in the yard. He dismounted and hailed him. John turned to come towards Edward.

"Can you supply me with oats, John, reg'lar like?" he asked.

"Yus, we've plenty of oats. You'll collect 'em when you comes fer the hay, will you?"

"Yus, I be obliged." He went to mount his horse and said, "I'll come with the cart termorrer."

On their return from Bathurst's evening engagement, Edward stabled the horses and retreated to his cottage. Before retiring he sat at the table and opened an account for Mr Dewe, entering in his book the cuts of meat which Thomas would deliver tomorrow and their price. He would need to keep a strict record. It was not uncommon for bills to remain outstanding for months, sometimes years. This would be a good source of income for him and a basis on which to build up savings, pending a future marriage.

He sat back in his chair in the flickering candlelight recalling the girl he'd seen walking up the lane to The Butts. He must find out more about her.

His mind wandered to more general things. His role here with Mr Bathurst was a mixture of manservant, groom, butler and messenger. Edward invariably accompanied his master, being in charge of the spaniel and the horses and seeing to their care when they were out and about. It was a life far removed from Slade Farm. He had to get accustomed to wearing kneelength breeches and a restricting jacket instead of his loose round frock. His shoes were tight on his feet.

He felt angry with his brother Thomas for putting him in this position. Guilt hung over his shoulders for having to abandon Slade Farm and his father.

Chapter Three   1698/9

In which Edward gains a friend.

John Paris had told him that his father was considering selling a horse.

Edward set off one winter's evening with money in his purse. It was a long trudge up the hill to The Butts.The weather was damp but not raining and Edward enjoyed the exercise. He strode up the lane and into the yard where the stables were, expecting to meet John and his father, but the place was deserted. He heard the rustling of straw in one of the stables and strolled over to look over the half door. A grey nose came to greet him. He fondled the horse's muzzle.

Hearing a light step behind him, he turned.

The girl he'd seen on the lane was standing there.

She curtseyed and said, "Farder en John will not be…" and hesitated.

She had raven black hair. Her mouth was shaped like a rosebud. Her eyes were dark.

Edward wanted to put a hand out to touch her blushing cheek.

"M-much obliged," he said. He didn't want her to slip away. "Er, d'you know which horse yer farder be sellen?" Perhaps she would show him, then he could get closer.

"Nay, beg pardon," she said. She didn't walk away but stood awkwardly, looking at him with sorrowful eyes.

Time seemed to stand still.

John came across the yard, followed by his father. The girl curtseyed and went back into the house. There was the faint scent of lavender and an aura of sadness in the space she left.

The grey mare he'd seen in the stable was the one for sale. They led her out into the yard for Edward to look her over. He was aware that his judgement might be clouded by his disturbed feelings. However, he trusted John Paris and decided to buy her. After paying for the horse he rode slowly home, getting to know her. He would call her Faithful.

Mr Bathurst was planning to take a party to Tunbridge Wells. It was rumoured that Princess Anne would be bringing her son William, the Duke of Gloucester, to take the waters. The thought of catching sight of Royalty intrigued Edward. He looked forward to accompanying the party as groom.

Rain poured down for several days beforehand. It was a relief to wake up that morning to bright sunshine. Steam rose from the roofs of the buildings and the air felt fresh and clean. Edward brought his new grey mare and his master's chestnut out of their stables and brushed their coats before putting on their saddles and bridles. He left them with hay bags then went to let Ming out of her stable to take her for a short walk.

On his return he heard the sound of hooves on cobbles. Lady Hanby came into the yard riding side-saddle, accompanied by a servant. Mr Bathurst emerged from the house to greet her, then turned to Edward.

"Are we all ready, Edward?"

"Yus, Sir." He put the dog back into the stable, checked her water bowl and shut the door. He led the chestnut to the jossing block where his master was waiting to mount.

"We'll meet the Longleys and the Newnhams when we get there," said Bathurst as they set off.

There were crowds of people already there, eager to see the princess. The atmosphere was brimming with expectation and Edward was carried along with it. Bathurst dismounted, then led Lady Hanby's horse to the mounting block and handed her down. Edward took the horses with his own to the tethering posts, where there was competition for places. He caught sight of Mr Longley and his wife riding in and hailed them.

"I'll teck yer horses," he called above the clamour. "'Tis a rush fer tetherin' places."

The Longleys dismounted and he took the reins. Other grooms were jostling each other. Horses were tossing their heads and snorting. Edward entered the fray. There was a danger of hooves treading on feet. At last he found free posts further along the railing and went to find hay.

His party had walked off in the direction of the well where most people were gathering. When he'd given the horses their bait, he went towards the covered walkway. He always enjoyed the exhilarating atmosphere at The Wells: the shops selling toys, china, rich clothes and the aromas of coffee, chocolate and other unfamiliar drinks and food coming from the cafés and eating houses. Most was far beyond his means but the experience of being there was enough to satisfy him. He'd heard of the town's scandalous reputation in the reign of King Charles II. His father had forbidden him to come here when he was a young man, afraid that he'd fall in with disreputable company. Even now he wasn't a regular visitor. Today the ground was deep in mud from the trampling of many feet. It was almost impossible to find a dry place to walk. The mud spread upwards, covering shoes and stockings and the hems of skirts. The walkway was no better and the floors of the shops had a coating of slippery paste. Edward strolled under the leafless trees, peering in the shop windows at the candle flames reflected on shiny trinkets. Everyone was excited, dressed in their best clothes, waving flags, laughing and singing. Children played tag in and out of the pillars which supported the roof of the walkway.

Edward saw a group of richly dressed men and women surrounding a large lady and a boy coming towards him. He was about to meet Princess Anne and her courtiers. He stood aside together with the crowd, gazing in wonderment at the dazzling jewels and rustling of full skirts of silk and velvet. He'd never seen such extravagance. The boy must be the Duke of Gloucester; the princess' only surviving child. There was something not right about him. He was the size of a ten-year-old boy, but behaved like a toddler; walking haphazardly on the treacherous ground, his limbs flailing like a doll's. Two attendants were attempting to keep him close. Edward watched as the inevitable happened. The child slipped in the mud falling flat on his back. His hat rolled off as he wailed pitifully. His nurses picked him up, trying to wipe the dirt off his clothes. The Princess cried out and came to comfort her son.

Edward was amazed at the haughtiness of the princess and at the lack of care given to her son, who should be kept away from the public eye in his opinion. All the people who had reached out to touch her drew back to retreat into the shops.

She called to the bailiff, who was among the party. "The condition of this walkway is appalling, Sir. My son could have been injured. Why have you not paved it? The people should not have to walk in this mess."

The bailiff bowed low, removing his hat. "Beg pardon your Highness. There is not sufficient in the coffers for such luxuries. The people are already paying high taxes for living in this town."

"I will donate a sum for paving along the walkway." She turned to one of her attendants. "See to it, Ralph."

The man nodded and bowed. The bailiff bowed deeply.

"I will not return here until the work is done," said Princess Anne. The Royal party moved on.

The people round Edward nodded their heads. Some stepped forward and presented posies of flowers, saying, "Thank 'e yer Highness, God bless thee," curtseying or bowing low, their clothes trailing in the mud. Princess Anne nodded and smiled as her maids took the gifts. She strode on regally with her sobbing son.

Edward heard a voice in his ear, "'Er be in a hurry ter get away, beant 'er?"

He turned round to find John Paris behind him. Edward laughed and they shook hands.

"Come for a beer," said John.

The crowd was still discussing the accident which had occurred. The two walked away to find a tavern. They bought their drinks and went to sit at a table outside.

"'Ow be yer young mare?" asked John.

"Bravely," said Edward. I be main pleased wiv 'she. 'Er be gentle en strong."

John was a gangly youth. He had the black hair and brown eyes of his sister.

Edward said, "They gave you the day off today then, John."

"Yus, there beant much farmin' ter do in the winter en the land be over-wet ter work on prensley," said John.

Edward took a mouthful of his drink and said, "I surely miss husbandry; the fresh air, the ploughen en the sowen en the birth of young animals in the spring."

"Will you be agwain back to farmin' one day?" asked John.

Edward nodded. "Betimes Farder passes on. He has anudder farm in the Faircrouch quarter that I'll have. There be tenants there prensley."

John said, "There'll be naught left fer me. Farder only has The Butts en me brudder Gerald'll have that."

"D'you have any other brudders en sisters apart from him en the gal I met?"

"Nay. There be but three of we." John sat quietly for a while.

Edward said, "That sister of yourn be main purty, ain't 'er?"

"Yus, Mary be my twin. But don't think you've got a chance with she. Farder's abouten wed she off to Robert Bat'rst, yer master's nephew. It be all arranged."

"Be she agreeable?" Edward asked.

"She don't know the man. He be supposed ter come a-courten she, but I ain't seed un."

Edward hid his disappointment. He would have liked to become more acquainted with Mary.

Just then a vagrant shuffled round the corner and came towards them, holding out his hat. He brought with him an aura of unwashed body and soiled clothes and seemed out of place in this town crowded with rich and genteel people, bewigged and scented with heady perfumes. His weather-ripened face was surrounded with grey, matted hair and beard.

He bowed and held out his hat, "Can ye spare a groat, gents?"

John and Edward did their Christian duty and found some coins in their money pouches to throw into the beggar's hat. He bowed again and went on his way looking for more people to badger.

"'E be come to the right place today," remarked Edward. "I ain't seen any other badgers hereabouts."

"Shouldn't be surprised if 'e collected a hatful," laughed John.

They watched him spring out into the path of a gentleman sauntering along a grassy path away from the sea of mud, with his lady on his arm. The beggar walked backwards in front of them, getting in their way so that they must divert to avoid him and muddy their feet in the process. He changed his position accordingly, holding out his hat and pleading, "Spare us a groat, Sir, Lady. I ain't ett fer free days."

The gentleman said, "Get out of my way, scrounger," waving his cane menacingly.

But his lady let go of her husband's arm and found some small coins in her purse. She tossed them into the beggar's hat. He bowed deeply, showing a leg and waved them by.

John and Edward were amused at the man's bravado and Edward remarked that he was a more attractive character than the princess who was at the other end of the social scale.

They chatted about the experiences of the day. Edward enjoyed John's company. They both had the same sense of humour and interests. They agreed to meet before long and he went back to his master and his party.

Chapter Four   1699

In which Bathurst holds a Ball

The master's mare was sick. Edward had tried taking her to Bewl Bridge to be flayed, but she was still moody and wouldn't eat. He bought malt and beer for her. She supped it down by the gallon and over the next few days began to lift her head and take notice.

He went to Bathurst and said, "The mare's looking better, surely, Sir. 'Twas the beer what did it!"

"Good man. Keep account of what you spend. I'll pay you when I give you your wages. Let's go and have a look at her." They walked to the stables together.

On the way, Bathurst said, "I'm planning a Ball, Edward. There'll be invitations I want you to deliver and you must be ready to receive the guests on the night. I'll hire a boy to take their outer garments. You will show them to the reception room and announce who they are. I'll provide you with a butler's uniform."

"D'you have a man fer takin' the horses when they arrive, Sir?" Edward did not like the sound of butlering. He would make a better groom.

"Ah, yes, I'll hire a groom for the evening. And we'll need a supply of hay in bags."

"When will this be, Sir?" enquired Edward.

"May the first. I'll see that you get the invitations to deliver well in advance."

They reached the stables and Edward opened the door for his master. The mare looked up and snuffled a greeting, nodding her head. Bathurst examined her eyes and looked into her mouth. He lifted one of her forefeet to check the shoe.

"You'll need to take her to the blacksmith before I ride her out," he said.

"I'll see to that, Sir, when she be eatin' reg'lar again, like."

"Of course." Bathurst patted his mare on the neck and left.

Edward anticipated his role as butler with trepidation. Bathurst gave him a list of the people expected to attend the Ball. He practised reading them out loud every night before he went to bed.

"Mr Thomas Longley and Mrs Longley; Sir James Oxenden; Mr Robert Newnham and Mrs Newnham; Lady Elizabeth Hanby; Mr Robert Bathurst and Miss Mary Paris..." Edward's throat tightened. He'd caught glimpses of Mary over the past few months, on his visits to The Butts, but had'nt spoken to her. He was trying to avoid even thinking of her.

He was measured for a butler's uniform and his master went through the procedure with him the day before. The extra groom, David, arrived in the afternoon on May the first. Edward showed him where the hay bags were and where to tether the horses.

Edward went to his cottage to get dressed. His fingers fumbled with the brass buttons on his coat and the buckles on his shoes. He'd trimmed his hair and beard and bought some hair powder and new hose. He dragged a comb through his brown thatch. It wouldn't lie down. He wondered whether he should have worn a wig. He walked as calmly as he could to the house and went in by the kitchen door. Cook turned round to see who had entered.

"Oh, my! What a sight!" she cried, clasping her hands together.

"You needs ter tie yer hair back," announced the parlour maid. "Bide there." She disappeared into a little room off the kitchen and came back with a wide black ribbon. She turned Edward round, reaching up to gather his hair into a bunch behind his head, tied the ribbon in a big bow, stood back and said, "There, that be better."

Cook nodded approval. Edward felt even more trussed up, like a chicken ready for the oven.

"Best go through," he said. His voice came out husky and he coughed to clear it.

In the entrance hall the boy was waiting to take the guests' cloaks. He was also dressed up looking as uncomfortable as Edward felt. The wait seemed interminable. The front door stood open for the first arrivals. They heard the musicians tuning up their instruments two rooms away.

At last a two-horse carriage rolled up the drive with two horsemen following. Edward watched as the groom helped the ladies alight. He stood to attention, ready to receive them. The gentlemen dismounted and came to offer their arms to the ladies. They approached the door, two by two.

"The Lady Elizabeth Hanby and Squire Campion of Combwell," said Squire Campion to Edward.

Edward bowed and led the way to the drawing room. Lady Hanby removed her cloak with Edward's assistance and he handed it to the waiting boy. He led the guests to the open door of the ballroom where there was a quiet atmosphere of expectation. Flickering candles in reflective sconces surrounded the walls, revealing richly coloured drapes and a spacious wooden floor. Dim figures at the far end arranged their musical instruments.

"Lady Elizabeth Hanby and Squire Campion of Combwell," he announced in a loud voice.

Bathurst came over to greet his guests. Edward turned back to the drawing room where more people were removing their cloaks. The evening had begun.

There was a lull in the arrival of guests. Edward paced the floor, anxious for the occasion to pass quickly. Another carriage drew up. Dusk was falling and he couldn't make out the identity of the lady stepping out on her escort's arm. As she came towards the lighted doorway he saw it was Mary and his stomach lurched. She was lavishly dressed in a full skirt. Her dark hair was scraped back and arranged in a pile of curls on top of her head. Her face was ashen and her lips were tightly closed. She was as nervous as Edward.

The couple stepped over the threshold. Robert Bathurst announced, "Miss Mary Paris and Robert…"

A small brown and white shape emerged from the gloom behind them, dived under Mary's skirts and into the hall.

Mary gave a sharp cry as she fell forward.

Edward tried to save her but wasn't nimble enough.

Robert said, "Zounds, Mary! What're you doin' down there? Pray, rise and contain thyself." He stood staring at the crumpled heap of lavender satin.

Edward wasted no time in helping Mary to her feet, enjoying the closeness of her body.

She gasped and sobbed, but held back the tears. He helped her hobble into the drawing room. Her escort followed.

"A chair for the lady!" called Edward to the boy, who snapped into action and placed a chair behind Mary.

As Edward lowered her into her seat she whispered into his ear, "Oh, Edward, thanks be 'tis you!"

One of the other lady guests had seen what happened and came to Mary's aid with smelling salts and kerchief. Robert Bathurst stood by, scowling.

Edward went into the ballroom where Ming was causing consternation among the guests. No-one could catch her.

"Ming, come here!" Edward commanded.

Ming stopped in her tracks and looked at Edward, her ears laid back. She hung her head and came to him. He breathed a sigh of relief, bent down to pick her up, then walked briskly out of the room.

David, the temporary groom, was in the entrance hall in a state of agitation. "I went to the wrong stable fer the hay bags," he groaned. "The dog ran out before I..."

"Teck she en have she back." Edward handed the miscreant over to David, brushed the hairs off the front of his jacket, breathing deeply to gather his composure. He went back into the drawing room where more guests were waiting to be announced. He glanced at Mary, still sitting on her chair with the ladies fussing round her.

"Sir Thomas Morland and Lady..." was whispered in his ear. He went to the door of the ballroom and repeated the announcement in a loud voice. The guests proceeded through. The musicians struck up with a sarabande, dancers spilled out onto the floor. All was going smoothly once more. Edward turned his attention to the next arrivals, Mr Robert Newnham and Mrs Newnham.

There were no more interruptions that evening. Edward observed the proceedings in the drawing room, unable to take his eyes off Mary. She recovered from her ordeal and took her place beside her fiancé who led her into the ballroom on his arm. She was still limping. Edward saw that she didn't take part in the dancing. Robert Bathurst enjoyed himself dancing with other beautiful women who seemed to appreciate his company, simpering and laughing at his conversation. Mary remained seated talking to the women who came to sit at her side, before being approached by the next dancing partner. She didn't look happy or comfortable. Edward longed to go to her and carry her away from the scene which neither of them was enjoying.

At the end of the evening the couples started collecting their cloaks from the boy in the drawing room before leaving. It was Edward's duty to summon the waiting coachmen and tell David which horses to bring from their tethers. He caught a glimpse of Mary as she and Robert came past him. He was sure she looked his way and smiled as she left.

Chapter Five   1699

In which Edward's hopes are raised

A few weeks later, Edward drove his master's cart up to The Butts. The birds were shouting out their evening song. The sky was turning a rosy pink and the light breeze blew ripples across the field of ripening barley. He breathed the cooling air into his lungs to disperse the tensions of a busy day. This was the last task before his work was done.

Swifts flew low, swooping and diving to catch the insects in the air, their screams echoing in the yard. Edward drove the empty cart through to the hay stacks, where he was expecting John to meet him. He was collecting hay for Bathursts horses. Before he jumped down from his seat he saw a figure in the distance that he was sure was Mary. She was walking towards him. He alighted and went forward to greet her.

"'Tis a pleasure ter see you again, Miss."

Mary blushed. "I were main glad ter see you at the Ball, Edward. Thank you fer pickin' me up." She smiled a warm smile that lit up her face.

"Pleased t'ter be of help," Edward stuttered. "Is yer foot recovered?"

"Yus, 'twere naught, but it saved me from havin' ter dance…"

"I b'lieve we was both feelin' ockard that evening." Edward was warming to the conversation.

Mary nodded. "'Tis likely I mun get accustomed to that life…" She hung her head and shuffled her feet.

John came round the corner and hailed them. "Sorry ter keep you waiting, Edward," he said.

Mary smiled at Edward and walked on.

John said, "'Er beant happy," and shook his head.

"When be the wedding?" asked Edward.

"Come next Lady Day," replied John. "Mayhap Robert will come a-visitin' en pay she praper attention afore then. 'Er might come ter like un." John looked at Edward and smiled grimly. "The closer it comes the more upset 'er becomes. Muvver don't seem ter notice, or don't care."

Edward could see that John was almost as distressed as his sister. He felt sad for them both. John helped him load the hay onto the cart, then Edward made his way home.

Mr Bathurst had a visitor, a Mr Weller from London, who wished to visit The Wells. Edward was asked to accompany him as groom. Bathurst was away on business in Maidstone that day.

Mr Weller was a gloomy companion. He dressed in black and wore a grey wig. He made no effort to converse with Edward as they were travelling. Perhaps he looked down on servants. When they arrived Edward tethered the two horses, agreeing to meet Mr Weller in the afternoon. That gave Edward enough time to have a pot of beer and do some other shopping for himself.

The summer had lasted into September that year. The population were out enjoying the hazy warm days before they would have to retreat to their firesides in the cold of winter. Some people were sheltering in the relative shade of the trees along the walkway, which were beginning to change their colours to reds and yellows. Customers were queueing at the doors of coffee houses for refreshments. Carriages, coaches and horsemen were arriving, jostling to find a space where their passengers could alight in comfort. Gentlemen and ladies stood around the well, supping the Chalybeat from elegant glasses.

Edward walked to the covered market to find a fisherman who would take a letter to Hastings for Mr Bathurst. Vendors were busy selling fowls, fish and meat. There were tables and chairs set out, waiting for people to dine. Edward soon found a man who was delivering to a stallholder the fish he had brought from the coast overnight. He hailed him. The smell of fish rose to Edward's nostrils and caught his breath.

"Where be you a-travellin' to next, Sir?" he asked.

"I be headin' back to Hastings," said the fisherman.

"I'd be obliged if you'd help this letter to this address," Edward said, pointing to the writing on the envelope. He gave the man sixpence, touched the brim of his hat and hastened away from the offensive stench. Going towards the apothecary's shop he saw John Paris coming down the walkway. He raised his hand in greeting.

"John! Good to see you. Will you come en have a beer with me?"

"John said, "Yus, Ed. Shall us go to The Red Lion? I'll meet you 'forelong, betimes I've found bait fer me horse."

They carried their beer outside and sat at a table in the sunshine. Although Edward had seen John many times since his last meeting with Mary, he'd only heard small items of news. He'd avoided asking too much, as there was no hope in that direction. But the date for the wedding was looming closer. He couldn't resist asking John how Mary was feeling.

John shook his head. "She be maudlin', but showen a brave face. I b'lieve she be resigned to 'er fate en will meck the best of it. Us ain't seen much of Robert, though 'e came ter dine a few times. Muvver be all of a fluster over the weddin'. I be come ter buy some more bits en pieces she wants." He took several mouthfuls of his beer and was silent.

Edward gazed into his tankard for a few moments, then looked up to watch the people coming and going. For once, he and John had little to say to each other. His attention was drawn to a couple going towards the walkway.

He reached out to touch John's arm. "Beant that Robert Bat'rst, John?"

John looked up. His eyes widened in surprise. "Yus," he said, "en that hussy beant Mary."

They watched as the couple passed them. The woman was gazing up into Robert's face in admiration. She was gaudily dressed, her face was highly made-up with cosmetics. Robert chattered away, putting his hand to her cheek affectionately. They laughed together, oblivious of their surroundings. Robert indicated a coffee house and they turned towards it. The woman tripped. Robert supported her while she regained her footing. Edward was reminded the man's lack of care when Mary fell at the Ball.

John took in a long breath and said, "Well, Farder will surely not be pleased ter hear about this."

The couple went out of sight into the coffee house.

Edward's interest was aroused. "What will un do?"

"I rackon this'll spoil Robert's chances of weddin' any respeckable young lady," remarked John. "'E'll not be abouten give up liaisen with those women after un be wed, will 'e?"

"D'you rackon the weddin' be off, then? John." Edward asked eagerly.

"I can't see Farder allowen that behaviour... In public en all! En Muvver will not want ter 'ave the family name soiled. There be no knowin' what nasty diseases 'e be pickin' up from the likes of she." John was carried away by his enthusiasm for the idea that the wedding should be called off.

"I'll tell Mr Bat'rst." said Edward, "'E'll have summat ter say en all. 'E gives that young varmint an allowance, 'im being 'is guardian."

The two finished their beer, agreeing to meet again tomorrow in the Star and Eagle in Goudhurst. They went their separate ways, hoping for a better future for Mary.

Back in his cottage that evening, Edward took out his account book and entered his expenses, knowing that his master would reimburse him. He recalled the revelation of the morning and the possibility that Mary would be free from the engagement to Robert Bathurst. He was relieved for her, but his hopes of her ever becoming his wife were slim. He was a servant. Her parents would plan a marriage to a person of Quality. His savings had gone down and Mr Dewe hadn't paid him recently.

Chapter Six   1699

In which situations change.

Edward took Ming for a walk the next morning before taking her to her master. When they entered the parlour Bathurt was sitting in his chair by the fire smoking his first pipe of the day. He wore his skull cap and an elaborately decorated silk smoking jacket. Ming jumped onto his lap as usual, settling down to sleep on his knee while he fondled her behind the ears.

Edward stood and waited.

"You wish to speak to me, Edward?" asked Bathurst.

"Yus, Sir," said Edward. "I seed summat at The Wells yusterdy that I b'lieve you should know about."

Bathurst stopped stroking his dog and said, "Go on."

"I were with John Paris, enjoyin' a jar outside The Red Lion, Sir," said Edward. "We seed yer nephew Robert, Sir, wiv a woman on 'is arm." He described the details, adding, "'E bein' abouten wed a respeckable lady, I beleft you should know. John Paris will be able ter support this. 'E be agwain ter tell 'is farder."

George Bathurst's face became flushed. He took his pipe out of his mouth. "The young fool!" he exclaimed. "I'll go to see Gerald Paris as soon as I've dressed." He pushed Ming to the floor and stood up. "Thank you for passing on this information, Edward." He knocked his pipe on the side of the hearth and put it down. "Please take Ming back to the stable and have my horse ready."

Edward called to Ming and picked her up. "Shall you be here fer luncheon, Sir?"

"No. I'll be going to talk to Robert afterwards. Tell Cook I'll be back for dinner."

"What shall I tell Mr Weller, Sir?" asked Edward.

His master had evidently forgotten his guest. "Oh, tell him to amuse himself. I'll see him at dinner." He hurried out of the room. Edward heard him striding noisily up the stairs.

He sighed as he took Ming out to the stable.

It wasn't until the evening that Edward went to The Star and Eagle to meet John. He arrived to find the tavern filling up with farm workers on their way home from a day in the fields. He bought a drink for himself, found two empty seats and waited.

At last he caught sight of John with a full tankard, squeezing past men standing around the bar. Edward caught his eye and waved from his quiet corner.

"Beg pardon fer me tardiness," said John as he sat down. "I had Farder's work to do, him being moithered, like." He took a long draught from his tankard.

"So, what did they say when you told 'em?" Edward asked.

John grinned. "You never saw such a start as there were in our parlour, 'smarnen. I telled 'em after we'd eaten, afore Farder en Gerald en me were abouten go ter work. Muvver had the vapours en had ter use 'er smellin' salts. Farder were in a tarble hike en swore 'e'd give Robert Bat'rst a bannikin' en Mary swooned away. I had ter pick un up off the floor. Gerald just laughed." John chuckled at the memory.

Edward said, "Mr Bat'rst rode to your place in a rage after I telled un."

"Yus, 'e came after Muvver en Farder had quieted down a bit. Muvver were weepin' en Mary went to 'er chamber. Gerald en me was sent off ter work. We left the three of 'em talken. Come luncheon time they'd decided ter call off the marriage. Mr Bat'rst were gone ter tell Robert en that 'is allowance were stopped."

"What of Mary?" Edward asked.

"'Er's been in 'er chamber all day. Muvver's been weepin' on en off. Farder be main moody. I'll miss dinner en find some food in here." John smiled wryly at Edward.

They both took long drinks of their beer, absorbed in their own thoughts for a while.

John spoke first. "Be you minded ter come a-courten betimes the shock has died down?"

Edward shook his head sadly. "I be but a servant. They wouldn't consider me as a suitor. I ain't got no money or prospects prensley." He took the last few drops from his tankard and stood up. "I wish 'er well, John. You en me will meet again." He shook hands with his friend and walked out into the evening sunshine.

It was a few weeks later that he met John again at The Butts. They loaded up five bags of oats which Edward paid for. He'd been trying to push the picture of Mary out of his mind, without success.

Before he left, John said, "Can you be at The Star and Eagle this evenin'?"

"Yus, said Edward. "Be Mary orright?"

John said, "Muvver en Farder sent she away ter bide with Aunt Louise in Eastbourne. I'll tell you more later." He was in a hurry to attend to work on the farm and couldn't stop.

Edward was shocked. Was Mary in disgrace? It wasn't her fault that the wedding had been called off. He went back to his cottage to find an old round frock to wear. It was more comfortable than the groom's waistcoat over a shirt. He hoped there would be no callers while he was dressed like this. Bathurst was away on business all day.

The first task was to take the horses out of their stalls and tether them each with a bag of hay. He shovelled their muck into a large barrow and heaved it away to the dung heap. Then he brought buckets of water from he well, silling and sweeping until the hard earthen floors were fresh and clean. Some of his anger and frustration had dispersed by the time he started grooming the horses. He left Faithful to last, then saddled her up for a ride to Slade Farm. It was time he went to visit his father and mother. He spread straw for the horses before putting them back in their stalls, then he washed at the well and changed into a clean shirt.

At Slade Farm they welcomed him into the parlour. Even Eliza came to hear all his news. Then Ann happened by and the parlour was crowded. Thomas was attending to the dwindling herd of sheep with James, choosing the next ones to be slaughtered. He'd be back for coager. Edward noticed that his father was looking tired. He declined to say anything about Mary or his feelings for her, as he had no prospects in that direction. But his mother noticed something about his countenance and said, "Be you a-courten, Son?"

Everyone stopped talking, waiting for an answer.

"Nay," said Edward, knowing that he wouldn't convince his mother. He started telling them about his visits to The Wells, repeating the story of the visit of Princess Anne for those who hadn't heard it. Martha was especially intrigued, she kept asking him to repeat his description of the princess and all her jewels and rich clothing.

They had coager together. Edward felt comforted by having his family round him. He heard that Ann was courting and Martha, though secretive, was flushed and blooming with something special in her heart. Thomas came in. He was presumably keeping up with meat supplies to Mr Dewe. Edward was reluctant to question him in case it started an argument.

He had to leave. He'd more work to do. He asked Dorcas for butter on the way out and she accompanied him to his horse.

"Muvver," he said, "be Farder ailen?"

"'E beant as strong as 'e were," she said. "'E don't help with the butcheren no more. But we both be gettin' in years. You be lookin' broody. Be aught amiss?"

"I be fair to middlen," Edward said. "I miss the fambly, surely. But I be in paid work en have some friends." He smiled at her.

She gave him a hug before he mounted Faithful and trotted away. It had been good to see them all.

John was waiting in The Star and Eagle for him when he arrived. Edward bought a beer and went to sit down.

"Tell me more about Mary, John," he said. "Be they punishen she?"

John looked ruefully at Edward. "They be angry on account of she didn't encourage Robert. They rackon 'e lost interest in she so 'e went to console hisself with that woman. If 'er'd paid un more attention 'e would've took more notice."

Edward felt his anger rising again. "She be only a young gal," he said. "'Ow could 'er know what ter be at?"

John nodded. "Muvver said 'er beant fit ter wed a dacent man en would be better as a nurse fer people's children. Aunt Louise bides in Eastbourne. 'Er'll teck Mary ter muvver 'er fambly. Mayhap 'er'll like it there en the sea air will perk she up. There'll be young men ter meet en 'er's partial to liddle uns." The expression on his face showed Edward that he had not convinced himself.

Edward sighed. "Mayhap you be right, my friend."

They chatted about farming and the weather. Edward told John about his family and his difficulty with his brother Thomas. They passed the evening comfortably while sharing the same concerns about Mary.

Edward spent the next interminable months tending Bathurst's horses and Ming; taking visitors to The Wells; butlering at lavish receptions and delivering letters to places he'd never heard of. Every week he looked in at Slade Farm, where all seemed to be proceeding smoothly. Mr Dewe was still happy with the arrangement but was often reluctant to pay his bills when Edward called, giving the excuse that he had no cash in the house.

The memory of Mary faded but an ache remained in the recesses of his heart. He'd never felt like this about any of the girls he'd walked out with.

Chapter Seven   1701.

In which Edward reckons with Mr Dewe.

One day while Edward was collecting supplies from The Butts, John appeared looking more cheerful than he had for a long time. "Mary be a-comen home!" he announced.

It was a fine sunny day in midsummer. A gentle breeze ruffled his horse's mane as Edward trotted her from Finchcocks, across the bridge and along the road towards Lamberhurst. When they came to The Parsonage he rode into the entrance and dismounted, leaving Faithful tethered. A servant opened the front door when he knocked.

"Be Mr Dewe at home?" he asked.

He was shown in and told to wait.

Soon the old man appeared wearing a robe of dark blue silk. An emerald skull cap perched on his bald head.

"Forgive my appearance, Edward," he said. "I rose late this morning. Will you come into the parlour? Your money's ready." He hobbled into the room he'd just left. Edward followed and stood waiting. A spicy aroma hung in the air. Dewe sat at a bureau and pulled down the lid. He searched in one of the pigeon holes and brought out a pot, the contents of which he emptied onto the green leather inlay of the writing surface.

"Here, take this." He counted the money out into Edward's hand. "This is what I owe for the year of 1700. I have your reckoning here and will pay the rest in due course. He closed the lid of the bureau.

"I be obliged, Sir." Edward put the money into his purse. "Be the supply of meat to your satisfaction, Sir?"

"Yes, yes. I'm not entertaining as often these days. My wife is ailing much of the time, but the rest of the household needs to eat." He smiled apologetically and led Edward to the front door.

Edward's next call was to Slade Farm. The geese set up a rumpus when he rode into the yard. He dismounted and shooed them away. Two horses were tied up near the jossing block. Who could the visitors be? He hitched Faithful up to the fence post and went through the close to the back door. Martha was on her way out.

"Oh, Ed, 'tis thee." She remarked. "There be all sorts a-doin' in the hall. 'Tis a blessin' you come round this way!" She turned and pattered after Edward into the parlour.

"What be a-goin' on then?" he asked.

Martha, wide-eyed, lowered her voice. "Farder's a-scribin' 'is will."

"Oh." Edward stood deep in thought while he absorbed this information. "Be un failin', Martha?"

"Nay," she said, surprised at the suggestion. Mas Thomas Tapsell en Mas John Feavour be in there wiv Ann en Muvver."

"Oh," Edward said again.

This might change everything, for all of them, he thought. Then he said, "Beant you be agwain ter be wed to that Crownage feller soon?"

Martha blushed. "Yus, us fixed the day. Next month. Be sure to be there, Ed."

"I be hem happy fer thee, Martha. God bless thee." He drew her plump body to him and gave her a brotherly hug.

They sat at the table. "Why be Ann in there with 'em?" Edward asked.

"She be 'is eggy chicks, or summat, whatever that be," said Martha, crumpling up her face.

The hall door opened. Their father and his two friends came into the parlour. Ann followed, with Dorcas carrying three empty tankards.

"Edward!" His father's face lit up. "Us was talking of you just now." He came and sat in his chair by the fire. "You knows Thomas en John d'you not?"

Edward said, "Yus farder." He went to shake each man by the hand.

Ann said, "D'you need me fer aught more, Farder?"

"Nay, Lass. But don't go abroad so soon. You ain't seed yer brudder fer I dunn'owlong."

Ann looked at Edward and smiled, then said, "Nay, Farder, I'd best be bodgen." She nodded to Tapsell and Feavour then left by the back door. Dorcas followed to the kitchen.

Thomas shook his head. His glasses slipped to perch on the end of his nose. "You can never pin she down," he said. Then to his friends, "Can ye stay fer a few minutes, or will ye be bodgen off en all?"

Edward indicated the benches round the table. He sat down. Tapsell and Feavour followed his example.

Thomas filled his pipe and lit it, taking long, deep sucks to get it going, producing a fragrant cloud of smoke.

"Edward, I've been putting me will together with the help of me friends, 'ere." He nodded towards where they sat. "They'll be the overseers, what see to it that me will is follered through, like. Ann's the executrix. She'll do the dolin' out of the bequests after I die." He took a puff of his pipe and looked at Edward over his spectacles.

Edward nodded. "Yus, Farder."

His father continued. "As I said afore, Junior will have Slade Farm dappen yer Muvver en me be put in. En if 'e dies with no heirs, 'twill come to you. But that's all in the future." He took another puff.

"Now, I've anudder property of thy Gaffer's in Wad'rst that I've been rentin' out. Savages it be. That, I want thee ter 'ave, Edward. The tenant passed away en you could teck it on now. 'Twould save me seekin' a new tenant en 'twould keep the place a-workin'. What d'you say?"

Edward couldn't say anything. He looked at his father open-mouthed. He knew change was round the corner, but not as soon as this. He swallowed. The sound of Martha going to the buttery brought him down to earth. The others waited patiently.

"Y-yus, F-Farder." He coughed. "I-I be obliged, Farder." Then he wondered whether he'd heard aright. Martha came in with a full tankard of beer and gave it to him. He took a sip.

"You mean... I can have Savages... now?"

Thomas Tapsell and John Feavour laughed. "Come now, Edward," said Tapsell. "Yer farder is giving you the farm at Savages, this day. 'Tis surely yourn!"

Edward was laughing, so was his father. They were all laughing. Edward slapped his thigh and stood to go and shake his father's hand. He raised his tankard. "To the future!" he said.

"To the future," they all echoed.

"I'll want some rent from thee, mind, betimes I be put in," his father reminded him.

Edward rode home in a lighter mood. His father was not about to die soon. He'd made his will so that Edward would be able to plan his life at last.

He must keep calm and take this step by step. First of all he would go to Savages to see what he was taking on, what he'd need to do to make it into a working farm and whether he could afford it with no wages coming in. Then he would have to disentangle himself from Bathurst's employ. It would not be fair or courteous to leave immediately. And his master owed Edward money he'd borrowed, as well as his wages. He needed to move into Savages with a full purse.

That night, before getting into bed, he opened the account book at Mr Dewe's bill of meat. He read the last entry:

Then reckoned with Mr Dewe.
   There is due to me
   7   -   13   -   8

He wrote below:

Received of Mr Dewe   2 guineas and a pistol
   It comes to   3   -   0   -   0

The next time he met John in the tavern, they both had exciting news to tell. John took a long draught, wiped his mouth on the back of his hand and said,

"Mary be a-comen home termorrer. Aunt Louise don't need she no more."

Edward said, "I rackon her'll be walkin' out along of another man by now. 'Er's too pretty ter be overlooked."

"'Er didn't say aught in the letter," said John. "What be your news? You looks main chirpy."

Edward smiled and sat back in his chair. "Farder's scribed 'is will en left me a farm."

"You told me you was expecting it a while back."

"Yus, but I've got tenancy from now." Edward couldn't contain the excitement bubbling up in his voice.

"Well! That be good news. So you'll be leaving Gowd'rst." John caught Edward's excitement and laughed, banging his fist on the table. "I shall be ernful ter see you gone. But 'tis good news, surely."

Edward leaned forward companionably. "The bidance'll need fixin' up, but I be anxious ter be there en start farmin'." He paused and sat staring into his tankard, his fingers restlessly turning it round.

The two sat in silence, supping their beer. Both at once they started to say something. Edward stopped and waited.

John said, "You had a hankerin' after Mary afore..."

The words tumbled from Edward's mouth. "If her beant walkin' out wiv nobody, I be partial ter

67

makin' she's acquaintance, like. But I ain't got naught to offer she yet en if I leave Bat'rst, there'll be no money a-comin' in. Yer farder'd send me packing fer certain sure."

John nodded and went back to his reverie. "You be right," he said. "Us mun bide while 'er be home."

They finished their beer while Edward told his friend about his ambition to grow wheat and keep sheep on his farm. It was time to go. The next time he came to The Butts for supplies, Edward was hoping to see Mary again to find out what his chances were.

Chapter Eight   1701 August

In which Edward meets his nephew.

As soon as his master could allow him a day away from Finchcocks, Edward rode through Wadhurst then along the Mark Cross road to Savages. He had no idea what to expect.

On the right of the road he found a farm track with a notice hanging askew on a tree trunk. This was Savages. That must have been the name of a previous owner. Grass grew in the middle of the track and brambles reached out their new shoots beyond the verges. There had been little in the way of farm carts along here for some time. It wasn't far to the house. Shutters covered two windows on the ground floor and two above. A trellis over the front door supported the remnants of a rose. Two paving slabs led the way to the door from a grassy track. Edward tied Faithful to a gnarled apple tree and went to go into the house, doubts filling his mind. He'd need to spend a lot of time and money to bring it back to a working farm.

He pushed on the door which obstinately resisted. When it opened wide enough to squeeze in, he saw that a bundle of old clothes had been left on the floor. He kicked them away. A mouse ran out and into the shadowy depths of the house. The door opened to its full extent and he left it to let in the fresh air. The earthen floor was damp. A musty smell pervaded the place. He turned to the right, entering what looked like a parlour. He felt he was intruding. Someone had spent the last days of his life in here, perhaps with relatives at his bedside. Or had he died alone, to be found later? A table and a couple of rickety chairs stood in the middle of the room. The grate had been cleaned out. There was nothing on the mantle-shelf. The bed in the corner was stripped down, leaving a simple wooden cot.

Edward came out of this room into the one he'd entered by the front door. There was an iron range with ovens backing onto the parlour, sharing its chimney. A low bench stood along the opposite wall. The doorway ahead of him led to a lean-to which had been added to the main house, running the full width. This was evidently the food preparation area cum dairy. Old iron cooking pots and utensils and pewter dishes, tankards and plates lay on a table with two wooden spoons. A milk churn and two barrels for beer huddled in the corner, pushed to one side like abandoned children.

He went out of the back door, leaving it open. He stood in a cobbled courtyard surrounded by cow stalls, barns and stables. His heart gave a little jump of excitement. This was to be his very own farm. The buildings were empty and cleaned out, except for piles of old hay and straw. A couple of hens chuckled as they pecked at the grass growing among the cobbles. Edward wondered where they'd been laying; somewhere there was a pile of addled eggs. He'd look for those later. He peered down the well, then drew up some water. It looked clean enough.

Indoors again, he found the stairs in a dark corner of the entrance hall and climbed up to the first floor. Cobwebs brushed his face as he walked by. There was no furniture up here, only dust. He went to a window to open the shutters. The bang of a door downstairs startled him. It was only the draught. He put his face to the wooden bars of the window, breathing fresh air. The view was of fields allowed to run to seed. They hadn't been worked for a couple of years. As he pictured a herd of quietly grazing sheep, his spirits rose. Near the house there was a meadow which wasn't as overgrown. Perhaps the tenant had kept a few cows.

Edward came out of the house and mounted Faithful. He walked her round the yard then through to the surrounding fields, following the lane. The hedges were in a poor state but there was a small copse with some good rods he could use for repairing them. To his surprise he found a field of corn ripening. He would need to cut that soon. He'd seen a plough in a barn behind the other buildings, with an old cart. He would prepare some ground ready to sow cowgrass for feeding animals.

Ideas and plans chased each other round in his head. He finished his tour then followed the track back to the road. He wanted to visit his brother in Riseden before returning to Goudhurst.

Richard was walking to his farmhouse from the fields when they saw each other. Edward dismounted and they warmly shook hands. They were both of medium build with the same thatch of brown hair. Richard was looking older.They led Faithful to tether her then Richard showed his brother into his house.

"Molly, we have a visitor," he called to his wife. She came out of the dairy wiping her hands on her apron. Her freckled face lit up when she saw Edward. Her curly auburn hair was tied back loosely.

"My! What a surprise!" she exclaimed coming to give Edward a hug.

Richard led the way into the parlour and showed Edward a seat. He took two tankards from a shelf and went to fill them. Edward was brimming with news for his brother, who he'd not seen for months.

Richard returned, followed by a small boy. "This be yer Uncle Edward, Sam," he said as he handed Edward his beer.

"Pleased ter meet you, Uncle Edward," said Sam. He grinned and showed Edward the wooden horse he was carrying.

"That be a cushti horse," said Edward. "D'you have oats ter feed un on?"

The boy wrinkled his brow, puzzled. He shook his head.

Edward looked in his purse. "Here, take this. It'll buy un some oats." He gave the boy a penny.

"Say thank you, Sam," said Richard.

"Thank you, Uncle Edward." The boy ran out shouting, "Muvver, look what I got…"

Edward said, "Fine boy you have there, Brudder."

"Richard nodded his head. "Molly's with child again. The last un died…"

"Behopes the next un'll do better," Edward said.

"So what's to be at in Lamb'rst?" Richard leaned forward in his chair. "I don't want ter run into Thomas. It allus ends in argifyen. Best keep away."

"Farder's scribed 'is will." Edward started to tell Richard his news.

Molly came in and said, "Will you eat with us, Edward? 'Tis time us catched up with fambly."

"Yus, I'd be main partial ter that," Edward agreed.

It was a pleasant evening. Edward had forgotten how much he and Richard enjoyed each other's company. He looked forward to seeing him more often now he'd be living nearer. Maybe Richard could give him some advice about how to get started on Savages Farm.

The meetings with John in the tavern had become a regular part of Edward's week. The time they met became earlier as the days became shorter.

Edward told John all about Savages and what he planned to grow there. But he was eager to find out how Mary was, since coming home. Did she have a suitor? Or was she content to remain single? He took a mouthful of beer and said,"Be Mary a-courten yet?"

John stared at him, his eyes troubled. He looked down. "Nay, she be unaccountable anxious en us can't get she ter talk." He paused.

After a few minutes he raised his head. "I believe 'twould raise 'er spirits if un knowed you had yer sights on she. Next time you comes to Butts, I'll make sure she can meet you somewhere ye can talk." He looked at Edward for his approval.

This gave Edward new hope. "I be obliged to you, John. 'Twould mean a deal to me if I knowed she were well disposed towards me."

They laughed, knocking their tankards together before draining them. John took them to be refilled.

Chapter Nine   1701 September

In which Edward gives in his notice at Finchcocks

Edward needed to spend a day at Savages planting the soft fruit bushes he'd bought. He woke up early and made the decision to talk to his master.

He did the usual rounds of the stables, mucking out, feeding and grooming and took Ming for a walk. The swallows dived and swooped to catch insects in the yard and perched in rows on the roof ridges, twittering to each other. They would be disappearing soon. Edward took Ming into the house and found George Bathurst sitting in his parlour smoking his first pipe of the day, a black smoking cap on his shaved head. Ming leapt onto his knee and he made a fuss of her.

Edward waited, hat in hand. Bathurst looked up at him.

"Sir, I be minded ter leave Finchcocks 'forelong. Me farder has a farm agin Wad'rst he's offered me. I'll work out me notice fer you, but if you beant in need of me today, I'd be obliged if I could go..."

Bathurst interrupted. "Edward, I know that you would rather be farming than working for me. 'Tis good news that you have that prospect now. You've been an honest and loyal servant. I shall miss you, so will Ming." He looked down and stroked his pet. "Take today to do what you need to do. I'll make enquiries about hiring another manservant. Could you stay here for another week or two while we settle your wages? I've a few more errands for you, but they can wait until tomorrow. I wish you well, Edward."

"Thank you, Sir. Thank you kindly." Edward bowed his way out of the room, relieved that his news had been received so amicably.

In the yard, he threw his hat into the air, caught it and ran to collect the plants he'd left in a pail by the well. He wrapped the dripping bundle in an old sack, took Faithful from her stable and went to the cottage for his knapsack and money. They trotted from Finchcocks to the bridge over the river in Lamberhurst and up the road to Wadhurst. There was no time to call at The Slade today.

He stopped in Wadhurst, tethered Faithful in the market place and went to Tom Stapley's shop. The bell above the door tinkled as he walked in. The place smelled of tanned leather, beeswax and oil. Harnesses and their attachments were draped around the walls. On the right of the door by the window, Stapley, wearing a leather apron, sat on a stool behind a workbench, holding a donkey clamp between his knees. He was bending over with his spectacles on the end of his nose, a needle in each hand, stitching the pieces of leather which were held in the clamp. He worked quickly, his hands flying to each side in turn as he pulled the thread through.

Edward stood and watched.

"En what can I do for you, young Sir?" asked Tom without looking up.

"I be minded ter mend a pair of bellows," said Edward. "Can you sell me a piece of leather?"

Tom stopped stitching, took the clamp from between his knees and propped it up on the workbench. He slipped off his stool, but gained nothing in height, as his back was permanently hunched from years of bending over. He shuffled to the back of the shop, rummaged around for a few minutes, then came back carrying a piece of hide. He rolled it up and tied it with thread before giving it to Edward. "That'll be fower pence," he said.

"I be obliged, Tom," Edward said as he looked in his purse for the correct amount and handed it to the leatherworker.

They both nodded and smiled. Edward picked up his purchase, put it in his bag and walked out into the sunshine.

He needed tools for cutting corn and walked down the road to the ironmonger's. The front of the shop was wide open. Edward shouted, "Hello," and waited at the entrance for Jim to come to him, as he was unable to see anything after being out in the bright sunshine. The sound of Jim's heavy footsteps preceded him and a strong smell of oil reached Edward's nostrils.

"Can I help?" roared Jim, emerging from the darkness.

Edward regarded the oil-stained figure standing before him. "I want harness fer cutten corn," he said.

Jim disappeared into the darkness. Edward heard him crashing around to find scythes, sickles, hooks and a drag-rake which he brought into the light at the front of the shop. "Be these what you be a-seekin'?" he asked.

Edward looked at the variety of corn-cutting tools laid on the floor before him. He picked out a sickle and a drag-rake. "This'll do fer now," he said.

"They be one pound and six shillen tergether," said Jim.

Edward paid for his tools, said, "Much obliged," then went to Bartlett's the seed merchants to buy cowgrass seed. That would do for today. The seed was expensive and he'd plenty to do without buying anything else.

He went to release Faithful from her tether and used the rope to secure the drag-rake along the saddle. "We'll have ter walk," he said.

Edward strode up the lane to Savages, his heart glowing with pride. This was a new beginning. He was Master here. He could run the farm the way he wanted. He tethered Faithful on the grass in front of the cottage by the old apple tree where there were some windfall apples for her to savour.

The door opened more easily this time. This place needed cleaning and re-organising but it would have to wait. He propped the doors open to let the air in and went to see what tools there were in the barn. He found a spade and fork and took them with the young fruit bushes to the vegetable garden. The soil turned over easily, falling friably from his fork, releasing the weeds which had accumulated. This garden had been well cared for.

As he dug and planted, enjoying the exercise, the loamy smell of the soil and the autumn air, his mind wandered to the impending meeting with Mary. A stir of excitement in his breast caused him to stop and straighten up for a moment to take a breath. Dare he hope that she would welcome his attention? Dare he picture her here as his wife, surrounded by their children? He pushed the thoughts away, turning his mind back to the planting.

He sat on the back step eating the bread and cheese he'd begged from Cook, watching the hens busily pecking. They came running when he scattered crumbs. There were four healthy birds and two which he guessed were past their laying life. They would give him a few meals. He planned to build them a coop and keep them in a run so he could keep track of where their eggs were laid.

The day passed quickly. He'd sharpened some tools and the ploughshare. He now had a good idea which jobs to tackle next and what he would have to buy in order to live here. He secured the doors of the cottage and the barn, mounted Faithful and made his way back to Finchcocks.

Mr Dewe had paid all that he owed for the meat up to date. Edward was expecting to be paid his last wages at the end of the week. He was preparing to leave Finchcocks. There was one last visit to make.

He walked up the hill into Goudhurst and along the track leading to The Butts. His heart fluttered with excitement. But he must bear in mind that Mary might not welcome his advances. He thought of her bright eyes, her rosebud mouth, the scent of her and how disappointed he would be if she showed no interest.

John, seeing his approach from the house, came out to meet him.

"Be Mary at home?" Edward asked.

"John nodded. "'Er be agwain to the copse. You can meet she there where ye can be private.

"Be 'er well disposed?" Edward needed re-assurance that he hadn't built up his hopes too high.

John smiled. "'Er seemed anxious ter see you." He led Edward through the yard and indicated the direction of the copse.

Edward waved his hand as he walked on. His heart was thumping by the time he reached the grassy track leading to the copse. There was a movement among the trees. He lowered his head to avoid a branch and followed, shuffling through the carpet of dried leaves towards a figure standing under a beech tree in the height of its autumn colour. She wore a blue dress with a white apron and cap. She held out her hand as he approached. He took it, feeling the warm soft skin against his roughness. She led him to a fallen tree trunk where she sat and patted the space next to her. Her hand was delicate, the fingers long and slender. He sat looking into her smiling face.

He took her hand and kissed it.

She said, "I be main pleased ter see you, Edward. 'Tis a long time..."

"Oh, Mary! I did not dare ter hope that you would want ter meet me. I'd dearly love ter be a-courten, if you be agreeable."

She turned her hand over and squeezed his. "Edward, you be often in me thoughts. I be anxious ter make yer acquaintance, surely."

Edward let go her hand and drew a deep breath. "Me prospects be good, Mary. But yer muvver en farder wouldn't agree to a courtship prensly, as I've no property or work." He told her that he was leaving Finchcocks and that Savages was to be his when his father died. "I'll never be wealthy like Robert Bat'rst en 'twould be a hard-working life ter be a farmer's mistus, as you knows..." His voice trailed off. He looked anxiously into Mary's eyes.

A blackbird flew down and disturbed the leaves by their feet, searching for worms in the soft humus. The scent of rotting vegetation rose to their nostrils. They sat close together, absorbed in the quiet of the wood.

Mary spoke. "I be more fitted ter be a farmer's wife than gentry. I beant Quality en have no wish ter be. Farder en Muvver had high expectations, but now they believe I've no prospects at all. They'd be relieved ter get me off their hands."

The blackbird rose from the ground. His alarm call echoed through the trees.

Edward's spirits rose. His heart swelled. "Will you wait fer me, Mary? I mun fix up Savages ter make it fit fer you ter bide there. 'Twill take a while ter turn it into a working farm."

Mary's eyes glistened with tears. "Surely I'll wait, Edward. Behopes 'twill not be long. But I'll be patient. Come en see me now en again, so's I don't disremember yer handsome face."

Edward planted a soft kiss on her rosy cheek. He felt protective towards her. "Come the time I thinks fit, I'll go en talk to thy farder, so's us can walk out together."

They strolled hand-in-hand to the edge of the wood. Mary went towards the house, not looking back in case someone was watching. Edward gazed after her, before he made his way along the grassy path and through the yard.

John was attending to the horses and came to meet him. "Good news?" he asked.

Edward nodded and beamed at John. "Good news!" he said.

The day arrived when Edward was to say goodbye to Finchcocks. Bathurst and Ming stood in the yard as he loaded his belongings into the cart he'd borrowed. Cook and the parlour maid came from the kitchen and embraced him. He felt something which was wrapped in a cloth being slipped into his hand.

"You'll need ter eat, m'dear," said Cook.

"Thank you, God bless thee," said Edward, touched by the affection shown.

Bathurst stepped forward to shake hands. "I wish you good fortune in your new life, Edward. I hope you find a good wife to share it with."

Edward felt his face flush. "I have a young gal in mind, Sir." He smiled. "I needs ter fix up the bidance afore I can go a-courten."

"I'll miss your gentle company," said Bathurst. "Come and tell us your news from time to time."

"Thank you, Sir," Edward replied. He turned to climb onto the cart, anxious to find a home for himself at Savages.

He would go straight there and call back at The Slade when he returned the cart. The journey took longer pulling his howsell. It was half way through the morning when he drove up the lane. A light drizzle covered everything in a wet film and he hurried Faithful into the yard where he unloaded his belongings. He took her to graze in her very own pasture then put the cart under cover.

Edward walked in by the back door. He stood in the hall, looking round. It was dark in here. He shivered as the damp seeped through his clothes. Best light a fire first, then sweep the floor and bring a small table and a stool from the kitchen. He would live in this room to start with. The cot would fit nicely against the wall by the stairs where the bench stood now.

By the time he'd made the room habitable his stomach was telling him it was time he ate. He unwrapped Cook's parcel to find a meat pie. He knew it would contain carrots as well as her best gravy, so decided to heat it up for his dinner. He had a loaf of bread and some cheese which was enough for several days' coager and there might be eggs. He found a plate and a knife in the kitchen and sat on the bench at the table facing the fire, which was warming the room up nicely.

As he began to feel more at home he started to make plans for the next few days. He needed to find candles and make up his bed. There was dry hay in the barn, which would make a good mattress. He had a coat to throw over himself if he got cold.

The next thing was to go shopping. He had to find a cow and a cart horse and some provisions for his meals until he was able to produce his own. Then there was the corn to cut and thresh, it was already late in the season. He would take some to the mill to be ground for flour. That should provide him with bread for the winter. The rest of the corn he would sow in the spring for next year's harvest. And it was urgent that he build a coop for the chickens.

Chapter Ten   1702   Autumn

In which Father reveals a secret.

The months slipped by and before he knew it the days were shortening again. He'd ploughed and manured, sowed and mowed and was building up his reserves. Visits to Slade Farm had been less frequent as he'd hardly time to rest. His father was right; he needed a woman to make the bread, butter, cheese, beer and cook the meals.

He met John Paris on market days for a drink in the Grazehound in Wadhurst and had sent messages to Mary who was constantly in his thoughts. He couldn't go courting her yet. His money was running low. He would soon have nothing left to buy meat or pay the rent.

He'd heard of a farm nearby where they were selling up today. There were a few sheep and a ram which would eventually provide meat and wool. He had plenty of pasture and had repaired the hedges. He hoped to buy the little flock for a reasonable price. He set off down his lane to the road with a stout stick. There were other people walking in the direction of Mark Cross. He suspected they were all going to the sale. Sure enough, some of them turned into the entrance of the farm.

Edward found himself walking alongside an older man with a bushy white beard and eyebrows to match. He had a pipe hanging from his mouth. He looked at Edward and nodded.

"Be you minded ter buy?" asked Edward.

"Yus, there be harness I'll have a look at. You buyin'?"

Edward nodded. "I be settin' up me own farm, like. There's sheep fer sale, but I know naught about sheep. 'Ow will I know they be fit ter buy?"

The man took his pipe out of his mouth and turned to Edward, holding out his hand. "Ed Wag'orn, from Bewl Bridge. I'd be pleased ter show thee what ter look fer."

Edward shook the man's hand. "Pleased ter meet you, Ed. I be Edward Lucke. I've taken over Savages on Best Beech Hill."

Waghorn nodded. "I knows the place. Gone down these past few year. I rackon you'll have a job ter get it goin'. Be you Thomas Lucke's son from Lamb'rst?"

"Yus," said Edward. It was good to meet a friend of his father. "'E be failin' prensly. Me brudder Thomas runs Slade Farm."

They chatted until they reached the farmyard where all the goods for sale were laid out, filling the yard. Farmers and their wives peered and poked at the tools, animals, machinery and some worn out furniture. An occasional voice was raised in protest at a price quoted too high, followed by loud discussion.

Waghorn said to Edward, "Over there. There's sheep in a pen. Come, I'll show you."

They walked over to the pen, where half a dozen woolly bundles bleated plaintively. It appeared that they hadn't been shorn that year. A sad collie dog lay beside the pen, its nose between its paws. The eyes rolled around, watching people coming and going.

Edward saw a man who looked as if he was in charge and went up to him. "Can us have a look at the sheep?" he asked.

The man came over to the pen and opened the gate. Waghorn had his pipe in his mouth again. He examined the eyes, ears, teeth and feet of one of the sheep. "You can tell soon enough if they beant healthy," he said. "Look fer flies, maggots en ticks in their wool. Wait 'til the spring ter shear 'em, mind. Feel their bellies en look at their feet. If you sees aught that looks unnat'ral, like, you've got trouble." He turned to the supervisor. "D'you mind what be their age?"

"I'd say fower or five year."

Ed said, "They've been unaccountable neglected, like, but with care, you should be able ter breed from 'em en get a healthy flock a-goin'."

Edward and Waghorn examined the rest of the sheep, finding nothing that pointed to disease.

The supervisor said, "Dog comes with 'em."

Edward looked at the thin creature. "What's 'is name?"

The supervisor shrugged. "Danged if I knows." He quoted a figure for the lot.

Waghorn took his pipe out of his mouth. "They be half-dead, man! They be worth half that!"

The supervisor agreed a lower price and Edward went to pay. He thanked Waghorn for his help and walked back to the sheep. Now he had to get them home.

Shep proved to be a well-seasoned sheepdog. He knew his charges.There was no trouble keeping them together along the road which was crowded with people returning home. Edward guided the sheep into Savages lane with his stick and went ahead to open the gate into the pasture. Shep herded them in, then came to sit by his new master, tongue lolling.

"Good dog!" Edward was amazed at how easy it had been. He bent down and patted Shep with enthusiasm. "Come en have some dinner," he said. "You looks like you needs it."

Edward counted the money in his purse. He had to go to collect some trees he'd ordered from the nursery at Hunton. Then he'd have just enough money left for a good meal at The Bull in Frant. He would share it with Shep. They hadn't eaten properly for several days. All his money was going on rent and taxes.

He called at Slade Farm on the way home. When he arrived, he left the horse and cart with Shep in the yard before going through to the court. Dorcas and Eliza were milking the cows.

"Hello, Muvver. Thought I'd happen by ter see Farder."

Dorcas smiled ruefully. "'E be middlin'. Go on in. I'll be with thee afore long."

Thomas's cot had been brought down to the parlour. He appeared to be sleeping, but when Edward pulled a chair up to the bed his father's eyes snapped open. He put a frail, shaky hand up to greet him. Edward took it in his two warm ones and put it gently back under the covers.

"I be breathin', but that's about all," croaked Thomas.

Edward sat and looked at his father. He couldn't imagine life without him. He searched the sallow features, looking for any small part of the man he knew. Thomas' eyes continued to be as sharp and warm as ever.

He cleared his throat before starting to talk. "I've been minded ter tell thee summat you should know afore I pass on." He tried to raise his head, but fell back.

Edward helped him to sit forward while he re-arranged his pillows. "Teck yer time, Farder," he said.

Thomas asked for a drink and Edward went to fill a mug with beer.

His father took a draught then lay back again, giving the mug to Edward to hold.

"'Tis summat yer Gaffer said to me afore 'e died. 'E told me 'ow 'is Uncle Thomas, what passed the farm on to un, like, said on 'is deathbed that if 'e were ever short of money, desperate like, that there were summat hidden that would solve all 'is problems." Thomas took the mug from Edward and had another sip.

"Where's this treasure hidden then, Farder?" Edward was getting interested.

"That's what 'e never said. 'Is last words was *'You'll find it in the cl...'* Then 'e coughed en died!" Thomas' eyes opened wide. His brow wrinkled as he looked at Edward.

Edward stared at his father in disbelief. What was the point in telling him only half the story?

Thomas spoke again. "Me farder searched for a while, but was never in such need, so 'e jacked it in. 'Tis unaccountable puzzlin'. I've tried ter work out what 'e could mean. But I weren't that desperate neither. Farder said that we mun pass the message on to our sons. 'E believed that when it were really needed 'twould show itself."

Edward took a sip of his father's beer then handed it to him. "Do my brudder Thomas know of this?"

"Nay, Son. I don't reckon 'e'd be sensible with it. No amount of money would solve his problems. En Richard's not likely ter need it."

Edward said, more to himself than to his father, "I'd dearly like to know where 'tis. I could do with some help prensly." He looked down, regretting letting it slip out.

There was nothing wrong with his father's hearing. His mind was as sharp as ever. "Edward, you should tell me when times be hard. I don't need no money. I can't teck it with me. Would it help if you didn't have ter pay me rent?"

Edward nodded. "Yus, Farder, that would be hem agreeable. But you needs money ter feed Muvver en yerself."

"I've plenty put away. En I helps Junior out now en again. I don't see why you shouldn't have a share."

Dorcas and Eliza had come into the milkhouse, bringing the pails of milk. There was a clatter as they set them down. Dorcas came to stand at the parlour door. Thomas beckoned her over. She bustled over to him. He pulled her close to whisper in her ear. She nodded and hobbled up the stairs. A few minutes later she re-appeared and went over to Edward. She took his hand, opened the fingers then closed them over some coins.

"Not a word," she said.

Edward swallowed back the surfacing emotion. He put the money in his pocket.

"'Ow's that wench of thine?" his mother asked.

He smiled. "'Twill be a while betimes Savages be ready. But I mean ter ax she ter walk out along of me afore long."

"You'd better get yerself well fed afore then. I can see yer ribs through yer shirt." Dorcas poked him where it was sensitive. He caught her hand in the act, held it up to his face and pressed it to his lips. She put her arm round his waist to give him a hug.

"Muvver, d'you have a cockerel I could use fer me hens? They've a'most gived up layin' fer winter en I could do with raisin' chicks come spring."

Dorcas said, "Follow me."

Edward gave his father a wave and followed his mother out into the court. They went through to the chicken run and the hens gathered round them for food. Dorcas caught one of the cockerels unawares. He squawked in protest.

"Will this do?" she said. "I've more'n enough. You can keep un en may 'e farder a fine brood fer you." She tucked the bird under her arm, closing the run behind them. They went to the barn where chicken peds were stacked in one corner. She popped him into one of them, secured the latch, then handed it to Edward.

"Thank you, Muvver. I'll pay you..."

Dorcas put her hand up to his mouth. "No need," she said. "Don't leave it too long afore you comes again." She gave his hand a squeeze as they walked to the cart together. Edward loaded up the cockerel and patted the waiting Shep before climbing up.

"That dog looks as hungry as thee," Dorcas said, watching as he drove off.

One evening a few days later, sitting at the table in his parlour in the flickering candlelight, Edward opened his account book. He took his quill, dipped it in the ink and wrote:

Then laid out of my pocket at the Bull at Frant for myself and the dogs eating 0-------2--------6
More for fetching the trees at Hunton to give the nurseryman 0-------0--------6
More for a pair of stockings 0-------4--------0

Paid for a cow's going to bull 0-------0--------6

Chapter Eleven   1703   Summer

In which Edward agrees to fell beeches for his brother.

Mary sat on the window seat in her chamber, reading Ben Johnson's poem:

> *Drink to me only with thine eyes,*
> *And I will pledge with mine;*
> *Or leave a kiss but in the cup,*
> *And I'll not look for wine.*
> *The thirst that from the soul...*

She sighed, closed the book and put it down on the table by her side.

The view from the window was of the little copse where she'd met Edward, nearly two years ago. She pulled a paper from under her low-cut bodice, unfolding it as she'd done many times since she received it two days ago. Her heart gave a flutter.

Dear Mary, [she almost knew it by heart.] *I hope you are well. I have Savages running as a farm and bought fruit trees for the garden. I planted them yesterday. Last week I bought a liddle flock of sheep. They come with a dog. I call him Shep. He be good company. But there beant any money a-comen in betimes I can sell summat. Behopes next time I write, 'twill be with good news. You be always in me thoughts. I be anxious to know that you be a-biding for me still.   Edwd Lucke*

Mary folded the letter carefully, kissing it before slipping it back into its hiding place. She stood up shook out her skirts, picked up a shawl and left the room. She went downstairs and out of the house through the kitchen. A chilly breeze whipped up her skirts and she wrapped the shawl round her shoulders as she walked towards the copse. There was nothing she could do but wait. But for how long? It was easy at first, with the recent memory of him sitting beside her in the copse. Life was tedious here. Her parents had nothing to say to her. John was a dear, bringing her news when he had some. She longed to go to see Edward at Savages. Perhaps there was something she could help him with, though she'd no idea about farming activities and her parents wouldn't allow it. She wanted to see the little cottage where she would share her life with Edward. She'd built up a picture of it in her mind. A neat little brick path led to a front door which had a rose growing round it. There was a garden with flowers and now some fruit trees. Inside there was a blazing fire in the hearth and a soft padded seat for two, where they would cuddle up in the evenings.

She made her way through the trees to the log where they sat together that day. Here, she could feel closer to him. She could recall the country scent of him, the warmth of his body, his voice saying the words she wanted to hear again, his promise to return. Her eighteen-year-old heart longed for romance, someone to love her. She knew hardly anything about him, except that he was kind and he liked her. He wasn't dashing and handsome as Robert was, but that didn't matter. He had kind blue eyes, a warm smile and a gentle nature.

It was a long time since that day. She was weary of waiting. She'd little idea what would be required of her as Edward's wife. They wouldn't have enough money for servants, at least to start with, so she imagined she would have to keep the house clean and do some cooking. Her mother never did these things. She spent her time embroidering and entertaining her friends. Occasionally she would accompany her husband into town to buy frivolous nick nacks, a dress or a hat. Mary enjoyed sewing. She made her own dresses which were simple and homely. She didn't feel comfortable wearing rich clothing or gossiping with her mother's friends. She would always find some excuse to be elsewhere when they came to visit.

She got up from her seat and walked slowly and despondently back to the house. She climbed the stairs to her chamber and closed the door behind her. Her quill and ink stood waiting on the table by the window. She found paper in the drawer and sat down to write to Edward. She took a deep breath. It would be a mistake to tell him how desperate she was to be with him. He might think she was weak and couldn't wait if she confessed. She'd made her promise. She had no choice but to keep it.

My dear Edward, I was pleased to receive your letter and to hear that you be making good progress on the farm. I look forward to seeing the lambs skipping in the pasture come spring and to sharing with you the fruit from the trees.
I be well, thank the Lord and Mother and Father also. It is nice to have news of you from John now and again. Life here is mortaceous dull and I long to be near you. I send my best wishes. Mary.

≈≈≈

Edward read Mary's letter with an aching heart. He needed to see her again soon. It would be spring before there were lambs skipping in the pasture with one or two calves. There would also be chicks, hopefully. In the meantime he would go visiting.

He collected Faithful from the pasture and saddled her up to ride over to see Richard. Molly came out of the house to greet him, carrying her daughter in her arms.

"Richard's fallin' trees by the copse," she said. "Wait there." She went back indoors, coming out again with a bundle of food and a costrel. "'E disremembered 'is bait. I've put some in fer you." She handed it over, directing him to the copse.

It was a cold November day but the sun shone brightly, throwing Edward's long shadow across the stubble field. He heard the sounds of chopping and voices and soon came upon his brother and a farm worker. Three stately mature beech trees stood where the field met the copse. Their tall straight trunks reached up to their branches spreading out, fingering the sky. Edward felt sad to see the great gash at the foot of one of them, where the axes had chopped into living flesh. Soon, the handsome tree would be stretched out on the ground, its branches crushed by the fall, to be carted away to build houses and furniture for rich men.

He stood to one side as the tree groaned.

"Timber!" shouted Richard.

The tree creaked, falling slowly at first.

The farm worker ran through the copse, away from the danger. He tripped on something hidden deep in the undergrowth, gave a terrified howl and plunged face down.

The tree fell with a splintering crash.

Silence, as all other sound was sucked into the void.

Richard and Edward ran to where the man lay.

He was moaning with pain.

Richard bent down. "Zach, hold on. We'll get you free."

A branch had pinned Zach's leg to the ground.

Richard went for his axe to attack the branch at its base. Edward tried to hold it still. Every chop sent vibrations through to Zach's leg. He screamed in agony.

At last the branch let go. Edward heaved it aside. Zach passed out.

Richard crouched down. Edward helped to roll the man onto his back and Richard examined the damaged leg.

"'E'll not be footin' it again," Richard remarked. He stood up. "Thanks be you were here, brudder. I'll go en fetch the horse en cart. Bide with un in case 'e wakes." He shook his head sadly. "'E were an upstanding, steadfast worker."

Edward sat on one of the branches of the fallen tree, musing upon the morning's events. The man was lucky to be alive. Or was he? How would he earn a living? Richard had lost a good farm worker. Farming was a dangerous business, Edward knew, but he'd never witnessed an accident like this. His whole body trembled with the shock. He tried to control himself. He didn't want his brother to see him in this state.

Richard brought a bottle of brandy with him. He and Edward took a mouthful before pouring a long trickle down Zach's throat. He came to, gulped, gasped and coughed. He tried to sit up, but lay back again with horror on his face as he remembered what had happened.

He looked at Richard. "I be no good to you now, Mas Richard," he said.

"Nay, but us can't leave you here, Zach," said Richard. "This'll pain you. We have ter pick you up en lay you on the cart. Here, finish the bottle if you have to." He handed Zach the brandy, nodded at Edward then went to heave Zach up by his shoulders.

Edward said, "Wait." He took the belt from around Zach's waist, using it to strap his two legs together. The good leg would now support the injured one.

Zach howled as they lifted him off the ground. He took a draught from the bottle. The cart was only a few steps away. Richard had laid straw down to soften the motion. The journey to the house over the field would not be smooth.

Molly was waiting for them in the yard. "I brought a cot down to the parlour," she said. "We'll get the doctor here. Zach beant fit ter tend hisself at 'is cottage."

When they'd settled Zach on the cot and Richard had sent for the doctor, the two brothers sat on a bench in the yard with their bait.

"What'll you do now with no labourer?" asked Edward.

Richard finished his mouthful. "I've got a buyer fer those beeches en 'e wants 'em dracly-minute."

Edward considered for a moment. "I beant over-busy prensly. I could come en work fer you betimes spring, when the birthen starts.

Richard looked at his brother and nodded. "That'd be hem agreeable. I'll pay you what I pays Zach."

They shook hands on it before they continued eating.

Edward said, "Farder's ailing. 'E be hankerin' after seein' you afore 'e passes."

Richard nodded. "I'll take Sam along dappen we've fallen those trees."

"I be minded ter see a friend in Gowd'rst 'sarternoon," said Edward. "I'll come termorrer betimes I've done me business."

Richard agreed. When they'd finished their bait, Edward went into the house to say goodbye to Molly and Sam and little Meg.

He trotted along the road through Lamberhurst to Goudhurst with a lighter heart. He'd be earning some money soon. He rode up the track to The Butts towards his heart's desire and into the yard. Faithful's hooves clattered on the cobbles announcing his arrival. But the place was quiet, seemingly deserted.

He dismounted and hitched the reins over a post. His throat was tight. What if they were all out somewhere? He'd come all this way for nothing. He should have written a letter first. Someone must be there; it was late afternoon and time the cows were milked. He wandered round the house, not knowing what to do.

But why was he creeping round like a thief? He summoned up his courage and strode purposefully to the front door. He raised the big brass knocker, then let it drop. The sound echoed through empty rooms. He waited, then knocked again, feeling less confident.

The sound of patens on stone floors came from the depths of the house, becoming louder. He stood back in anticipation. A maid opened the door, mouth agape. "Please, Sir, Mas en Mistus be abroad for the day en the men be a-worken in the fields. Who shall I say called?"

Edward cleared his throat. "Be Miss Mary at home?"

"Yus, Sir."

Relief tingled through his body. "Tell she Edward Lucke be here," he said.

"Yus, Sir." The maid curtseyed, shut the door and her footsteps clacked away.

Edward took a deep breath. He told himself to stop shaking. All would be well.

More footsteps. The door opened. His sweet Mary was standing there, all rosy smiles and glistening eyes. "Come in," she said.

He entered the cool, spacious hall. He could see nothing but her face and her arms outstretched in greeting.

He took her hands, saying, "Mary, I be sorry it's been so long. I should've written, but…"

She put her fingers to his lips. "Hush, now. You be here en I be dearly glad ter see you."

Edward stood for a moment looking at her, enjoying the warmth of her hands in his. "I be come ter ax yer farder if I can walk out along of you."

Mary gasped with excitement. Her hands tightened on his. She recovered herself, saying, "'E be abroad with Muvver. When can you come again?"

"I be minded ter come visiting Sundays, if that be agreeable. I'll come next Sunday en ax un then," said Edward.

"That be good news. I'll tell them you be a-comen. "She squeezed his hand and kissed it. "Come Sunday, Edward."

He took both of her hands, kissing them many times, excitement welling up in his chest. He released her and turned to go. "Come Sunday, Mary," he said.

Chapter Twelve   1704   July

In which Mary is kept waiting.

It was a lovely bright sunny morning, nearly a year later. Mary threw back the bedcovers, sat up, breathed deeply and stretched her arms high above her head. Edward would be visiting today. She could stay in bed no longer.

These weekly meetings were a Godsend. They kept her going during the waiting time. She and Edward were getting to know each other, their likes and dislikes, hopes and dreams. She was sure they were right for each other. Furthermore, he was her only chance of her escaping from this life of tedium. He'd told her how she would be expected to help him on the farm and in the dairy, where there would be butter and cheese to be made and beer to brew. She went to watch the maid doing these things here and felt that with a little help at first she would master it. She loved the farm animals and looked forward to feeding chickens and collecting eggs. As a child she had a pet lamb which she fed with a bottle until it grew up. And she'd always hoped to have a dog.

By the time she finished dressing, her excitement had mounted so that she wondered how she would contain herself until he came to meet her outside the church. She went out into the garden, breathing the fresh, sweet air. She picked a daisy to put in her hair and bent to smell a newly opened rose.

Breakfast was waiting when she came indoors. Her brothers were already out on the farm feeding the animals. Her mother and father sat moodily awaiting her arrival before starting to eat. She sat down at the table and helped herself to a small portion of game pie and some bread.

"Are you ailing, child?" her mother said. "There's not enough on your plate for a bird. Come, there are some beautiful quails eggs here." She handed the dish to Mary, who took one egg and declined more.

"I haven't the stomach this morning, Mother. But I'm quite well, thank you."

"She be pining for that man of hers," her father smirked before putting a large forkful of meat into his mouth.

Mary felt herself blushing and bowed her head.

"'Tis a beautiful day," remarked her mother. "We should take a stroll round the village after church. I've invited George Bathurst to dine with us."

Mary struggled through her breakfast while her parents made small-talk. She heard little of what they said. Her mind was anticipating her meeting with Edward; the sight of him as he approached her, their greeting, the warmth of his lips kissing her hands, the feel of his hands holding hers, her longing to touch his face and move closer, but aware that all eyes were upon them.

The church bells were ringing. Mary and her parents climbed into the carriage to be taken down the long drive to the village. People were gathering, greeting each other and chatting before going into the cool stillness of the church. Edward had not yet arrived.

"I'll wait out here," Mary called to her parents as they alighted.

They waved and left her standing anxiously by the door.

Late-comers hurried by.

The bells stopped ringing.

She went to the litten gate straining her eyes to catch sight of him riding up the road. The village was deserted.

Music came floating out from the congregation. She should be in there with her parents. She went in reluctantly to take her place in the family pew next to her mother, leaving a space by her side for Edward. She joined in the singing.

Her thoughts were far away as she went through the motions, reciting the responses and prayers of the service.

He surely would not have forgotten to come. Something had held him up. He was never late like this. Perhaps he'd had an accident and was lying in the road somewhere, having been flung from his horse…

They sat for the address. Mary tried to concentrate, to take her mind off her racing heart and the lump in her throat. Every little sound from the back of the church prompted her to turn round to see if it was Edward. Her mother nudged her and gave her a withering look.

Mary looked through her tears at the watery sun filtering through the stained glass window, certain now that he would not come. The vicar's voice droned on, saying nothing of meaning to her. How would she live through the next week, not knowing what had happened? Her thoughts were now a blur.

As everyone stood for the final hymn, she automatically followed. She fancied she could smell his earthy aroma of milk and horses and felt a touch on her arm. She looked down to see his feet standing next to hers. She looked up. He was there, smiling down on her. His hand found hers and gave it a squeeze.

She clung onto his hand as music filled the cavernous space, tears rolling down her cheeks. She was unable to sing. When they knelt for the final prayer and blessing, she mopped her face with her handkerchief. No-one should see she'd been weeping. They rose and he stepped aside for her as she came out into the aisle. He bowed to her mother as she passed. Mary kept on walking, hoping that her unsteady gait would not be obvious.

They emerged into the sunshine. Everyone stood in little groups, gossiping amicably, relieved to be in the fresh air, releasing the emotions stirred up by the vicar's words.

"I be sorry ter come so late." Mary heard his voice over her shoulder.

She turned to face him. "You crept in so quiet I didn't hear you!" she burst out happily, disguising with a laugh the state she'd been in.

≈≈≈

Edward went to greet her parents. George Bathurst joined the family party. "Shall we take a walk round the village?" invited Mistus Paris in a commanding voice. She wanted to be seen in the company of gentry and with a daughter who had a suitor, however lowly.

The men replaced their hats and the women adjusted their bonnets. They strolled down the path through the litten, nodding to acquaintances, Mistus Paris leaning on the arm of her husband. Mary came behind them, Bathurst and Edward on each side. They squeezed through the lych gate along with the rest of the congregation, spewing out into the village street, each group going their separate ways. Mary walked by Edward's side. Bathurst came to walk next to Edward and they exchanged news, Edward giving

Bathurst an update on the farm's progress. Mary listened.

Back at The Butts the company assembled round the table in the dining room with Mary's two brothers who had joined them. Mrs Paris carved the spit-roast beef which was served with spicy sweetmeats made with dried fruit, a carp and a chicken pie. A servant passed the plates round to Mr Bathurst first, followed by her husband, her two sons and lastly Mary and Edward. They drank Madeira wine. Bathurst proposed a toast, first to his hosts then to Mary and Edward as a couple.

The conversation covered the latest politics. There had been a General Election earlier in the year. Bathurst, as he worked in London, had news of riots between the Tories and the newly-emerging Whigs. Mary sat between her brothers, opposite her mother, who had Bathurst and Edward on either side of her. Edward had little interest in politics and judging by the look on Mary's face across the table, she felt the same. They pretended to listen while gazing into each other's eyes when they thought it wouldn't be noticed.

"And who did you vote for, Edward?" asked Paris throwing his loud voice across the table.

Edward was embarrassed. He cleared his throat. "Beg Pardon, Sir. I beant a voter betimes I inherit me farder's property."

Gerald Junior sniggered.

John said, "Me too en I be doubtful 'twill make a lot of difference who us votes fer. Parlyment will do what they think fit without consulting we."

There was an uncomfortable silence.

Mistus Paris said, "Your plate is empty Mr Bathurst. May I offer you some more?"

Bathurst accepted. "The meal is perfectly delicious, Ma'am. You have an excellent cook." The company broke into pairs, talking among themselves. Gerald talked to his father and Bathurst engaged Mistus Paris in conversation.

John said across the table to Edward, "How be the new sheep, Edward?"

"Middlin'," said Edward. "Behopes the ram will take to 'em en give me some lambs ter sell next year. You found a farm yet?"

"Nay, I be a-seekin' summat down your way. Small to begin with. Then I'll be in the same position as you. We could back each other up, like. I be partial to be near to you en Mary after ye wed..." He looked at his sister affectionately.

≈≈≈

Mary had been listening as she toyed with her food. "That would be hem agreeable," she said. She was longing for the meal to be over so that she and Edward could walk round the garden together.

The table was cleared and the sweets arrived. Mary picked at titbits of tarts, crystallised fruit and sticky puddings, hoping her mother wouldn't notice and persuade her to eat more.

At last the meal was over. The men retired to the drawing room for a glass of port and a smoke. Mary and her mother made their way to the parlour.

"Your man was unaccountably late this morning," her mother said disapprovingly.

"I believe 'e stayed at the back of the church for the address, Muvver, so's not to disturb people." Mary picked up her embroidery to relieve the tension of waiting.

"He's a very rough young man. Heaven knows how he'll treat you when you're wed and I dread to think what conditions you'll have to live in."

Mary was tired of her mother insulting Edward. She raised her voice, "He be kind and gentle. He wouldn't hurt a fly, Mother. And he loves me, which is more than anyone does round here." She put her embroidery down and stood up. "I shall wait for him in the garden."

"Don't you lead him on, my girl! We don't want any bastards here before I get you off my hands!" Her mother said loudly as Mary left the room.

She went to sit on the garden seat in full view of the parlour window, but facing towards the roses. She watched the bees visiting the flowers and began to calm down.

Soon she heard the whisper of footsteps across the grass behind her. Edward came to sit by her side and held her hands. She looked up at him.

"Oh, Edward, I so long to be away from here and in your arms. They're all anxious fer me ter leave. Mother has said as much just now." She clutched his hand desperately.

"Behopes 'twill not be long, my love." Edward's gentle voice soothed her. "The house beant ready for you yet en money be short. I be workin' fer me brudder agen betimes spring, then I'll be better off. I long ter have you with me, Mary. These Sundays be a trial for both of we, I b'lieve."

"Better ter see you now-en-agen than not at all," said Mary.

They wandered round the garden hand-in-hand and talked about how it would be. Edward told her that his father was dying and though he dreaded losing him, it would open a door to their marriage, as he would then be a man of property. After a time he took his leave once more to go to see to his animals before dark.

"At least I'll not have ter cook meself a meal," he said. "That dinner will last me a few days I reckon!"

Chapter Thirteen 1705/6

In which a will is read and a proposal is made.

Shep was barking. Edward left his plate of porridge and went to see who was calling so early in the morning. As he opened the door the drizzling rain blew into his face. He peered out, not wanting to get wet.

A horseman rode into the yard, dismounted and came to Edward with a letter in his hand. He took it asking if a reply was required. This might be from Mary, he hoped nothing was wrong.

The horseman shook his head and returned to his horse, mounted and turned to go back down the lane.

Edward called Shep and let him into the house before closing the door. He went back into the hall, sat at the table, pushed away the half-eaten porridge and unfolded the letter. He read the brief note:

> *"Farder be ded. Muvver ses tell Richrd.*
> *Yer brudder Tho."*

The room appeared to spin round for a moment. He couldn't see for the water in his eyes. His chest felt as if it would burst.

Shep came to put his paws up on his master's knee.

Edward automatically put out a hand to stroke the dog. He looked round at him, tears falling from his eyes. "Farder be gone," he said.

His hands were shaking now as he put them up to his face and drew a long breath. Sobs shook his body. He stayed there letting the grief flow.

He milked the cow and fed the fowls and beasts before going to tell Richard. His brother was greatly saddened by the news and Molly came to join them in their sorrow. Then the two brothers rode to Slade Farm together to comfort their mother.

It seemed as if the family had wept all their tears at the funeral. The church was packed with friends and neighbours as well as family.

A week or so later the mourners sat around the table in the hall at Slade Farm. Dorcas, as first executrix, held the will in her trembling hands. Ann sat next to her. Opposite them, Thomas Tapsell, yeoman and John Feavour, tailor, were the overseers. Thomas Lucke, now head of the family, sat next to his mother, his brothers and sisters filling in the gaps.

Dorcas read the will, stumbling over the words now and again:

"...to be buried in the churchyard of Lamb'rst...

...my loving wife my said house and lands lying in...

...not to fell or cut down any timber but only for reparation of my said house...and shall not cut down any fruit trees but preserve them and all the said coppices...my wife do happen to marry again...my said son Thomas Lucke shall disendow her and enjoy it to himself....for want of a male heir of his body I give and bequeath...to Edward Lucke my youngest son all my said house and lands lying in Wadhurst...I give and bequeath unto Richard my middle son the sum of twenty shillings to be paid..."

Dorcas' voice pattered on and Edward's attention took a diversion. Savages was now his own property, officially. He could at last go to Mr and Mrs Paris and ask for their daughter's hand in marriage. Since they started courting Mary had shown interest in everything Edward was doing at Savages and they made plans for their future together. But he wasn't bringing in enough money to support the two of them. All his wages from Richard were being spent on the farm.

His mother was coming to the end, *"...last will and testament renouncing all other wills...my wife and Ann my daughter paying all my...and funeral expences. I make my..."* She laid the will on the table and the company bowed their heads in silence. The clock's ticking was the only sound in the room.

Thomas was the first to speak. "That be it, then. As Master of this house I invite ye all ter take a jar

119

with me in the parlour. 'Tis a gloomy place in here."
He stood up to make his way through. Edward went
to his mother, who was quietly weeping and being
comforted by Ann.

"Be still, Muvver," he said. "You did well." He
sat down beside her and held her hand.

"I be orright, Son. 'Twill pass." She dabbed her
face with her handkerchief, took a deep, shuddering
breath, put her hands on the table and pushed herself
up to standing. She picked up the will to hand it to
Edward. "Put this in the drawer, Edward, where
'twill be safe."

The others had gone through to the parlour.
Edward followed his mother and sister after he'd
deposited the will in the dresser with his father's old
account books.

The fire was giving out a warm glow and the
room was filled with the gentle hum of voices. As
Edward helped himself to beer he found Thomas
Tapsell at his side.

"How be you getting on at Savages, Edward?"

"Middlin'. 'Tis becoming a workin' farm. But 'tis
not hem productive. I be scrapin' by. Come next year
there'll be produce."

"I be avised you be a-courten," said Tapsell.

"Yus. 'Twill be better with a mistus about the
house." They both chuckled.

Tapsell said, "What would you say to the offer of work on my farm? 'Tis not far from Savages en we could do it barterin' like."

Edward looked at Tapsell and smiled. "I'd be partial to that, Mas Tapsell. 'Twould help me considerable." He held out his hand and shook Tapsell's gratefully.

"We be good neighbours, Faircrouch way. You'll find us shares the work en produce like for like en helps each on us when 'tis needed."

Edward and Tapsell talked for a while about the work needing to be done at Savages. Edward began to feel more confident about the future.

On his return home, he looked around his cottage, admitting to himself that it didn't come up to the standard of living to which Mary was accustomed. The floors downstairs were bare earth. There was little furniture. This suited his bachelor life. He didn't know how to improve things to make it more comfortable for her. There wasn't even any glass in the windows. He would ask his mother's advice.

"Make sure everything's clean, Son," said Dorcas. "Strew dried herbs on the floor. That'll keep the air fresh. Polish the furniture with beeswax until it do shine and brighten up the walls with a coat of limewash. If she loves you, she'll surely be happy to put her own touches to the place. En keep the fowls out of the kitchen en dairy."

Edward worked for his brother all winter. By March he was busy on his own farm, ploughing and sowing. The animals started birthing, keeping him up at night. He worked on the house in the evenings when he could. He was surprised how much dirt gathered in corners where he couldn't see it.

He continued to visit Mary on Sundays. Though he was not comfortable with her parents in their house, he could tolerate it, knowing that it would not be long before he could carry her away to have her all to himself.

One day, they were strolling round the garden after dinner. Edward felt that the time was right. He turned to face her, holding both her hands in his.

"Mary, 'tis abouten time I asked thee the question that's been in me mind fer so long...Be you ready ter be my wife?"

Mary blushed with pleasure. "I be aching fer the day, Edward," she squeezed his hands. They kissed.

"I'll go en ax thy farder, dracly-minute." He led her back to the house. Mary went to the parlour to join her mother, Edward to the hall where Gerald Paris would be smoking an after-dinner cigar. He knocked on the door, opening it when he heard the word "Enter."

Paris was sitting reading the newspaper. He looked at Edward over his spectacles and removed the cigar from his mouth. "Edward," he said.

Edward stood before the man he hoped would become his father-in-law, though neither had any liking for the other.

"Sir, I believe my intentions toward Mary, yer daughter, have been eye-proof. I wish to ask for she's hand in marriage."

Paris removed his spectacles to stare into the fire. Then he looked at Edward. "I had realised that was your intention, Edward," he drawled. "I do wonder, however, if you are able to support her in the way she is accustomed."

Edward was waiting for this. "Sir, me way of life does not equal yours prensly, but I be buildin' up me farm. It be thrivin' en can only get better. I wish to share it with the woman I love en who loves me. I believe we can make it prosper together."

"Mm." The cigar went back between Paris' teeth. He sucked deeply, inhaled, then puffed out clouds of spicy smoke which billowed round his head. "When d'you plan to wed?"

Edward took this as a confirmation that the answer was "*Yes*". His heart gave a thrill of excitement. "We'll have to speak to the vicar, Sir. Would sometime in May suit?"

Paris nodded and sighed. "Come and see what the women say, Lucke." He led Edward to the parlour, where Mary and her mother were sitting quietly. They both looked up expectantly when Paris and Edward entered.

"Wife, Mary, it seems we have an engagement to celebrate." He went to the dresser and poured wine into four glasses. Mary and her mother embraced, then Edward went to shake their hands.

Paris handed the glasses round. "A toast to the future of this young couple," he said.

"Hear, hear!" exclaimed Mrs Paris, clinking her glass against her husband's.

Edward would rather have taken Mary into his arms and swung her round than drink wine, but it didn't seem appropriate. They looked into each other's eyes and were briefly alone together. Edward went to stand by Mary. He took her hand, brought it to his lips and kissed it.

Chapter Fourteen   1706 May

In which Thomas disgraces himself.

Edward and Mary walked up the aisle of the church in Goudhurst as man and wife, their arms linked at last, their hearts glowing. They were hardly conscious of their surroundings as they climbed into the chaise. As soon as it was proper they kissed long and fervently then sat close enjoying each other's warmth. On their arrival at The Butts Edward handed Mary down from the chaise and they went arm-in-arm into the hall.

Mistus Paris had come to the house ahead of them to see that all had been suitably prepared. Edward and Mary stood at the front door to receive the guests. The dining room was cleared for the reception, with chairs lining the walls. Mary's two brothers were the first to arrive and they greeted the happy couple with affection.

Thomas Lucke, having drunk two tankards of ale before coming to the wedding, lurched into the hall shouting to Edward, "You'll be gettin' all high en mighty now, Brudder, with yer Quality folks." He roared with laughter, took Mary's hand then bowed low as he kissed it, showing a leg. He said, "Pleased ter meet you Ma'am," then wandered into the reception room where the string quartet was tuning up. He performed a few unsteady twirls in the middle of the room, tripped and fell into the nearest chair. Edward flinched as he saw the shocked expression on his mother-in-law's face.

By now, Ann and her mother were embracing Mary. "Don't take no heed of un, my dear," Ann said in a low voice. "'E be rough , but don't mean no 'arm."

Martha and her husband followed close behind. Martha curtseyed and said, "Pleased ter meet you, Ma'am, surely." She blushed and made way for the next guests.

Dorcas embraced Edward, saying, "Behopes you won't be putten on airs en graces, Son, now you're Quality." She held Mary's hand for a few seconds and said, "En behopes you'll be happy bein' a farmer's mistus."

John Paris was in the reception room showing the guests to their seats and offering them wine or beer. George Bathurst mingledwith them, being expertly sociable. The Paris guests; Mary's uncles, aunts and cousins, sat stiffly on the other side of the room, staring at the Luckes in their homespun clothes and whispering about the uncouth behaviour of Thomas.

The music struck up. Thomas Lucke went to pull a young girl of the Paris family from her seat. He proceeded to gallop round the room with her. Mary and Edward were already dancing. Other guests joined them. Eliza jumped up and walked bravely onto the floor. She stood in the path of Thomas and dragged him away as the young girl ran back to her family, red-faced and sobbing.

Mary and Edward hardly noticed what was happening, they were so absorbed in each other. The music stopped and they walked hand-in-hand towards the Lucke side of the room. George Bathurst came striding over to Mary."Mistus Lucke, may I have the pleasure of the next dance?"

Mary reluctantly let go of Edward's hand as Bathurst said, "I'll look after her Edward." He whisked her away and danced her round the room. Mary's heart was singing as Bathurst's dancing skills raised her spirits until she was soaring. He twirled her and skimmed her across the floor. When the dance finished she breathlessly laughed with pure delight as she was delivered back to Edward.

Eliza had taken her husband in hand. He was sitting obediently by her side. On the other side of him was Ann, who scolded him roundly.

"Just behave yerself, Brudder. 'Tis no place ter be tight. Don't you touch another drop, mind."

Thomas shook her hand off his arm. "Adone! I beant a child. I shall do as I pleash." He stood up and walked unsteadily to where the wine was being poured into glasses. He took a glass and threw the contents down his throat, put the empty glass on the tray and took another. He looked round the room for another victim. His eyes rested on his hostess. The second glass of wine was quickly consumed before he staggered over to Mistus Paris.

Edward watched with horror as Thomas said, "Can I have the pleshur of this dansh, Madam?" He attempted to lift the lady out of her seat.

Mary, sitting next to Edward, chuckled at her mother's discomfort. But Gerald Paris had been watching. Before Thomas knew what was happening his arms were held from behind and he was pulled away. He swung round to make an ill-aimed swipe at his host's head, missed and fell sprawling onto the floor. George Bathurst came to help and the rebel was removed from the room. Eliza rushed after them. She and Thomas were not seen again that day.

Edward breathed a sigh of relief and looked at his brother Richard.

"Thanks be 'e be gone," said Richard. "'E were mecking fools of us all" He stood up and asked Mary for a dance.

There was a break in the dancing and the guests rose from their chairs to take some of the sweetmeats and cakes that were on offer. Mary and Edward mingled with their families, greeting people and introducing each other to their relatives. After more dancing, it was time to take their leave. The celebrations were over. They embraced and shook hands with everybody, then climbed into the waiting chaise.

Mary's trunk had been packed into Bathurst's chaise beforehand. His groom drove Edward and Mary to Savages and he helped Edward carry the trunk into the house and up the stairs. On the way back from the bedroom Edward lit candles in the hall. The groom handed Mary out of the chaise and drove off, leaving the newly married couple on the doorstep. Edward lifted Mary into his arms, stepped over the threshold and put her down gently.

"Welcome home, Mistus Lucke," he said and held her close. They kissed passionately.

A flickering glow lit up their humble surroundings. Their feet crunched on the herb-strewn floor, sending scents of lavender, rosemary and thyme floating into the room. He picked up a candle and held it to Mary's face.

To his astonishment he saw tears coursing down her cheeks.

"Oh, Edward," she sobbed. "I didn't know 'twould be so lowly. 'Twill be like living in a barn."

Part Two

Chapter Fifteen 1706

In which Mary finds a friend.

Momentarily, Edward was shocked and offended. He'd worked hard and had done everything he could think of to make it the way she would want. But he couldn't bear to see Mary distressed. This was their wedding night. He put the candle down and took her in his arms again. She sobbed on his shoulder.

"Mary, my love, this be the best I could make it. You be tired en it be dark en gloomy in here. 'Twill look better come mornen when the sun will lighten it." As he rocked her gently the sobs subsided. "Dost want ter rest awhile in the parlour, or shall I take you to bed where 'twill be warm? I put goose down in the mattress especially for thee."

Mary lifted her head and dried her eyes. "You be kind, Edward. I be a pampered young woman. Shall us take a look in the parlour en sit en talk? I needs time afore you takes me to bed." She managed to smile, then kissed Edward on the lips.

They each picked up a candle. Edward opened the parlour door. He hadn't lit the fire that morning, as he would be out all day. He put his candle down on the table and showed Mary a chair. She appeared to brighten up.

"I'll find a faggot en we'll soon have a fine blaze a-goin'," he said. "I've ter shut the fowls up en feed Shep, but 'twill not take long."

"I can light the fire if you'll bring me the faggot," said Mary.

Edward nodded as he left the room. He felt more hopeful.

≈≈≈

Mary sat watching the flames leap up the chimney as the faggot took hold. Her anxiety subsided. She realised that, although there were no home comforts here, she was safe with Edward at last. The most important thing was that they loved each other, she was sure of that. She determined to be a good wife.

Soon they were sitting together with mugs of beer warming on the hearth. Mary's cheeks were pink again.

Edward pulled his chair closer to hers, taking her hand in his. "Mary, this be your bidance now en I'd be hem obliged if you'd fix it up the way you wants it. I be no home-builder. I needs you ter make it homely." He kissed her hand.

"Ed, I unnerstand what you be a-sayin'. I knows we can be cosy here. This room be better than the hall. I'll do me best ter do as you ax."

They sat quietly supping their hot toddies, watching the flames licking up the chimney. Mary's eyelids began to droop and Edward led her upstairs to bed. She allowed him to take off her dress, then she lovingly removed his outer garments. They settled into the goose down nest, exploring each other's bodies until arousal led to consummation.

≈≈≈

It became clear to Edward that although she'd been raised on a farm, as she had two brothers Mary hadn't been needed to do any heavy work and they had a maid who did most of the cooking. She loved the young animals at Savages and learned to milk the cows and to feed them all. But she was finding the cooking difficult. She frequently had accidents in the kitchen. Rather than leave her to her own devices, they had to do the cooking, beer brewing, cheese and butter making together. This took up his time when he should have been out working on the farm.

Some weeks had gone by. Edward had spent a restless night trying to work out how he would catch up with the farm work. It was still dark when he crept out of bed. He took his clothes downstairs to dress, then went through the kitchen into the yard. Shep stretched his stiff limbs and came to greet him. Edward spent some time fondling the dog who had become his friend. How simple and trusting this relationship was compared with his marital one. He sighed and went towards the barn in the grey dawn. He needed to sharpen the tools before the mowing season started. This was a task he hoped would calm his nerves. When it grew lighter he would sow some seeds in the vegetable garden, something he would expect his wife to do, if she knew how. He pushed away his feelings of irritation. This was a new day.

When he'd finished sowing the seeds he went to the barn to look for the hoe. There were weeds coming up between the vegetables. It would be prudent to remove them at once, while they were small. Now where did he put that hoe? He'd heard Mary come out to feed the hens and went to the chicken run to ask her.

"Mary, hast seen my hoe?... What be you a-doin' with that pail? That be the one fer milken. It mun be kept clean..."

Mary turned to look at him with eyes blazing. He'd said the wrong thing again.

"Good mornen, Mas Lucke," she said testily. "I have not seen your hoe. I'm using this pale acause the handle of the other one be broke." She turned her back and continued feeding the hens.

"You could've mended it!" shouted Edward. "There be plenty of rope in the barn!"

Mary swung round to face him, letting the pail drop. It fell onto its side, spilling the contents in a heap at her feet. The hens crowded round to feed on the grain. "I can't do nuffin' right, can I? You can do it yerself as you're so partic'lar." She pushed past him out of the chicken run, lifted her skirts and ran into the house.

Edward sighed in exasperation. She'd gone off in another paddy. He took the empty pail from the chicken run and shut the gate. He would have to clean this before milking the cows, a job Mary should be doing. He walked towards the well and noticed the hoe leaning against the wall of the house where he'd left it yesterday.

Edward strode through his fields with Shep, moving the sheep to a new pasture. The lambs skipped and frolicked in the sunshine as they followed the small flock. Everywhere was lush and green. The May blossom had shed its petals. Buttercups were dotted about in the grass. He loved this time of the year. His heart should be singing, but it was being weighed down. He didn't know how to make Mary's heart sing with his.

Shep brought the flock into their new pasture, then Edward turned to go and look at the calves in the next field. The dog barked, wagging his tail. Molly was walking up the lane with Sam and his little sister, Meg. Edward waved and they waved back. But he continued in the direction of the calves. Mary would have to deal with visitors, he thought angrily.

Later, he came through the kitchen into the parlour to find Molly comforting a tearful Mary. He quickly withdrew, realising that this was women's business. He went back to his work with a sense of relief.

Sam was in the yard throwing sticks for Shep, who was showing little interest.

Edward said, "Come with me, lad. We'll go to see if the corn be a-growen'" They walked off together, leaving Shep lying in the sun.

It was time for coager. At least Mary was now capable of providing that meal without his help. They sauntered back to the house, entering through the kitchen. A smell of fresh bread filled their nostrils.

The hall had been transformed. The fire in the range was lit. The big table from the parlour stood in the centre of the room and the bench had been brought to its side, facing the fire. An array of pewter plates and mugs and bread, cheese and cold meat lay ready for their eating. Mary stood by the range with a cloth in her hand. Her eyes were sparkling and she chuckled when she saw Edward and Sam in the doorway. Molly stood in the shadows, away from the table, watching.

"My word!" said Edward. "That be a welcome sight, surely!" He went over to greet Mary, who gently pushed him away.

"I be abouten take another loaf out, Ed. You sit down, I'll be with you dracly-minute." She opened the door of the oven, took out a big brown loaf with the cloth and carried it out to the kitchen to cool. She came back, sat next to Edward and squeezed his hand. "Molly be a Godsend," she said.

"You look to be in fine shape, Edward," said Molly. "Marriage do suit you." She lifted Meg and sat down next to Mary with Sam. "You'll need another bench fer this table, afore more liddle Luckes do start a-comen." She filled her plate with food and gave some to the children. "En a few more plates en mugs wouldn't go amiss." She grinned at Edward before filling her mouth with warm bread and cheese.

They all tucked into the meal. Edward's head was reeling at the change in Mary's demeanour. She was taking the initiative at last, with confidence.

"Molly's axed me to go to her house to larn me how ter brew the beer, Edward. En us took one of the hens fer today's dinner," she said.

Mary and Edward sat by the parlour fire together after their dinner that evening, finishing off their hot toddies.

"Mary, I be so proud that you cooked that dinner yerself. 'Twas main tasty," said Edward.

Mary blushed. Her eyes were still sparkling. "'Twere Molly showed me. She made it easy. I've been so afeared of displeasin' thee that it's made me all of a boffle. I knows I've a lot ter larn. But she says she'll show me."

They sat quietly, relaxing for the first time for weeks.

Mary broke the silence. "Edward."

"Mm?" he said, looking up.

"Us could do with a dresser in the hall, ter keep the things fer eaten. En one day afore winter, I'd be partial to paven the floors. I brought me dowry along of me when we was wed, so I can pay fer that."

There was a long silence. Edward saw the need for these things, but wasn't sure where the money would come from.

At last he said, "Mary, I don't want you ter pay fer things fer the house. Thy dowry is fer thee ter buy dresses en all. We've not much money a-comen in prensly. I'll have ter seek work with Thomas Tapsell, but that would mean leavin' thee here ter do the meals en work in the dairy by thyself, like..."

A cloud passed over Mary's face. She nodded, sighing, "I beant ready fer that, Ed. Gimme a few more weeks en see how I gets on."

"Orright, love. I'll wait fer you ter say the word." Edward was feeling his way, hoping they could come to some agreement without quarrelling. Since their marriage he'd almost lost sight of Mary ever becoming the farmer's wife he'd dreamed of. But now there seemed to be a glimmer of hope.

Chapter Sixteen

In which Mary learns how to brew beer.

A few weeks later they were finishing their breakfast.

"Mary, that were a good dish of porridge," Edward said, pushing his bowl to one side. "Today I be agwain ter see me brudder Thomas at The Slade. 'Twill not take all day. Will you be orright on yer own, or dost wish ter come along of me?"

"Yus, Edward, I'll be orright. I'll milk the cows en feed the young animals. Then I be agwain to Molly, ter larn how ter brew beer." She grinned before she put the last spoonful into her mouth. She cleared the table and took the bowls and spoons into the kitchen. Edward checked the fire and put more logs on. They bumped into each other in the doorway. He put his arms round her waist.

"I do believe you be startin' ter like being a farmer's Mistus," he kissed her.

"'Tis fair to middlin'." She giggled. "'Til dinner time, Edward." She disentangled herself and went into the parlour.

"I'll bring the cows in fer you afore I go," Edward called. He suddenly didn't want to leave her. She was becoming independent too quickly.

He found his mother sickly when he came to Slade Farm.

"I should have happened by afore," he said guiltily. "Mary needed tenden en I've been busy."

Dorcas was sitting in Thomas' chair by the fire. She looked at her son. "'Tis only a cold on me chest. 'Twill pass." She coughed. "So yer new wife be trouble, like?"

"Nay, Muvver. Not trouble. But her beant accustomed ter farm work or cookin' en all. Now Molly's larnin' she, things be easier."

"Molly's a fine woman," Dorcas remarked. "I'd like ter see more of Richard en 'is fambly, but I don't rackon 'e has the time."

"I rackon 'e don't come on account of Thomas. They don't call cousins, never have," Edward said. "Be Thomas in the fields?"

"Yus, Eliza's helpen un get the hay in, with Esland." Dorcas coughed again. "'Twill soon be harvest. They'll have ter get help."

Edward said, "I want ter talk to un about Esland. Come winter I'll be needin' help with some heavy jobs, like. I'll go en find un. I'll happen by afore I goes home, Muvver."

Edward walked up the whapple way and soon found the hay wain. Esland was pitching up great forkfuls of hay. He was a stunted man, well-built, with considerable strength and stamina. But he had such a severe cleft palate that clear speech was impossible.

The dwarf looked up, his distorted face wreathed in smiles. "Nash Ed," he spluttered.

Edward patted him on the back. "I be come ter ask Mas Thomas summat. Bythen I'll talk to thee Esland."

Esland nodded and Edward went to find Thomas. His brother was raking hay from the windrows into heaps ready for Esland to take them to the cart. Eliza was not far off, doing the same. Edward raised his hand as he approached. Thomas stopped raking. His face was red and he was breathing heavily.

"What brings you here, Brudder?" Thomas enquired.

"I be minded ter have Esland over to Savages dappen you've finished harvestin'. You'll not be needin' un come winter en I've work fer un."

"Yus. 'Twould save me payin' un fer nuffin'. Go en ax un." Thomas went back to his raking.

Edward returned to Esland, who was carrying another forkful to the cart. Edward waited until it was loaded, then said, "Esland, how would you like ter work fer me at my farm come winter? I've some tasks I need help with."

Esland nodded vigorously clapping his hands. "Yush, Shur!" he said, slapping his thigh.

Edward laughed with him. "I'll come en tell you betimes I be ready." He waved and turned to go.

His mother was still by the fire when he returned. "Son, will you go en get me a few things from the village? Eliza hasn't the time."

"Of course. What be it you wants?"

She took off her shoes and handed them to him. "Take these to Watson. He be maken me a new pair. Collect those en ax him ter mend these. En us needs tow fer spinnen'. You'll get that from Lawrie Foster."

"Beant there wool from the sheep, Muvver? You can do better than tow."

"Nay, Son. Us sold all the wool after shearen."

Edward shrugged his shoulders. "I'll be back 'forelong." He left the house with the shoes in a bag over his shoulder, untethered Faithful and rode down into Lamberhurst.

He had a jar with some friends in the alehouse before returning to Slade Farm in time for coager with Thomas and Eliza. Dorcas sat at the table but ate little. Eliza soaked some bread in milk and took it out to Esland in the court. He wouldn't eat indoors as it was such a messy business.

The geese heralded the arrival of a visitor. Ann came clicking into the parlour in her patens. It was years since Edward had seen her smiling.

"I have news," she announced after she'd greeted Edward. She sat at the table, took a piece of bread and popped it into her mouth. The others stopped eating.

"I be betrothed to Joseph Collins. We'll be wed a year come spring. I'll be leavin' the cottage. I thought mebbe Esland could bide there. 'Tis time 'e jacked up bidin' in the barn."

Edward was pleased for her. He jumped up and went round the table to shake her hand. She was not partial to shows of affection. "That be good news, Ann," he said.

Dorcas smiled. "It be time you was wed, Darter," she said.

"Esland can't pay rent fer the cottage," said Thomas indignantly.

"He could if he had praper wages," remarked Ann.

"We'll sort that out betimes you move out, Sister," said Edward, before his brother and sister fell into an argument. "I be agwain have Esland a-worken fer me come winter."

≈≈≈

Mary had a good day with Molly, learning how to brew beer. Molly was kind and patient. She understood the difficulty Mary was having settling in to her new role as a farmer's wife. Mary was alarmed at the number of tasks she was expected to do. She couldn't imagine how Edward managed all of these chores on his own for the last two or three years.

But she was improving every day. The release from the boredom she had suffered at The Butts spurred her on. She was discovering new skills. She enjoyed coaxing the warm milk from the cow's udder and transforming it into butter and cheese. It was satisfying to prepare and cook raw ingredients to bring them out of the oven as wholesome, edible food.

She was stirring the hot-pot on the stove when Edward came in. He approached her from behind and held her close. She put the lid on the pot, then turned round, spoon in hand.

They kissed. He asked, "How was yer day with Molly?"

"Middlin', thank you Ed. I rackon I could manage the brewen' meself 'forelong," she said proudly. "I be quite taken with Sam en Meg. 'Twill be wunnerful ter have some of us own." She put the spoon down and went to fetch bowls and spoons from the kitchen.

"Then you'll have even more work ter do!" Edward exclaimed.

He sat at the table while Mary dished out the meal.

Edward said, "We'll be harvesten' soon, love en I'll need thee ter come along of me. Dost think you can do it?"

Mary nodded. "I be a farmer's Mistus prensly, Ed. I be ready ter do whatever work you have fer me."

"'Twill be hard, Mary. 'Twill take time ter build up yer strength."

Mary lifted her chin, pursed her lips and looked directly into his eyes. "I be agreeable."

"But first, I've fixed up ter collect beef from Wad'rst termorrer. I'll buy a powderin' tub en salt en we'll do some curin'. 'Twill be summat ter larn fer each on us."

"My! Then I'll have ter larn how ter cook it!" she said laughing.

"En another thing; our neighbour, Robert Smith, he's jackin' up keepin' sheep. I'll help un drive 'em round here termorrer arternoon with some geese. We'll need ter prepare a shelter fer the geese, like."

"Termorrer be a hem busy day, surely," said Mary.

≈≈≈

A few days later, before he went to bed, Edward took out the account book and entered the money owed, before he forgot:

Lamberhurst in debted
Joseph Tiast for a gridiron 00-------2---------0
more to Lawrence Foster for tow 00-------2---------3
more to Watson for solen
of a pair of shoes & for a new pair 00-------5---------0
Then received of Henry Plaster
3 stone of beef 0-------3---------0
more to Magar the cooper

145

for a powdering tub	0--------8--------0
more to Ned Burges for a peck of salt	0--------1--------6
more a gallon of salt	0---------0---------9
Indeted to Robert Smith	
for sheep & geese & work	1--------0-------6

Chapter Seventeen   1706   September

In which Mary meets Esland

In the front garden at Savages, the fruit trees were laden with apples and pears. It was a fine day in September. Edward and Mary rose early. They were already hard at work when Molly came up the lane with Sam and Meg. Sheets lay on the grass under the trees, waiting to catch the fallers. Edward was up the ladder with his head among the branches picking rosy red apples, carefully placing them in the basket which hung over his shoulders. A rich fragrance was released as he disturbed the sticky bloom. Sunshine trickled through the leaves, dappling his face. He stopped picking and looked down to watch the women take the fruit off the lower branches. Sam sat on the ground to sort the fallers from the unmarked apples, putting them into separate baskets. Meg ran around among the daisies, her auburn curls flying.

A shout from the lane distracted them and John Paris came round the corner. Mary ran to meet her brother when she saw him. They embraced and walked back towards the orchard. Edward climbed down the ladder, putting down his full basket before going to welcome his friend.

"Hey, John! You be just in time ter do some gatherin'!" Edward slapped John on the back. "Good ter see you."

Mary said, "I'll bring a costrel of ale en some mugs out here. We can have a break en hear John's news. Come, Sam."

Edward and John sat among the bulging baskets.

"Mother be asking after Mary," said John. Her ain't had a letter from she for a while."

"Us have been hem busy, 'er's been helping harvesten," Edward explained.

Mary emerged from the house with two costrels. Sam followed laden with mugs. He put them down on the sheet and went to fetch some more. The others picked up a mug each, holding them out for Mary to pour their drinks.

"Why don't you go en visit yer muvver fer a day or two, Mary?" Edward suggested. Dappen we've finished the fruit picking there'll be less ter be at.

"Muvver'd be main pleased ter see you," said John.

Mary's face lit up. "I'd be partial ter that, if you be agreeable, Edward."

"That's settled, then." He would be glad to have the place to himself for a few days. He was planning a surprise for Mary.

They continued picking the fruit with John's help. When they were having coager, John announced that there was a small farm to let, not far away. He'd be moving there sometime soon. His elder brother was now Master of The Butts Farm as their father was ailing. John felt it was time he moved on.

Edward and Mary were storing the apples in the empty chamber in the cottage, checking each one carefully for bruises and insect inhabitants before placing them on the clean floorboards with a space between each. They worked well together as a team when they were in harmony. Edward took an apple from the basket and put it to his nose. It smelt of roses and lavender. Instead of placing it on the floor with the others, he sunk his teeth into it and tore a piece away with a crunch. He relished the juices flowing into his mouth as he crushed it.

Mary looked up at the sound, surprised and saw the twinkle in his eyes. She laughed and followed Edward's example.

"They be woundrous tasty, surely," she said between juicy mouthfuls.

The two of them sat back on their heels enjoying their stolen snack until their apples were no more, then went back to their task.

"I'll tell thee a story, Mary," said Edward. "It be both sad and happy and you mun hear it afore termorrer."

Mary looked up at him and nodded in anticipation. "Be it a true story, Ed?" she asked.

Edward nodded. "Yus," he said. They continued sorting apples as he spoke. "There were a young woman abidin' in a poor dwellin' in Lambr'st about thirty year gone. Her got money from sellen besoms, what un made from pickin's in the woods. Some people were kind to she en brought un food. 'Er was with child en when the babe were birthed it had the mos' ugly face you can imagine. There were a great split from 'is mouth up to 'is forehead en one eye were buried in 'is cheek. 'Is muvver kept un hidden for years. No-one saw but a glimpse of un now en again, until 'e were a man en she were an old woman. 'E be short in height, but hem stocky, en helped 'is muvver with all the heavy jobs until 'er dyin' day. Then people were afraid of un. They said 'e were conceived of the devil en they druv un away. Me farder, 'e felt sorry fer un en took un in. 'Es been a-workin' on the farm at The Slade to this day."

Mary sat up straight. "I rackon yer farder did the right en praper thing. What's the man's name?"

Edward was relieved that Mary had responded to the story so positively. "Esland," he said. He took another apple and studied it, before putting it on the floor. "I've axed un if 'e'll come en work fer us over the winter," he said casually. "Thomas ain't got much work fer un en I could do with some help with the heavy jobs."

"But 'e'll want somewhere ter sleep en we've just covered the floor in here with apples!" Mary exclaimed.

"'E can sleep in the barn," said Edward. 'E be accustomed to it en 'e don't like comen into the house. 'E be ashamed of 'is looks."

"Us can't let un sleep outside in the winter," Mary persisted.

Edward shuffled over to her and put his arm round her shoulders. "It'll be orright, Mary. You'll see. There's just one more thing you needs to know..."

Mary cuddled up to him and he kissed the top of her head. "The man can't speak praper. 'E knows what you be asayin' en understands, but 'e beant able ter make words.

"Now I rackon 'tis time we was agwain below ter fix us summat ter eat."

Mary had been vomiting the last few mornings. Edward heard her retching into the chamber pot. He knew about morning sickness and was quietly joyful. But he would wait until she announced her pregnancy herself.

He made sure he was busy in the yard when Esland came walking in as arranged. Mary was in the kitchen washing the breakfast dishes.

"Mary," Edward called, "come en meet Esland."

She came out of the kitchen drying her hands on her apron. She looked directly at Esland. She hid her horror with a bright smile and walked towards the newcomer, holding out her hand.

"Esland, welcome to Savages. I hopes you'll be happy here."

Esland shook her hand vigourously, nodded his head and said, "Ush , Nishus Ucke," and returned her smile with twinkling eyes.

"I've saved you some porridge," said Mary. "Shall you have some afore Mas Lucke puts you to work?"

Esland nodded and put his hands together and bowed. "Nnnn," he said.

Mary went indoors and brought out the bowl of porridge with a spoon. Edward found a wooden stool in the barn and placed it outside the back door. They went inside to give him privacy. Edward held Maryclose as she lay her head on his shoulder and shuddered.

"You did well, girl. I be praper proud of you," said Edward.

"'Tis monstrous that Nature could do that to a person," she said. "How can that happen? Has God no mercy?"

"That be a question I cannot answer," said Edward. "Us must carry on with us work now en treat un like one of we. Didst say you was agwain to yer muvver's termorrer?"

Mary sighed and straightened her apron and cap. "Yus, John's a-comen fer me in the marnen. I can

feed the fowls en do the milken en all afore I goes."
She reached up and kissed Edward on the lips, then
went out to see if Esland had finished his porridge.

Chapter Eighteen

In which Edward dries Thomas Tapsell's hops

Edward knew of a cottage which was being demolished nearby. It had been destroyed by fire fifty years ago, when his great uncle and namesake, Edward, died in the flames. The Lucke family in Wadhurst, who intended to sell the land, agreed to let Edward have the undamaged stone slabs for nothing, if he could cart them away. It took him three days to lay them in the kitchen, hall and parlour with Esland's help. It gave him pleasure to install them in another Lucke property, where they would hopefully see happier times. There were enough left over to pave round the well, where it was regularly swampy in the winter.

Mary was expected home the next day. They put the furniture back in place and Edward picked some late roses from round the front door and put them in a mug of water on the table in the hall. Then he and Esland had their supper and sat together in the yard with their jars of ale, enjoying the last rays of the setting sun.

Next morning they went to look at the plough to see if it needed attention before being put to use. Esland was happy to clean off the rust and sharpen the blades and Edward went to check the cart horses' bridles. The geese ran round to the lane, screeching. Shep pricked up his ears and followed them. Edward guessed that this must be the cart bringing Mary home and went to meet John as he turned into the yard. Mary sat next to him, smiling happily. Edward helped her down and they embraced.

"I missed you," Edward said, "considerable so."

"I be glad ter be home," said Mary. "'Tis dismal at The Butts, with naught to be at all day." She turned back to the cart. "Muvver wanted us ter have this. She don't need it no more."

Edward looked in the cart. There was the dresser Mary had dreamed of. He looked at her and said, "You be main chuffed ter have that I rackon."

Mary nodded. "It'll take three of you ter lift un en carry un in. Behopes 'e don't rock around on the earthen floor.

Edward said, "Wait. First you mun shut yer eyes en I'll guide you indoors. I've a surprise fer you, too."

Mary obeyed and was led towards the house. John followed, curious to see what was in store for her. They stopped at the back door.

"You can look now," Edward said and opened the door with a flourish.

Mary stared and gasped, clutching her hands to her bosom. She walked onto the stone slabs and stood in the hall doorway. The sun was shining through the window onto the table, lighting up the roses. Mary clapped her hands and said, "Oh, my!" Then she ran

156

round to the parlour. "Oh, Edward!" she exclaimed. "'Tis beautiful!" She ran back to where he stood watching her and flung her arms round his neck.

"It be all ready fer the dresser!" she said.

"Behopes the slabs be level," said Edward. He lifted her, swinging her round as she shrieked with laughter.

They brought the dresser in with Esland's help. He quickly disappeared as soon as it was in place and Mary couldn't stop twirling round on her new floor.

"John, will you stay fer coager?" asked Edward

They rustled up a snack of stale bread and cheese, washed down with ale.

≈≈≈

Mary was busy baking and attending to the neglected dairy that afternoon. She seemed happy to take charge of the kitchen again and soon filled the dresser with items which had had no home until then.

Over dinner she said shyly, "I be with child, Edward."

He put his hand over hers, squeezed it and said, "That be wunnerful news, my love"

"Muvver told me all manner of things I didn't know," she said. "It explained why I've been feelin' latchety lately. I wunt be so worritted prensly."

They discussed what they would need to get for the baby and Edward told her that she must be careful not to do anything strenuous, reminding her that they now had Esland to help him.

"I told Muvver about Esland en she said I shouldn't look at un while I be with child, in case it affected the baby en it came out crippled."

Edward was horrified. "That cannot be! There be no harm in the man. 'E beant no witch!"

"It's made me afeared though, Ed. I can't get it out of me head."

"Yer muvver don't know what she be sayin'. She ain't even met Esland. What about all the animals 'e's helped ter birth? None of <u>them</u> was malformed."

Mary couldn't answer. She pursed her lips and got up to clear the dishes away.

≈≈≈

Some days later, Thomas Tapsell came calling. He had urgent need of someone to dry his hops. The man who generally did it had been taken ill. Edward consulted Mary.

"I'll be away day en night fer a week, love. But Esland be here. 'E can help if need be, like en I'll tell un what ter be at while I be gone. You knows what ter do with 'is food now, don't you?"

Mary's face blanched. She hesitated before replying. Edward was afraid she would say no.

She nodded hesitantly, took a deep breath, then said, "That be orright, love. Us needs the money en I can go en talk to Molly if I gets lonesome. There's beer en cider to brew en cheese ter make... I'll be fine." The colour came back to her cheeks. She nodded more positively and turned away to busy herself in the kitchen.

Esland was happy with the arrangement. Edward gave him instructions to keep an eye on the Mistus and not to let her do any heavy lifting. He left the next day with a light heart, confident that all would be well.

≈≈≈

Mary said goodbye to Edward after they had breakfasted. Esland was doing some work on the barns, making them rain and windproof before the winter storms. Edward had left him with plenty of work to do and she would have little contact with him.

Except for mealtimes. This she dreaded.

It was not that she disliked the poor man. He could not help the way he looked. She wondered whether he had ever seen a reflection of himself. The safety of the child she was carrying was of paramount importance. She wanted to believe Edward when he scoffed at her mother's warning. But she would not take the risk.

She busied herself in the house and cared for the animals. She brought the cows in, milked them and took them back to pasture. She made the meals as normal, sharing them with Shep and Esland. But she avoided any sight of Esland. She left his meals outside the back door by his stool and waited until he had gone back to his work before bringing in the dirty bowl.

Once or twice he appeared in the yard while she was out there and she saw him wave his hand in greeting. She hastily covered her eyes and turned away to avoid seeing his face. She hated doing this but could not help herself. The third time Esland did not wave. When he saw her he turned his back abruptly, as if he knew. She fancied she heard him whimper like an injured dog. As the end of the week approached she saw nothing of him.

It was more difficult at night. She lay alone in the dark with her eyes shut. But it was as if his face was imprinted on her mind. She slept only fitfully until exhaustion took over. Then she woke up in a cold sweat. It seemed a long week.

≈≈≈

Edward had never dried hops before. Living in the hot oast, turning the dusty hops continuously and stoking the fire below was taking its toll. His meals were brought to him and he snatched a breath of fresh air now and again when he was sure the temperature would stay constant until he returned. Another worker came to bag the dried hops when they were cooled, while Edward spread more on the oast hair, to start the process all over again. He had nearly finished and would be glad to get back home to Mary.

It took the best part of the morning to cool the last batch. He let the fire die down and went outside to report to Thomas Tapsell. He had coager in Mistus Tapsell's kitchen then went back to the oast to shovel the hops into the hop pocket. He forced them down with the press, before sewing up the top and dropping it down onto the waiting wagon, ready to take to the brewer. He climbed down the ladder, shook hands with the others in the team and wearily marched off towards Savages.

Shep heard him coming and ran into the lane to greet him. Edward bent down to fondle him and they continued up the lane together. He came into the yard and found Esland sitting outside the back door, his head in his hands.

He got up, making urgent noises and rocking an imaginary child in his arms, shaking his head.

He stuttered, "Nishush," and pointed towards the house.

Edward dashed indoors, calling, "Mary, Mary!"

Chapter Nineteen

In which Edward and Esland fell the Littlewood.

Mary sat in a chair in the parlour, all of a heap. Her face was ashen and awash with tears. Her skirts were bloodstained. Edward was at her side, holding her hand to his lips.

"Fegs, Mary! Hast catched hurt?" he asked.

Mary's tears flooded her face. "The child," she sobbed. "'Tis dead and gone, Edward." She put her arms round his neck and wept onto his shoulder. He held her close and rocked her soothingly.

When she had composed herself, she held both of Edward's hands in hers and told the whole story: That morning she felt well and happy that Edward would be home. Esland was replacing doors on the barn and stables. Mary needed potatoes and vegetables for the meal that evening. She took a spade and fork from the skillon and went into the vegetable garden with a basket.

Mary dug some turnips and carrots then started on the potatoes. "All of a sudden, like, I felt a pain in me stomach. I stood up en the pain went round to me back. Worse, it was. Then I felt summat trickle down me leg en I looked down. It were blood. I were tarble afeared, Ed. I shouted fer Esland. It were pourin' out of me en I had ter crouch down, there in the garden. Gurt lumps of blood came en a tiny liddle white thing, no bigger than me finger nail. It looked like a child, all curled up. 'Twere our baby, Ed!" She wailed and moaned rocking herself backwards and forwards.

"Esland come en picked me up en carried me into the house. I've been 'ere ever since. I be bleeden still. Canst find some paddin' en help me upstairs?"

After cleaning up the mess, Edward left Mary sleeping in bed and went to look at the evidence in the vegetable garden. He dug a deep hole and buried the remains of the miscarriage. He was stunned. The future had been turned upside-down. Their eager plans were now futile. Still wearing his dusty clothes from the oast, he stripped them off at the well, brought a bucket of water up and had a good wash. The cold jerked him back to immediate tasks. He went to fetch some clean clothes from the chamber.

Mary was awake and looking better. She sat up.

"You stay there, Mary," he said. "You lost a lot of blood. You needs ter rest. Yer body will replace it, bythen you'll feel better."

Mary said, "I rackon 'twere on account of Esland being here that I lost the child, Edward. Muvver did warn me. I tried not to look at un."

Edward attempted to control his anger. How could Esland be blamed for this? It was that wicked mother of Mary's who put the idea into her head. "Mary, I dunnow whatsoever caused it, but that baby were not ter be. 'Tis not for we ter know the reason. Only God knows that. There'll be more, love. Us needs ter bide the time." He went to her and gave her a kiss. "Rest now. I'll bring thy dinner 'forelong."

She lay down obediently and he went to see what Esland had been doing while he'd been away.

≈≈≈

The next day she woke to hear Edward talking to someone in the hall, then footsteps on the stairs.

It was Molly. How glad she was to see her. Tears welled up again and she was unable to speak. Molly put her arms round her holding her until the sobbing abated. Then she sat down on the edge of the bed.

"Mary, you feels bad now, but 'twill pass. These things happen to us women en 'tis mortaceous cruel. But life do go on. You've plenty of time. Richard en me was married fer five year afore I had Sam."

Molly's voice was soothing and brought Mary down to earth. "I still be bleedin'," she said. "When will it stop? It makes me feel dirty en I can't love Edward like I should."

"Why dost feel dirty? 'Tis the same as having a monthly."

"'Tis on account of Esland. Like 'e put a spell on me when I looked at un."

Molly's brow wrinkled, her eyes widened. "What made you think that?"

Mary explained what her mother had told her.

Molly shook her head. "Oh! no, I don't b'lieve the poor soul is a witch." She held Mary's hand in hers. "Listen, Mary, if you believe summat bad is agwain ter happen, mayhap it will. The idea were planted in yer head en you imagined that Esland put a spell on thee."

"You mean I made that thing happen? How could I? 'Twas the last thing I wanted." Mary started sobbing again.

Molly said, "Nay, nay, love. I beant sayin' you did it a-purpose. Only that you was over-worrited en were frettin', like." She held Mary and rocked her until she calmed down.

Mary was not sure she understood. She didn't want to talk about it any more. "Be your fambly well?" she asked.

She was grateful to be brought back into the real world, where ordinary things happened. The two young women talked about families, work and the weather and how many eggs the hens were laying, until it was time for Molly to leave. She was like the sister that Mary never had and Mary was grateful. She settled down and slept peacefully for a few hours.

≈≈≈

Edward left Molly with Mary, talking women's talk and went with Esland to fell some of the trees in the Littlewood. With the timber, they would post and rail round the hollow field and the watery field ready for pasture next spring. They would have more animals come the summer. The wood that was left over they stacked in the dry, ready for winter fires. Edward would keep the bullocks in half the barn. The other half they filled with straw from the harvest. They prepared the open barn for housing the cows in bad weather and made a wooden trough to leave in the yard for fodder. Edward worked through his grief and anger and came back to Mary feeling better.

By the end of the week Mary was back in the kitchen and dairy working with grim determination. She couldn't look at Esland, even though the danger had passed. Mealtimes were quiet. There was little to say.

Edward spent the darkening evenings sitting at the candlelit table with slate and chalk, planning how many beasts to slaughter, which fields to plough and which he would need for pasture next year. The ram had already been in with the sheep and he and Esland would soon be putting up temporary pens with hurdles ready for lambing time. They'd brought the shepherd's hut from The Slade and Esland was willing to stay in it at night.

Mary went into town with the horse and cart to market once a week, taking butter, cheese and eggs and a batch of bread she'd baked that morning. Those were the days when she came home with rosy cheeks and bright eyes and she talked about all the gossip she'd gleaned and the new friends she'd made.

"I seed John in town today, Edward," she said as she served the meat pie and gravy. "'E were looken hem spry. 'E'll be a-comen ter see you 'forelong."

"What be un so happy about?" Edward enquired. "Has 'e found a girl at last?"

"Nay, 'e don't consider much of girls. 'E be a-settin' up 'is farm."

"That be good news. Did 'e say where it be?"

"I b'liv 'tis down Riseden way, near yer brudder's farm."

They continued eating their dinner. Edward realised that he was missing companionship. He'd been burying himself in work and he felt he needed a break.

"I'll be a-comen to market with you next week, Mary. We'll be slaughteren some beasts en I'll teck some meat along fer sellen."

"'Twould be good ter have some salted up fer winter," Mary commented.

At last they were talking again. Edward marvelled at the change in his mistus. They were beginning to be a partnership, working together instead of separately.

"Us needs ter harvest the vegetables afore the frosts," he said.

"I can do that, Edward. You've work enough ter be at."

"Orright, love. I'll give thee a hand carryin' them indoors en storen 'em."

Chapter Twenty   1706/7

A Family Christmas.

Autumn rain and wind delayed the outdoor work. Esland spent time undercover maintaining the tools, grooming the horses and installing mangers in the places where the animals would be sheltered in the winter.

A break in the weather and a few colder, fine days allowed them to plough a couple of fields and manure them ready for sowing wheat, clover and turnips in the spring. Esland went in front with the cart, spreading the dung and marl and Edward followed, holding the plough and letting the horse do most of the work. They slithered and squelched in the cledgy clay. Their boots became caked and the horses' legs were covered up to the knees. The wheels of the cart took a trail of mud back to the yard when they had finished and it needed several buckets from the well to clean it off. Dusk was falling by the time they had stabled the horses, filled their haybags and put the cart and plough away.

Esland made his way to his hayloft and Edward trudged to the house. A welcome aroma of cooking food met him at the door as he entered. Mary was busy over the stove in the hall, her back towards him.

A wave of affection flowed through him. He went and put his arms round her waist to give her a hug. She turned round, her face flushed with heat from the fire. A wisp of hair had crept out of her cap and hung down her cheek. She had a spoonful of stew in her hand, with the other hand held underneath to stop the drips falling onto the floor.

"Here, have a taste," she said.

While he was savouring the promise of dinner, he saw her eyes sweep down his body to his feet and to the trail of muddy footprints he had inadvertently left across the newly-paved floor.

"Get out of here!" she screamed, taking the spoon back and thwacking his retreating shoulders with it. "Teck yer boots off at the door and mop up that mess afore I gives you yer dinner."

It was half an hour before he was allowed to sit at the table. He was annoyed that she should treat him so, after a tiring day in the fields. He cursed the day he laid the paving. Until then, they hadn't had to worry about bringing mud in.

"You ain't cleaned it praper," she said when he sat down. "I'll have ter do it again when we've finished eaten."

They ate their meal in silence.

One day they were riding home from market on the cart exchanging news and talking about the people they'd met that day. The tensions between them were melting away. They were enjoying each other's company again.

Mary said, "Ed, Christmas be a-comen en I'd like ter give the fambly dinner. They've been woundrous kind this year, especially Molly. What d'you say?"

Edward thought it was a splendid idea. "Mary, I be main proud of you ter want ter do that. Us could ask thy brudder ter join the party."

They agreed that they should celebrate on Christmas Day with a roast goose, boiled bacon, meat pie and a pond pudding which Mary had learned to make recently. Edward found a yule log for the parlour fire. He and Esland foraged for holly, ivy and mistletoe to decorate the house and they made another bench for the hall table.

They were up before dawn on Christmas Day to prepare for the feast and left it all cooking before going to church. Mary put on her best dress and wore a blue cape over it. They rode into Wadhurst on the cart. The church was full to overflowing. Everyone was in festive mood, greeting friends and waving to each other across the crowds. Edward and Mary squeezed into a pew with a family they didn't know. They sang the hymns lustily and Edward prayed that this was a new beginning for his relationship with Mary, that they would find long-lasting harmony together and eventually have a healthy family to raise with pride.

Somewhere among the congregation there were Richard and his family and John. They all met up in the church litten. John had walked into Wadhurst He joined Mary and Edward in their cart for the ride to Savages, with Richard following with his family in his cart. On their arrival the women dashed into the house to attend to the meal.

Edward and Richard drove into the yard and left Esland to stable the horses and carts. They made sure there was no mud on their shoes before entering the house. Edward took wine and glasses from the dresser in the hall and the three men went through into the parlour. Meg played by the fire with a doll she had brought with her. Young Sam helped Mary and Molly in the hall, taking plates and knives, forks and spoons and placing them on the table.

In the parlour the yule log quietly crackled as it smouldered. The men sat smoking pipes and sipping their wine. They talked about their farms, the problems they had with their crops and beasts and how they resolved them, giving each other advice and sympathy when needed. The warm air was heavy with spicy smoke and they relaxed in a glow of contentment.

The door opened and Sam entered.

"'Tis time ter be a-comen to table," he said.

The men looked at him and nodded and continued their conversation.

Sam stood helplessly in the open doorway.

A voice from the hall called, "Dinner be on the table."

The men stood up and knocked their pipes out on the hearth. Richard picked up Meg and they came into the hall carrying their glasses. Mary and Molly were taking off their aprons, their faces flushed. They'd already supplied themselves with glasses of wine.

"Sit ye down," Mary said. She was enjoying being hostess.

They seated themselves round the table and Edward raised his glass. "A toast to our women. Good health and God bless ye all," he said and knocked back the remains of his wine. He sat down suddenly, realising that it had gone to his head and the sooner he started eating the better.

It took all afternoon for them to do justice to the food and wine. The talk became louder, the laughter merrier. They ate until they could eat no more. Then amid more laughter, they cleared the table and pushed it to one side. Mary mashed up potatoes, vegetables and juices from the roasting tin and soaked some pudding in milk for Esland. Edward took it out to him in the hayloft with a mug of ale. When he got back to the hall, John was playing his mouth organ and the women were dancing with Richard, Meg and Sam. Edward sat on a bench and watched, clapping his hands to the music. Then they played a few games of Blind Man's Buff before retiring to the parlour, exhausted. Meg sat in her mother's lap and fell asleep.

The evening ended with the company telling stories and reciting poems. Sam went quiet, his eyelids started to droop and Richard said it was time they went home. He offered John a lift in the cart. Edward and Mary waved them goodbye from the back door.

They were alone together. The house was abruptly quiet. They wandered into the parlour and sat gazing at the diminishing yule log. Little tongues of flame flicked and hissed as it settled into its bed of red ashes. Their minds reverberated with the day's festivities.

Mary yawned and said, "John said that Muvver were snuffy on account of us didn't invite she en Farder to the party,"she said.

"We've no room fer no more," said Edward. "She wouldn't like it here anyhows."

Mary looked at him and smiled. "I be fallin' asleep a-sitten here."

Edward rose from his chair. "Shall us go to bed, love? We can clear up en put things to rights come mornen."

"Yus, I be a-comen. There's summat I needs ter be at first." She stood up and went through the hall into the kitchen where she picked up a parcel and a candle.

Edward watched, curious to know what she was doing. She went out of the door and over the yard to the barn, opened the door and disappeared inside. He heard her calling Esland. This was so unexpected that he crept after her and listened at the door.

He heard her speaking. "Esland, I be hem thankful to you fer yer kindness to me. I wants ter give you this. 'Twill keep you warm in the cold weather that's to come. God bless you."

Edward, astonished, dashed back to the house, anticipating her coming out of the barn. He managed to get back into the hall and was riddling the fire when she came in.

"You've been a-spyin' on me," she said, smiling shyly.

Edward went towards her and cuddled her. "Couldn't resist," he said. "Can't wait ter see what it is."

They giggled and made their way upstairs.

The next morning Esland appeared wearing a blue woollen hat and a long scarf wound round his neck three times, covering his mouth, the ends tucked into his coat. He chuckled and clapped happily.

Chapter Twenty One   1706/7

In which Robert Smith meets Esland.

There was little to do on the farm in the winter except feed the beasts and milk the cows. Molly and Mary visited each other, exchanging produce and recipes. Mary made her own dresses and learned to spin. Her brother John was also a frequent visitor and he entertained Edward and Mary at his house. They all shared their supplies through the harsh weather.

Esland installed himself in the shepherd's hut as it had a small stove, which made it warmer than the draughty barn. He kept an eye on the pregnant sheep and let Shep stay with him in the hut.

Robert Smith, their neighbour, came round and he and Edward sat in the parlour smoking their pipes, talking about farming. Robert, older than Edward, was a small, rugged man with a ruddy face. His mop of greying black hair crept down the sides of his face to his thick beard. A bachelor, he'd managed his smallholding single-handed since his parents died. He kept enough stock to be self-sufficient and he had a maid, Alice, who lived in. Robert mentioned a half-brother, who rarely visited.

Robert met Esland when he came to call one day. Edward watched as Robert stared at the dwarf, unable to take his eyes off his face. Edward quickly ushered Robert away, not wanting to embarrass Esland.

"Whatever happened to 'is face?" asked Robert as they went indoors.

Edward explained briefly that the man was born like that.

"I be surprised 'e can do work fer you," Robert said. ""Be un in his right mind?"

"There be naught wrong with his brain," said Edward. "'Tis a malformation."

Robert grunted and made no further comment.

Word came from Thomas Tapsell in March. He needed a team of men to carry out some coppicing and hedging. Over the next few weeks Edward, Esland and Robert Smith went to do the work together. It was good to get back to physical activity. Every day they met before dawn and walked over to Tapsell's, arriving as it was getting light. Thomas was there waiting for them with a horse and cart, loaded up with mallets, bill hooks and axes. When he saw Esland his face lost its colour. Esland turned his back.

They did the coppicing first, cutting rods to be used for the hedging which was the next task. Robert avoided eye contact with Esland, pushing him to one side when they were taking the tools off the cart. When Esland went to take the bill-hook, Robert snatched it out of his hand.

"I be agwain ter use that. It be dangerous work," he said.

Esland shot a look of contempt at Robert and took the fagging hook instead. He went to the end of the hedge and vigorously slashed the brash off the top, collecting it to be made into faggots. Edward took the rods they'd cut from the coppice and sharpened the ends. He followed Esland, beating them into the ground inside the hedge. Robert came behind cutting the stems of the hedge almost through, leaving a thin piece of bark still connected. Then he laid the top part over to weave through the stakes.

They worked until the sun told them it was midday when they stopped to eat their bait. Esland took his milky porridge away to eat in privacy. The afternoon was spent continuing the hedging in the same way. They built up a rhythm, following each other along the hedge. It wasn't necessary to converse, they were each concentrating on the job. The only sounds were the chopping of the bill hook and hammering of the mallet, accompanied by spring birdsong.

Edward thought of Mary and how their relationship was blossoming, each finding their own role in the partnership. It had never occurred to him that this process would be so complicated. He wished he'd had more time to get to know her when they were courting. He was discovering her strong personality. She could be stubborn at times and ruled the roost indoors. But she was also fiercely supportive of him and gently loving when the occasion arose.

The next day the routine was repeated. They worked until midday and ate their bait sitting in the sunshine. Then they continued along the hedge. Edward was following Esland with Robert behind him. He heard a cry of pain and turned round. Robert was sitting on the ground, holding his leg.

Edward dropped the mallet and went to Robert's aid. There was a split in his trouser leg and blood oozed from the wound.

Robert turned a shocked face towards Edward. "Me bill'ook slipped. I've cut me leg," he wailed.

"Us mun stop the bleedin'," Edward said. "Let's cut off yer trouser leg."

Esland was on the scene by now, still holding the fagging hook he'd been using. Edward grabbed it and used the point to cut a slit in the fabric. He tore it all round Robert's leg and pulled it off. There was a deep gash on Robert's shin. They tore a strip off the trouser leg and he tied it tightly round the leg above the wound, saving the rest for a bandage.

"You needs ter keep un raised. Can you get onto the cart? Us'll teck you home." Edward didn't give Robert a chance to answer. He and Esland helped him into the cart. He sat leaning against the side, his legs stretched out in front. His face was pale. He was breathing heavily.

Esland collected the tools and carried them, following Edward who led the horse to the farmhouse. He went in and told Tapsell's wife what happened.

"Us'll teck Robert home en bring the cart back termorrer ter finish the hedge." Mistus Tapsell said she'd pass the message on and they set off back to Robert's house.

Alice was alarmed when she saw the state of her master. They took him in and sat him down with his leg propped up.

"D'you have any brandy?" Edward asked.

"Yus, in that dresser there," Robert indicated.

Edward poured him a large dose and said to Alice, "Me mistus'll call later en dress the leg praper, like." He went out to where Esland was waiting with the cart. "Us'll have ter finish the work tergether," he said.

Esland nodded, "Nnnn."

They took the horse and cart round to Savages.

"Robert's catched hurt," Edward said to Mary as he walked into the kitchen, having removed his shoes at the door.

She stopped chopping vegetables and looked at Edward, concerned. "Oh, my!" she said. "Be it bad?"

"It'll teck a while ter heal. 'E's took a piece out of 'is leg with the bill-'ook."

Mary gasped.

Edward said, "Us bound it up as best us could, but it'll need a praper dressin'. Canst do that Mary?"

She nodded. She'd learnt simple first aid years ago when her father injured his leg. Her aunt Louise had shown her how to use herbs for the healing of wounds. "I'll have ter cut up a sheet fer bandage." She put down the knife she was holding, washed her hands in the bucket of water nearby and dried them on a towel. "I've some salve that'll help ter heal it," she said and disappeared into the parlour to collect the things she would need.

"Meck sure Alice knows what ter be at, Mary," Edward said as she was leaving. "I'll see thee 'forelong."

≈≈≈

Over the next few days Mary went to dress Robert's wound and Alice learned how to tend him. Edward and Esland went to finish the hedge-laying.

One morning as Edward was preparing to set off for Tapsell's, Esland came to the door. "Shee... shee..." he said and pointed to the sheep field. He cradled his arms as he had done before, as if holding a baby.

Edward asked, "Lambing started, Esland?"

"Nnn... nnnn," he nodded his head.

"D'you need any help?"

Esland shook his head. He waved Edward away.

"I'll finish Tapsell's job by meself," Edward said.

"Nnn... nnn," nodded Esland and turned to go back to the sheep.

Before he left, Edward told Mary that lambing had started.

She clapped her hands and said, "Oh! That be exciting! I'll go en see if Esland needs help."

There was a little more coppicing to do, then Edward spent the rest of the day tying up bundles of brash to make faggots. He was excited to think that there would be lambs skipping in the fields very soon. He also needed to get back to his farm to attend to the expectant cows.

He led the horse with the cart laden with cordwood and faggots to Tapsell's yard that evening.

Tapsell came to meet him. "I'll settle up with you later, Edward. That's a good job done, despite you losing your team."

"It took a liddle longer," said Edward. He shook hands withTapsell and strolled home.

Mary met him in the yard. "Come en see the fambly," she said, taking his hand, pulling him towards the sheep field.

Three proud mothers and their offspring sheltered in one of the pens. Shep lay at the entrance on guard. Esland came out of his hut, his eyes twinkling, his cheeks puffed out in the best he could do for a happy smile. They went into the pen. Edward checked the four lambs, which were healthy and already showing signs of skipping and playing together. The ewes lay down chewing the cud contentedly.

"Well done, Esland!" said Edward, slapping his shepherd on the back. At that moment another sheep started bleating and Esland rushed away to be midwife.

"I'll be here ter help you 'forelong," Edward called after him, "if you needs it." He and Mary walked hand in hand to the house together.

"Did Tapsell pay thee?" she asked.

"Nay, us'll have ter wait awhile. I rackon he'll pay we in kind."

That evening Edward took his account book out of the drawer in the dresser. He sat down with it at the table and recorded the last few weeks' work:

1707 Then dried Thomas Tapsel's				
hops 6 days which was forgot	0	9	0	
Esland & myself for hedging 26 rods				
we three together for faggots 100 half & 20				
faggots	0	2	7	0
for Cutting of Cordwood	0	3	0	0
for hedging 33 rods	0	4	0	0
more for cutting of bushes	0	1	0	0
more for hedging against the Tared				
more myself for cutting of that wood				
& making the faggots by myself	0	0	10	0
This was left to reckon				

Chapter Twenty Two   1707   March

In which a vigil is held.

It was time Esland went back to The Slade. Thomas would be needing him. Edward was home and Mary could help him with the lambing and the calving. One bright morning in early April, after a sharp frost, they stood at the door and shook hands with the man who'd helped them through some troubled times. Their breath steamed into the cold air. Edward gave Esland his last wages and he bowled out of the yard, turned to wave, then disappeared round the corner.

There was an empty space where he had been. They would miss him.

The sheep were bleating and Edward ran to the pasture leaving Mary to do the morning chores. She went to feed the hens and checked the broody, who sat tightly on her nest, blinking at Mary and making motherly clucks. A fluffy yellow head peeped from her breast feathers and cheeped.

"Oh, you clever hen!" Mary threw her some grain. There would be more chicks by the end of the day. She carefully shut the door of the coop. They would be able to run in and out between the bars, looking for insects on the ground. Their mother would call them back at any sign of danger.

Mary made the rounds of the other animals. There were two expectant cows in separate stalls. One of them was rolling her eyes and mooing in distress. The calf was evidently about to be born, but something was wrong. Mary dashed out of the stall and up to the pasture.

"Edward! Come, dracly-minute!"

Edward was up to his arms in birthing the second of twin lambs.

"The cow's in trouble! I b'lieve 'tis breech," said Mary.

"Fegs!" said Edward, withdrawing his arm and straightening his back. "This sheep needs help. Can you take over?"

Mary gulped. "I've watched Esland enough times," she said. "I can't help the cow. You go, Ed." She bent down, took a deep breath, rolled up her sleeves and inserted her fingers cautiously into the slimy opening, sliding her hand in until it met the head of the lamb. It was warm and soft inside the womb. The sheep was busy licking the first twin. Mary reached further and slid her fingers round the lamb's body, easing it into the outside world. Her heart was beating fast. In a trice, the sticky bundle slithered to the ground at her feet. She picked it up and wiped its nose and mouth the way Esland did.

Tears streamed down her cheeks as she placed the lamb by its mother's head. She'd helped to bring a new life into the world. The afterbirth came out easily.

She cleaned her hands and arms in the bucket of water nearby, then sat on the step of the shepherd's hut watching the little creature come to life with its twin. They staggered to their feet, sneezed, shook their heads and uttered the first feeble cries.

A horse was coming fast up the lane. This sounded like another emergency. Mary left the sheep and her lambs and hurried to the yard to meet the visitor.

Ann dismounted, her face flushed with exertion. "'Tis Muvver!" she called. "She be failin' fast. Where's Ed?"

Mary was already on her way to the cowshed, hoping she wouldn't have to take over again. She opened the door to the warm smell of soiled straw and animal breath.

Edward was struggling with the back legs of the calf and getting nowhere. Ann came to the doorway. She quickly understood the situation.

"Let me help," she said, rolling up her sleeves.

As brother and sister attempted to prise the calf away from its mother, Ann said, "Muvver's failing, Brudder. I have ter go en tell Richard…"

Edward looked aghast at Ann. "I can't leave Mary with this."

"Wait, I believe 'e's on 'is way." Ann twisted her arm and slowly brought another leg out.

Edward did the same. The calf tumbled to the floor. There was silence. They all looked at the newborn lying still. Mary moaned. Edward bent down and picked up the limp body. He desperately cleared its airways, then breathed into its nose and mouth. The baby was dead.

Ann came to her senses. "Sorry, Brudder," she said. "I'll be bodgen. You come to-wunst." She went to swill her hands in the bucket by the well, mounted her horse, then called, "Behopes Muvver waits fer you," as she cantered away.

Mary watched Edward wearily deal with the afterbirth and take it away with the little body.

"I'll go en fetch Faithful en saddle 'er up fer you, Ed," she said and left him in his disappointment and sorrow to grieve with the mother for a few moments.

≈≈≈

Faithful took Edward swiftly along the road from Wadhurst towards The Slade. It was unbelievable that his mother was dying. He'd always thought of her as indestructible.

As he clattered into the yard, Eliza came out to meet him. He dismounted, tethered his horse and hesitated before going into the house. He could not face what he might find.

Eliza re-assured him. "Her be waiting fer you," she said.

"Richard be a-comen," said Edward. He went round by the back door and into the parlour.

Martha was sitting by the cot holding her mother's hand. Thomas was in his father's chair supping ale from a tankard. His face appeared smooth and grey, his eyes gazed into the distance. Edward remembered he'd always been his mother's favourite.

Dorcas was lying propped up with pillows. Her body had lost all its bulk. Her face was hardly recognisable. Edward placed himself where she could see him. She stretched out her free hand.

"Come closer, Son," she croaked. "'Ow be yer lovely Mistus?"

"'Er be shapin' up bravely, Muvver," said Edward as he took her hand and sat on a chair by the bed. "Her be a praper husbandwoman prensly. 'Er birthed a lamb 'smarnen."

"You teck care of she en her'll tend thee. Will there be any liddle uns on the way?"

"Not yet. The time will come."

Voices sounded in the court. Richard and Ann came through the door.

"'Ere be Richard, Muvver." Edward got up from his chair and let his brother sit down.

Martha was weeping softly. Ann came to gently nudge her out of her seat. "You go en seek us summat ter eat. Edward'll help you."

"Hast been here long?" asked Edward as he and Martha went into the dairy.

Martha turned to him and wiped her eyes. She sniffed and said, "Ann called fer me first thing. I got here dracly-minute. Will Muvver die soon, Ed?"

She was like a child again. He recalled taking care of his little sister when they played together. He'd defended her from Thomas who bullied all of them. Edward was the mediator. Ann was more independent and fought back.

"Behopes 'er'll not suffer long." Edward gave his sister a hug then went to look for some bread and cheese, though he doubted that any of them would feel like eating.

It took a long time for Dorcas to let go of her life and her children. They took it in turns to sit with her. Eliza provided what sustenance they needed. Dorcas declined all food and would only accept a sip of water to quench her thirst.

Edward took a blanket and lay down by the fire. His heart was aching, but his thoughts were with Mary and the animals. The death of the first calf was a blow, but they had to take the rough with the smooth. He was proud of Mary, the way she was facing up to farming tasks so willingly. He hoped she wouldn't have any emergencies to deal with while he was away. This was the first time he'd left her with no support from Esland.

Thomas said nothing. He sat in his chair, occasionally nodding off, then jerking awake. Once or twice he went out to relieve himself, coming back with his tankard slopping over with more ale. The others came and went as they needed, saying little, each absorbed in their own thoughts. The candles flickered, died down and were replaced as the night wore on.

Dawn broke with the crowing of the cockerels. Eliza went to see to the animals. The geese squawked and hissed as they were let out of the barn. The sound of hooves reached into the parlour. Edward got to his feet, stretched the stiffness out of his limbs and went to see who the visitors were.

Two big strong men dismounted, leaving their horses in the yard. News of Dorcas had reached her brothers. The older ones had died some years ago, but the remaining two lived and worked in the smithy in Lamberhurst. They were dressed in their best dark clothing. They removed their hats as they bent their heads to go through to the parlour. White-haired now, they were still handsome and had the same florid complexion as their sister. Their bulk filled the room. Martha and Ann left their chairs to let the two men sit either side of Dorcas.

She opened her eyes, disturbed by the movement around her. A gentle smile lit up her tired face. She didn't speak, but reached for her brothers and put their hands in theirs.

"God bless thee, Sister," said Abraham.

Moses echoed the blessing.

All was quiet. Eliza put more wood on the fire, which crackled and spat. Tankards of ale were brought for the visitors.

Dorcas' chest rattled as she struggled to take her last breaths. Ann came to raise her on her pillows. They all watched as she closed her eyes and relaxed. Peace at last. The vigil was over. A life complete.

Chapter Twenty Three

In which Mary's night is disturbed…

As Edward galloped down the lane, Mary found herself alone and responsible for the management of the farm as well as the household tasks. There was no knowing how long Edward would be away. She would tend the animals and had proved to herself that she could birth a lamb if need be. The remaining expectant cow was a different matter.

She went back into the cow stall and stroked the bereaved mother. She was reminded of the loss of her own unborn child. The udder would be filling up with milk. Mary decided to take the cow to join the others in the pasture, where there was grass and company.

She completed the remaining morning tasks and went indoors. When she'd found something to eat there would be the cows to milk, the butter to churn and a number of other chores which would keep her busy all day. As she worked she recalled her life before her marriage to Edward. How naïve she'd been, spoilt by her mother. She led the life of a lady, sitting most of the day with her embroidery or reading a book. Her meals were provided and her clothes were laundered. She hadn't been prepared for this drastic change. Now she was doing things she never dreamed were possible. How much happier she was. Her hands were red raw in the winter, but she could put up with that. And now the spring was here she would love to work side by side with Edward in the fields, doing what she'd always considered was man's work. She felt stronger, more confident and proud of herself.

Her one desire was to have a family. She and Edward enjoyed their love-making. Every month she watched for a sign that a child was on the way. Then she remembered the dreadful experience of the miscarriage and she saw Esland's face and heard her mother's voice. *Your child will be born malformed...* Perhaps this was the reason for her failing to conceive. Today they'd said goodbye to Esland and future babies would be safe.

In the afternoon she had time to make a brief visit to Robert Smith next door. His leg was taking a long time to heal and he blamed the lotion Mary used on the dressings. He was angry that he was unable to work. Mary continued to visit him, taking small gifts of butter and cheese which he grudgingly accepted. Today she would take a freshly baked loaf wrapped in a cloth. She looked in on the sheep before leaving. All was quiet and Shep was on guard.

Mary let herself in to find Robert limping round his parlour, holding onto the furniture, peering into corners and under piles of papers and discarded clothes. He looked up.

"Oh, 'tis you," he said and continued his search.

There was a smell of stale urine.

"What art a-seeking, Robert?" Mary asked. When he didn't reply, she said, "You should get Alice ter tidy up a bit. This place be in a fair hike. 'Tis no surprise you can't find aught."

"I don't want nobody a-rummagin' through my things. They be private." He flicked through the pages of a book he'd picked up, then slammed it down on the table.

"Cannot yer brudder help you, like?" suggested Mary.

Robert went back to his chair and sat down with a sigh. "What business is it of yourn, anyway?"

"I brought you some bread. 'Tis a lovely spring day out there, Robert, 'twould do you good ter get some exercise en fresh air. Be you doin' aught ter tend ter those animals; milking the cow or feeding the fowls?"

"Alice does it all," Robert admitted. "I s'pose I could be at they things. Me leg's still bad." He looked at her woefully.

"I rackon the leg would improve if you used un. En when didst last change yer riggin'?" Robert looked away.

Mary said, "I've left the loaf on the table out there. I'd best be bodgen. Ed's away with 'is muvver.

She be failin' en I be left with the lambing. I'll leave the door open to get some air in the place." She turned to go. "If you'd been fit I could've paid you ter help with the work while Ed's away," she called on the way out.

She strode back to Savages thinking Robert needed a good bannicking. She had been a little hard on him, but he did exaggerate his difficulties. This was the first time she'd seen him walking around. She'd caught him unawares.

The day was drawing to a close and Edward wasn't home. Mary milked the cows, put them back in the pasture, fed the fowls and the expectant cow. She went across to the sheep field to examine all the sheep while it was still daylight. There was no sign of an imminent birth. Shep came to follow her round, he was missing the men, too. Mary sat on the step of the hut and watched the sun go down. Shep lay by her side until a chill in the air chased her inside.

She didn't want to spend the night without Edward in their bed. If she took Esland's place in the hut she'd be near the sheep if they needed her. She sat down on the small cot. It was cosy in here. The stove was still warm from last night's fire. She opened the door to find a glow smouldering among the ashes. A few twigs thrown in burnt up. She added a small log and there was soon a good blaze going. She caught sight of a little pile of shredded candlewax on the floor among the logs. As she swept it up and threw it on the fire, she wondered if there were mice in here.

She went into the house and heated up the remains of yesterday's dinner, fetched the blankets from the bed upstairs and took them into the shepherd's hut with Shep. He shared the stew with her, then she wrapped herself in the blankets and lay down. Shep leapt up and arranged himself on her feet. It had been a busy day. She was tired. Her eyelids closed and she drifted off to sleep.

She woke to a great hullaballoo. The geese were shrieking, the sheep bleating. Shep scratched at the door, barking. Mary got up, opened the door and pulled her boots on. She grabbed the torch from its corner, thrust it into the fire, the tar caught light. She carried it, flaming and smoking, out into the night.

Shep dashed over to the yard, barking. The torch flung long dancing shadows across the walls of the buildings. A dark figure stood by the door of the house, shielding his eyes from the glare.

Mary called Shep away. The geese in their shed cackled and hissed.

"Go back, Shep," Mary ordered. She didn't want foxes around while she dealt with the intruder. Shep trotted away.

"What d'you think you be at?" she shouted angrily.

"I er… I w-were minded, er…" He shuffled his feet and sniffed.

"You was abouten go into my house," said Mary. As she drew nearer she realised that the intruder was Robert Smith. "Was you minded ter find what you was a-seekin' in yer parlour?"

He shrugged and turned away to limp back to his cottage.

"If there's summat you wants ter ax me, you can get yerself over here come mornen. There's naught much wrong with yer leg if you can walk this far in the middle of the night."

Mary watched him go. Her heart was racing. The fear was subsiding, but she was angry; relieved that the intruder was Robert, but had he intended to steal something? He'd seen the pot of money on the mantelpiece in the parlour when he came round in the winter. There was little in it now. She went back to the shepherd's hut, wishing Edward was there. Shep came to her and she stroked him for a while before going back to bed.

≈≈≈

Edward was on his way home, leaving the women to prepare his mother's body for burial. He was tired and sad, but a feeling of relief mingled with his bereavement. Dorcas was released from her suffering. She'd gone to meet her Maker with patience and courage. He was sure that, whatever lay beyond the grave, she would be cared for. She'd been a loving mother and a dutiful wife, giving good advice when needed. Thomas was the one who would miss her most. She was always at his side, comforting and cajoling him. She understood his obstinacy and laziness and she'd never stopped loving him.

Esland had returned and was helping Eliza with the routine work around the close and garden. Edward talked to Ann before he left.

"Esland be the only help on the farm now that James be gone," he said. "Will Thomas be able ter manage?"

"The farm's a-runnen right down." Ann said. "I be minded ter come en bide 'ere ter give 'em a hand, like. Joseph en me beant ringlin' betimes April next year. Esland can have my cottage if 'e's a mind en can pay the rent."

Edward nodded. "Esland'll be hem partial to that, I'll be bound. Thank you, Sister. Thomas beant bringin' in enough ter pay un a praper wage. I can pay his rent." He held Ann's hands in both of his. "If there be aught else I can be at, send a message. I'll see thee anon."

Thankfully, Ann was a strong-willed woman with a good business sense. She would help Thomas get the farm into a manageable state before she left. As Edward rode through Wadhurst life continued as normal in the town, oblivious to the latest events in Edward's life. He spurred his horse on. He wanted to get back to Mary.

There she was standing in the yard, a pail hanging from each hand, waiting for him to turn the corner. His heart jumped with affection. Shep greeted him as he dismounted. Mary put her pails down and ran towards him. They embraced.

"Oh, I did miss thee, Ed!" she said into his shoulder.

He squeezed her a little tighter, then made space between them so he could see her face. "Is all well?" he asked.

She relaxed her hold on him and held his hands. "Us had a liddle adventure," she said and looked down at the dog. "Didn't us, Shep?"

Shep stood up from his waiting pose on his haunches and wagged his tail, ears pricked, eyes bright and tongue hanging out.

Mary looked at Edward seriously. "Yer Muvver?" she queried.

Edward shook his head and told Mary of Dorcas' death that morning.

Mary took his hand and squeezed it in sympathy. "God rest 'er soul," she said. They stood with their heads bowed until Mary sighed and said, "I be agwain ter feed the beasts. Art a-comen?"

Edward tethered Faithful and went to pick up one of the pails. He followed Mary into the stall where the expectant cow was still waiting. He gave her some chopped turnips and felt her belly. "She be near birthen," he said.

The two went on the rounds together. Edward checked the condition of the sheep and nodded in approval. "They lambs en their muvvers can be let loose in the pasture," he said. "Us'll bring 'em to the fold come night-time."

On their way back to the house, he said, "So what be this adventure?"

While she made porridge for their breakfast, Mary told him about Robert Smith and his intrusion during the night.

Edward was angry. "After all you've been at for un, tenden 'e en all," he said to Mary. "I be minded ter go en give un a good bannickin'."

"'E were middlin' ashamed of hisself," Mary said." I told un ter come en ax if there be summat 'e wanted. I rackon 'e be short of money, like us all be."

"There be nobbut a few shillin' in the pot," agreed Edward, "en there beant much wheat left fer bread. I'll go over ter Tapsell's with the cart 'smarnen. 'E be indebted to us fer all that work."

The geese set up their alarm and Edward went to see who the visitor was. Robert stopped when he saw him, turning to go back. Edward strode across the yard and took hold of Robert by the shoulder.

"Come here, you file!" He turned the man round and marched him, limping, into the house. "What d'you mean, a-comen sneakin' round here in the dark, frittin' the mistus en all? I bluv you was a friend."

Robert covered his head with his arms. When Edward released him he said, "I be short of money, Mas Edward. En I ain't been paid fer worken fer Mas Tapsell. I bluv mebbe…"

"Us all be short. I be abouten call on Tapsell 'smarnen. Be you a-comen along of me?"

Robert nodded.

Mary doled out some porridge into a bowl. She put it down in front of Robert, who was sitting at the table.

"Thank you, Mistus Lucke," he said.

"You don't deserve it," Edward said as he emptied his own bowl.

They went to Tapsell's and collected a bushel of wheat in part payment for the work they'd done. Robert was paid in money. Tapsell agreed that Edward should have a heifer and a sheet, which would be delivered to him this week. So started a partnership between Thomas Tapsell and Edward Lucke, in which Edward worked for Tapsell, mowing grass and clover, marling and drying hops. He was paid in wheat, malt, meat and peas and sometimes in money. Edward supplied Tapsell with lamb and mutton when he had it to spare and was paid in money. He kept an account of all these transactions, valuing work at a shilling a day. Each time an account was complete, he crossed it out in his account book.

Mary worked alongside Edward in their own fields and sometimes went with him to mow grass on the other farms. She took charge of the garden and grew potatoes, peas and beans as well as a few flowers.

There was no sign of a child on the way.

Chapter Twenty Four   1707/8

In which Thomas signs an agreement

The seasons rolled by and soon it was autumn again. The harvest was inned, the fruit was stored, the lambs were all grown up and the new pigs had settled into the hog pound. The hedgerows were decorated with the berries of hips and haws and dew sparkled on the cobwebs stretched across the branches. Mary and Molly were picking blackberries in the lane with Sam and Meg when Edward approached on his horse.

"I be agwain to Lamb'rst ter see Ann," he called as he rode by.

He could hear shouting as he rode into the yard at Slade Farm. The geese surrounded him, making a fuss. He shooed them away as he dismounted. It was Ann's voice he heard, raised in anger.

"What d'you want these hop poles for anyways? There's been no hops grown on this farm for the past two years."

Ann and Thomas were standing outside the barn. The door was open and he could see piles of stored wood, bundles of faggots, rods mixed with rusty, dusty old farm machinery, twine and gardening tools. Straw was spread over the spare floor where the geese spent the night, covering everything with their juicy green droppings.

Thomas's face was red with anger. He looked up to see Edward standing there. "I can't let this stuff go. When I feels fit I can get the farm worken en it'll be needed."

Ann laughed in disbelief. "You be a-dreamen, Brudder. Who's agwain ter use these rusty old things? They be no good fer aught by now. Ed, tell un not ter be such an old fool."

Edward said, "I could buy some of they things off you, Thomas. I be minded ter grow hops. Those poles would come in handy. En we be short of faggots if you beant abouten use 'em."

Ann said. "There be plenty more in the copse. Esland en me did some coppicing last week. 'E's fetchen more rods en wood in the cart prensly."

Thomas said stubbornly, "You can have some of 'em, but I don't want ter sell 'em all.

Ann shrugged her shoulders and sighed in resignation. "Come in en have a jar, Ed. I be all-in trying ter get un ter see sense." She turned and walked to the back door, leaving Thomas staring at the decaying remnants of better times on the farm.

"'E can't seem ter let go of aught," Ann said as she took two tankards off the shelf and filled them from a barrel in the buttery. "I'll be leavin' come April en want ter get the place cleared en manageable fer Eliza afore then."

"Once 'e's made 'is mind up, 'e wunt be druv," commented Edward, taking his drink into the parlour.

"'E be like a mule with a sore head," agreed Ann.

They sat down at the table.

There was a creak on the stairs as Eliza came down slowly. She smiled when she saw Edward. "'Tis me knees," she said holding onto the edge of the table as she sat down. "I can't get around like I did. En Thomas be hardly better. I can't think how us'll manage without yer sister here."

"There be Esland. 'E be strong en can manage the few beasts when I've sold the rest. There won't be no farming work to be at..." Ann was interrupted by Thomas coming through the door.

"You beant sellen me kine!" he shouted. We needs 'em fer milk en next year's calves." He sat down heavily on his father's chair.

"En who's agwain ter teck 'em to bull en birth en raise the calves en have 'em to market?" Ann's voice was raised again.

"Don't upset thyself, Thomas," purred Eliza. "I'll get thee a drink." She pushed herself to her feet and hobbled out to the buttery.

"I be minded ter settle up with you fer Esland's rent, Ann," said Edward.

"We'll go over to the cottage," said Ann. "There's a few things there I've a mind ter let you have. Esland's no need of 'em."

She got up from her chair and Edward followed her out into the close. Esland drove in with the cart, laden with wood from the copse. Edward chose 300 hop poles and some bundles of faggots. Esland agreed to put them to one side for him to collect later with his cart. They all three walked over the road to Esland's cottage.

Edward recalled the days when his aunt Tamsen lived here with his cousins. They were older than he and Richard, but he enjoyed going there and romping in the neighbouring fields playing hide and seek. It was a happy household. There was always something going on: visits from older cousins, days when they helped Tamsen with the baking or harvesting the fruit. As he entered the parlour he fancied he heard the echoes of laughter and children's voices.

But this was Esland's place now. The place was tidy and clean. The items on the shelves were things he used; bowls, spoons in a mug, a tinder box, knife, scissors. Scattered among these everyday objects were many beautifully carved wooden figures of animals and birds. There were cows, a herd of sheep, pigs, horses pulling a cart and wild things like foxes, rabbits and owls. Ann had left him her clock. It stood on the mantleshelf ticking quietly and steadily, enhancing the peace of the surroundings.

A few chickens scratched around outside. Ann went to what used to be the cowshed and came out with some tools. "There's a sheep and her lamb in the field. You don't need 'em, Esland, d'you?"

Esland shook his head. "Na," he said and indicated that Edward should have them.

"The rent's five pounds a year to Ladyday," Ann said to Edward. "The hop poles en faggots I'll let you have fer twelve shillin' en nine pence en the sheep en lamb, six shillin'."

Esland nodded in agreement. Ann would let him have the money for the sheep. They all shook hands on it.

Edward found the money in his purse and handed it over to Ann. "I'll pay the rent come Ladyday," he said.

They walked back to Slade Farm together. Edward mounted Faithful, said goodbye and rode home.

There were a few things he wanted to buy in Wadhurst. After leaving the horse tethered by the market cross he walked up the main street. Coming towards him was a neighbour of Thomas Tapsell, William Ashdown. He was a stocky man of middle age with a florid face and a thick black beard. He always walked with a stick, swinging it as he went. His eyes twinkled when he saw Edward. The two exchanged greetings.

"When I seed you at the market you said you was willin' to exchange work en goods, William," Edward said.

"Yus, I be agreeable," said Ashdown.

"There be some wood ter collect from Lamb'rst fer me farm. I be takin' me cart to collect a sheep en a lamb. Can you teck yer cart along of me en bring the wood?"

"For certain sure,"

"Would termorrer be orright?" asked Edward.

"Yus," Ashdown nodded. "I'll bring me cart first thing in the marnin.'"

"Thank you," Edward said. "Give greetin's to Bella," he added as they parted company.

In April Edward went to Slade farm to settle up with Ann, who was to be wed the next weekend. They sat at the table in the parlour where Thomas was enjoying a beer and warming his feet by the fire.

"I've two ducks you can have, Edward. 'Twill save teckin' em along of me," said Ann, absent-mindedly wiping some crumbs off the table.

Edward nodded. "Us ain't got no ducks. The eggs will be a treat. I'd be partial to a piece of yer special cheese. En I've brought the butter you wanted. When be you agwain ter leave?"

"Termorrer marnen," Ann said. "'Twill teck the day ter cart me howsell to Joe's farm. I'll bide with 'is muvver fer the night. Then I'll ride back fust thing ter get ready." Her eyes sparkled as she looked at Edward.

"'Twill be good ter see you wed en settled," said Edward, covering her hand with his.

"I'll see thee en Mary Sadderdy, Ed," She stood to go out. "I'll go en put the ducks in a ped fer you."

"Will you stay en be witness to this?" Edward opened his account book and showed her the page headed: *Thomas Lucke's account.*

Ann looked at it and nodded, "Yus, I be willin'." She smiled wryly as she glanced at Thomas who was dropping off to sleep.

Edward said, "Thomas!"

His brother jerked his head up and became alert.

"Thomas, you ain't paid me fer all that's owin'. I'd be obliged if we could come to an agreement." He showed Thomas the pages on which he'd recorded the outstanding debts.

Thomas studied them and nodded. "I can't pay prensley, you knows that." He looked at Edward defiantly.

"I'd be obliged if you'd sign this agreement, so's us knows where us be at." Edward turned to the next page where he'd written:

April 10   1708. Then reckoned with Thomas Lucke
for all accounts and there is due to me Edward Lucke
the sum of fourteen pounds and eighteen shillings.
I say indebted to Edward Lucke

by me Thomas Lucke which I promise to pay
to Edward Lucke upon demand
Witness my hand
           14-------18--------00

He placed the book on the table and went to fetch quill and ink from the dresser in the hall.

Ann stood and watched as Thomas rose from his chair and came to the table. He sat on the end of the bench and took the quill in his right hand. He dipped it in the ink and with a trembling hand wrote: *Tho Lucke.*

He put the quill down, looked at Edward and said, "There, do that satisfy thee?"

It was a large debt. Edward wondered how his brother would find a way of paying him. It would take a long time, but Edward was determined to have what was owing.

A few months later, at the end of the summer, Edward went to call on his brother to find out how he was getting on. He tethered Faithful in the yard as usual and walked through the close to the back door. All was quiet. He knocked and went in. Eliza was in the dairy churning butter. Her face was red and wisps of grey hair had escaped from her cap. She looked up and her eyes brightened. She stopped churning.

"Hello, Edward," she said with surprise. "Us ain't seen you fer a while. Come en sit in the parlour." She led the way.

The room was empty. The only sound was the fire crackling. An aroma of baking bread met them as they came in.

"I come ter see how ye be faring," said Edward, sitting down at the table.

"Thomas en Esland be out there a-mowen the hay. Summer's been good en this be the second cut." Eliza nodded her head with satisfaction.

"D'ye have any help on the farm?" Edward could hardly believe what he'd heard.

"Nay. Thomas did a big turn-around when Ann left. 'E had a good talk to Esland en said 'e'd give un better pay if they could keep the farm a-goin' together, like. They've got wheat en oats a-growen en plan to grow hops again next year. We be fitter with all this work," she said, grinning.

"Whatever brought this on? 'E's never worked like that." Edward was shocked.

"I rackon 'e's allus had other bodies ter do the work for un en 'e couldn't see the need. There be none but we prensly."

She looked directly into Edward's eyes and he saw that the two of them were making a last bid to prove that they could do it, despite all the scoffing and badgering over the years.

Eliza continued, "Us don't have no beer in the house no more. 'E says if it's there 'e'll drink it. 'E beant had a drink all summer. It saves me brewen it."

Edward said, "I were wondering if 'e could keep a calf fer me in his pasture. Calf's a good un en I want un fattened up fer sellen."

"Don't see why not," said Eliza. "'E can go in with our calves. There be plenty of pasture now the sheep be gone. Bring un over somewhen. I'll tell Thomas."

"Tell un I'll knock it off what 'e owes me." Edward got up to leave. "I be considerable impressed that ye be makin' a go of it," he said.

He followed her out to the dairy and said goodbye as she went back to her churning. His head was reeling with the news of Thomas' reformed character. He wondered how he and Esland were getting on together. Thomas had been unkind and sometimes cruel to Esland in the past and Esland took it badly when he was treated with disrespect.

Chapter Twenty Five   1709 April

In which Thomas Lucke delivered in…

Every Sunday Edward and Mary took the cart into Wadhurst to attend the church service. This was becoming quite a social occasion. They met their farming neighbours afterwards and stood around in the litten chatting, before returning home. Ed Waghorn and his wife were often there. One day they were all deep in conversation when William Ashdown and Edward Benge approached.

"Mas Lucke, may we interrupt you for a moment?" asked Benge. Edward left Mary talking to the Waghorns and raised his hat to the two parish officers.

Ashdown said, "Edward, I rackon I knows you well enough to be an upstanding, God-fearin' man. Us be seekin' fresh faces in the parish vestry en I've recommended you as suitable."

Edward was taken by surprise. He was not sure he was the right person for the job, but flattered that they should consider him. He said, "I thank ye fer yer attention. I beant familiar with the work that's needed, but I be willing ter larn it."

Benge said, "'Twould only be your attendance at vestry meetings to start with, Lucke. That would familiarise you with our procedures. There are various offices available. We need at least two overseers to tend the parish chest and distribute to the poor. What do you think?"

"I be main agreeable, Sir. When d'ye hold the meetings?"

Ashdown said, "Good man! Once a month we go over to The Grazehound after church. It takes no longer than an hour. Can you join we today?"

Edward hesitated. "I -- I'll talk to the Mistus. She'll want ter be bodgen home. If not today, for sarten sure I'll be there next month." He shook the hand of Edward Benge before turning back to Mary and the Waghorns.

"I've been asked ter join the parish vestry!" he said proudly. "'Twill mean agwain ter the meetings once a month after church."

"I be hem proud of you Edward," said Mary.

The Waghorns agreed and shook Edward's hand.

"'Tis a great honour, surely," said Edward. "But how will you get home, Mary?"

"I'll foot it," she said. "'Tis not far. You go en see what 'tis all about, Edward."

"Yus, yus, I be agwain drecly." He waved to them all as he went out of the litten, through the market place and over the road to The Grazehound.

The parish officers were gathered in a quiet corner of the bar, sitting round a table. There were eight or nine of them.

Benge stood up when he saw Edward and said, "Here be our new officer, Edward Lucke. I'll fetch you a beer, Lucke. You sit yourself down."

Edward found a vacant chair and sat down. He looked at the men sitting round the table, recognising some of them: John Feavour the tailor, his father's friend. There were streaks of grey in his black hair which was smoothed sleekly against his head and falling to his shoulders. He looked over his spectacles and nodded unsmilingly. Nicholas Fowle, the ironmaster, was there. He was the tax collector.

Some were staring at Edward as if summing him up. He nodded and smiled in embarrassment. "Good marnen, Gentlemen," he said. He looked round the rest of the bar. The place was nearly empty. All taverns were made to close during the church service, so that those who should be at church were not tempted away. There was a trickle of them arriving. Soon the place would hum with voices, some discussing the vicar's sermon, others gossiping about the latest scandals.

Benge, a bulky man wearing a grey curled wig, a velvet knee-length jacket and buckled shoes, brought a full foaming tankard and set it down before Edward. He was the brother of William Benge, another ironmaster and owner of considerable property. "Shall we procede, Gentlemen?" he said.

Glad to have their attention diverted to business matters, Edward picked up his tankard of beer, took a mouthful, then sat back in his chair to listen. The first discussion was of a girl in the parish, Susan Newnham, who had become pregnant. She had asked for poor relief, but was refusing to disclose the name of the father.

"Comber and Duplock," Edward Benge addressed two men across the table from him. "I suggest you seek out this hussy and get the name of the father. We cannot afford to support bastard children in this parish."

The vicar, John Smith, cleared his throat. "I know a little about the background of this girl," he said quietly. "She's a servant in the house of William Cruttal."

"Oh, well. 'E be well-knowed fer taken 'vantage of 'is servants," a thin man with a large Adam's apple burst out. "Though God knows 'e's enough children from 'is late wife." His mouth opened wide and he laughed mirthlessly. Edward was reminded of the bleating of one of his sheep.

Benge put his hand up. "We're not here to discuss gossip, Pitkin. If the girl's master is responsible he must be made to..."

He was interrupted by Comber, a clean-shaven man with red hair cut straight across below his ears and a fringe across his forehead. He and Duplock, who sat next to him, were the churchwardens. "I will investigate the matter with Mas Duplock, here. Let no more be said until we know the facts."

Edward was hearing periodic rumbles as of distant thunder, until he realised that it came from the stomach of the neighbour on his left. The man nudged him and whispered in his ear, "Benge be acquainted with Cruttal en won't have naught said agin un." He chuckled and Edward smelled a whiff of rotten eggs coming from his mouth.

"Quite so, Comber," Benge was saying, "Now there's a fellow by the name of…" he peered at a piece of paper in his hand, "…Jude Scrase, from Ticehurst, wants to come and set up a business in Wadhurst. He has no experience and might not be able to support himself. Should we arrange for him to have a settlement order?"

"What business would that be?" squeaked a small, mouse-like person opposite Edward. He was bent almost double with a curvature of the spine. His chin was so near to resting on the table that he had to hold his fist between the two to support it.

Duplock, wearing a short grey wig and dressed in purple, had the answer. "I'm well avised that 'e be a saddler."

The man on Edward's right chipped in, "But we a'ready have a saddler in Wad'rst. Tom Stapley would lose custom."

There followed a discussion on the merits of introducing competition in so small a town. There was a pause while two of the company struggled out of their chairs and lurched over to the bar to replenish their tankards.

Voices rose in anger and Nicholas Fowle shouted, "That be enough argifying! There will not be sufficient custom in the town for two."

Benge banged his fist on the table and the noise subsided. He said, "I believe Stapley is getting in years. He'll not be in business much longer. Let us have a show of hands. Those in favour of giving the man a chance in Wadhurst..."

The vicar and the man on Edward's left put their hands up.

"That settles it," said Benge. "The man will have to go back to Ticehurst. Now we will review the contributions to the parish for poor relief, which we must do every year." He looked at Edward to pass on this information. "I say we leave it as it stands."

There were mumbled protests among the company and shaking of heads. The two drinkers waved their fists in the air. One of them said, " There be barely enough in the chest ter pay the people who needs it."

Ashdown spoke up, "It's stayed the same for several years now. Us should put it up accorden to the rise in prices."

Duplock agreed. "The reserves are runnen low. If there were a crisis there wouldn't be enough."

Benge was becoming agitated, strumming his fingers on the table. "Perhaps we should be less generous. There are those receiving poor relief who could be working," he sneered.

The man on Edward's right raised his voice: "If you would pay yer workers a dacent wage they wouldn't need poor relief." There were shouts of "Hear, hear!" "En what's more, be you payin' more into the purse since you bought that piece of land at Mark Cross? I reckon we should get a surveyor along ter measure the land you own..."

Beads of perspiration broke out on Benge's forehead. He shouted, "Pah! And how much do you pay in taxes, John Day? I've heard you added rooms to your house with three more windows. Feavour, put him down for a raise in window tax!"

John Feavour, who'd been crouched over, feverishly writing all this down in a large ledger, sat up and looked at John Day over his spectacles. "Is that a fact, John?"

"Yus," admitted Day. "But I b'lieve we should get a surveyor to look at Benge's property."

Several people shouted "Hear, hear!"

Fowle stood up and shook his fist. "Don't you think you can get away with it, Benge!"

Benge stood up and shouted, "Mind your business, Nicholas Fowle!"

Richard Comber said quietly, "Gentlemen, calm yourselves."

The two rivals sat down.

Comber continued, "I will see that the right thing be done. I propose that we raise the rates by one penny per acre of property. All in favour, raise yer hands."

All but two of the company agreed and Feavour recorded the result.

The meeting was closed. Benge and another landowner called Watson walked out. John Day chuckled. Others had smirks on their faces. Three of them stayed behind, continuing the discussions. Some went to the bar and ordered more drinks. Ashdown invited Edward to join them, but he declined, waving his goodbye as he left. He hoped he would come up to expectations but dreaded getting on the wrong side of Edward Benge.

He mulled over the morning's events as the horse trotted him home in the cart. He felt it was his duty to work for the parish as a responsible member of the community and wondered how much this would encroach on his already busy life.

≈≈≈

Mary was walking home along the road when Richard drove up on his cart. Molly called, "Can us give you a lift, Mary? Where be Edward?"

Mary climbed into the cart and sat next to the children on some sacks. "Ed's gone to a vestry meetin'," she said. "'E's been invited ter be a parish officer."

Richard clicked the horse on and said, "So 'e'll be a-comen round collecting rates en taxes, then."

"Oh, I s'pose so," said Mary. "I hadn't thought of that." She laughed.

"'E'll do the job well, I rackon," remarked Molly. Some o' them officers can be unaccountable skrow. Full of their own importance, they be."

The cart clattered into Savages yard and Mary jumped down. She waved as they drove away. Shep came to greet her and she went to change out of her Sunday dress before she cleaned the goose house. Coming down the stairs, she heard a cart driving into the yard. Thinking it was Edward, she was surprised when Thomas Lucke jumped down and came towards her. He'd lost weight since she last saw him.

He looked at her and said, "Mary, be it you?"

She nodded and smiled.

"I didn't recognise you. You look quite the farmer's mistus by now."

"You've changed considerable, too," she remarked. "Will you pull the cart over agin the barn? Edward'll be a-comen drecly."

Thomas led the horse and cart closer to the barn. "I've brung the corn what 'e asked fer. Where d'you want it put?"

At that moment Edward drove in. His mouth dropped open when he saw Thomas and his loaded cart. Edward drove round behind the barn and came back leading his horse which he tethered by the back door.

"I be hem pleased ter see you, Thomas. You be looken spry."

"I've brung yer oats en wheat."

Edward opened the door of the corn store and went to take one of the sacks from the cart. "How much didst bring?"

"'Tis what you asked fer. Four bushels of wheat en eight bushels of oats. Meck sure you puts it in yer book." Thomas was not in the mood for pleasantries. They unloaded the sacks and he drove away.

Chapter Twenty Six 1709 Summer

In which Edward reckons with Thomas Tapsell

When Edward and Mary had mown the grass in their hay meadow, Edward left Mary to turn it and rake it into windrows. He wanted to settle some accounts with Thomas Tapsell, who'd been slow paying his dues lately.

Edward walked into Tapsell's yard where there was an argument going on between the farmworker and his master. Edward stopped where he was, intending to wait until things calmed down.

"I paid you last week," Tapsell was shouting. "You'll get the rest dappen you've mowed the other fields."

"I beant doin' aught more betimes I gets paid what I be owed," said the labourer stubbornly. He started to walk away, calling over his shoulder, "I can find better work otherwheres."

Tapsell took his hat off and scratched his balding head. Then he looked at Edward standing by.

"Ah, just the man I be needen'" he said. "Joseph's bodged off en there's more mowen ter do. Can you do it, Edward?"

"I needs ter rackon up what be owin' first, if you please," said Edward firmly.

"Come indoors a minute, I needs ter sit down en get me breath after all that argifying." He led the way. His wife was in the parlour. She produced two tankards and filled them with ale from a jug.

The two men sat at the table and Edward brought out his account book. "In March," he said, "I did some hedgin' and cuttin' of wood fer you. He showed Tapsell the page:

1709   March 17   Then reckoned with Thomas Tapsell
For hedging & for cutting of wood
& for faggots & for bushes which was forgot
& my part is 7 pence so the whole sum is due
to me for all this---------------------------- -0-----7-----8-----0
March 26 more one day dressing of hops--0-----1-----0-----0
                                        0------8-----8----0

Tapsell nodded and supped his ale.

Edward continued, showing Tapsell another page. "Now in November last, you delivered oats, malt, wheat and peas. That be the last time I had what was owed. You still owes me fer the work I did in March." He sat back, picked up his tankard and took a long draught, swallowing it slowly.

Tapsell said, "Orright, I'll pay you in money, but you'll have ter wait fer it. Prensly I needs a body ter mow my meadows. Be you agreeable?"

Edward hesitated before he said, "I be agreeable. But I can't wait long fer the money. You be hem forgetful en I can't afford ter work fer naught. I'll start on the mowen termorrer. Be minded, I have it all writ down." He waved the book under the old man's nose before draining his tankard. He stood up and left.

On his return home, he found Mary in the kitchen.

"Hello, love." He greeted her with a kiss. "Hast finished fer today?"

"'Forelong. There's the geese and ducks ter put to bed later. That duck that's disappeared, I rackon 'er's gone into the woods ter find a place ter lay."

"We can leave she be. 'Er'll come back when 'er be hungry." Edward laughed.

"Did Tapsell pay thee? Or will un bring us some corn?" Mary asked.

"Nay. 'E be unaccountable cantankerous prensly. 'E's asked me ter mow 'is meadows. The labourer's bodged off in a hike acause 'e ain't been paid."

"I rackon old Tapsell's losen his mind." Mary said. "I be advised 'is mistus be justabout worritted on account of the farm. 'E beant fit ter manage it praper, like."

"Where didst hear that?" asked Edward.

"Oh, talk goes round the market," Mary said vaguely.

Edward went to put his account book away and made a mental note to be wary of Tapsell. He'd no need to continue working for him. William Ashdown and he had struck up a good partnership and just lately he'd done some work for Ed Waghorn at Bewl Bridge, digging and hoeing his hops.

In due course the missing duck appeared in the yard, marching proudly towards the feeding station as predicted, quackering gently. Following her was a troop of six small balls of yellow fluff, complete with bills in proportion to their size. The one in the rear leapt into the air, unfledged wings spread, to catch a mosquito.

Mother duck increased the volume of her commands, "Jaack, keep in step!"

Jack ran to catch up.

The mother and her brood reached the grain being scattered on the ground by Mary, who exclaimed, "My, you kept that quiet!"

Edward, standing by the barn door, said, "How did 'er manage that? There be no drake!" He laughed as he followed after the newcomers. "I reckon 'er was broody when I got 'em from Ann. 'Tis time I cleaned out the duck pond."

Meanwhile young Jack had picked a fight with one of the chicks. Mother Hen chastised him with her beak, whereupon Mother Duck pounced in defence of her wayward son. Feathers flew, accompanied by squawking and quacking, until Mary scattered grain a few feet away. The birds were distracted and gathered their young to peck in peace.

Robert Smith had been coming round to help with small jobs for Edward and Mary. Edward paid him with supplies: grain for his hens, bread, beer and meat.

The next day they met in the yard. "I'll be cleaning out the duck pond 'smarnen, Robert. Be you willin' ter help?"

"Yus," said Robert, "Though I be ornary today. "

Edward was getting used to Robert's complaints about his health and took little notice. They went to collect forks, spades and shovels from the skillon.

"I were hem middlin' in the night. Didn't get no sleep." Robert continued to grumble.

Edward attempted to lift Robert's spirits. "Mayhap you'll feel better 'forelong. 'Tis a wondrous fine marnen."

They reached the duck pond at the lower side of a sloping field. Rainwater drained from the field to collect in the pond. But it was showing serious signs of neglect, being choked with rushes. This would be heavy work. Edward stuck his fork into the ground where he thought the edge of the pond should be. Robert followed his example. The forks sucked up vegetable matter from the sludge it was growing in, to be thrown into the hedge to rot down. As they worked and the sun rose high into the sky, they stopped frequently to mop their brows.

The edge of the pond became visible. They had to wade deeper into the mud to reach the remaining rushes. Edward welcomed the cool water seeping into his boots. But wading back out, the mud sucked at his feet, restraining him. He had to use all his strength to bring the forkful to the bank.

At last he flung down his fork saying, "'Tis time us had a break."

He looked round to see Robert stagger as he carried a laden fork out of the pond. His face was purple, his eyes bulged, his mouth opened as he groaned, falling forward into the mud.

Edward took three strides, but failed to catch Robert as he fell.

The fourth stride took him knee-deep into the pond. He grasped Robert under the arms, dragged him onto the bank, rolled him over and wiped the sludge from his face.

Robert didn't move.

He lay there staring at Edward, mouth ajar.

Edward knelt beside his neighbour, horror seeping through his whole being. "Robert?" Edward shook the man's shoulders, picked up his arm and let it drop, lifeless, onto the ground by his body. He stooped close to the man's face, hoping to feel his breath. There was nothing.

Edward closed Robert's lids over his staring eyes and said, "Oh, God, forgive me."

Why had he not taken Robert seriously when he said he wasn't well? He'd caused the death of a man through his thoughtlessness. The events of the morning coursed through his brain. Tears of remorse flowed down his face.

"Robert, I be mortaceous sorry," he sobbed.

Edward brought himself back to practicalities. He had to get Robert's body back to his house. He had to find his brother to let him know what had happened. He got to his feet, picked up the spades and forks and made his way to break the news to Mary, leaving Robert spread out on the ground.

≈≈≈

Mary was baking bread, wishing it was not such a hot day. She wanted to be out in the fields, making hay with Edward as she was last week. They'd mowed all Tapsell's hay and were waiting for payment. They would soon have enough in the pot to buy glass for the windows of the cottage before the winter.

She heard the well pump squeaking and glanced out into the yard to see Edward washing. He'd stripped naked. Surely it wasn't time to stop work? She'd only just eaten her coager.

Something must be wrong.

Where was Robert?

She scraped the dough off her fingers. With a damp cloth she covered the lump she'd been kneading then went out into the yard.

"Be there aught amiss, Edward?" she called.

Edward looked up, his face puckered. He shook his head.

"Edward, what is it?" Mary ran towards him and took his head in her hands.

Edward coughed and sobbed. "Oh, Mary! Robert be dead!" He sobbed again and went indoors, leaving his soiled clothes on the ground.

Mary ran in front of him to fetch a towel, returning to wrap it around Edward and clasp him to her. She rocked him gently until he was able to speak, then sat him on the bench by the table.

He spilled out the story. "'Twere my fault. I didn't take no notice when 'e said 'e were ailing. I bluv 'twere just 'is grumbles. But 'twere hot en tejus hard work. 'E collapsed en were gone. I dragged un out of the pond, but 'e were dead." Edward shivered, though they were close to the hot stove.

Mary said, "'Twere not thy fault, Edward. 'E should have knowed better en stopped work if 'e were feelen that bad. You beant responsible fer all that happens. You wasn't drivin' un was you? I'll away en fetch you some riggin', then us'll talk about what ter be at." She went to get a tot of brandy and gave it to him to drink while she fetched his clothes. When she came back he was rubbing himself dry.

She gave him the clothes and said, "I'll finish off this batch of bread while you gets yerself tergether, Then we'll teck the barrer ter carry un to 'is cottage."

≈≈≈

With the help of William Ashdown, Edward tracked down Herbert Smith, Robert's half-brother. They

232

hadn't spoken for years. He called on Edward to hear the account of Robert's death and seemed annoyed that he would now have to wind up his affairs. Edward and Mary were the only other people at the funeral apart from his landlord, William Ashdown and Alice, the maid.

Chapter Twenty Seven 1709 Autumn

In which Edward installs glass in the windows.

It was not until autumn that Edward was called upon to carry some deliveries for the parish. He was on his way back from one of these journeys when he decided to stop in Wadhurst and have a drink in The Grazehound. There were few people in the bar. As he sat alone, he saw John Paris walk through the door. They greeted each other with a wave and John brought his drink to sit with Edward.

"'Tis main quiet in here today," remarked Edward.

"Yus. Just now I were a-talken ter the blacksmith. 'E were sayen there be smallpox in Teec'rst en folks have took fright. Many of 'em be bidin' indoors."

Edward was alarmed. A smallpox epidemic could be disastrous. "Be there any in Wad'rst?" he asked.

"I ain't heard, but I'd keep Mary away from the market next week."

"Mm. Behopes it won't get this far."

The two men stared into their tankards for a while before their conversation turned to other things.

"Be there new neighbours yet, in Robert's cottage?" asked John.

"Nay. I believe the landlord's minded ter be sellen."

Before leaving Wadhurst Edward called in at the glazier's to buy some glass for the windows.

"I be well avised the school's closed on account of the smallpox." The glazier commented as he cut the glass to size.

"I've not heard of any who's catched it in Wad'rst," said Edward

"They say Cruttals fambly be down with it," answered the glazier.

"That be bad news, surely," said Edward, paying for his purchases.

He carefully wrapped his panes of glass in sacking and put them in the cart, tipped his hat to the glazier and climbed up to drive off.

Edward and Mary kept away from Wadhurst where the smallpox reached epidemic proportions. Some didn't survive. Others were scarred for life. The doctors were powerless. The charlatans were making a fortune selling dubious remedies.

It took Edward over a week to install the glass. They couldn't believe how much warmer the house was. They were throwing off the bed covers in the night.

"You wait come winter," said Edward to Mary. "We'll be hem glad not to hear the wind whistlen through the shutters en seein' the snow a-blowen in."

He was finishing off the last window in the second bedroom where a good store of apples covered the floor. They should last the winter. He was enjoying the scent of them. The sound of a cart caused him to look out to see Richard coming up the lane with the two children. He dropped his tools and made his way down the stairs.

Mary had heard the cart roll into the yard. She was greeting the children as they ran into the house, clutching their favourite toys. Richard unloaded a bag and followed them in.

"We be comen ter bide here, Aunt Mary!" Sam shouted excitedly.

Richard said, "I've come ter ask if ye'll have the children. Molly's catched the smallpox. Us don't want 'em gettin' it."

Edward stopped in his tracks, trying to take in the situation. Was Molly in danger? Could the children pass the disease on to Mary? The apples in the bedroom would have to be moved. How would Richard manage his farm and tend Molly?

Mary spread her arms open wide and welcomed the children. "Well now, what a lovely surprise! What fun us be agwain ter have." She led the two into the parlour and left Edward and Richard together.

"I be sorry ter be so sudden," Richard said, dropping the bag on the bench by the table. "Molly be showen early signs: fever en all. She avised me ter bring the children here dracly-minute. They don't know she be ailing..." He sat down on the bench and covered his face with his hands.

Edward put his hand on his brother's shoulder. "'Tis the best thing you could do," he said. "Us'll muvver 'em praper fer as long as needs be. You tend Molly en be sure she gets well agen." He went and filled two tankards with ale and brought them back. They sat quietly for a while.

Mary and the children came out of the parlour and through the hall. "Us be agwain ter wrap up a few things fer Molly," she said to Richard. They disappeared into the kitchen and Edward heard Sam and Meg's voices chirupping away happily.

"'Twill be good fer Mary ter be a muvver for a while. She so longs fer a child," he said.

Richard took a bag of herbal remedies, little spicy cakes and a crock of soup with the lid tightly secured and wrapped in a cloth. He thanked Mary and Edward, said goodbye to the children and drove the cart away.

The rest of the day was spent transferring the apples to the loft in the barn and making a rough cot for the children. Their bedding was in the bag that Richard had brought. Sam helped Edward with the carpentry. Meg went with Mary to dig up some vegetables from the garden. She helped her to clean them and prepare a big hotpot for their dinner.

≈≈≈

Mary's daily routine changed drastically, as she squeezed in caring for the children and the extra washing between her everyday chores. She was grateful that it was late in the year, with less work to do outside. The children played happily on their own for short periods, but Meg missed her mother and needed Mary to distract her with games with pebbles, drawing pictures on a slate and telling stories about kings and queens and princesses. They made little figures with bread dough and played hide and seek in the parlour. Sam went with Edward to the fields and helped him feed the beasts, dig ditches and mend fences.

Edward was still working for William Ashdown, being paid with oats and wheat. He took supplies to Richard when he passed by and each time he came away with worse news of Molly.

Mary knew from the look on his face when he returned that he had little hope to give them. One day she decided that she had to prepare the children for the worst. She gathered them to her in the parlour.

"There's summat important that I have to tell ye," she said.

Sam said, "Muvver be agwain ter die, beant she, Aunt Mary?"

Mary's heart jumped. She felt tears prickling her eyes. She didn't know how to answer. Her courage failed her.

After a few moments, she took a deep breath and said, "'Er be failin', Sam. Us will pray for she every day en ax God ter save un."

Meg was quiet and Mary wasn't sure whether she understood. "It might be that God wants ter take she away from we," she said. "Us mun all be brave."

"I don't want Muvver ter go to God," said Sam. Silent tears welled up in his eyes and spilled out to fall on Mary's lap.

She hugged them both close to her, hiding her own distress.

"I want my muvver," cried Meg, catching the sadness.

Mary rocked them until they calmed down, then took their hands in hers and said, "Let's ask God to let she rest in peace."

They all closed their eyes and Sam's lips whispered, "Please don't take Muvver away, God."

Mary said, "Amen." She got out of her chair and took them by their hands into the kitchen, saying, "Shall us go en feed the fowls afore it gets dark?"

≈≈≈

The little family continued to go to Church every Sunday. They needed to demonstrate that they had put their faith in God. Mary and Edward prayed earnestly for Molly and Richard. There were fewer people in the congregation each week. No-one stayed after the service to gossip in the litten. Edward went to the vestry meeting, leaving Mary to take the children home in the cart. She was beginning to show the strain. Neither of them was sleeping well. Her eyes were surrounded with dark shadows and her face had lost its glow.

At the meeting there was news of more families requesting poor relief as the wage earners became ill and died. One Sunday, Richard Comber announced that William Cruttal was sick. He'd confessed that Susan Newnham's unborn child was his. He'd requested that if he died she would be allowed to remain in his house to tend all the remaining children. Two of them had died of the smallpox. Until his will was proved they would need poor relief. Some of the officers objected to this.

"Surely there be enough in his purse ter provide fer 'em," insisted Pitkin.

There followed a lengthy discussion and Comber eventually said he'd go back and find out if Cruttal could arrange for an allowance to be made before his possible decease.

Edward walked home with an uneasy mind. The weather seemed to reflect the turmoil in Wadhurst. The November wind roared up the road, buffeting all in its path. Trees rocked, bravely clinging on to the earth with their roots. Some had already fallen. Leaves chased around in the air. Squally rain stung his face, stopping as suddenly as it started, giving way to glimpses of bright sunshine as the clouds flew across the sky. He had to pull his hat firmly down, to prevent it from blowing away.

Chapter Twenty Eight   1709/10

In which Edward reckons with Mistus Tapsell

With December came the rain and the mud. Working outside became almost impossible. Stores were running low and so was the money in the pot. Edward rode Faithful over to Tapsells with his account book, to see if he could persuade him to pay what he owed.

His wife had heard Edward's horse's hooves in the yard and stood waiting at the door. "What do you want?" she asked. She was unwilling to let him in.

"There be money still owin', Mistus Tapsell. I can't wait no longer…"

"Orright. Come in. You'll have ter deal with me. Tapsell beant fit…" her voice trailed off as she showed Edward into the parlour.

He looked over to the chair by the fire. He could hardly recognise the figure sitting there, hunched over with his mouth open. A string of saliva oozed out and dribbled onto the towel which was draped over his knees. Edward looked at Tapsell's wife.

"'Is mind be gone," she said as she indicated a chair by the table.

"How be you managing?" asked Edward. He was concerned for the woman.

"Middlin'." She looked directly at him, her lips a thin line across her face.

"D'you have the money ter pay me?" Edward was prepared to forgo his payment if it meant the Tapsells went without.

"Yus." She nodded. "I be sellen off the beasts en some of the harness. Come spring there'll be land ter sell. I can manage a smallholden with one worker." There was the glimmer of a brave smile round her mouth.

Edward brought out his account book and they counted up the outstanding debt.

"Who be that?" A sudden shout came from the chair by the fire.

"'Tis Edward Lucke, Thomas. "'E be here fer his money."

"Don't give un a penny. I don't owe un naught."

"Take no notice, Edward. 'E don't know what 'e be sayin'."

They went back to their calculations.

Finally, Edward said, "'E owes me seventeen shillin'."

Mistus Tapsell went to a drawer in the dresser, counted out the coins and gave them to Edward.

He thanked her and said, "If you needs help, send fer me, Mistus Tapsell. Mas Tapsell helped me get on me feet when I needed it. I'll do the same fer ye."

She nodded and said, "Thank you. You be a considerable upstanding man, Mas Lucke."

Edward left feeling sad that this couple should be in such a state. They had no family to support them in their need and she could end up in the poor house. But she was a determined and capable woman and might survive. He prayed that he and Mary would not come to this. His brother Thomas and Eliza were in a similar position; struggling to keep the farm working so that they could be independent. There would be more families in need after this smallpox epidemic had passed.

He rode into his yard and put Faithful back into her stable with a bag of hay. As he opened the back door he could hear voices in the hall.

Richard was there.

They looked up when Edward came in. They were smiling.

"Molly be better," said Richard. "She be hankerin' after seein' the children."

"Heaven be praised!" Edward's heart bounded with relief.

"'Er beant well enough ter tend 'em. 'Er be hem weak, but behopes 'twill not take long ter build she up. I footed it here, thinking you can take we all to our farm in your cart." Richard had his arms round the children. His face had lost some of the tension of the last weeks.

Mary got up from her seat by the table. "I'll pack up a bag of sweetmeats ter tempt she ter eat," she said. The children followed her into the kitchen to help.

Edward sat down next to Richard and shook his hand, not able to speak through the lump in his throat.

"'Twere a near thing," said Richard. "There were one night when 'er come out of the ague. 'Er were that still en quiet I bluv 'er were gone. I come close en could feel the breath like a feather on me face."

"Thank God that be over!" said Edward.

They sat quietly for a few moments, then went out to prepare the horse and cart for the short journey to Richard's farm.

≈≈≈

Mary sat in the cart with the children, wrapped up against the cold. "Muvver will look different to the last time ye seed she," she said. "'Er's been mortal sick en 'er face be scarred from the pox."

"'Be 'er still purty? Like 'er was afore?" asked Sam.

"'Er be purty in 'er heart en that will show in 'er eyes. 'Er'll be hem leary for a while. Betimes 'er be recovered ye can go ter bide at home."

"But not yet?" Sam looked sad.

"Nay, ye can bide along of Uncle Edward en me awhile longer." Mary hugged him. "I shall miss thy company when ye bodges," she said.

The cart pulled into the yard and stopped. Mary's heart was beating fast as she helped the children to the ground. She picked up the bag of gifts and followed them into the house, excited to see Molly again, but afraid of how she would be.

The children reached the chamber before her and were on the bed in their mother's arms when Mary came through the door.

"'Tis good ter see thee lookin' perky," she said as she sat on a chair by the bed.

Molly put her hand out to hold Mary's tightly. "Thanks fer tenden the children," she said.

Sam was stroking his mother's face.

"'Twill get better," Molly said. "I ain't looked in the mirror yet. Be it awful?"

"Middlin'," re-assured Mary.

"Richard bathes me every day," Molly said. "'E be a good husband."

The children told Molly all about their life with Mary and Edward. Sam could read quite well now. He'd started working with figures and learning to write. Meg proudly counted up to ten.

Richard and Edward came into the chamber and Mary shepherded the children downstairs to put together a nice meal for their mother. Then they took it up to her to say goodbye.

"Come en see me again," said Molly. She smiled as they left the room.

Mary was concerned. Her beloved friend looked as if she would fade away at any moment. When they arrived back at Savages she went to her chamber and knelt by the bed, praying fervently for Molly's recovery. As she did so, tears welled up in her eyes and she wept.

The atmosphere was sombre in the hall as they ate their dinner that evening. They were all immersed in their own thoughts. The children picked at their food.

"Richard said it be time Sam were larned ter ride a horse," Edward announced.

Sam's eyes lit up. He stopped eating.

Mary said, "Us'll need ter find a pony for un."

"I be agwain ter ax around. There'll be somebody us knows who has a pony," said Edward.

Sam said, "I be main partial ter that, Uncle," and started eating with enthusiasm.

Meg piped up, "Can I larn ter ride too?"

"You can have rides on the pony betimes you be growed enough ter ride praper," Edward said.

"When us goes home ter Muvver, can I take un with me?" Sam said with a worried frown.

"Surely, 'twill be yourn betimes you be ready ter ride a big horse, then Molly will have un."

The atmosphere relaxed and the conversation turned to choosing a name for the proposed addition to the family. The future had become more promising.

≈≈≈

Edward came back from vestry meeting one Sunday. "William Cruttal be deceased," he said to Mary. "Susan Newnham's birthed the child en she's muvveren all the children."

"How many be there?" asked Mary as she put the bread and cheese on the table for coager.

"There were eight, but two died of the smallpox. There be six now, seven with the baby."

"Susan will have 'er hands full," commented Mary. "Be there anyone ter help?"

"The two older ones be able. Trouble is, Cruttal didn't have no money left ter pay for their care. 'E were deep in debt."

Mary stopped what she was doing and looked at Edward, hands on her hips. "Oh, No! What will happen to 'em? They can't send 'em to the Poor House, surely."

Edward shook his head. "They'll have ter survive on poor relief until the will be proved. Us might have ter sell the property ter pay the debts."

Mary sighed and continued to prepare the meal. "There's allus them that be worse off than we," she said. "Poor liddle children."

Chapter Twenty Nine

In which Edward becomes an overseer

It was a small funeral. Nobody wanted to gather in large numbers at this time, though the smallpox epidemic was abating.

Molly's brother came from Ticehurst and helped Richard carry the coffin into the church.

That day, as they all stood round the grave, Mary came out of her state of shock. With the full realisation of what had happened, she allowed her grief to spill over. The children stood and watched the coffin being lowered into the hole. Their faces were white and lifeless.

A few days after their visit, Molly had begun to weaken. The doctor said that her heart had been under too much strain. She died peacefully in the night with Richard beside her. He came to break the news the next morning and stayed with Mary and Edward until after the funeral, going home in the day to attend to the farm animals.

Now they all rode back in the cart together. No-one spoke. Meg whimpered in Mary's arms. Back at Savages, Mary took the little girl with her to prepare a simple meal of cold meat, cheese, bread and pickle. She perched Meg on the table to watch. The child was so cold Mary worried that she had taken a chill. She talked about what she was doing and what they would do after they'd eaten. She told Meg she would be going home to stay with Father soon and that she would have her own bed all to herself. Meg looked at her with sad hazel eyes and clung to the doll in her arms.

They sat round the table and stared at their plates of food.

"Where be Sam?" asked Mary.

The two men looked blank.

"I b'lieve I know where 'e'll be." Mary stood up and left the table.

It was pouring with winter rain. She ran across the yard, opened the stable door and shut it quickly behind her.

There was Sam, sitting on the straw by his pony, feeding her small handfuls of oats. Tears streamed down his cheeks. He looked up when Mary came in. She went to sit next to him.

"You beant had a chance ter ride 'er praper, like, have you? Didst think of a name?"

Sam took a deep, sobbing breath. "Nay, I can't think of aught 'cept Muvver en that makes me weep." He burst into more floods of tears and collapsed into Mary's arms.

She rocked him, humming a tune she'd heard Molly singing. Sam stopped crying and looked up.

"Muvver sings that song!" he exclaimed.

"Yus. Every time you sings it she'll be by thy side, singing it with thee. Let's sing it tergether."

They wrapped their arms round each other and swayed together as they sang:

"Greensleeves was all my joy,
Greensleeves was my delight;
Greensleeves was my heart of gold,
And who but Lady Greensleeves."

"I knows what ter call 'er!" said Sam suddenly: "Greensleeves!"

The pony lifted her head, nodding in agreement.

"En now us must go to have summat ter eat en talk about you en Molly bodgen home ter keep Farder company. 'E'll need you more than ever now."

They stood up and dusted the straw off their clothes. Mary opened the door and said, "Run, now, or you'll get wet!"

The mood in the hall was lifting. Richard had persuaded Meg to eat by telling her stories about each mouthful as he put it in.

"En this liddle frog jumped right into the cave where Meg gobbled it up."

Meg chewed the bread, wrinkling her nose with pleasure.

Richard said, "I've been missin' these two, surely. I'll be pleased ter have 'em home." He put his arms round them. Dost want me ter play frog in the hole with thee too, Sam?"

Sam grimaced. "Nay, Farder. I beant a baby no more." He started eating hungrily.

Without the children, Mary's bereavement was threefold. She found herself standing in the hall wondering what to do next. She worried about them constantly and cooked treats to take to them.

Richard found a housekeeper who doubled up as a nanny for Meg. Sam started school and found new friends. Occasionally Mary would tend them for the day with the Ashdown children, who'd all survived the smallpox.

The days were dark and short, the nights were long and cold, though the new windows did make a difference. Christmas came and went. There seemed little to celebrate.

≈≈≈

In March the spring began to show itself and spirits were raised. Frost continued to cover the ground in the early morning, but by midday the sun had burned most of it away. The birds paired up and foraged for nesting material. Clumps of snowdrops nodded their heads in the hedgerows and the catkins on the hazel branches danced in the wind.

Edward was out in the yard breathing in the clean air, when he saw Herbert Smith walking up the lane, whistling.

"I've found a tenant fer Robert's cottage," he announced.

"That'll be welcome, surely," said Edward. He didn't like living next door to an empty house. "When be they a-moven in?"

"Behopes next week. The name's Winder. 'E needs somebody ter cart 'is housel. I told un mayhap you'd be willin'. 'E be a-comen from Mark Cross."

"'Twill be a day's work," said Edward. "Tell un ter let me know which day."

Smith nodded and stroked his chin. "William Ashdown be minded ter buy the cottage. Then I'll have it off me hands." They went over to the cottage to make sure it was ready for new residents.

Before he left, Herbert said, "I've a few bits of work fer you, Edward, a-dressin' hops en some gardenin' en the like. Can you start next week?"

Edward agreed, glad to have another job, now he'd finished at Tapsell's.

At the vestry meeting the following Sunday, Edward was appointed Overseer along with William Ashdown. They were to pay allowances to the poor in their allotted area each month and sometimes provisions. They were responsible for the funeral arrangements of the poor, of finding apprentice positions for the young people and providing clothes and the means to earn a living. These duties would be their responsibility for a year, at the end of which others would be appointed.

Edward's first visit was to Susan Newnham and Cruttal's children. He collected the money from Ashdown, who held the purse, then walked down the road to Walland, a beautiful mansion of considerable size. There were three gable ends facing the entrance and timbers with plaster between them across the upper floor, the lower being built in brick. Two clusters of tall, decorated chimneys adorned the roof. It seemed strange that the residents of such a place should be paupers. He opened the grand iron gates and let himself into the entrance yard. A group of three screaming children came running round the corner of the house, pursued by a slightly older boy. They stopped when they saw Edward.

The older boy piped up, "Be you from the parish?"

"Yus," Edward answered.

The children raced each other round to the back of the house, shouting, "Susan! 'Ere be relief!"

The boy who'd spoken, said, "Foller me, Sir," and led Edward in the same direction to the back yard. Chickens flew squawking from under their feet. By the door there were two smaller children rocking a cradle from which came the sound of a baby heartily excercising its lungs. A young woman came out of the house. She was slim, tall and elegant. Her chestnut hair was tied back under her cap revealing a pale face and brown eyes, dark-circled with exhaustion.

"I be Mas Lucke, from the parish," announced Edward. "Be you Susan Newnham?"

"That I be," a strong, musical voice answered. "You be come with the money, I rackon. Come in." She picked the screaming child out of the crib to sit it on her hip, supported in the crook of her arm.

Edward followed her into a capacious kitchen. This was evidently where most of the day's activities took place. There were clothes hanging on a line above an extensive iron range on which a pot of bones bubbled steamily. The table was strewn with dirty bowls and spoons and the remnants of a loaf of bread. A black cat, which had been helping to clean the dishes, leapt from the table when Edward appeared and darted out through the door.

Susan reached over to tear a piece of crust off the bread and gave it to the baby, who immediately stopped bawling and sucked greedily at it.

"She be ready fer a feed," Susan said apologetically.

Edward took the little bags of money from his pocket and emptied them onto the table. "'Ere be nine shillin' fer the children en eight shillin' en six pence fer you, that being what you allus have. Be there aught else ye needs?"

"Well I'd be main obliged if I could 'ave a liddle more. 'Tis hard ter make it stretch. The children be a-

growen en we needs more riggin' fer the older ones."
She sat down on a chair and opened her bodice to
reveal a full breast, to which she attached the baby.
Edward fancied he could hear purring as the child
drank hungrily.

"I'll see what I can do," he said. It seemed to him
that seventeen shillings and six pence was a small
amount for feeding and clothing seven growing
children and one adult for a month. He suspected that
Susan was not feeding herself properly. He left the
house and wound his way out through the children
and chickens in the yard.

That evening he wrote in his Account Book:

1710   April   Monthly pay   (poor relief.)
23   Critls children   00--------09--------0--------0
           Susan Newnham   00--------08--------6--------0
                              00--------17--------6--------0

Mary and Edward went to meet their new neighbours
one evening. Winder opened the door to them. He
was a wiry man with a grey face and thin lips. His
eyes were covered by the thick lenses in his spectacles
and his back was curved over below the shoulders.
He did not look pleased to see them.

"Us be yer neighbours," said Edward. "Come ter
welcome you en yer fambly en enquire if there be
aught ye needs."

Before the man could answer, a voice came from indoors. "Who be that, Josiah?"

"'Tis the neighbours," Josiah called back.

Footsteps made their way to the door. Mistus Winder was as thin as her husband. Her greying hair was tied back under her cap. Her face was tired and drawn.

Mary held out the cheese she'd brought with her. "Mistus Winder, 'ow be ye settling in? Teck this as a welcome gift." She handed over the cheese.

The woman took it and said, "Thank you kindly, Mistus Lucke. Us'll not be in no need of help. The children be gone to bed prensley en I be tidying up, like. Good night to ye." She pulled her husband away from the door and shut it.

Mary and Edward looked at each other and shrugged their shoulders. "They be partial ter keepin' theirselves private, I'll warrant," said Mary. They walked back towards their house.

Mary asked, "What do Winder do fer work, dost know?"

Edward said, "'E be a cobbler in Wad'rst, I b'lieve. I've seen un walk down the lane with three boys in the marnin', but they never speak. There's a girl bides with 'er muvver. Will Ashdown bought the cottage en they be renten off un."

"Well, it don't look like they'll be bovveren we. Behopes we can be friendly otherwhiles," said Mary

Chapter Thirty 1710

In which Mary mows hay with Edward

One evening in May, Edward sat at the table with Mary after a day attending to the needs of the Wachas family. Goodman Wachas had injured his leg and was unable to work, throwing his family into the hands of the parish.

"What happened to the muvver?" enquired Mary.

"I b'lieve she died in childbirth, years back," said Edward. He took a long draught of beer before continuing. "The daughter be the housekeeper en the son, Joseph, 'e be but a young lad. 'E does all the heavy work, choppin' wood en a-fetchen en carryen, like. I teck 'em a tovet of barley en some milk every week en one shillen a month."

Mary sighed. "It don't seem much fer the three of 'em ter live on."

She put her spoon on her empty plate and pushed it to one side to finish her beer. "'Ow be Susan en the children?"

"I've been considering givin' 'em the use of one of our cows," said Edward. "They've plenty of meadow for un. What d'you say?"

"You be over generous otherwhiles, Ed. But it mun be hard watchen the young struggle like that." She supped her beer, elbows resting on the table. "Mayhap you could let 'em have the cow what's lost 'er calf. Us can manage without un."

Edward leaned over the table and held her hand for a moment. "'Twill help ter keep 'em healthy," he said.

The next day it was pay day for the Cruttals. Edward led the cow into Wadhurst and down the hill to Walland. He hadn't asked Susan if she would like a cow.

The children came to meet him at the gate. They crowded round Edward and his charge.

"Don't come all of a rush," he protested. "Give we space ter come in."

They backed away and followed him round to the yard. Susan was on the doorstep holding the baby over her shoulder, singing in a low, dulcet voice. Her face lit up when she saw the cow.

"Will this help?" Edward asked.

"Surely, Mas Lucke. 'Er be a fine beast."

"I'll lend un to you. No need ter pay me. 'Er'll feed well in yer meadow en I'll larn the lads ter milk un." He handed the leading rein over to the boys, who took the cow away.

Susan's eyes filled with tears and she put a hand on Edward's arm. "You be a kind en thoughtful man," she said, leading the way into the house.

Edward paid Susan the money, then went to find the boys. They took the cow into an empty barn and found a pail and milking stool. Edward showed them how to clean the pail, then demonstrated the milking process. The children gathered round, whispering and giggling when the milk squirted, hitting the side of the pail. Then he summoned Mark, the eldest, to the stool. Mark, embarrassed to be handling a full breast, fumbled for a few minutes.

He looked up at Edward, his face red. "I can't do it," he announced.

Edward took hold of the boy's hands and placed them on the warm, soft udder. "Think of the milk in that gurt sack, awaiting ter pour out. Get a hold en pull down firmly, squeezing with one hand, then t'other." He helped Mark squeeze. The milk came in little squirts at first. Then the boy got the hang of it and the pail started filling up with frothy white milk, to the delight of the children.

It was Luke's turn. He sat down with confidence and imitated the process he'd been watching. It didn't take him long to produce the milk. Everyone cheered, except Mark, who was tired of being upstaged by his younger brother. He turned round and kicked a stone, which flew over into the yard.

Edward told Luke to take the pail of milk to Susan and called Mark to bring the cow to the meadow. On the way he gave him instructions about when to do the milking and how to keep the pail clean. "You be in charge," he said. "If you want ter leave the milking to Luke that be orright. But you mun see that 'e do it praper."

Mark nodded. They walked back to the house. Edward said goodbye and left, satisfied with the morning's work.

≈≈≈

The midsummer sun shone on the green and gold hayfield. A cooling wind blew fluffy clouds across the sky and ruffled the uncut hay. Mary and Edward worked with a gentle rhythm, swishing their scythes through the green stalks, leaving hay lying in swathes on the ground behind them. A raptor circled above, hunting the disturbed mice as they fled from the destruction of their nests.

Mary was at peace here in the fresh air, working in unison with her beloved Edward. It seemed that their love grew deeper over the years together, caring and supporting each other through the dark times. She still missed Molly. Every time she saw Sam and Meg, she could see their mother's likeness and mannerisms showing through: her hazel eyes in Meg and a way of tucking her hair behind her ears; her caring nature in Sam and of always saying the right thing at the right time. She missed a woman's company and Molly's ability to find solutions to difficult problems. She'd hoped that Mrs Winder would prove to be a friendly neighbour in whom she could confide, but it seemed that was not to be. Mary had a feeling that the family had something to hide, but she was at a loss to imagine what it could be.

It was time to eat their bait and they sat down in the shade of a great oak tree, overlooking the farm buildings below them and a long view of the Lower Weald stretching far into the hazy distance. The calls of cows and sheep drifted up to them and the rumble of the wheels of a cart trundling along a stony road accompanied by the clop of horses' hooves. The raptor mewed overhead.

"I be seekin' a 'prenticeship fer Joseph Wachas," said Edward when he'd eaten. "If you hears of any master looken fer lads ter larn 'em a trade, I'd like ter know."

Mary finished her mouthful and said, "Mm, now en agen I gets ter know betimes I be at market. Be un knowledgeable?"

"'E knows numbers en can read en write middlin' well, like. 'E be willin' en strong."

They stood up and shook the crumbs from their clothes before going back to work.

The harvesting was finished, both at Savages and Smiths. Edward was away distributing poor relief.

Sam and Meg came over to Mary for the day and they collected crocks and bowls to fill with blackberries.

"Where shall us go ter find 'em?" asked Meg.

"There be skits of 'em along the lane," replied Mary. "That be allus a good place ter start."

They loaded the crocks into a basket and Sam said he would carry it.

The lane was shared with the people next door. The Winders didn't have a cart. When they passed Mary or Edward walking along the way they only nodded. Today, Mary hoped there would be a chance to speak to them if they passed.

She set off with the children and they came to the entrance gate to Winder's land. Robert used to leave it open. These days it was kept firmly shut. Mary noticed a movement behind the gate and went to see what it was.

A girl, a little older than Meg stood there, staring with beady eyes. Her cheeks were unusually red and her straight black hair was matted. Tufts of it surrounded her round face.

"Good day," said Mary. "What be yer name?"

A big grin spread across the girl's face. She said nothing. Her hands twisted and turned a corner of her grubby apron. She giggled.

A voice shouted from the door of the cottage. "Peg! Come you here, dracly-minute!" Mistus Winder ran out and grabbed Peg by the arm, pulling her away.

Peg screamed a hoarse, animal scream. She struggled as her mother dragged her into the house and banged the door shut.

Mary could still hear the screaming and shouting. She turned away to see Sam and Meg staring with shocked, pale faces.

"Come," she said. "Let's seek those blackberries. Who can fill a crock first?" They walked down the lane and found the berry-filled branches leaning out of the hedge, offering themselves to the pickers.

"What be amiss with that girl?" asked Sam as they started gathering the soft, sweet treasures.

"I dunnow, Sam. There be all manner of things that be private in some famblies. Mebbe it be best not ter know." Mary was upset by what they'd just witnessed and didn't know if there was anything she could do. She worried about it for the rest of the day.

≈≈≈

At the November vestry meeting Edward reported his poor relief activities to the assembled company.

"I sold the deceased widow Bellingham's goods at the almshouse at Walard. Ed Chapman paid six shillen fer a mantle en a riding gown. I give the money ter the warden."

One or two of the officers nodded their heads in approval.

Edward continued. "The Wachas fambly have received two tovets of barley since July and four shillen in money. Then I bought Joseph Wachas a pair

267

of breeches en spent nine shillen en nine pence a-putten un out as 'prentice."

Duplock said, "It be high time too. That lad would be a-runnen wild afore long."

Edward continued, "Mary Bishop I haved to Battle where she do belong. I had to hire a horse fer she. It come ter one pound, four shillen en tuppence with the settlement order en the eatin'."

The list continued, including Susan Newnham and Cruttal's children. Edward didn't tell them about the cow. That was his affair. At the end of his report, Benge said, "Well reported, Lucke. Thank you. Are there any questions?"

"I don't believe we agreed ter supply young Wachas' breeches," bleated Pitkin.

"'E couldn't be took to a master in rags," retorted Charles Day.

"Quite right," agreed Comber. "'Twere a good decision, Lucke."

Edward smiled. He could do no less than what he felt was necessary. "There be one more thing, Sir." He turned to Benge. "Goodie Wachas be anxious ter start worken as a spinner. 'Er do know some as would give she the work. But she ain't got no spinnin' wheel. Also, 'er needs a gown menden, on account of 'er tore it on a spike. Can I agree ter pay fer these things? If 'er can earn a bit a-spinnen, we could pay she less relief."

There was silence in the room and Edward wondered whether he'd overstepped the mark.

Benge said, "She should pay the money back for the spinning wheel when she's earned it."

This set off a great deal of nodding and shaking of heads, grumbling and affirmatives.

"If 'er be made ter pay it back, that defeats the whole purpose. 'Er'll still need poor relief until 'er can make the money up," said Day in a loud enough voice to be heard above the din.

"One of our duties be ter set up the poor in their trades en support them until they be able ter do without us," declared Comber.

"Hear, hear," a few agreed.

Benge said, "Do we have enough in the parish chest to do this?"

"Well, us could allus pay a bit more into the chest," said Fowle.

There was uproar. Edward was unwilling to withdraw his request. He knew it was the right thing for Goodie Wachas.

Benge had gone red in the face. He banged his fist on the table. There was silence. "I believe we should take a vote." His voice was shaking as he tried to control his anger. Fowle was always making inflammatory remarks. "Who wishes us to pay for a spinning wheel?"

All but Pitkin put their hands up.

"Should she be made to pay the money back?"

There was another show of hands. Feavour counted them.

"And those against this."

Again a show of hands. Feavour counted them and announced the result. "The decision is that Goodie Wachas should not be made to pay the money back for the spinning wheel."

Edward breathed a sigh of relief. "Thank ye, Gentlemen," he said.

It was Ashdown's turn to give his report. This was not as controversial as his fellow overseer's. There was no further business and the meeting was closed.

Edward caught Ashdown before he left. "There be payment outstanding for pulling of poles en hopping atwixt you en me, William. Can us rackon it prensly?"

Ashdown looked surprised. "Oh, I be agwain home dracly, Edward. Can us do it another time?"

Edward sighed and nodded. It was always the way, having to pursue people for his payment. One day he would have a farm large enough for him to employ other people.

Chapter Thirty One   1710/11

In which Edward and Mary get wet.

November storms lashed at the windows in Savages
cottage. Edward continued to work for Herbert Smith,
hedging and cutting poles. One day he arrived in the
pouring rain, hoping there would be no work for him
today. Smith met him in the yard.

"The sheep breached the hedge in the night,
Lucke. They be a-roamin' abroad. Us'll have ter go a-
seeken 'em en have 'em back."

Edward said, "I'll go en fetch Shep."

When he got back they trudged up the lane
together to the pasture and found the breach. There
were a few sheep remaining. Edward went to find a
hazel branch to fill the gap. That would be another
day's hedging.

Herbert went off in one direction. Edward took
Shep in the other. They slithered and squelched
through saturated fields looking under hedges and in
ditches. Shep realised what they were looking for and
put his nose to the ground, leading the way. Soon
they came to a disused barn. There they found five
sheep munching the remnants of hay. Shep rounded
them up and Edward led them back towards the
pasture. He was soaking wet and the wind threw

stinging rain at his face. His boots were full of water. He met Herbert coming back with another two sheep. They put them into the pasture and Smith counted them.

"There be fower missin'," he said.

They agreed to go together. Edward said to Shep, "Go seek." Shep sniffed around the breach in the hedge, found a scent and followed it up the hill towards the coppice. Edward and Herbert went close behind.

It seemed as if they would never find the sheep.

"Be you sure 'e knows what 'e be a-folleren?" asked Herbert.

"Middlin' sure," said Edward, hoping that Shep was not leading them astray.

They skirted the coppice, thankful that the wind was now behind them. Drops of rain fell off the brims of their hats to run down their necks. The dog turned a corner to go through a gateway into a field of turnips. There were the sheep, having a feast. One had already sat down and was looking dozy.

"They be hovin'," said Herbert. "Us mun get 'em out dracly-minute!"

Shep started herding the sodden animals. The sleepy one stubbornly refused.

"Git up will you!" shouted Herbert, prodding the sheep with his stick. Then he resorted to kicking. Edward came and the two of them hauled the bundle of wet wool to her feet. Herbert gave her an extra prod as she started following the others.

At last all were heading home. Herbert said in admiration, "That be a wondrous knowledgeable dog, Lucke. I would never 'ave believed it if I 'adn't seed it with me own eyes."

Edward breathed a sigh of relief that Shep hadn't let him down.

The light was fading as the last sheep was encouraged through the gate.

"Good dog," said Edward, rubbing Shep's head and patting his back.

Herbert asked, "Will you come in fer a beer?"

"Nay, I be anxious ter get out of this rigging en be in the dry. En the dog will be wantin' his dinner. Termorrer I'll be deliverin' poor relief. I'll come en repair the hedge nexty." He called Shep and made his way home, thinking that Herbert must lead a lonely life without a Mistus to welcome him home with a kiss and a hot dinner.

≈≈≈

Mary opened her eyes and put out her hand to Edward's side of the bed. It was cold and empty. He was so busy these days that he was starting out well before sun-up. She turned over in the cosy bed and knew it was time to step out onto the foot-freezing floor. The dark mornings were getting darker. She sighed and folded the warm covers back, swung her legs over and stood up. Dizziness came over her and she sat down again. Taking a deep breath, she found the second attempt more successful and walked over to the window. She opened the shutters and saw rain dripping down the glass. It was impossible to see the end of the field, the cloud was so low. She washed in the bowl of cold water on the dresser, put her clothes on and took herself downstairs. As Edward had left so early, the beasts would need feeding. Mary wrapped her cloak round her, raising the hood over her head, then pulled her boots on and went out into the yard. The barn door was ajar. Shep was nowhere to be seen. Edward must have taken him.

It took a long time to fill the trough in the yard with turnips and vegetable trimmings, let the steers out for their breakfast, scatter grain for the fowls and take chopped turnips to the pigs and the sheep in their pasture. There was dry hay in the shepherd's hut and she filled their trough, slipping and sliding through the mud where they'd poached the grass away. They came running from their sleeping huddle and munched gratefully. Mary, now soaking wet, left the gate open for the cows and trudged back to put the steers indoors with new hay. In the house she kicked her boots off and went to get the fire going. She didn't feel like breakfast this morning. Memories of the comfortable life she'd left floated through her thoughts and a little spark of rebellion flickered in her chest. She riddled the fire crossly, then brought it to life with a faggot to heat the oven for baking.

It was milking-time. The cows were already gathered round the trough. Mary went into the stalls and called them. They came in to munch the hay she'd left in their racks. She milked each one, then drove them back to the pasture, closing the gate behind her. She picked up the pails of milk and carried them into the house. Then she took off her wet clothes and hung them on a line over the fire and put on a dry dress and apron. The fresh milk was warm and comforting as Mary drank a cupful before she started on the bread-making. She still felt angry, but didn't know why. Kneading the dough on the table by the fire helped to calm her and she soon warmed up. She thought of Edward, out there in this rain, getting soaked. He would want a lovely hot meal when he came in. Mary began to plan what she would cook.

Some lumps of soot fell down the chimney, startling her. She continued to knead the dough. There was a rumble and soot and dust fell with a whoosh, filling the room with smoke. Mary screamed and ran to the other side of the room. The rumbling stopped. A few more bits rattled down.

Everything was quiet. When the air had cleared, she went back to the fireplace. There were no flames, only a pile of black soot. A blanket of it covered everything, including the floor, the table, the dough she'd been kneading and the wet clothes hanging overhead. The stench of soot was overpowering. Mary sneezed and coughed as she gazed at the mess in bewilderment.

It had to be cleaned up before Edward returned home. She went to the kitchen and found an iron jam pan. She picked up the brush and shovel they used for cleaning the ash from the fireplace and shovelled up the soot, dust and ashes into the pan, then carried it out into the pouring rain. As she was crossing the yard to throw it onto the garden, a figure appeared at the top of the lane and came towards her.

It was Mistus Winder. She wore only her indoor clothes, no head covering and was wringing her hands in distress. Mary dropped the pan and ran to meet her.

"Oh, Mistus Lucke, I be mortaceous worritted. My liddle Peg has gone abroad en I can't find un. Be 'er hereabouts?"

Mary said she hadn't seen Peg. They looked in the barn, cowshed and other buildings and found nothing.

"How long be it sen she be gone?" asked Mary.

Mistus Winder sniffed and wiped a string of wet hair away from her face. Her forehead wrinkled. "I... I didn't notice. Her were in the parlour a-playen with a doll en I slipped upstairs ter bring some soiled riggin' down ter be washed. The water-bucket were empty en by the time..." She moaned. "What'll I do?"

The rain was relentless. There was no point in going to find a cloak to put on over her already soaking dress. Mary said, "Where've you looked? 'Er can't have gone far."

"Down the lane." Mistus Winder hesitated before saying, "Peg, 'er beant right in the head, like. 'Er can't talk en 'er has the devil in her."

"How do you know that?" Mary was shocked. How could an innocent child have the devil in her?

"'Er be possessed. 'Er goes into rages en foams at the mouth. I have ter tie un up ter stop she hurten 'erself en me, like." Mistus Winder was now distraught.

"Calm yerself," said Mary. "This'll not help us find un." She grabbed the woman by the arm and led her behind the farm buildings to where they kept the cart and farm implements in a lean-to. There was no sign of Peg.

They went to the pasture and looked under hedges, then to the duck pond. It had overflowed and flooded the surrounding area. If Peg had drowned, her body would be floating. There was nothing.

The next place to look was the copse. They peered between the trees in the semi-darkness and fought their way through bramble trailers. What was that moving ahead of them? When they reached the spot, Peg was not there.

A high mound of earth skirted the copse, with a ditch on the outside, to discourage animals entering to eat the tender hazel shoots. The two women walked round looking into the ditch which was filling up with water. They'd almost completed the circuit when Mary caught sight of a whisp of black hair. A wooden doll floated nearby.

She ran to have a closer look. The child was submerged.

Mistus Winder let out a howl of pain.

Mary caught hold of the little girl's arm and dragged her out of the ditch. There was foam round her mouth. The body was still warm. Mary lay it on the slope, head down, hoping to drain the water out. Peg remained lifeless.

Her mother was by her daughter's side. She took her in her arms and rocked her, moaning and sobbing. The child's head lolled to one side.

After a few moments Mary put her hand firmly on the woman's shoulder. "Come, us mun carry un home."

Mistus Winder took a deep breath, lifted her daughter's body and started carrying her towards the yard. Mary picked up the doll and followed.

In the Winders' parlour, they laid the body on the table and covered it with a sheet. Mistus Winder was inconsolable. Mary stayed and held her for a while. Then she started talking to her.

"Peg be at peace now, my dear. The devil has left she en 'er be in no more pain or distress. There'll be no more seizures or screamin'. Your child's soul be gone to God." She continued to say calming words until the shaking and moaning quietened.

They were both cold and wet. Mary went to build up the fire.

"Dost have dry riggin' ter wear, Mistus Winder? You should get that wet dress off en warm yerself."

The evening was drawing in and Mary felt tired, cold and hungry. The thought of returning to a soot-filled room with no fire and no fresh bread filled her with dread. But she couldn't stay here. There were the beasts to feed and the cows to milk.

Mistus Winder was sitting watching her with shadowed eyes. She said in a steady, calm voice, "Me name be Prudence en I believe you be Mary. You've been unaccountable kind, Mary. Thank you. You'll be wanten ter get back to yer house en change yer riggin' too. Me fambly be a-comen home prensly. I be orright." She got up and showed Mary to the door.

Mary walked out into the dusk and groped her way through the gate where she had met Peg a few weeks ago. She was so exhausted she wondered if she would make it home.

Chapter Thirty Two   1710/11

In which a secret is shared.

Edward trudged up the lane in the twilight, hoping that Mary had milked the cows and fed the beasts. He put Shep in the barn and gave him some oats, then started to walk across the yard. There was no light in the house and a foreboding crept into his throat. The door to the kitchen had been left ajar. He kicked off his muddy boots and went through to the dark hall. A strong smell of soot hung around. The foreboding turned to alarm. He called Mary, but there was no movement in the house. He found tinder and lit a candle, revealing disaster.

Where was Mary? Perhaps she was taking the cows back to pasture after milking. There was no point in going out to look for her in the dark. She'd be back soon. He searched around for the brush to find that Mary had begun to clean the fire out. He went out to fetch a pail for the soot and ashes. A figure appeared from the direction of the cottage next door. She was staggering and Edward went to catch her before she fainted.

He carried her into the parlour, put her gently into a chair and went to find another candle, lit it and placed it in the hearth. He kissed Mary's forehead, wiping the wet strands of hair from her pale face. Her eyelids flickered and she gasped for breath.

"Edward!" she moaned when she'd regained consciousness. "I be mortal ashamed that it's all of a hike. The beasts beant fed, nor the cows milked. She put her hand up to his arm. En you be soaked to the skin, love."

Then she remembered and gasped. "Mistus Winder lost 'er liddle girl. Us went a-seekin' un. En, oh, Ed! Us found un in the ditch, drownded!" She burst into tears putting her wet apron up to her face.

Edward sat on a chair by her side. "That be tarble, Mary. That poor woman!"

Mary said through her tears, "Us carried the body to the cottage en I did the best I could fer un. Prudence said she could manage en I left. That's when you found me." She shivered. "I were minded of when we carried Robert's body back, en thought mebbe there be a curse on the cottage or summat."

Edward grasped her hand. "Hush, Mary. Calm thyself. I'll get the fire a-goin' in here en fetch us both some dry riggin'. Hast eaten today?"

She shook her head. "Mebbe that be the cause of me c'lapsen. I'll go en…"

Edward put a hand on her shoulder. "I'll fetch bread en cheese en us'll eat it in here. You stay there." He lit a couple more candles to show his way, went into the kitchen, and found ale to go with the bread and cheese. The state of the parlour was not as bad as the hall, but there was a thin film of soot over everything.

"Eat some of that," he said as he put the food in front of her. Then he went to find a faggot and lit the fire. They changed their clothes and sat munching their snack while Mary told Edward about the soot fall. He remembered that the summer had been so busy he'd neglected to sweep the chimney.

"The rain be abated," he said when they'd finished. "If you can clear up indoors, I'll go en milk the cows en feed 'em en all."

It was late evening by the time all the jobs were done and the hall fire was relit. Mary found some cold meat which they ate with the remains of the bread. She would have to spend the next day baking and making cheese and butter with today's milk.

They sat in the parlour with hot toddies before going to bed. Edward told Mary about finding Henry's sheep with Shep's help.

≈≈≈

Mary called on Prudence Winder a few days after Peg's death, to offer her condolences. Prudence opened the door but didn't invite her in.

"Be there aught I can help you with, Prudence?" Mary asked, giving her a crock of her best butter.

Prudence took the gift and said, "You be a kind woman, Mary. I be busy a-clearen out Peg's riggen en all. The funeral be termorrer. I've no need of help, thank you." She offered her hand. Mary took it and held it for a moment.

"You come along en ax if you be in need," she said, and turned to go.

The door closed. Mary felt rejected.

≈≈≈

The rain turned to sleet and then to snow as the winter closed in.

It was just before Christmas that Thomas Lucke delivered the annual supply of wheat and oats in part payment of his debt to Edward. He looked tired and older. There was no brotherly exchange of news between them as they unloaded the sacks into the grain store. Thomas said as little as possible, driving away without even a wave.

Edward was sad that Thomas continued to be so unfriendly. He went back into the house and entered Thomas' delivery into the account book, then sat for a while wondering if he'd been unfair to his brother, insisting that he paid his debts after so long.

Soon after Thomas' visit the ground froze solid and more snow covered everything in a thick white blanket. The road into Wadhurst was not impassable but longer journeys were out of the question. They wouldn't see Richard and the children until it thawed. Edward continued to deliver supplies to the poor, grateful that the grain stores were well stocked after a plentiful harvest. He'd made sure that he and Mary had enough beef and pork salted down to last a few months. The money they'd accumulated over the harvest period was dwindling, only being added to when Mary sold produce at the market when she could get there.

Edward spent hours staring into the fire. He tried to read passages from the Bible, but was unable to concentrate. He envied Mary who seemed to be able to occupy herself most of the time, making dresses and spinning when she wasn't baking and cooking. He helped her with the brewing, making the cheese and feeding the beasts, but all the time morose thoughts clouded his head.

At the beginning of March there were signs of a thaw. Slowly the trees lost their frosty decoration, water trickled into puddles in the yard where Edward had cleared the snow. Icicles dripped. There was a soft stirring as Nature came back to life. Then it froze again overnight, turning the puddles to ice.

Edward found Mary clinging to the door post one morning, white-faced and shaking.

"Whatever be the matter?" he asked.

"I don't want ter slip en fall, Ed," she said.

He helped her indoors and sat her down in the hall.

"If you go careful en mind the ice you'll be orright," he tried to re-assure her.

She sat for a while, then said, "Edward, I be quick with child. I don't want ter lose annuver." She would have preferred to share her secret at a more congenial moment.

Edward sat down next to her. "I be main glad ter hear that, Mary. En you be right ter be anxious. You leave the outdoor work ter me betimes the weather be better." He took her in his arms and held her close.

She looked up and they kissed.

Edward went to feed the beasts and milk the cows with a lighter heart.

He'd been unable to plough the fields in the autumn, but now the earth would start to dry out and warm up it was time to sharpen the ploughshare. Edward hitched up the horse and cart, loaded the share and drove into Wadhurst. Water streamed down the road leaving little gulleys in the frozen earth and the going was difficult.

He called at Goody Gessop's cottage on the way, delivered her poor relief and made sure she had plenty of dry wood stored indoors for her fire.

Wadhurst was beginning to come alive in the sunshine. Edward stopped outside the blacksmith's to offload the ploughshare. Elliott emerged from the dark depths of his shop and tipped his hat with a black hand. Edward thought that it was a good job to have, working with fire through the winter. He leaned forward to lift the heavy share, unaware that he was standing on a sheet of wet ice.

The weight of the share threw him off-balance. He twisted round. His feet slipped from under him, the share flew over his head landing on his outstretched leg. He heard a sharp crack. Searing pain shot from his shin up his spine and flooded his body.

Elliott was by his side lifting the ploughshare away. Edward sat up and looked at his right leg. The foot was not in line with his knee.

People gathered round. He tried to get up, using his good leg.

"Stay there! Don't move!" shouted Elliott. "You've smashed yer leg, Mas Lucke."

He heard Herbert Smith's voice. "Us'll get you to the bone-setter, Edward."

There were hands under his arms. He was being lifted onto the cart. He cried out in agony. Someone poured brandy into his mouth and he was grateful.

The cart moved off. The pain persisted.

After a while, Edward began to realise what had happened and the implications of this. Horror filled his whole being. The cart stopped. He lay back, his head swimming. The brandy was taking effect.

A voice told him that the bone-setter was ready to see him. He felt himself carried into the house and laid on a table. More brandy was administered. There was a tearing noise as one leg of his breeches was ripped away. Hands held his shoulders and head firmly.

The pain of the next few minutes rendered Edward unconscious.

When he came to, his head was swimming again. A voice in his ear told him he would be taken home on his cart. He was lifted from the table and carried out into a cold damp afternoon. Herbert Smith made Edward as comfortable as possible on the cart with some sacks and climbed up to drive him home.

Chapter Thirty Three

In which friends are supportive

Mary put her sewing of tiny garments down and came from her chair in the parlour through the hall and into the kitchen for the sixth time. She opened the door and looked out into the icy wetness in the yard. There was no-one there. She'd finished the morning's work, put clean sheets on the bed and washed the soiled ones. She would wait until Edward returned and ask him to hang the sheets outside to blow in the breeze. She'd taken a newly-baked batch of bread from the oven, putting it in the kitchen to cool and she'd prepared the food for coager.

She could tell that Edward was late from the position of the sun, as its slanting beams shone through the hall window directly onto the table. Her appetite had returned and she was looking forward to sitting down to eat. She was restless, wondering whether to start without him. There were apples in the spare chamber upstairs. It would be nice to sink her teeth into one of them while she waited. She started to climb the stairs, then hesitated as she heard a noise outside. That must be him. She continued on her mission and found two perfect apples, a little wrinkled but not yet decaying. She picked them up and put them to her nose, enjoying the fragrance, then tucked them into her apron pocket and started the descent of the stairs. There were two corners to negotiate and she was particularly careful to keep her balance. As she came into the hall she heard voices. Two figures entered, one supporting the other. She stared in disbelief.

Edward looked up at her as she stood on the second step. His face was white. He hung onto Herbert with his arm round his shoulders, limping badly. His leg was in a splint.

Mary gasped. Her hands flew up to her face.

"I'll teck un through to the parlour, Mistus Lucke," Herbert said.

She regained her senses and walked quickly to the parlour door, opened it and went to prepare a chair for Edward.

When they'd made him as comfortable as possible he lay back with his eyes closed.

Herbert said grimly, "'Is leg be broke. The bone-setter did 'is best. I dunno if 'e'll walk on it again." He shook his head, not able to look Mary in the eyes.

A strong voice came from the chair. "Mary, t'will be orright. T'will teck awhile, but us'll scratch along."

Mary went to kneel by Edward's side. She stroked his forehead and kissed his hand. "You be hurt turble bad, Ed. Do it pain thee?" She went to fetch a stool and gently placed it under his splinted leg. Edward winced.

Mary stood up and looked at Herbert. "We be hem grateful to you fer a-carten him home, Mus Smith. Can I pay you fer the bone-setter?"

"Another time, Mistus Lucke. I'll have the cart home with me dappen I can fetch me horse from Wad'rst. You'll need some help with the farm, like. I'll see what can be done." With that he tipped his hat and left.

Mary listened to the cart as it rolled out of the yard. There was silence. She took a deep breath, glanced at Edward who'd closed his eyes again and went to get a faggot and some wood to light the fire. She was relieved to remember that the beasts had been fed that morning. She would have to do it this evening, but the sun might have melted the ice by then.

Herbert returned with the cart a few hours later, leading his horse. Mary showed him where to put the cart and he stabled the horse for her.

She said, "Before you go, Mus Smith, I'd be obliged if you could carry a cot down for Edward ter sleep in the hall. 'E wunt get up the stairs."

Smith brought the spare cot down and asked if there was anything else Mary needed.

"That be all, thank you," said Mary. "I fed the beasts earlier en put 'em away fer the night, like. You've been considerable kind." She touched his arm. "I'll bid you goodnight."

As Henry mounted his horse she waved and went back into the house feeling dreadfully alone. Edward lay on the cot in the hall. She would miss his company tonight.

Early the next morning, when Mary was preparing to do the outside jobs, there was a knock on the kitchen door. Prudence Winder stood there with her youngest boy.

"This be John," she said. "Mus Smith told us of Mas Lucke's accident. You'll need help with the beasts in your condition. Show John what's ter be done. 'E be a good worker."

Mary glowed all over with gratitude. "Oh, you be a Godsend. I'll pay you fer the work, John." She looked at Prudence. "How didst know I be quick?"

"I knew it that day Peg died. You had a look about you. You was kind to me then. If you needs a woman's advice, just ax." She turned away, having said more than she was accustomed.

Mary turned to the boy. "Come, John, I'll show thee. Canst milk a cow?"

John nodded and smiled shyly. He was even more reticent than his mother.

The jobs were finished and John went home with one of Mary's best cheeses. She was about to go back into the house when she heard the clatter of a horse and cart coming up the lane. William Ashdown appeared round the corner with a load of provisions. He jumped down and came over to Mary, his ample figure towered over her.

"Mary, I be ernful shruck to be avised of Edward's accident. There's a load of wheat, hops en straw in payment of what I owes un. Where shall I put it?"

Mary showed him the barn and the cornstore. He unloaded the wheat and straw and carried the hops into the kitchen ready for the next brewing. They went into the hall, where Edward was sitting on the edge of the cot, his leg extended in front of him.

Mary went to him. "Ed, what be you a-doing? You can't walk."

Edward looked at Ashdown. "I b'lieve you be just the man I needs, William. Can you fashion me two bats that I can lean on, to walk with one leg?"

Ashdown's eyes twinkled. He laughed. "There'll be no holden you down, Edward, will there? For certain sure I can do that fer you." He planted his bulk on the bench by the table.

Mary went to get a mug of ale and handed it to William. She looked at Edward. "You won't get any of that dappen you've et summat, husband." She went into the kitchen to prepare porridge for them all. When she came back to cook the breakfast on the stove, William and Edward were deep in conversation.

"I'll do the last few of yer deliveries to the poor," William was saying. "En there'll be lambing prensly. I've a spare labourer. I'll send un over ter stay in yer shepherd's hut. Was there aught else needs doin' dracly?"

Edward shook his head. "When the ploughshare be..."

Ashdown said, "Nay, there be no need fer you ter worrit thyself. Herbert Smith said he'll plough yer fields."

Mary had been listening. "Us surely haves some unaccountable generous friends, ain't us, Ed?" She handed round the steaming bowls of porridge.

"Well!" Ashdown exclaimed, "I believe my good wife gave me breakfast awhile ago. But I wunt say no to more." He chuckled and spooned the food into his mouth.

A few days later, Edward was practising walking round the hall with the crutches Ashdown had made him, in a dot-and-carry-one fashion.

Mary had said goodbye to John Winder for the day and was preparing to churn some butter when they heard a horse's hooves approaching. Shep ran across the yard, barking. John Paris leapt off his horse and strode into the house. Mary met him and they embraced.

"I can't stay long. I happened by on me way ter meet someone. What be this I hear about Ed?" he asked, taking off his hat.

With his arm round Mary's waist, they went into the hall. Edward stopped in his tracks, grateful to sit on a bench. He leaned his crutches on the table. John put his hat down and joined him. Mary went to fetch ale for them both. When he'd heard Edward's account of the accident John assured him of any help he needed on the farm.

"That be unaccountable good of you, John," said Edward. "Goodman Ashdown en Henery Smith be a-ploughen fer we. They'd be glad of yer help, surely, if you can spare the time."

John nodded. "I've got me smallholding working well en I be considerin' lettin' it en findin' a place where I could raise a fambly," he said and took a long draught of ale.

Mary looked at him in surprise.

Edward said, "Be you a-courtin', John?"

John pursed his lips. "Mebbe." He stood up. "I'll be bodgen. Mayhap I could sow yer corn when the ploughen's done." He drained his mug and picked up his battered hat.

Mary said, "You can't go a-courten with that hat, John."

He looked at her with a bland smile, hugged her and left.

It wasn't long before Richard and the children visited. Mary was enjoying all this attention. Sam came on his pony. He'd grown a few inches since they saw him before Christmas.

"I can come en help with the heavy jobs when I beant at school," he assured Mary.

They left the two brothers talking and went to see the new lambs. They met Gideon, Ashdown's shepherd, who was only a few years older than Sam. Meg regarded him with admiration. He showed her a lamb that had been born that morning and she held it in her arms. It nuzzled up and sucked her fingers, which made her giggle.

Sam started talking to Gideon who told him all about shepherding and birthing lambs. Mary sat on the step of the hut, enjoying the brief respite from the daily chores. She was beginning to feel the presence of another life inside her, feeding on her energy and getting in the way when she bent down. She watched the boys emulating manhood, while still gangly and awkward in their movements and gestures. Sam stood with his legs apart, knees braced and his hat pushed back and Gideon had his hands in his pockets. Meg, who was outgrowing her babyhood, crouched among the lambs which had gathered round, talking to them in her chiming voice. All around there was young life and motherhood and Mary felt a part of the scene, nurturing a vision of the future and her own children.

Chapter Thirty Four

In which Anne Paris meets Esland.

Spring turned softly into summer and Edward's leg began to heal. He drove Mary into town and helped her with the market, but he couldn't walk steadily enough to carry heavy loads. He became frustrated. He watched his friends come to plough, spread dung, sow wheat and hill up the hops. He was critical and complained to Mary that he could have done it better.

"You be so ungrateful, Edward," she scolded. "If 'tweren't for them the farm would be barren. We'd have ter sell stock ter survive." She stormed out of the house to cool off and went to see the lambs.

Gideon stood outside the hut staring at a dreadful scene. The sheep were cowering in the shelter of their pen. The lambs' bleating could be heard from the yard. One lay dead with its head mangled and bloody. Another had a gash in its side and was missing a leg. Part of the hurdle fence had been ripped away. Shep was nowhere to be seen. Mary felt faint and had to hold onto the fence post.

Gideon spoke with a hoarse voice. "Fox had 'em, Mistus Lucke. Got away with one. Shep's agwain after un." He sat down on the step of the hut and put his head in his hands.

Mary's anger melted away, to be replaced by sorrow and concern for Gideon. "Us maun weep over what can't be put right, Gideon. Us has work to do to-wunst. Those sheep be frit to death en the lambs what's left. The hurdle needs replacen en us mun have the dead en injured lambs away. I'll show you where the barrer be."

Gideon recovered himself and set to work making the fence secure. Mary picked up the dead and injured lambs and laid them on the grass in the meadow. Gideon came and despatched the badly injured one by wringing its neck and together they checked all the survivors for injuries. Shep came back, panting, his tongue hanging out of his mouth. He was limping and it crossed Mary's mind that the dog was getting on in years. She wondered how old he was as she made a fuss of him, then she went with Gideon to find a barrow. He would take the lambs and bury them, right away from the sheep.

≈≈≈

Edward sat in the parlour brooding over his misfortune when Mary came in and told him of the disaster in the sheep field. He felt his blood begin to boil.

"I could tell that lad were over-young fer the shepherdin'. Ashdown should've knowed better. How many lambs died, didst say? Us can't afford ter lose 'em." He stood up, grabbed his crutches and started to go towards the door. "I'll give that young man summat ter think on."

Mary stood in front of him. "You'll lose a shepherd if you do that. 'Tis not as if 'e let it happen a-purpose. En I be in no fit state ter shepherd."

Edward was shocked. Mary was right. This was another mishap he had to accept. He sat down again and burst into tears.

"I be no good as a husband to you, Mary. How can I sit by a-watchen you struggle en not get angry?"

She went and held his head against her already swollen belly and stroked his hair. There were no more words to be said. They must manage as best they could. They both knew that.

≈≈≈

Their loyal friends came and went all summer. They mowed the hay, tended the hops, took lambs to market and cut the corn. Richard and the children came to help gather the fruit. Edward walked with only one crutch and was able to feed the beasts and milk the cows. John Winder continued to work for them and played his part with the routine jobs around the farm.

Prudence Winder became a frequent visitor as Mary's pregnancy advanced and Mary was glad of her womanly understanding. Come September, Mary herself would become a mother.

Her brother John came to help with the harvest. He told Mary that their mother intended to visit and be there for the birth of her first grandchild. It was over a year since Mary had last seen her mother. The news of her impending visit was not welcome. Anne Paris's head was full of old-fashioned notions about childbirth. Mary did not want her near at this time. But how could she refuse?

Prudence helped her to prepare the spare chamber for the visitor. Edward could use the stairs now and this year they had stored the apples in the barn. Mary knew that her mother would have plenty to say about the lack of comfort in her house, but there was nothing that could be done about that. She picked some sweetly-smelling roses from the garden and put them in a pot by the window.

The day dawned. It was raining and dread crept its way into Mary's stomach. Her mother arrived, driven in her carriage by her husband. Mary and Edward went out to greet them and showed them into the hall where Mary had laid out a simple meal of cold meat, bread, cheese and pickle.

Her father declined the meal and left his wife sitting at the table, looking around her with distaste.

"Do you not have a kitchen, Mary?" she asked.

"The kitchen is there, Mother." She indicated the lean-to. "I prepare the meals in there en do the cooking on the stove in here."

"I would have thought your husband could have built a better kitchen than that." Anne spoke as if Edward was not present.

Edward said, "Did you have a pleasant journey here, Mother?" He accentuated the last word.

Anne did not look at Edward as she deigned to reply. "It was pleasant enough."

The meal proceeded with little conversation. Mary and Edward glanced at each other across the table and raised their eyebrows.

After coager Mary showed Anne into the parlour where she sat with her embroidery all afternoon. Mary cooked a chicken for dinner with vegetables from their garden, which John Winder had proudly grown for them.

When the time came, Mary accompanied her mother up the stairs to the bedchamber. Anne looked at her daughter in horror. "Is there nowhere else I can sleep? I shall not sleep a wink in here. And take those flowers away. There will be nasty creatures on them from outside."

Mary resisted making a sharp retort and said gently, "There be nowhere else, Mother." She wished her goodnight, left the room carrying the pot of flowers and closed the door behind her. She breathed a sigh of relief and went to join Edward in their bed.

The next day, when Mary woke, she felt different. Something had happened to the child inside her. She turned over and woke Edward.

"Ed, I believe my time be near. Can you go fer Mistus Winder?"

Edward roused himself, dressed hastily, crept quietly through Anne's room and limped downstairs.

Mary heard a movement from her mother's chamber and sat up. She must get dressed and go down before her mother realised that she'd sent for Prudence. Mary only needed to hear that everything was as it should be, that the child was not ready to be born. She didn't want her mother interfering with her horror stories.

She swung her legs out of bed and sat on the edge for a few moments. She reached over gingerly to her clothes which were on a chair and dressed with care. She crept quietly downstairs and went into the kitchen to get a drink of milk.

Prudence and Edward came in and they all went into the parlour.

Mary said to Edward, "Can you keep Muvver out of here until we've finished, love?"

Edward understood, nodded, left the room and closed the door.

Mary heard voices in the hall. Her mother was downstairs. The voices faded, Edward had taken Anne into the kitchen.

Prudence examined the swollen belly. "'E beant ready ter come yet. Any day now." She patted the bump and lowered Mary's skirt to cover it. "You send fer me when you feels the birthen pains."

Mary nodded and Prudence left. She was a good woman, gentle and kind, but a very private person.

Mary sat and mused for a while. She really should be going to prepare breakfast. The noise of a cart coming up the lane brought her back to earth. Who could that be so early in the morning?

≈≈≈

Edward heard the cart and said to Anne, "I'll see who that be, then we'll have some breakfast. Mary'll be here anon." He walked out into the yard and found Esland arriving with Thomas Lucke's annual delivery. Esland climbed down from the cart and was coming towards Edward when a shriek came from behind. Anne had followed him out. She continued to shriek hysterically and Edward stared at her in amazement.

Mary came out of the house, pale with shock. "Mother? What be the matter?" She ran to her mother who collapsed into her arms, throwing them both to the ground. Mary was underneath. Edward and Esland came to pick the two women up.

Anne opened her eyes and stared straight into Esland's distorted face.

She screamed again. "Mary, don't look at it. It's the devil himself."

Esland snorted and whimpered before retreating.

Edward helped Anne to stand up. She covered her face and fled into the house.

He pulled Mary to her feet. She was shaking with fright. He took her into the parlour where her mother had sunk into a chair. He poured them each a glass of brandy and went out to attend to Esland.

Anne Paris said nothing for several hours after the incident in the yard. Mary went about her usual morning tasks, grateful that Edward and John Winder were attending to the beasts. She was suffering from severe shock. The scene in the yard repeated itself over and over in her head; the screams reverberated in her ears; the bruises she'd received when her mother fell on her continued to remind her of her ordeal.

The time came for coager and the three of them sat round the table. Anne declared that she had no appetite. Then a stream of abusive accusations and derisive comments about Esland poured from her mouth, mainly directed at Edward.

"How could you let that monster anywhere near the house with your wife in her condition? I dread to think what sort of creature she will produce now. I sincerely hope she did not see it close to as I did. I have never seen such a beast. It should have been destroyed at birth. Its mother evidently had coupling with the devil…"

Mary could bear to hear no more. She rose from the table and wearily climbed the stairs to her chamber where she lay on the bed and sobbed.

≈≈≈

Edward looked at Anne. His patience was giving out. The woman was mad and the sooner he could get her back home the better. He stood up and cleared the table of food. Anne was about to launch into another tirade. He banged his hand on the table which startled her into silence.

"I'll thank you to stop that insulting talk in my house, Mistus Paris. Go en pack your things. I will not have you anywhere near Mary when the child be birthed. Stay in your chamber betimes I get the cart ready to have you home."

Anne quivered with anger. She stood up, slapped Edward on the face and marched away up the stairs.

Chapter Thirty Five   1711/12

In which Edward loses a friend

When Mary heard the cart roll away she lay on her bed savouring the peace. Her distress abated and at last she slept, exhausted after the strain of the past few days. That night she and Edward clung together and slept in each other's arms.

Still shaken, the couple endeavoured to get back into a normal routine the next day. Mary felt the need of some fresh air and went to feed the chickens in the autumn sunshine. They rolled towards her like small boats on choppy water. Their clucks and gurgles comforted her and she thanked them for the warm brown eggs they'd laid in their boxes. She placed the eggs gently in the straw-lined basket she'd brought with her and walked back to the house.

A sharp pain stopped her in her tracks. She cried out and staggered to the open doorway, where she gratefully leant on the frame. Before long, the intensity of the pain dispersed. She was able to put the eggs down and make her way into the parlour, where she sat in a chair and rested.

Edward had heard her cry and followed her.

"Be you orright?" he asked anxiously.

"I had a pain, Ed. It be gone now. If I have another, mayhap you should fetch Mistus Winder." She lay back with increasing foreboding as her mother's words echoed round her head. *I dread to think what sort of creature Mary will produce now.* She dreaded the birth of the beautiful child she had nurtured for nine long months, which might now be malformed. She tried to reject as suspicious nonsense the notion that her mother had planted, to no avail.

There were voices in the hall and Edward came into the parlour with Herbert Smith.

"Herbert's agwain into town en happened along ter see if us wants aught," Edward said to Mary.

Mary couldn't think of anything. She looked at Edward blankly.

Herbert said, "Us were amenden my ploughed field en John's hat blew clear away! 'Twas a dunover auld thing like, so I said I'd buy un a new un."

Mary said, "We'll pay fer the hat, Herbert, seein' as 'e be my brudder."

Herbert nodded. "I be minded ter borrow some money if I could. I left me money purse at home."

Mary was distracted from the conversation by another wave of pain. She gasped and held her belly.

Edward said, "I'll get John Winder ter fetch his muvver." He left the room and Herbert stood staring helplessly at Mary.

"Beg pardon, Mary. I be sorry to intrude. You be nearin' the birth, beant you? I wish you a healthy delivery." He raised his hat and retreated hastily, leaving Mary in the throes of another contraction.

≈≈≈

Edward called John from mucking out the stables. "Go fetch yer muvver. Mistus Lucke be in pain."

John dropped his shovel and ran over to the cottage.

Herbert Smith came out of the house. "I weren't aware yer mistus was abouten birthen, Edward. Why didn't you tell me?"

"I weren't aware, either, Herbert. I mun stay here prensley. I'll lend you the money." He went in, took some coins from the jar in the parlour and gave them to Herbert.

John and his mother came into the yard.

"She be in the parlour," Edward told Prudence.

Between them they helped Mary up the stairs and into the chamber. Prudence said, "Get towels en boil a kettle of water, Mas Lucke."

Edward did as he was bid and left the women to bring his first child into the world. At first he hung around the kitchen but Mary's shouts of pain disturbed him and he went to help John with the mucking out. Every so often he went in to listen for the cries of a newborn baby.

They finished the work in the yard. It was getting dark and Edward realised that he hadn't eaten all day. He took John into the house and found some bread and cheese which they shared, sitting at the table in the hall.

The shouting from upstairs had stopped. The door of the chamber opened and Mistus Winder called for more hot water.

Edward leapt up and took the kettle to her. Prudence would not let him into the chamber.

There was now no noise at all. Edward and John sat and listened. The tension increased.

Edward went to light some candles.

At last the door upstairs opened and Prudence came down. She shook her head and said, "There be naught more I can do. Go en comfort she." She beckoned to John and they left.

Mary and Edward buried their stillborn son a week later. He was perfectly formed. Mistus Winder could give them no reason. She assured them he had been quick two days before. "These things do 'appen."

Edward was convinced that the fall of Anne Paris on top of Mary had killed his child. Mary couldn't help wondering if her sight of Esland that day had anything to do with it.

They struggled through the next few months, keeping the farm going and supporting each other in their grief. Then John Paris came to tell them that Anne had suddenly collapsed and died. The doctors thought it might have been her heart. The news came as a shock, but they didn't grieve for her.

Herbert Smith and John Paris had struck up a good working relationship while working for Edward. They continued to work on each other's farms and came to Edward to give a helping hand when needed. The money in the pot was dwindling. There was little wheat or fodder in the barns. John Paris brought them faggots before the winter set in and Herbert brought oats and peas.

Edward's leg had healed, but it was weak and sometimes caused him pain. Herbert and John came to help with the ploughing in March. The frosts had broken down the earth and now the sun was warming it ready for sowing. Edward brought the two horses out of the pasture and harnessed them to the plough. The three men proceeded to the field that had grown wheat last year. John, wearing his new hat, held the plough and Herbert led the horses. The coulters sliced through the clay soil as if it were butter, rolling it over into furrows, ready for the peas. Edward followed, limping over the rough ground, scattering the peas into the furrows and kicking the earth to cover them. Blackbirds accompanied the work with their spring songs, diving down to gobble up disturbed worms. A robin joined them, until a gang of crows crowded him away and stole the peas which had escaped being covered. It was good to be back in the open air, working his farm again.

They stopped at midday and went to the house where Mary had prepared bread and cheese. They sat outside to eat it in the sunshine and chatted about this and that.

"'Ow be you fairen with yer lady-friend, John?" asked Edward through a mouthful of bread.

"Fair to middlin'" was all that John would say with a grin.

When they asked whether she was comely and what colour her hair was, his replies were vague.

"I don't rackon 'e be courten at all," declared Herbert. "'E's 'avin' us on."

"I never said I were a-courten. 'Twere Edward said it." John grinned again and took a long drink.

Shep appeared from his resting place in the sun, wagging his tail. He came to Edward and nuzzled under his arm, asking to be fondled.

"'E be looken like 'is days be over," commented John, glad to be able to change the subject.

Edward pulled the dog towards him and rested his head on his knee. "I don't know what I'll do without un," he said.

≈≈≈

April brought sunshine and the birth of animals. Edward and Mary nurtured them as tenderly as they would have done their lost child. Their friends gathered round giving comfort when needed and Edward wrote in his account book again, recalling all the work they did for him when his leg was healing.

He planned to repay them with produce in the coming year.

Soon, Mary was able to announce that she was pregnant again. This time it would be alright. Edward was reluctant to let her do any outdoor work.

"Don't mollycoddle me," she said. "I can't spend months indoors. I'll be careful." She squeezed his arm and kissed him.

She spent time over the summer months sitting in the sunshine in the sheep pasture, watching the lambs growing up. She took walks down the lane and back, sometimes meeting the Winder boys and their father. They were interested to hear how the pregnancy was going. Prudence called regularly to re-assure her that all was well.

On the 10th of November 1712 a child was born to Edward and Mary. He was a fine, dark-haired boy with a lusty voice.

Mary handed him to Edward and said, "Take un. 'E be yourn, my love. 'E'll be our pride en joy."

"'E'll be named Thomas," Edward announced, taking the little bundle gently into his arms. "...after me farder. En 'e'll foller in 'is footsteps en become a working husbandman."

A steady stream of friends and relatives called to admire the firstborn. The christening, a few days later, was a joyous celebration. Prudence Winder helped Mary to prepare a feast for the guests. The last of them stayed on until the evening. Sam and Meg were especially excited to meet their little cousin. Meg held him in her arms and Sam took his tiny hand into his young man's fingers, roughened with farm work.

He looked at Mary and asked, "Was my hands as purty as this when I were a baby?"

≈≈≈

The November winds were strong that year. Some trees were blown down in the copse. Doors and windows rattled and smoke blew down the chimney. John Winder helped to secure roof tiles and barn doors. Shep spent most of his time in the barn and Edward saw him limping when he took him to the pasture to help drive the sheep to their winter enclosure.

One day Edward opened the barn door and didn't receive the usual greeting. He found the tired old dog lying stiff and cold on his bed of straw. Edward laid a hand on his head and closed his eyes. He sat on the floor by his side and remembered Shep's loyal companionship and his skill with the sheep. He would miss him dreadfully. He stood up and went to tell Mary.

≈≈≈

She was sitting in the parlour giving Thomas his first feed of the day. "What be troublin' you, Ed?" she said as he walked in.

"Shep's gone," he said and sat down heavily.

"What? Gone abroad? 'E can't be dead, surely?" Mary released her nipple from the grip of a sleeping Thomas and covered her breast.

"'E were old en tired. 'E couldn't go on fer ever," Edward said. He shrugged his shoulders and sighed.

Mary wrapped up her son snugly and placed him in his cradle. "Can you manage without un?" she asked, putting a comforting hand on Edward's arm.

"I be minded ter sell the sheep, like," Edward replied." 'Twould bring in some money. I don't know how we'll manage otherwhiles."

Mary sat still, taking in Edward's words. She'd been so engrossed in her baby and how he'd changed her life that the everyday running of the farm had passed her by. At last she said, "'Ow much be there in the pot?"

Edward said, "Come en see." He stood up and led Mary into the hall, taking the money pot with him. They sat with the account book and emptied the pot onto the table. Edward showed Mary how much was still owed to John Paris and Herbert Smith for their help on his farm, over a year ago. It amounted to three pounds and four pence. They counted the money, which came to one pound and a few coppers. The two looked at each other.

Edward said, "That beant enough ter pay fer wheat en young John over winter."

Mary said, "If us waits betimes spring afore sellen the sheep, us'll get money fer lambs en all."

"What else do us have ter sell?" asked Edward.

There was a movement in the yard. They would have to get used to the lack of Shep's barking. Herbert Smith appeared at the door.

"I happened by on me way to Wad'rst..." He took in the scene in the hall. "Be ye in moil?" He waited in the doorway.

Edward stood up from the table. "Considerin' sellen the sheep," he said. "Shep died."

"That be ernful news, surely. Be ye short of money?"

"'Twill not last betimes spring," Edward admitted.

Herbert came and sat opposite Mary. "Times be hard en you've a nipper ter fother. Next year I'll need help on my farm, Ed, if you be willin'. 'Til then I can lend ye some money ter feed yerselves. You've done it fer me afore." He brought out his money purse, delved into it and placed five pounds on the table.

Mary stared. "That be unaccountable good of you, Herbert. Be you sure you can spare it?"

Herbert smiled and nodded. "Can't let ye starve, can us? Now, be there aught ye wants in town?" He got up and raised his hat to Mary before going out with Edward.

Chapter Thirty Six 1713 April

In which Edward sells a cow

Edward hated being in debt. He remembered what his father had said on his deathbed and wondered whether, if he went to Slade Farm, he could find the money Uncle Thomas had hidden somewhere. It was worth a try.

It was early April. The birds were singing and the sun was shining. Edward went to the pasture to check the heifer he was keeping for Herbert Smith. She was looking quite at home with his cows and the lambs were doing well. It would be a while before they were ready to take to market. He went to saddle up Faithful and brought her out into the yard. Screams of childish laughter came from the house and he went to say goodbye to his family. Little Thomas came skidding across the hall floor on his bottom and held out his hands to be picked up. Edward bent down and lifted his son high into the air, to shouts of joy.

"I be agwain ter The Slade, Mary. I might be all day, but I'll be back fer dinner." He went to kiss her and put Thomas down on the floor. The child screamed in protest until Mary picked him up and gave him a crust from the bread she'd taken from the oven. She put her hand up to wave to Edward while singing a little tune to Thomas.

At the vestry meeting the previous week, John Tolast told Edward that his cow had died. He needed another. Edward remembered the cow he'd lent to Cruttal's children and said he might be able to help. He would go there on his way through town and see how they were managing.

When he called at Walland the gates were closed and there was no sign of life. He left Faithful and went round to the back yard. He knew that the older children had been apprenticed to various people in town, but what about Susan Newnham and her child? Edward tapped on the back door. There was no reply. He opened the door and stepped into the cool deserted kitchen. A few old clothes had been tossed onto the table. The black cat emerged from a cupboard next to the abandoned fireplace and came to rub itself against Edward's legs, mewing pitifully.

Edward called up the stairs, "Anyone there?"

A slight movement above him became a shuffling sound and the grey figure of a woman appeared at the top of the stairs, wrapped in a blanket. Her bare feet came down towards him and Edward gasped as he realised that the white face surrounded by bedraggled dark hair was Susan.

"Lord 'ave mercy!" he exclaimed. "'Ow come you ter be in such a state?"

Susan crept wearily to the bench by the table and sat down. She coughed and shook her head. The movement set off a paroxysm of coughing which rattled alarmingly in her chest. Susan held her arms round herself until she could breathe freely again.

She looked at Edward. "They be havin' me away (gasp) to the poor house today…The children be gone to apprentice en fosterin'. (gasp) I can't tend 'em. They be agwain…" She broke into more coughing…"They be agwain ter sell the house…"

Her rasping breaths shook Edward to the core. "Can I get you a drink, Susan?" he asked.

She nodded and he went to find a cup and some water.

He came back into the kitchen, sat on the bench opposite her and gave her the drink.

When she'd finished she put the cup down and looked at Edward. "I were abouten send word to you ter teck the cow back. She be gone dry."

Edward nodded. "Can I get you aught while I be here?"

She shook her head. "There be naught in the house." She coughed again. "They said they'd come today…" Her voice trailed off. Then she took a deep, shuddering breath. "Thank you fer yer kindness." She put out her hand and laid it on his arm. The icy cold seeped through his sleeve.

He got up to go. He would remember for a long time the thin smile she gave him and the fear in those big brown eyes.

The cow was grazing in the lush meadow. He went to find a leading rope and tied it round her muzzle. "You'll have ter come home with me en we'll teck you ter the bull," he said to her. "I'll fetch one of me other cows fer John Tolast."

It took the rest of the morning to exchange one cow for the other and deliver it to Tolast. Edward stopped for coager while he was at home, bounced Thomas on his knee for a while, then set off for The Slade, thinking of Susan and Cruttal's children.

The geese met him in the yard. He shooed them away and went into the house to see if Eliza was there.

She was working in the dairy and was surprised to see him. She looked thin and tired.

"I be come ter find summat I might have left here, years ago," said Edward. "Can I look round the house?"

Eliza nodded. "Thomas be out in the fields with Esland. Don't let un see you here. 'E be hem tempersome en I rackon you don't call cousins no more."

"Us never did," Edward commented, as he went through to the hall. Thomas was still angry with him for insisting that he paid his debts.

He searched all the drawers and cupboards in the dresser, looking for false backs where things could be hidden. He examined the fireplace for secret compartments and paced up and down the floor, listening for loose flagstones. He noticed the clock was missing and thought maybe Thomas had sold it.

The parlour was next. He wasn't even sure what he was looking for. He hunted everywhere for hiding places and found nothing, then went up the stairs to look in the chambers. The place was in a sorry state: plaster dropping off the walls and cobwebs hanging from the ceilings. Everything was covered in dust. In the corner of the milkhouse chamber he found the model of a horse: a child's toy. There was a leg missing and it had holes in its sides for the attachment of a cart. A little boy had slept in this room, years ago. Edward felt unaccountably that it was his fault that the horse had been lost. He picked up the toy, brushed off the dust and put it in his pocket.

In the garrett there were a few rotten apples left over from last year's store. The place smelt of cider. There were two cots up there. He could remember his sisters sleeping in this room. His search continued. He found the clock, silent and abandoned. He picked it up and brushed the dust off. He ran his fingers over the carving in the wooden casing. The metal round the face was tarnished. He remembered his father telling him that old Uncle Thomas had given it to Gaffer William on his wedding day. It had been loved and cherished then. There was a rattle as he turned it over. There must be something loose in there. It needed the attentions of a clocksmith, but it wasn't his. He didn't want to upset his brother by taking it now.

Edward went out to the court and searched the stables, cow stalls, up between the rafters and behind beams. Nothing there. There were no loose cobbles as far as he could see and the last resort was to dig them all up. That would be going too far. He'd have to manage without Uncle Thomas' treasure. At least he'd be paid for the cow and keeping Herbert's heifer. But he still had to pay back the money Herbert lent them.

They slaughtered some of the sheep for selling and eating, then sold the young ones for a good price. The lambs went with them. Mary was able to help with the haymaking while Prudence kept an eye on little Thomas. Edward would now not need as much hay next winter and he carted twelve loads of it to Herbert Smith, as well as some dung.

He spent some time on Herbert's farm, cutting clover and tying up the hops. Herbert was looking smarter lately. His parlour was tidier and his hair and beard were trimmed neatly. One evening after work Edward walked back to the house with Herbert, expecting a draught of ale and a gossip before he went home. But Herbert didn't go and pour the ale as usual and Edward was not invited to sit down. They both stood in the parlour looking at each other, Herbert standing uneasily on one leg, then the other.

"You'll be wanting ter get back to Mary en the liddle un, like, Edward," he said.

"Well, yus," Edward said in surprise. "Will you need me termorrer, Herbert?"

"Yus. Us'll get the rest of the hops tied." Herbert walked to the door and showed Edward out.

Edward replaced his hat on his head and said goodbye. He sauntered off down the road in the evening sunshine, whistling a tune and puzzling over Herbert's strange behaviour.

The next time he entered Herbert's parlour there were flowers on the table. Edward called on John Paris on the way home.

"Be Herbert Smith a-courten?" he asked John.

"You've got courten on the brain," said John. "You'll have we all married off afore long."

Edward reported what he had noticed. John said that he hadn't seen Herbert in the alehouse lately, so he couldn't tell Edward anything more.

By his first birthday little Tom was walking and saying a few words. Mary and Edward found that he was as stubborn as his Uncle Thomas. Mary didn't allow his wilfulness to upsides her. She also had a contrary streak. He couldn't stay in one place for long and soon discovered ways of opening doors. He constantly disappeared, to be found sitting in a puddle in the yard or in the chicken run, having left the gate open allowing the hens to escape. When found, he required firm handling to persuade him to come back to the house.

"I'll have ter put up some hurdles en meck a pound to keep un in," said Edward, laughing as he watched Mary carry the child kicking and screaming into the hall. He found the three-legged horse in his pocket. He brought it out and showed it to Tom, who stopped crying immediately. Edward made it gallop along the bench. Mary put the toddler down and he watched, then tried to grab the horse. Edward galloped it to the other end of the bench and Tom followed. This game of chase went on for a while until Edward gave in and left his son to continue the galloping game on his own.

"'Tis time I fashioned un some toys," he said to Mary.

The following February Mary and Edward were sitting in the parlour on the settle, enjoying hot toddies before going to bed. Flames flickered in the grate, lighting up their flushed faces and sparkling eyes.

Mary said, "I be considerin' givin' up breast feedin', Ed. 'E be eaten well en getten teeth. 'E can manage without my milk."

Edward nodded. "Mm, I rackon I could start havin' un with me on the farm come spring. That way I can larn un some husbandry."

Mary looked at her husband. "'E be too young, beant 'e? 'E'll get under yer feet like 'e do mine."

"'E can sit in front on me horse, or ride in the cart. I wouldn't teck un ploughen or hedgen, but 'e can ride on me shoulders when I be sowen, like. 'Twould give you a rest."

"Hark at we, fighten over who should have un!" Mary giggled. "Us'd better make some more, so's us can share 'em."

Edward laughed and reached out to her, pulling her onto his knee. "That be a tremenjous good idea!" He cuddled and kissed her. "Be you ready?" He released her and raked the fire until the embers died down. Then he lifted her into his arms and staggered upstairs with her shrieking with laughter, until they remembered that Tom was asleep. They didn't want to wake him now.

Chapter Thirty Seven   1714 Spring

In which Edward buys a suit.

Mary stood in the kitchen washing the dishes after coager. Tom stood on a stool next to her, his hands in a smaller bowl of water, washing his horse. He was trying to make it lie on the bottom but, being wooden, it kept bobbing to the surface. Tom started splashing it around the bowl, wetting himself and everything in the near vicinity. Mary quickly lifted him onto the floor, gave him his horse and rubbed them both dry with a towel. She noticed a pulling sensation in her back as she stood upright. She'd better be careful.

Edward came through on his way out. "Cow's abouten birthen," he announced.

Mary stopped him. "Edward, I be with child again. I be afeared that liftin' Tom will make me lose un, like."

Edward's eyes lit up. "That be hem good news, Mary" He hugged her. "You be considerable careful. Don't do any heavy jobs. I'll do all the liften." He picked up Tom and cuddled him. "You be agwain ter have a brudder or a sister, liddle man."

The sound of a cow calling came from the barn and Edward put his son down, kissed Mary and went jauntily out to attend to the next birth.

≈≈≈

The pot in the hall was filling up. Edward paid Herbert what he owed in money and kind and continued to work for him when he was not attending to his own farm. Mary sold eggs, bread, cheese and milk at the market as well as a few broiler hens. Tom came with her and played with the children of the other standing holders. He sometimes went with Edward to the beast market, or to Herbert's farm to hoe the hops.

One day, Tom had been pulling his toy cart through the rows of hops, loading it with things he found and tipping it all out in another place. He was now sitting eating his bait with his father and Herbert, in the shade of a hedge foaming with May blossom.

Herbert said to Edward, "I be minded ter ringle me lady friend in July. We'll be asked in church come Sunday. Will you en Mary be a-comen ter the weddin'?"

Edward stopped eating to allow his mind to digest this revelation. He took a mouthful of ale from his costrel and wiped the foam off on his sleeve. "That be woundrous news, Herbert, surely. Mary en me'll be there fer certain sure. I be main pleased fer you both. Be you agwain ter tell me she's name?"

"Her be called Judith." Herbert's face had become a deep red and he got up to continue with the hoeing. Edward followed.

At the day's end he hurried home, carrying Tom on his shoulders, singing as he went. He was excited for his friend and yes, John was right, he did want them both to be happily married as he was himself. Life for him was rich with joys and laughter as well as hardship and fears for the future. That hardship was half the weight when shared with a loving wife and balanced with companionship.

Tom sang along with him until he was too tired. He wrapped himself round his father's neck and fell asleep.

≈≈≈

Mary met them at the kitchen door, took her son into her arms and carried him to a chair in the parlour. He would wake when he was hungry. She covered him with a shawl and went to prepare the dinner.

Edward came in, having fothered the beasts and washed himself at the well. He approached Mary from behind and put his arms round her waist. She rested the ladle in the pot and swivelled round to return the embrace.

"Herbert be ringlen in July," Edward announced. "She be named Judith. Us be invited to the weddin'." He lifted her, then put her down gently. "You be over heavy fer liften prensly," he remarked.

"'E's been unaccountable quiet about that," Mary observed. "I be main pleased fer 'em. Do us have fittin' riggin' fer a weddin'?" she asked thoughtfully. "I've some left from me dowry."

"Mm, nay. I've only been to Ann's weddin' en the riggin' I wore then were scraped tergether." Edward sat at the table and rested his chin in his hands.

Mary went back to stirring the stew. "I reckon we've got enough in the pot fer a new outfit fer you en stuff fer a dress fer me."

Edward looked thoughtfully at the pot on the shelf above the range. "I were abouten buy a wagon en other things fer the farm."

"Us needs decent riggin', Ed. There'll be another baptism come November. En us can't go to Herbert's weddin' in what us stands up in, like." She turned and gave him a look.

Tom appeared at the parlour door, rubbing his eyes and hugging Mary's shawl. "Mama," he said and raised his arms to be picked up. She hadn't seen him all day and had missed him. Edward went to lift him onto the bench but the child squirmed and wriggled, calling "Mama!"

Mary sat on the bench next to him and lifted him onto her knee. She hugged him and kissed him and said, "You be covered in dirt, young man. Farder will clean thee up en dinner will be ready prensley."

The hum-drum of life took over and no more was said about the possibility of buying new clothes. Mary knew that Edward would see sense when he'd mulled it over.

≈≈≈

Edward went to see John Feavour, his father's old friend and his acquaintance from the Parish Vestry, who'd moved to Ticehurst to carry on his trade as a tailor.

"I be in need of riggin' fit fer a weddin'. Not too houghy, like, but swish. Can you fashion me summat afore July?"

John looked at Edward over his spectacles with his beady eyes, his head on one side, birdlike. "Well now, Mas Lucke, you be a-comen up in the wurrell, I be avised. Come, let me show you the sort of thing I believe you be a-seekin'." He led Edward into the dark depths of his shop, between shelves of fabric of all colours on one side and on the other, rails of garments, some ready-made and others unfinished. John took three of these off the rail as he passed and carried them into a well-lit room with a large table in the centre. In the sloping ceiling above the workspace was a window which let in daylight. Round the walls were sconces with candles in them, some with flickering flames, lighting up a corner where there was a tall mirror. All sound was muffled and Edward felt as if he was wrapped in a blanket.

John laid on the table two of the garments he'd picked out and held up a long coat in front of Edward. It had small buttons all the way down the front and wide sleeves with deep cuffs. Edward had seen these coats worn by respectable gentlemen when he went into town.

He looked at it and nodded.

"This would be worn with knee length breeches, stockings and a shirt with lace round the sleeves, protruding from the sleeves of the coat," said John. "I reckon this one is about your size. Please remove your outer garments and try them on. I'll go and find some cloth for you to choose from." He discreetly left the room.

Edward stood in front of the mirror, gazing at the image of his transformation. He saw that his hair resembled a hay cock and that his boots might not be suitable to go with this outfit. But he felt good; upstanding and proud. John Feavour appeared behind him in the glass.

Edward smiled and said, "That will be praper perfect," and turned round to face the tailor.

"I will measure you now, Sir. Pleased take off the jackut." He took the tape measure from round his neck and proceeded to measure Edward's height, width at the shoulders, hips, waist and arm and leg length, writing down each measurement on a slate.

"Now you can put on your own riggin' and choose your cloth."

When he was ready, Edward went over to the table and looked at all the coloured stuff lying there. He chose a deep maroon for the coat and dark blue for the breeches. His stockings would be blue. The shirt with the lacy trimming and the cravat would be cream.

"I'll also need a hat en some shoes," he said.

"I can supply the hat, Sir. You'll get the shoes at Buttons', across the road. May I suggest you wear a wig, Sir? Your hair…"

Edward was shocked. He did not want to wear a wig. He'd have to shave off his mop of hair and he couldn't do farm work in a wig.

"Nay, I'll talk with the Mistus, thank you kindly," he said.

"As you wish. Come for a fitting in two weeks." John showed Edward out of his shop.

The fresh air slapped him in the face. He stopped in the street, wondering what he'd done. He would have felt more comfortable buying a wagon.

The time for the fitting arrived. Edward persuaded Mary to come with him and they went with Tom in the cart. The tailor had a young man assisting him that day. Edward tried on the finished garments and Mary clapped her hands and said, "Massypanme! I'll have ter fashion a dress fit fer a queen ter walk along of you in that!"

Tom clapped his hands too and reached up to his father to be picked up. Mary came to the rescue while Edward changed back into his working clothes.

John Feavour called the assistant to wrap up the new suit and announced the sum owed to him.

Edward felt a wave of cold pass through him and looked at Mary. She smiled and nodded. He took money from his purse, laid it on the table carefully, saying goodbye to his hard-earned cash. He took his account book from his pocket and opened it at a clean page.

"Will you write a receipt on there, Mas Feavour," he said.

John brought quill and ink and wrote;

June 29: 1714
Know all Men by those
present that I: John
Feavour of Ticehurst Taylor
Have received of Edward
Lucke of Wadhurst Yeoman
The full and just sum of
10 pounds of good and Lawful
Money of England where
unto I witness My hand
John Feavour

Chapter Thirty Eight

In which Edward receives sad news…

A peal of bells rang out as the happy couple greeted their guests at the church door after the wedding. The company went to the Grazehound where a space had been cleared and food laid out on tables. As well as Judith's close relatives, Herbert had invited all his friends, having no family of his own. John Paris was there wearing his new hat, but no lady on his arm.

Edward said to Mary, "I don't reckon aught come of that time 'e were a-courten."

William Ashdown seemed to fill the room with his great bulk and infectious laugh. He limped round leaning on his stick, greeting the ladies. Then he came to Edward and Mary who were talking to Ed Waghorn and his wife. Tom hung onto his mother's skirts, taking in his surroundings with wide-open eyes. Mrs Waghorn was saying, "'E be the bly of you, Mary…"

"There's a fine boy, surely," boomed Ashdown. He bent down and ruffled Tom's hair. Tom pushed the offending farmer's hand away and hid round the back of Mary's skirt.

Mary brought him back to the front and said firmly, "Say, 'how do you do, Sir,' to the gentleman, Tom."

Tom scowled, but obeyed, adding, "Be you a giant?"

Ashdown roared with laughter and said, "Nay, but me farder were. 'E were bigger'n me."He laughed again. He kissed the ladies' hands and said to Edward, "Has Wag'orn told you? 'E'll be joining us in the vestry come Sunday."

Ed Waghorn's face turned red and he nodded.

Edward said, "Oh, I be main glad of that, Ed. You'll be a worthy member of the company."

Ashdown wandered off and Mary went to talk to her brother. Edward tipped his hat to Waghorn and his Mistus, picked up Tom and followed Mary.

"You look hem swish, surely," remarked John Paris when he saw Edward in his new suit. Mary had put curling rags in his hair the night before and now it resembled a wig under his hat. "En Mary, I've never seen you a-lookin' so purty. It do suit you bein' a muvver, I'll be bound. When be the next un expected?"

"November," said Mary.

The fiddlers struck up with a bouncing tune like excited bees. Herbert and Judith led the company to form two lines, ready to start the dancing. Mary decided that this might not be a suitable activity for her in her condition. She sat watching the men whirling their ladies and leading them through arches with a whoop. The women's skirts swished and swung. The floor pounded to the rhythm as they cavorted up and down the room.

Tom and his mother clapped to the time of the music. A little girl came and whisked Tom away to dance by themselves, making it up as they pranced together. When they were tired the girl delivered Tom back to Mary. He climbed onto the bench and cuddled up. Before long he was asleep.

The caller shouted instructions as the next dance started;

Broomsberry Market
The first man cast back and take the third woman
by the left hand and turn then the second by the
right then his partner then the woman cast back
take the third man by the right hand and turn him
then the second by the left then her partner
then the first man hey on the woman's side then
lead in between the second couple then
the first woman hey on the man's side then
clap single cast down one couple and so it ends.

There was a break and Edward, who had danced with a young girl related to Judith, came puffing over with two mugs of ale to sit by Mary. The curls in his hair were dropping out and his brow glistened with moisture.

"I be justabout beazled," he said. "This jackut be over heavy fer dancen."

"You could've taken it off!" said Mary, laughing. Trickles of sweat ran down into his eyes. She took out her handkerchief and mopped them up. "I see you've lasted longer than Will Ashdown," she remarked. "En Herbert looks like he's bin dancen in the oast oven. 'E be red as a berry."

Judith came towards them and they stood up to greet her. Edward lifted Tom gently onto his shoulder where he continued to sleep.

"You be Edward en Mary Lucke," said Judith. "Pleased ter make yer acquaintance." She shook their hands.

"This be a fine celebration, surely," said Mary. "Behopes you'll have a long en happy marriage."

"Us both be gettin' in years fer marriage, but us be abouten make up the time prensley." She laughed.

They talked for a while until the music started again. Mary said, "'Tis a'most time us took the nipper home, Judith. 'E be all-in."

They went to find Herbert to say goodbye. He was sitting on a chair in a corner with his head in his hands.

"Herbert, be you orright?" asked Edward.

Herbert looked up. His eyes were watering. "I be feelin' ornary. Don't tell Judith. I'll be orright in a while."

They said goodbye and made their way out to the cart. Mary stepped up and took Tom from Edward. They were soon trotting down the road to Savages.

≈≈≈

On Sunday Edward greeted Waghorn at the vestry meeting and bought him a beer.

"Don't be worritted," he said. "There be a deal of unaccountable argyfyin' goes on, but genally it don't mean aught. You be well avised ter sit en listen at first, ter get the measure of 'em."

They took their places and Benge started the proceedings. The overseers made their reports and a few contravertial issues were settled.

"And now we have to appoint a new officer to collect conributions from the Cousleywood quarter, as Pitkin has left us. Do we have any proposals?"

Ashdown spoke up. "I believe Edward Lucke could carry out that duty admirably."

The company voted on it and Edward accepted the task.

Comber passed over a list of names to him. "You'll need to check on the amount of property they have and if that has increased or decreased since the last assessment. Some of them will pay in money and some in produce."

Edward nodded. "Be there a time limit for these ter be paid?"

Benge said, "As soon as possible. If they can't pay when you call give them one week."

Comber tut-tutted. "Don't be too hard on them, Benge. We all know you can't allus have the money or produce to hand."

The meeting was drawing to a close. Edward looked at the names and only recognised one; Thomas Button. But this might be a relative of the one he knew in Lamberhurst.

He came back from his reverie to hear Benge saying, "Sad to say that Susan Newnham died in the poorhouse last Friday. She'll be buried on Tuesday."

"I believe she had no relatives," said Comber. "One or two of us should attend the funeral."

Edward raised his hand. "I'll be there," he said.

Edward was deeply saddened by the news of Susan's death. She'd a hard life for a young girl. He wondered about her baby and if it was being cared for.

There were few people at the funeral. William Ashdown was there with his wife. "To represent the local community," he said.

A handful of young people clung together shyly. Edward saw that they were Crittall's children. He recognised Mark and Luke as the boys he taught to milk the cow.

He approached them in the litten before they left. "'Ow be ye fairin', you lads?" he asked.

Their faces lit up as they saw who it was. "Middlen, thank you kindly, Mas Lucke."

They told him who they were apprenticed with and the work they did. "That be me Master, there." Luke pointed to a well-dressed couple who, seeing Edward, strolled over to meet him.

The man spoke, "Mr and Mrs Newnham," he said and offered Edward his hand.

Edward felt a shiver run down his spine. "Edward Lucke," he said, taking the other's hand. "Be ye relatives of Susan?" He was shocked to think that they hadn't been there to help her in her need.

"I'm her uncle," said Newnham. "Call me Thomas. Susan was my brother's daughter. He was Robert and lived in Lamberhurst. I believe you were working for our friend Bathurst in those days. You probably met my brother and his wife."

Edward nodded. "Yus, yus." He paused. "How come Susan were so neglected these last few years?" he said boldly.

Mrs Newnham spoke up. "I can see that you are angry, Master Lucke. I believe you were very kind to the girl when she was at Crittal's. The fact is, we have only recently come to Wadhurst from Ticehurst and had no idea where she was. It was when Luke started talking about her that we realised, alas, too late."

Mr Newnham added, "Susan left home when she was fifteen with a young man from Lamberhurst. Her father told her she must stop seeing him, as he was not a suitable match. But Susan was strong-willed and left, leaving no trace. Since then my brother and his wife have both died. We had no way of knowing…"

Edward had calmed down. "I be main ernful. 'Twas a cruel end. Susan were a brave girl en tended those children as best her could. D'ye know what happened to the child?"

Mrs Newnham looked at her husband.

He said, "I was hoping you would know, as you're a parish officer. I would do anything in my power to see that she is cared for."

Edward said, "I'll make enquiries." He nodded and held out his hand. "Glad ter make yer acquaintance."

They all shook hands and walked out of the church litten to their homes, musing over the revelations of the morning.

It took a long time to trace Susan's child. The officer who had dealt with her adoption had left the vestry and moved away. He hadn't kept very good records. It was at the November vestry meeting that Comber announced that the child had been found and was thriving. The parish continued to pay for her keep and they would willingly pass this duty on to the relatives. Edward was given the task of delivering the news to the Newnhams.

Chapter Thirty Nine

In which Mary bakes two loaves.

A week later Mary, by now heavily pregnant, was walking back from collecting the eggs with Tom and found Edward saddling up Faithful for the journey into Wadhurst.

"'Tis the time of the year we get a delivery of hops from Thomas," Edward said. "John can deal with un if 'e comes while I be abroad."

Mary hoped it would not be Esland who came. A shiver travelled down her spine and a lump came to her throat.

Edward continued, "John be a-doen all the jobs 'smarnen. 'E'll fetch Prudence if you needs 'er. Don't go a- liften or doen aught ockard, like. I'll be back come coager-time. I'll take Thomas along of me."

Mary said, "I be considerable obliged." To Tom she said, "You be agwain along of Farder. 'E'll give you a ride on Faithful." She let go of the boy's hand and he walked over to Edward.

"Where be us agwain?" he asked.

"We'll ride into Wad'rst en call on a fine gentleman en his Mistus. Up you come." Edward lifted his son onto the horse's neck and mounted. "Hang on tight," he said, "Geewoot."

"Geewoot!" echoed Thomas. They rode out of the yard. Mary gave a wave and listened to the clatter of hooves going down the lane, accompanied by Tom tongue-clicking; "cli-clo, cli-clo.".

She smiled and went into the house, her heart brimming with pride. There was a different feeling in her belly today and she wouldn't be surprised if she were calling for Prudence in the next few hours. She had to bake bread and wash Tom's dirty clothes before it was too late. She pushed away the visions of Esland which rose to the surface and the image of her still-born child.

Mary enjoyed bread-making. She collected the ingredients; flour, freshly milled from wheat grown in their own fields, with the help of sun and rain. They'd had a good yield this year. There was water by her side, brought in earlier by John Winder. Yeast was also at hand, ready prepared and foaming nicely. She plunged her hands into the soft flour, adding the water and the yeast trickle by trickle and mixing until the dough formed. This always reminded her of the day Molly taught her to make bread. A wave of sadness passed through her as she lifted the dough onto the board and kneaded it, releasing morbid thoughts, until it felt right. She scraped the sticky dough off her fingers, covered the lump with a cloth and put it in a warm place near the fire to prove. It was the same shape as her belly, she mused.

The next job was the washing. The kettle was full of hot water. She carried it carefully to the kitchen and poured the contents into a bowl half-filled with cold, mixing it to a comfortable temperature. Having topped up the kettle and carried it back to the stove, she plunged the little breeches and round frocks into the bowl and rubbed them with soap. Soon she would have more small clothes to wash. When she'd finished she left the bowl of wet clothes for Edward to hang up when he returned.

Back to the dough, warm now and exuding a yeasty aroma, Mary stood at the table and kneaded, slapped, pummelled and pulled until she was satisfied. Then she divided the soft lump into two, folded each piece gently to the shape she wanted and with the smooth side up, placed them on the baking tray.

Her back was aching and she straightened herself, taking a deep breath before opening the oven door. She picked up the tray and carried it to the oven. Then she felt it; the first contraction. She breathed deeply again and, her hands shaking, put the bread in and shut the door. Clutching her belly, she let out a cry of pain. Water ran down her legs onto the floor.

"John!" she shouted.

There was no sound. She sat down on the bench and waited until the pain died away. It might be possible to get to the kitchen door and call John from there. She stood up and more water trickled out. On her way through the kitchen she grabbed a towel and held it between her legs with one hand while she opened the door with the other.

She leaned on the door frame and called, "John! John!"

But he was nowhere in sight.

≈≈≈

Edward and Tom found the Newnham's house. They dismounted and went to knock on the door. A maid opened it. Edward announced himself and the maid said "Come in." She indicated a seat in the entrance hall and Edward sat down.

Tom saw the black and white chequered floor and jumped from black to black, shouting "Hop, hop, hop!"

Thomas Newnham came through a door and greeted Edward with friendly familiarity. He said hello to Tom who turned shy and went to stand by his father.

"This be Thomas," said Edward.

Newnham smiled and said to the child, "That cannot be right, I am Thomas!"

Tom shook his head and said, "Nay, I be Thomas."

Edward said, "You be Liddle Thomas en the gentleman be Big Thomas."

The child nodded and stood quietly looking round the great hall with its grand winding staircase, a dresser against the wall, the shelves laden with decorated china plates.

"I be come ter tell you that Susan's child has been found," said Edward.

Newnham's face beamed all over. He called his wife and she appeared at the top of the staircase. She wore an orange dress with a wide skirt which rustled as she came down towards them. Tom gazed at her in awe.

Newnham introduced him to his wife and she shook the little boy's hand. "Would you like to come into the parlour and have some refreshment?" she asked Edward. "There's someone in here I believe you would like to meet."

They all went into the parlour, which was lavishly furnished with comfortable sofas and chairs, carpets and curtains. All noise was muted. A man stood up and came towards Edward, his hand outstretched.

"Edward!" he exclaimed. "You're looking well. And this must be Thomas. I've heard all about you."

Edward was overcome with surprise. He grasped the man's hand. "Mr Bat'rst, Sir. 'Tis a pleasure ter see you again."

Tom stood watching the reunion.

Edward said, "Say good day Tom."

"Good day, Mas Bat'rst," said Tom.

They all sat down and Tom stood by his father's side.

Mrs Newnham had called for the maid who now appeared carrying a tray of glasses of port wine and milk for Tom, with a large plate of biscuits.

George Bathurst and Edward exchanged news and George announced that he was at last betrothed to a woman of his choice.

"That be good news, surely," said Edward. "I wish you both health and happiness." He raised his glass. He told Bathurst that Mary was due to birth another child, then he turned to his host and another toast was called for.

He explained where Susan's child was fostered and suggested that the Newnham's might like to visit and arrange whatever help was needed.

"I would offer to have her here," said Mrs Newnham, "but our lifestyle is not suitable and if the child is settled where she is it would be a mistake to move her."

"Would you let the foster parents know that we'll call on them quite soon?" Newnham asked Edward.

Edward agreed and got up to leave.

Tom finished eating his second biscuit and went over to Mrs Newnham. "Thank you for the bait, lady. I like your house." He put out his hand and Mrs Newnham shook it.

"It was a pleasure to meet you, young Sir," she said.

They said goodbye to George Bathurst and left.

Edward and Tom called at the Carpenters' house on the way home.

"Will I get more biscuits?" asked Tom.

"Nay, we beant agwain indoors. You stand by Faithful. I'll be back dracly-minute."

Mistus Carpenter answered Edward's knock. He could hear children's laughter coming from inside. He said, "I be sent by the Parish ter tell you that kin of Susan Newnham have moved to Wad'rst. They heard about you fosterin' the child en want ter visit."

The woman raised her eyebrows in astonishment. "They beant abouten have she away, be they?"

"Nay. They be getten in years en they want ter pay fer the child's keep, like," said Edward.

Mistus Carpenter relaxed. "Be they Quality, then?" Her eyes widened.

Edward nodded and said, "They be a-comen 'fore long. They be good people." He raised his hat and turned to go.

The door was shut behind him.

Chapter Forty

In which Edward and Mary are surprised

Faithful clip-clopped into Savages yard. Edward dismounted then lifted Tom down.

John Winder came running out to meet them. "I were in the barn en couldn't hear she shouten... Muvver's with she now."

Tom ran indoors, "Muvver, us went to a grand house..."

John said, "'Er be roaren like a beast," then ran into the house to stop Tom going up the stairs.

Edward left Faithful tethered and munching hay from a bag hung on the stable door. He strode into the house. There were two plump, freshly-baked loaves cooling on the table. John was restraining Tom who was at the foot of the stairs, listening to shouts of pain coming from the chamber.

"Come here, Tom, don't be frit. Muvver be orright," Edward said.

Tom stayed where he was, holding onto the newel post.

Edward went to bring him away but he resisted.

The shouting continued.

Edward sat on the second step and persuaded Thomas to sit next to him. The child had seen lambs being born and Edward said, "Muvver be birthen a baby brudder or sister for thee. It hurts a bit en 'er shouts ter help un."

Tom was difficult to console.

The door of the chamber opened. Edward was reminded of Tom's birth.

"Water please, John," called Prudence.

John, who had been sitting by the table, grabbed the kettle and pushed past the two sitting on the stairs. He came back with the empty kettle.

All was quiet.

A thin wail pierced the tension in the room.

Instead of a shout from Prudence, another cry from Mary startled them. This time it was long and loaded with exhaustion.

The child continued to wail.

Another sound followed. Could there be two babies crying?

Edward could wait no longer. He grasped Tom and climbed the stairs as fast as he could.

The chamber door opened. Prudence popped her head out. "Wait a minute," she said and disappeared again. The crying stopped.

They waited...

Prudence opened the door with a flourish and Edward burst in.

He stopped. There was Mary sitting up in bed holding a bundle on each arm. She was laughing through her tears.

Tom shouted, "Muvver! You catched hurt."

Edward let him go and he climbed onto the bed.

"I birthed a brudder en a sister fer thee, liddle man," said Mary. "You en me will be busy tendin' 'em while they be a-growin'." She showed the now sleeping bundles to him.

Edward came and embraced all four of them.

Mary put her face up for a kiss and he wiped her tears away.

He said, "I be main proud of thee, my love." He took the nearest twin in his arms. They looked exactly the same; round heads, a fluff of pale hair and button noses. "How will us tell 'em apart?" he asked.

Mary had her spare arm round Tom. She suddenly looked terribly tired. She smiled and shrugged, shaking her head.

Prudence was tidying up around them. "That un you've got, Mas Lucke, that be the girl. You'd best find different coloured shawls fer 'em!" she laughed.

Tom was quiet, enjoying the comfort of his mother's arm, unaware of how much his little world would change from this moment.

A week later Edward drove the cart down the lane carrying Mary and Tom and John and Prudence Winder. The two babies wrapped in a yellow shawl for the girl and a green one for the boy were sleeping soundly in a large basket, end to end.

They drew up at the church. A crowd waited for them. All were dressed in their Sunday best. John Paris wore his smocked round frock. Richard, Sam and Meg were there and the Ashdown family, the Waghorns, Elliott the blacksmith, Henry and Judith Smith, Edward Benge, Mr and Mrs Newnham, George Bathurst and a host of local folk who'd heard the news. The successful birth of twins was a rare occasion in Wadhurst.

Mary and Edward, now holding their newborns, led the way into the church, followed by the godparents and their spouses; John Paris, Richard Lucke, Mistus Waghorn, Herbert and Judith Smith and Dolly Ashdown with her husband. They all stood round the font while the rest of the congregation filled up the pews.

The vicar, John Willett, was waiting by the font.

There was a disturbance at the door and everyone looked round.

Edward's sister Ann came in first, out of breath, then Martha, carrying a small child. They joined the congregation in the pews.

When all was quiet, the vicar dictated the promises for the godparents to make and took each baby in his arms, saying, "I name this child Mary…" while pouring water over her head. Baby Mary remained calm, but when the boy was given the same treatment, "I name this child Edward…" he shouted loudly. The noise echoed round the church.

His mother took him back and comforted him and all was quiet for Mr Willett to conclude the service. Edward carried his daughter out into the winter sunshine followed by Mary and John Paris holding Tom's hand. Everyone gathered in the litten to take a look at the babies. Mary felt proud of her family. Edward, dressed in his new suit, could hardly contain his delight. He suggested to Mary that they should go over to the Grazehound to drink the health of the children with their friends and family. Ann and Martha were full of their own news and were thrilled to see the newborns.

The alehouse sold a record number of beers that day. Edward and Mary and their family left long before the others, as they had to attend to the needs of the children. Richard and family and John Paris followed shortly after with Ann, Martha and her daughter. The celebrations continued at Savages. As the babies slept soundly after their feed a discussion arose on the subject of names.

"You can't call 'em Edward en Mary," complained John. "There'll be considerable confusion."

"There'll be other Ed's among our friends," said Edward. "It'd better be Eddy fer now."

Tom was looking at his brother and sister in the cribs. Meg said, "What will you call 'em, Tom?"

He thought for a moment. Everyone stopped talking. He looked up, puzzled, then back at the babies. "That be Mamie," he said, pointing to the girl. "En that be Ted, surely," he said, pointing at his brother.

"That be perfect," said his mother.

Mary was busy in the kitchen, churning some butter. The babies were sleeping and Tom was playing on the hall floor, building a barn for his horse with wooden bricks made by his father. Edward was away working for Herbert Smith and John Winder was in the barns and stables, mucking out and feeding the beasts.

Mary didn't hear the cart coming into the yard. She continued to churn until she was out of breath, then let go the handle and stood up straight. John was talking to someone and she opened the door to see who it was.

Esland was carrying a load of hops into the barn. When he came out he looked up to see Mary standing at the door. She felt unaccountably fearful and turned to go into the house. But he came towards her, beamingwith pleasure.

"Nishtush Ucke," he spluttered. He took her hand and shook it vigorously with both of his.

She tried to control the shaking which had overtaken her body and forced a smile.

Esland, still grinning, making his face look even more gruesome, made the cradling gesture she knew so well, nodded and clapped his hands, then held up two fingers. He was congratulating her on the birth of the twins.

Mary was touched. But how did Esland know about the birth? She nodded and said, "Thank you, Esland. They be sleeping prensly. They be a-growen well." She didn't want Esland in her house and stood firmly in the doorway. Tom was indoors. She'd rather he didn't see the man's hideous face.

Esland grasped her hand again and shook it, making Nnnn noises then turned at last to go back to the cart for another pocket of hops.

Mary went into the kitchen shutting the door behind her. She leant against it until her heart stopped hammering.

"Poor man," said Edward later when he heard what had happened. "'E means no harm. You should have let un see the liddle uns."

Mary knew that her husband would never understand her instinctive fear of Esland. Misfortunes often occurred after he'd been here, particularly when someone had offended him.

"Herbert be ornary," Edward said. "'E beant hisself nohows."

"'E beant accustomed to married life. 'Twill teck awhile fer un ter settle," Mary assured him.

Chapter Forty One   1714/5

In which Herbert Smith settles his debt

The icy puddles crackled as Faithful's hooves stepped on them. A white frost covered the hedgerows along the lane, sparkling in the January sunlight. Edward's breath came out in a cloud, joining the steam rising from the horse's nostrils. He shivered and spurred the animal on, then walked as they met the road going towards Herbert Smith's farm, avoiding the frozen ruts made by carts in the wet weather.

Edward had spent many hours last year working for Herbert, to make up for the help he'd given the year before. It was time he made the Savages fields more productive now there were five mouths to feed. He'd been making plans over the winter months and thought he would raise more pigs as there were no sheep. There were more fields that could be used for growing grain. He'd had a poor harvest last year and would need to get his wheat from other sources. First, he must reckon with Herbert.

He rode into the yard and tethered Faithful before knocking on the door. Judith answered.

"Come in out of the cold," she said.

Herbert was away in town. Judith poured Edward a beer and he sat at the table, pleased to have the chance to talk to her on her own.

"Herbert don't seem 'is rightful self these days. Be un orright?" he asked.

Judith shook her head. "'E beant as strong as 'e were. 'E's had to get help on the farm. I do's all I can. The cold weather don't help. 'E gets home all-in."

"I've come ter reckon up with un, Judith," said Edward. "I'll be buildin' up Savages next year en can't work fer un no more. I be ernful that 'e's ornary."

"'E's been talking about a-runnen the farm down, like," she said. There be only two of us. Herbert wants ter carry on this year en see if 'e be better come summer. Then 'e'll decide. How much do 'e owe you?"

Edward took out his account book and showed her. "It be one pound I reckon. I'll have need of wheat come spring. If 'e has any spare 'e can pay me that way. En I'll buy one of they sheets off un."

Judith nodded. "I'll tell un. 'E might happen by your place when 'e be a-passin'."

Edward got up to leave. He shook hands with Judith and let himself out. The cold hit him as he shut the door behind him.

Returning from the Smiths', Edward mused on Herbert's deteriorating health.They were the same age. Edward didn't want his own body to start failing him now. Life was only just beginning. Mary was around ten years younger and had many more ahead of her. Now that he had a family he must make sure that they would be well provided for in his old age and beyond.

The next time he saw John Paris Edward said he would buy a sheet, some clover seeds and eight bushels of wheat from him. This, with the supplies from Herbert, he hoped would tide them over until harvest time.

Over the next months the farm at Savages bustled with ploughing, manuring, sowing and haymaking. Herbert delivered a tovet of wheat each month until August. John Paris worked most days for Edward and became part of the family. Mary did what she could to help and Tom joined in. Prudence watched the babies who thrived and by the end of the summer were crawling around the floor like busy bumble bees. She spent more time at Savages these days. Her own family were working all day at the shop and she only had to cook the dinner for them when they came home.

One October evening Edward sat at the table with his account book in the flickering candlelight and recorded John Paris' work.

Mary had settled the twins in their cots and was sitting with Tom in the parlour, telling him a story before taking him upstairs. Edward listened to their voices while he was writing. His spirits rose with love and pride. All was well and prospects were good. John Paris had bought some land from Herbert Smith and Edward had promised to help him the next year. He had great plans of growing oats, clover and hops and needed to prepare the land, since it had been used as sheep pasture.

Tom came through the hall and climbed onto the bench beside his father. "What be you a-doen?" He looked at the page of accounts.

"I be reckoning up the money I owes to Uncle John fer the work he's done fer me," said Edward. "Look, that says *John Pares's work*." He dipped his quill in the ink pot and continued to write...*more for*

Tom watched. "What do that say?" he asked.

Edward read to him the whole account, pointing at the words.

"Will you larn me ter write like that, Farder?" Tom asked.

"I will. En dappen you be ready, you'll go to school en be larned ter add up the figgers en all."

Thomas breathed a big sigh and looked at his father.

"Come now, Tom. It be time you was abed," called Mary from the foot of the stairs. They climbed up together.

The following morning Edward and John Winder were in the hog pound, mucking out. The young pigs Edward bought in the spring would be adults next year and he hoped that, with the older ones, he would be able to raise a couple of litters, sell some of the piglets and kill an adult to salt down for the following winter. They would need another hog pound.

The geese were cropping the grass round the feeding troughs at the edge of the yard, where the cattle had spilled some of their feed. Gregory, the goose leader, raised his head and cocked it to one side. He'd heard a cart approaching. When it appeared round the corner he gaggled and hissed, setting the others off and they all spread their wings and ran screeching towards the visitor.

It was Thomas Senior with a load of hops. Edward watched his brother alight from the cart, moving slowly and stiffly. They met in the centre of the yard by the well. Edward held out his hand in friendship. Last time he'd seen Thomas he'd been broody and refused to talk. Thomas shook his hand, but showed no affection.

"'Ow be things up at The Slade, Brudder?" Edward enquired.

"Fair to middlen," answered Thomas. "We all be getten in years."

"Yer hops be a-doing well," Edward commented.

"Yus, they be better than aught else on our land. I have a man ter tend 'em en dry 'em in the oast." Thomas was being unusually chatty, but his face remained morose.

"How be Esland?" asked Edward, wondering if the dwarf was sickly. It was he who generally brought the hops.

"Same as ever," said Thomas. "Where d'you want these put?" he asked.

Edward went to open the barn door. "I'll give you a hand," he said.

The two men carried the full hop pockets into the barn and Edward found the empties from last year and gave them back.

When they'd finished Thomas said, "I be avised your Mary were birthed of twins." His face didn't change, but he did look Edward in the eye.

Edward smiled. "Yus, a girl en a boy. They be thriving. Will you come in fer a beer?"

This was pushing the good will too far for Thomas. He said quickly, "Nay, I'll be bodgen." He turned and climbed back onto the cart, waved and drove away.

The following March Herbert delivered three bushels of oats and fulfilled his debt. He was looking better than Edward had seen him for a long time. They had a beer together before Herbert went back to his farm.

"Us be a good team, Judith en me," he said. "En I be thankful ter have less work. Us haves time ter enjoy each other's company."

"Let's drink ter that." Edward raised his mug. This man had become one of his closest friends and he was delighted to see him happy.

Chapter Forty Two   1716 Summer

In which Old Ed Waghorn of Bewl Bridge is buried

Mary was expecting another child. She wouldn't be able to help on the farm this summer. The twins were on their feet and she and Tom were continuously rounding them up and bringing them back to the house.

Today it was pouring with summer rain. They needed it. The water in the well was low and the pasture was parched. They would have to supplement the cows' feed if the grass stopped growing. Corn and crops need rain as well as sunshine.

The children were in the hall where Mary could keep an eye on them. Tom sat at the table drawing on a slate, trying to make letters like his father. The babies were on the floor, surrounded by the wooden toys Edward had made. Mamie sat quietly turning a building block around in her hand, examining each aspect. She put it in her mouth, dribbling constantly, making everything she touched wet and sticky. Ted was making as much noise as possible, banging bricks together and on the floor, then on the bench, comparing the sounds. He crawled up to Mamie and banged a wooden brick on her head, triggering a scream of pain. This fascinated him. The sound was different to the others. He repeated the experiment, just as Mary came down the stairs with an armful of dirty clothes to be washed. Through his sister's screams, Ted heard his mother's voice.

"Ted! That be hem unfriend ter bannick thy sister. Adone!"

Ted was shocked to be told off. He was only playing. He threw the brick across the floor and accompanied Mamie's screams with his own.

Tom looked up from his drawing. His eyes met his mother's in exasperation and he got down from the bench, found Mamie's rag doll and walked it across the floor towards her.

Mary carried the laundry into the kitchen and came to fetch hot water from the stove. She didn't notice that Ted had crawled under the table. She turned with the full kettle and tripped over him.

She fell sprawling. The kettle flew from her hand, spilling its contents on the floor with a splash. Ted started screaming.

Mary's first thought was the safety of the child in her womb. But Tom was coming to help her.

"Don't touch the kettle, Tom!" she shouted.

Ted was hurt. She crawled over to see what it was.

The door opened and Edward came in to pandemonium. He stood, taking in the scene, then strode over to Mary.

"Ted's catched hurt! The hot water..." She caught her little son up into her arms and tried to calm him.

All the children were crying now, but Ted's screams were piercing. Mary attempted to prise his arms away from his face. She looked up at Edward.

"You take un while I gets to me feet," she said.

Edward took the little boy and crouched down to Tom. "You go en give Mamie a hug, while us sees to Ted."

Tom slipped easily into his caring role and went to Mamie, who was now sobbing and rubbing her eyes. He sat down on the floor next to her and put his arms round her in a hug.

Mary had gone into the kitchen to find her lavender salve. Edward followed her with Ted, who was still screaming. They took his arms away, revealing the cause of his distress.

From his eyebrow down the right side of his face, ending on his jawline, there was a red scald.

"Oh, my!" whispered Mary. "You poor love!" She gently spread the salve over the wound while Edward held Ted's arms. The lavender started to do its work and by the time Mary had finished Ted was calming down. She took him from his father and walked round the hall, rocking and soothing while Edward and Tom cleared up the mess and attended to Mamie. Soon they were all sitting on the bench,

Mamie in Edward's arms and Tom between his parents.

"Didst catch hurt, Muvver?" asked Tom.

"'Tis only me knees," she said.

He rubbed them and kissed them better.

"Time ter feed these nippers and put them to rest," Mary said.

"I'll take Tom along of me come coager," said Edward. "The rain's eased.

≈≈≈

Edward came back from the vestry meeting one Sunday. "Ed Wag'orn be ailing, Mary. 'E weren't at the meeting. I'll go over to Bewl Bridge 'sarternoon en see if I can do aught."

"Us'll all come," said Mary. "Us can take a liddle walk along the river while you be seeing the Wag'orns."

It was a lovely August afternoon. There was enough summer warmth lingering to keep it comfortable. Leaves were beginning to turn, birds twittered and swooped over the water and there was a plop now and then as a fish caught a fly, leaving a ring of ripples spreading across the surface of the river.

Tom ran on ahead while Mary held a little hand on each side of her. Ted kept stopping to pick up a stone, or to crouch down to watch a shiny blue beetle crawling across the path. Every time Mary looked at his scarred face she felt a wave of guilt. If only she'd looked where she was putting her feet... Mamie was content to walk alongside her mother, pointing out familiar things and saying their names, "Tree... duck... flower..."

Mary felt the child inside her shift its position and move its limbs across her belly. It wouldn't be long now.

Mary gave birth to Elizabeth before the harvest. She was small and frail. Her contant thin cries echoed round the house. Mary loved and nurtured her as best she could, but she could not take her milk as the others had. Prudence was helping out soon after the birth and saw Mary's concern.

"I reckon those twins took all yer strength," she said. "The poor liddle mite beant thriving."

Elizabeth faded away before the month was out. Edward and Mary laid her to rest in the church litten in Wadhurst, next to her stillborn brother.

The crying had stopped. Tom asked Mary, "Where be baby?"

"God has taken her, Son," she replied. "She weren't strong enough ter grow. She be safe now."

Only a few weeks later, Sarah Waghorn buried her husband. Mary and Edward went to the funeral, leaving the children with Prudence. Edward had lost a dear friend and counsellor. Ed had always been ready to give advice about failing crops or the health of the beasts. He'd saved Edward from a good deal of mistakes. There were many mourners and Edward suspected that he was not the only one who'd been helped by Waghorn's wisdom.

Sarah Waghorn was accompanied by her son. They came to speak to Edward and Mary after the service.

"This be my son, Ed," said Goodie Waghorn.

They all shook hands and Ed said, "I be main pleased ter meet ye. I've heard 'ow you've been friends with me farder fer many years."

Mary said to his mother, "I be hem ernful, Sarah." She took the widow's hand in hers and held it there. "Will you be orright by yerself, like?"

Ed said, "Muvver will come en bide with me. Farder let the farm go down en 'e advised we ter sell it. I have a working farm. I don't need two."

The old lady looked fondly at her son and said, "Ed will look after me. 'E be a good son."

"Us shall miss our little gossip in the litten of a Sunday," said Mary. "Do you bide in Wad'rst, Ed?"

"My farm's the other side of town, Ma'am. I'll bring Muvver to church now en then."

They all shook hands and Mary and Edward made their way home.

Chapter Forty Three   1716/7

In which William Ashdown gives advice

They dealt with their sorrow by putting all their strength into gathering the harvest, storing all the year's produce and taking stock of the beasts, selling some and slaughtering others for salting down.

The last day of the harvest, the whole family was there, cutting and stooking before the rain and the wind came. John, Richard, Sam and John Winder were reaping with Edward, while Mary, Meg and Prudence bound and stacked the stooks and kept an eye on the children playing at the edge of the field.

Edward took a break from his work and went to find a costrel of beer. As he sipped, he surveyed the golden scene.

A warm feeling of achievement and love for them all seeped through his whole being. He thanked God for his good fortune. The heavy weight of sadness over Elizabeth's death lay at the back of his mind, but he knew that Mary would bear him more children. His own parents had lost three girls before his brother Thomas was born. He was so proud of Mary. He watched her as she moved gracefully, stooping to gather the fallen stalks of wheat, skilfully binding them together and propping the bundle up against the others to form a stook. Her dark hair, tied back with a ribbon, fell down her back and the broad-brimmed hat shaded her face. She'd changed so much since the day he saw her walking up the lane to The Butts farm.

He went back to join the team, their sickles swishing rhythmically through the corn stalks as they moved forward as one, their harmonious voices singing harvest songs.

≈≈≈

The harvest supper was over, the children in bed. It was dark now, save for the light from the harvest moon which seemed to float across the sky with the skudding clouds. Mary stood at the kitchen door, watching Prudence and John Winder walk away across the yard to their home. Prudence had helped with the clearing up after supper; Meg was upstairs tucking Tom into bed; the men were in the parlour smoking their pipes, drinking and gossiping.

A roar of men's laughter reached Mary's ears. Tears welled up in her eyes. She had never felt so lonely. Her aching breasts, still producing milk, reminded her constantly of her lost baby, who'd left her imprint on Mary's nipples. She uncovered the throbbing lumps of flesh and expressed some milk to relieve the pressure, pouring it into a crock which she left by the door for the barn cats. Prudence had given her a potion to stop the milk coming but the effects had not yet benefitted Mary.

As she covered her breasts and wiped her wet face with her apron, she became aware of someone approaching from the hall. She turned and gasped. Was that Molly?

But no, the candle Meg was carrying lit up her young face; the image of her mother's.

"You be weeping, Aunt Mary." She placed the candle on the table and wrapped her arms round Mary. This produced another flood of tears. Meg was now as tall as her aunt and their relationship had changed as the girl matured.

"You be grievin' fer yer child," Meg said.

It was easier for Mary to nod her head in response than to try to explain all that she was feeling. She relaxed into the tender arms around her and remembered her dear friend Molly.

Meg poured a mug of beer for each of them and they went into the hall and sat down by the fire. Meg placed the mugs on the stove to warm. Mary mopped up her tears again.

"You be the bly of thy mother, Meg." She put her hand up and stroked the soft skin of the girl's cheek. It felt like a ripe plum before the bloom has been rubbed off. She smiled and kissed Meg's forehead.

"I were agwain ter ax you summat that's been on me mind, Aunt Mary." She hesitated.

"En what may that be, my love?" Mary grasped Meg's hand.

"Betsy, our housekeeper, when I were liddle, she muvvered me as best she could. But she beant a muvver. She tried to larn me all about what men do to women ter get babies, but I found out more watching the animals. I've seen our bitch Gemmy dropping blood when she be ready fer a mate and now I find blood coming from between my legs. Do that mean...?"

Mary stopped her there and started to explain what happens when a girl becomes a woman. Her mother had never been able to bring herself to talk about these things and Mary had always vowed she would not leave her own daughter in the dark. Meg needed her counselling too. They sat close together on the bench in the flickering candlelight, sipping their hot toddies and talking in low voices about women's things. Mary's heart lightened. She found it comforting to play the mother's part. Soon the talk drifted to other matters until the parlour door opened and Richard and Sam came in.

"There you be!" said Richard. "'Tis e'en a'most time us was bodgen, lass."

≈≈≈

Edward and his brother-in-law continued to work for each other and both their farms flourished. Edward started before sun-up every morning and was out all day, taking his bait with him. Mary saw nothing of him until sun-down, when he came in after washing at the well and collapsed into a chair, sometimes dropping off to sleep until Mary roused him for dinner.

After dinner he made a fuss of his growing children, playing with them and telling them stories until Mary whisked them off to bed before washing the dishes.

Edward was happy. His ambitions were fulfilled. If they had more children they would need to find a larger farm and start employing labourers. He'd always dreamt that they'd be able to move into Slade Farm in due course, but he couldn't turn his brother out, no matter how much mess he was making of running the farm. In the meantime the pot on the shelf was filling up and he could afford to buy better farm equipment and workhorses. Tom would be wanting a pony soon.

As soon as Mary had finished clearing up and washing the dishes after dinner, they were both too tired to sit and talk in the parlour. They trudged wearily up to bed. Edward looked forward to folding Mary's mature, curvaceous body into his arms. They felt so comfortable together. As the bed warmed up, so did his desires and it was not long before he was plunging his hard phallus into her juicy depths. He reached his climax and lay on her, relaxed in contentment, before he withdrew and allowed sleep to take over.

One day in April, Edward came home early. He and John Paris had been cutting and sharpening hop poles. They'd finished that task and it was too late to start the next job; putting the hop poles in the ground and tying up the bines.

He walked into his yard and splashed water over his face from the well bucket, then went into the house expecting to find Mary and the children. There was no-one there. He poured a beer for himself and sat out in the sun. There was something niggling in the back of his mind like a trapped gnat. What was it that Ashdown had said after last vestry meeting? He'd noticed that Mary was looking tired. Edward couldn't remember the last time he'd looked at her attentively. They were both so busy.

Ashdown's words came back to him. "It takes a lot out of a woman givin' birth. Be minded ter tend yer Mistus carefully. She won't let you down if you looks after un."

It was a strange thing for Ashdown to say to him. But he should know. He had enough experience.

John Winder came round the corner with a sickle. He looked surprised to see Edward.

"I finished early," Edward said. "You seen Mary en the liddle uns?"

"Last time I seed 'em they be headed over there." He pointed.

Edward nodded, put his empty mug in the kitchen and strolled towards the vegetable garden. A faint cry alerted him. Then he relaxed. It would be one of the children.

He came round the corner to find Mary with a sobbing Mamie on one arm, at the same time bending down to pick up the onion sets which had spilled out of the basket. Tom was encouraging Ted to gather the little onions and put them back. Ted was being rebellious and throwing the sets far and wide, laughing gleefully.

Edward shouted, "Ted! Stop that! Do as Tom says en help thy muvver."

Ted turned to see his father striding towards him. He ran away as fast as he could, tripped over and fell.

Mary straightened up, her hand on her back. She smiled bleakly at Edward and said, "My, you be come hem timely. We was abouten plant these sets." She handed Mamie over to him and went to see to Ted.

When she'd picked him up she walked him back to Edward. "You deal with un. I be all-in." She turned to help Tom gather the last of the onion sets and picked up the basket.

"That'll have ter wait 'til termorrer," she said and set off back to the house.

Edward followed with the twins, both subdued now. Tom walked behind his mother.

Mary busied herself in the kitchen. Edward settled the children in the hall with their toys. He could see things were not going smoothly. He went to Mary.

"Come en have a rest, Mary. We mun talk," he said.

"If I sits down now, I shall never get up. There be the dinner…" She looked up at him.

He could see tears in her eyes. He took the dishes and spoons out of her hands and put them down. He held her shoulders and steered her through the hall and into the parlour, where he sat her in a chair.

He went back into the hall and said, "I don't want to hear a squeak out of any of thee, d'ye hear?" They all looked at him and nodded.

"Yus, Farder," came the chorus.

Back in the parlour, he sat and held his beloved wife tight until she stopped sobbing. Then, while she dried her eyes, he started to talk.

"You be the most wunnerful wife in all the wurrell en the best muvver there ever was en I beant minded ter lose thee.The way you be agwain, you'll drive yerself into the ground. There won't be naught left fer meself when the children be growed. I be main ernful I didn't see it afore. I've been too wrapped up with me own work. I disremembered that us be a team en must work tergether.

"Most farmers' wives have a woman ter help with housework en whatever else needs ter be done. I be minded ter ask Prudence Winder ter help you reg'lar, like. Us'll pay her a wage like us do 'er son. What d'you say?"

Mary looked at him and nodded. She was still tearful. She struggled to speak.

Edward waited, holding her hand to encourage her.

She said in a very small voice, "Edward, I be quick with child again," and looked down at their hands, clasped in her lap.

≈≈≈

Prudence agreed to come and help Mary. She was glad of the money and she would be provided with clothes, as was the custom for servants. She didn't need to sleep in, as she lived so close, but every morning she was at the door before cock-crow.

Mary found that Prudence knew what needed to be done without being told and she would sometimes shoo Mary out of the house to have some time to herself. She would tackle any task and was as thorough and diligent as Mary would wish. She had two afternoons free every week to attend to her own family's needs.

Mary began to enjoy being a housewife and a mother again. She blossomed in her pregnancy and found Edward more attentive. But now, there were other things on her mind.

Chapter Forty Four   1717 Autumn

In which Edward and Tom visit Slade farm...

Edward and John Paris were working in Edward's fields, spreading dung and ploughing it in. John had brought along his labourer, Richard Stephens to help. Richard led the horse and cart in front, stopping now and then to allow Edward to heave the dung off the load with a grape and spread it on the ground. John held the plough while the oxen pulled it, following Edward. The plough shares sang as they sliced through the clay soil, leaving smooth, shiny ridges. The wind, frost and rain would spend the winter breaking up the clods.

Edward heard a shout and looked up to see John Winder approaching from the house. As he drew near, the wind carried his voice.

"Yer brudder be here with a load of hops, Mas Lucke. 'E wants ter speak with you."

Edward left his fork stuck in the load and trudged across the field. "I'll go en deal with un. You take me place a-spreadin', John." He kicked as much mud and dung off his boots onto the grassy verge as he could and made his way to the yard.

Thomas Lucke Senior was already off-loading the hops into the barn. He stopped when he saw Edward.

"This be the last load I can bring. There'll be no more hops. Me labourer's cut 'is stick."

Edward was concerned. "Why were that, Thomas? Can't you get another?"

"Nay, it be Esland. There be nabble in the village. So long as 'e stays, I can't get no labourers." Thomas lifted the last pocket of hops and carried it into the barn. He came back and climbed up to the driver's seat. "I can't do no more. I be jackin' up."

He drove away.

Edward stood and watched him go. All was not well at Slade Farm. He had to go and see if he could help. He felt responsible for Slade Farm. It had been the family home for four generations. His forebears had worked hard to build it up into a thriving farm. His brother had let them all down with his lazy, stubborn nature. When he died Slade Farm would pass to Edward. But Edward didn't want to inherit a failed farm.

The children burst out of the back door. The two three-year-olds ran screaming and shouting across the yard, followed by five-year-old Tom, wearing a lion mask and roaring, "I be a-comen ter eat thee!"

Mary came and stood in the open doorway, her hands on her hips, now heavy with child. She was laughing.

The twins ran three circuits round Edward, dodging Tom who pounced as they went past. Mamie hid behind her father, holding his legs, while Ted ran into the barn, not realising that he would be trapped in there. Tom followed and happy screams and giggles and more roaring reached their parents' ears.

Edward picked up Mamie, lifted her onto his shoulders and galloped round the yard, to shrieks of delight.

The two boys emerged from the barn, straw sticking out of them in all directions and saw what was happening.

"Me too, me too!" Ted shouted and chased after Edward.

Tom took off his mask and walked towards his mother.

"Well, well! I do believe 'tis my Tom en not a lion after all!" exclaimed Mary, bending down to hug him. "Be you over-growed ter play horses with Farder?"

Thomas nodded. "One day soon I'll have me own pony." He looked up and grinned at Mary and put his hand in hers.

Edward came and put Mamie down next to Mary. He lifted Ted and gave him a ride, then delivered him too.

"I be agwain back ter ploughing," he said. "I have me bait. I'll see you fer dinner." He planted two kisses on Mary's cheeks and walked back to the field.

Tom ran after him. "Can I come too, Farder?"

"Not this day, Son. There be naught you can help with. Mebbe I'll take you up to Slade Farm termorrer." Edward continued on his way.

It was not until the next week that Edward was able to visit Slade Farm. As promised, he lifted Tom onto the neck of the mare and mounted. They waved goodbye to Mary and the nippers. Edward swung Faithful round and they set off down the lane.

This was Tom's first visit to Slade Farm. On the way, Edward told his son about his childhood in Lamberhurst, about his brothers and sisters and about his brother Thomas who lived there with his wife, Eliza.

"Will there be children there?" enquired Tom.

Edward explained that his brother had no children. Then he said, "There be a farm labourer ter help yer Uncle Thomas with the work, as do John Winder fer I. 'E be called Esland. 'E has a wondrous ugly face en can't talk praper. But you have no need ter fear un. 'E be a kind en gentle man."

Tom sat quietly as the horse walked on.

Soon they came out through the trees to a view of the downs stretching into the distance. They came down the hill from the common and turned into the yard at Slade Farm. The geese made a fuss, but Tom showed no fear. They dismounted and shooed the birds away. The sound of men shouting came to them from the court. Edward went to the gate and lifted the latch.

Thomas Senior and Esland were in the throes of a fierce argument. Esland's noises were angry and he was shaking his head vigorously.

"Na! Na!" he seemed to say. His distorted face was bright red.

Thomas shook his fist at Esland. "You good fer naught! 'Ow d'you think the roof'll be fixed if you don't do it? I can't!"

A ladder stood up against the barn. Esland pointed up and shouted "Na!" He held his head and wimpered. Then he stamped his foot and stomped out of the court.

"If you can't do the work," Thomas shouted after him, "don't bother comin' back. You can starve fer all I care!" He threw down the hammer he was holding, looked at Edward and said, "What d'you want? Pokin' yer nose in, be you? Want ter see yer brudder in a hike so's you can have a laugh?" He went to get some tools out of the skillon and walked away towards the fields.

Edward and Tom stood for a moment in the silence. Tom said, "Can us go home now, Farder? I don't like it here." He came and took hold of Edward's hand.

Edward said, "Nay, Son. I mun go en talk to Eliza. You come indoors."

They entered the house. There was a smell of damp and the mud on the floors had spattered up to cover the walls. Cobwebs brushed his face as Edward went through into the parlour. The table was covered with the remains of the last meal and possibly the one before that. The windows let little light in. The smell changed to that of spoilt cooking. Eliza sat by the fire in the best chair, hugging herself and rocking backwards and forwards. She looked up.

Edward said to her, "I come ter see if there be aught I can do ter help."Then he remembered his son, still clinging onto his hand. "This be Tom, Eliza."

She stopped rocking and said, "I beant partial ter children, but 'e looks a fine boy. Sit down, the two of ye."

They sat gingerly on the bench by the table, which felt sticky to the touch.

"There be naught you can do, Edward. Thomas be lamentable ill-conditioned en Esland be gettin' the worst of it. There be no labourers will come near we. The villagers be nabble traps. They say 'e be a witch, or 'is muvver were. The men terrify un en 'e get's upset. There's been people catched mortaceous hurt en they say it be Esland putting a curse on 'em."

There was a noise of boots dragging on the floor and Thomas Senior came in carrying a tankard of ale. Edward looked at him in surprise.

His brother said, "I know. I started takin' me comfort in drink again. There be no other comfort round here." He went and sat down opposite Eliza.

She said, "You knows Esland can't go aloft, Thomas. Never has done. En if 'e went up on that roof 'e'd be that unaccountable afeared 'e'd not be able to do the work."

Thomas started shaking. He put his tankard down on the hearth. He doubled up, moaning in pain.

Eliza went and fetched a pail and put it by her husband's chair. He vomited into it and groaned.

Eliza sat down. "'E allus has stomach cramps after 'e's been at two with Esland. I don't know if it's the madness what do it, or the beer 'e beant accustomed to."

Tom had watched all that had happened with wide eyes. Edward saw the fear on his face and made a decision.

He stood up. "Us'll be bodgen. I don't rackon there's aught anyone can do to help you, Brudder. You be a cantankerous old mardy en I wish you good day." He took his son by the hand and they went out by the back door.

When they stepped out into the fresh air, he said, "Come, Son. I be minded ter have a look around while I be here." He led Tom round the court, looking in all the buildings. The hog pound had been abandoned, there was tackle for only one horse in the stable and the cow stalls were on the point of collapse.

A milking pail and stool occupied one compartment where there was hay in the rack.

They opened the door to the barn which had been left ajar. This was where the geese spent the night. Their mess had not been cleaned up for some time. A small amount of straw lay in a pile in one corner. In the corn store there was barely enough to get his brother and his wife through the winter, not forgetting that they fed Esland as well. A wagon full of hay occupied half the space and was in reasonably good condition.

The ground floor of the oast was cluttered with decaying farm equipment. Cobwebs adorned the rafters and a thick layer of dust covered everything.

"They don't tend the farm praper, do they, Farder?" said Tom.

"Nay," Edward replied. "'Tis hem ernful. My farder would be main ashamed. Come, I'll show you the woods."

They walked down the grassy whapple way, overgrown along its edges now. The hedges either side were ragged and breached in places. The echo of children's voices floated back to Edward; memories of days when they all helped with the coppicing, weaving hurdles and binding the brishings into faggots for the fire. Entering the wood, he remembered the charcoal burner and his pet; the mound of wood which smouldered away for days, to produce charcoal.

The copse was a tangle of brambles and wild clematis. The hazel stools were overgrown. They'd not been coppiced for a year or two. Some of the boles were rotting. Branches had fallen from the oak trees, breaking other branches off as they came down to block pathways.

Edward stood with his son and stared at the devastation and neglect. His eyes smarted with rising anger. A cold wind rustled the dead leaves and he shivered. This would have been a good farm to move his family to when they outgrew Savages. But his brother had allowed it to go to ruin. It would take years to bring it back into good condition. Thomas was the bain of his life.

But Edward still felt responsible for his brother's wellbeing. He pitied him for his shortcomings which were the cause of his downfall. If their father had left the farm to Edward...

"Come, Son," he said with a deep sigh. "Let's be bodgen."

They walked hand in hand back along the whapple way.

Chapter Forty Five

In which John gives advice

Mary woke early, before the winter sun had made its weary way into the leaden sky. She reached out and touched Edward's body beside her. His stertorous breathing became louder as Mary lay in the warm bed, reluctant to climb out. The child in the mound of her belly was waking up too and this became an urgent necessity. She lifted her legs over the side of the cot and reached for the chamber pot.

Her movements triggered the breaking of her waters and she hurriedly lifted her nightdress and sat down before liquid poured out of her. The next child had started its journey into the world.

Mary stayed on the pot for some time, gathering her strength for the familiar process of giving birth. She had no fear. The pain was almost a pleasure to bear. It was a creative process which was finite and there would soon be another child in her arms; a gift she would treasure; a little human with a whole life before it; a part of her and Edward.

But she knew that this child would also be another mouth to feed, another body to accommodate in this already crowded cottage. There would be more laundry and another little person to nurture and train.

Where would it sleep after it grew out of the crib? Where would she keep the extra clothes? She must talk to Edward.

She lifted herself carefully off the pot and lit a candle. She went to the table to swill cold water over her face from the jug and changed into her day clothes.

Edward stirred and sat up. "You be up en about a'ready," he commented, stretching and rubbing the sleep from his eyes, unaware that today he would be father of a fourth child.

"The birthen's started," said Mary. "But there be no hurry. 'E be takin' 'is time. I be agwain ter get meself a drink. Prudence will be here somewhen soon."

Edward leapt out of bed. He came to her and gave her a kiss.

She smiled and held his hand over her belly. "'Twill be orright this time, Edward, I knows it." She touched his cheek and kissed him again.

She took the candle and went through the children's chamber to the stairs. She stepped down one at a time, holding onto the rail that Edward had fixed there and walked through the hall to the kitchen. A touch of light in the sky showed over the barns. The cockerel was crowing and there was Prudence making her way towards her across the yard.

Mary opened the door and Prudence said, "The child be on 'is way, beant 'e?"

"How did you know, Prudence?"

"I knows," was all she would say.

They worked together in the kitchen, making porridge and pouring milk into mugs. Prudence took a faggot into the hall and brought the fire to life, then she went to rouse the children and prepare them for another day.

Edward came downstairs just as Mary sat down at the table holding a mug of milk.

"Watch that porridge on the stove, can you, love?" she said. She had felt the whisper of the first contraction.

Tom came down first, his mass of black hair tousled. He came to kiss his mother and she said to him, "Go en fetch the comb en I'll tidy you up."

He went into the parlour and brought the comb back. As she pulled it through his tangled hair, she said, "I be agwain ter birth a liddle brudder or sister fer you today, Son. Do yer best ter keep the twins in order, will you?"

Tom nodded and said, "This un won't die will 'e, Muvver?"

"Us'll do all us can ter nurture un into a strong en healthy child as you en the twins be. Now eat yer porridge."

The twins tumbled down the stairs in front of Prudence, who carried an armful of clothes.

"Us'll have ter hang these indoors when I've washed 'em," she said. "There be rain in the air."

Mary combed the twins' hair. Mamie's golden curls were down to her shoulders now. Ted wriggled and squirmed as his mother tried to smooth his fair hair into some semblance of tidiness, he would soon have a thatch like his father's. Edward served the porridge out and sat down. Prudence was starting the washing when John Paris knocked and walked in.

"It be rainin', Edward," he said. "Be you minded ter do the hedgen today?"

Edward finished his mouthful. "Nay, John. Come en sit. Now you be here we'll sharpen the tools in the skillon. Mary be abouten birth en I don't want ter go far abroad."

Mary said, "Will you have some porridge, John?"

John nodded. "Thanks, Mary," he said.

"I b'lieve you'll have ter get it yerself," she said, as the next contraction made itself felt. She got up and called,"Prudence!" and slowly made her way up the stairs. She had to lie down.

≈≈≈

As Prudence followed Mary, Edward and John were left in charge of the children. Tom finished his breakfast and got down from the table.

"Muvver said I mun look after the twins today," he announced. "Come, Mamie, let's find yer dollies."

The toys were on the floor by the stairs. Mamie and Ted climbed down from the bench and the boys started building castles. Mamie took her doll out of its crib and became involved with a pretend game of mothering.

John said, "You be main fortunate, Edward, with yer fambly around you en all. I be hem ernful I never found a girl ter make me Mistus."

"I be considerable proud of 'em, John. But this house will be too small fer me fambly anywhen soon. I were minded ter take Slade Farm on one day. 'Twould be good ter live in the old place again. Farder left it to me, after Thomas..." Edward felt his anger and frustration mounting, as he remembered the dilapidated state of the farm.

"Be yer brudder failin', then?" asked John.

"Nay, but 'e beant tenden the farm like Farder would wish. I've been thinking, mebbe I should've stayed en kept the farm a-going, as he wanted me to. 'Twould not have been in the hike it is now."

John had finished his porridge. He took a mouthful of beer and said, "But you wouldn't have met Mary, or me, if you'd stayed."

Edward shook his head. "Nay en if I had, I could never have took Mary to bide there with Thomas."

John said, "You can never go backwards, Ed. You have ter teck life as it do come. You've worked hard en brought this place on bravely. There'll be another place you can move to betimes you be ready."

Edward smiled at John. "You be a good friend, John. Come, we'll go en see to the tools. Tom, we'll be in the barn. You come en fetch me if you have need."

"Yus Farder," came the reply.

The two men went out into the pouring rain. They met John Winder on his way to fetch the cows for milking and waved as they ran round the corner to the skillon.

≈≈≈

Mary lay on her side, enjoying the warmth of Prudence's hands as she massaged Mary's back. The aroma of the herbal oils; Lavender, camomile and marjoram surrounded and calmed them both.

"Now turn to the other side," Prudence said.

Mary rolled over and felt another contraction start.

Prudence continued smoothing and kneading the muscles. "Breathe yerself through it," she murmured.

When Mary was lying on her back, Prudence told her she was going for a kettle of hot water. She left the room and Mary knew it would soon be time to start pushing.

Prudence came back. "I've told Tom to go en fetch 'is farder. Be you ready?" she said with a smile.

Mary said, "I be ready." She held onto the side of the cot and breathed through the next contraction, pushing when Prudence told her to. She let out a cry as the pain increased, shut her eyes and pushed.

The image of Prudence's smiling face stayed with her while she went along with the contractions and the pain. Prudence rarely smiled, she evidently enjoyed bringing children into the world. The next contraction bore down on her. And another...And another.

Mary concentrated on the process. Soon she felt the little body slither out of her and it was all over. Lying back, exhausted, she waited for the first cry. It seemed a long time coming.

She heard Prudence say, "Come along, liddle man. You can breathe

now." Mary was aware of the tension in the room. She opened her eyes.

Prudence was vigorously rubbing the baby with a towel, then hanging him upside-down and swinging him like they did with the lambs.

Mary's heart came into her mouth. Memories of her stillborn child came to her...

At last the baby spluttered and let out a long wail. Prudence laughed with relief, wrapped him up and handed him to Mary while she dealt with the afterbirth.

Mary sat up and gazed into the eyes of her newborn. He took a deep breath and his jaw shuddered. He screwed up his crinkled face and shut his eyes.

A rumble of feet came up the stairs.

"Wait a minute!" shouted Prudence.

When she opened the door the children burst in, followed by Edward. The twins scrambled onto the cot and crawled over Mary to see their brother. Mamie hugged him and planted a big kiss on his head. Ted looked unsure. He said, "'E ain't purty, like Elizabeth."

Tom said, "'E's got black hair like you en me, Muvver. What be 'is name?"

Edward came and bent over Mary to kiss her and took his new son into his arms. "I believe we'll call un John, after his uncle," he said.

Tom ran to the door and called, "Uncle John, come en see our baby brudder! 'E be called John!"

Chapter Forty Six   1717/8

In which Edward carries housel for Ed Waghorn

A week later Mary was sitting in bed, giving baby John his last feed of the day, hoping he wouldn't wake her too soon for the next one. Edward came up to the bed chamber, having checked the beasts and riddled the fires.

Mary said, "Edward, there be summat us mun talk about."

"What be that?" he asked as he took off his day clothes and climbed into bed. He lay with his hands behind his head and watched his son sucking hungrily at Mary's breast.

"The cot the children be a-sleepin' in, it be all of a solly. You fixed it in a rush when Sam en Meg came ter bide. I be worritted it'll fall to pieces somewhen soon. En when John be growed we'll have ter get another cot." Mary released the baby from her nipple and put him to the other breast. She waited for a reply.

There was irritation in his voice when he said, "I just now bought a harrow en there be naught in the pot. I put by enough ter pay Prudence en John fer a-comen ter help en I were minded ter start Tom at school come spring. I could fashion a couple of cots, but there be surmany other things ter be at on the farm..." Edward paused.

Mary said quietly, "En there be other things in the house needs fixen."

"Mm," he said. "I wish you'd told me afore I bought that harrow."

"How was I ter know you was agwain ter buy a harrow?" Mary allowed her voice to rise, then thought that they must not quarrel before sleeping. John had finished sucking. She took him off the breast, wrapped him up and laid him in his crib next to her. She leaned over to kiss Edward before she blew out the candle on the table and tucked herself in.

"I know you'll think of something," she said.

≈≈≈

Edward was angry. Mary had asked for the impossible. He was angry with himself for forgetting to include household needs in his plans. But why couldn't she have mentioned them sooner? He turned over with his back towards her. He knew she was right, but it seemed that however hard he worked and no matter how much money he earned it was never enough. He cursed himself for buying that harrow. It was a new idea, to make the job of sowing the seed easier in the spring. But he'd managed without before.

They had the winter to get through, but if he'd judged right they had enough supplies including salted meat, to last them until spring. He'd thought they wouldn't need much money, only what came from Mary's sales in the market. She used that to buy what they needed in the way of clothes. He and John Paris had settled all accounts and he knew no-one would employ him this time of the year, even if he had the time.

All night he thrashed around. The same thoughts travelled on a treadmill in his head with no solution.

The next morning he rose before Mary woke and went out to see to the beasts. Things didn't seem so bleak. Mary's needs were not life-threatening or urgent. The children's cot hadn't collapsed yet and what was the harm of them sleeping on the floor? He could fill more bags with hay and John wouldn't be ready for a cot for a few months.

The mending of the roof on the kitchen was far more urgent. The winter storms would blow it off if he didn't attend to it at once.

The baptism took place the following Sunday before the service. Mary and Edward were proudly showing off their latest addition to their friends when Goodie Waghorn approached them with her son, Ed. She looked frail and Edward thought she might not survive the winter.

Her son took Edward to one side and said, "We be clearin' the farm house at Bewl Bridge. There be some things that Muvver wants brought over to my house. Be you willin' ter fetch 'em in yer cart?"

Edward said, "Yus. Would one day next week suit?"

"That would be perfect. How about Tuesday?"

Edward agreed and they shook hands on it. That would be a day's wages, which would help.

It was frosty the next Tuesday when Edward drove down the lane on the cart. His breath rose up in clouds, dispersing in the cold air. The hedges sparkled in their covering of frost. As he progressed towards Wadhurst the sun shone through the trees and the blue of the sky intensified. He drove through the town, waving to folk who were preparing for another day, unlocking the shop fronts and businesses. Cousleywood Street was quiet, the only activity being around a wagon, delivering barrels of beer to the alehouse. Just before he reached Lamberhurst he turned down the lane to Bewl Bridge, a quiet little backwater with only a few houses and the river Bewl, which ran by the side of the road. Ed Waghorn was already standing in the yard. He was the image of his father except for his upright stance. Edward was reminded of the day they met at the farm sale, when he bought his first flock of sheep and Shep brought them home for him. He drove up to the door of the house and climbed down from the cart.

The two men shook hands and Ed said, "There be a few pieces of furniture Muvver wants for 'er chamber en I've bagged some chattels she needs."

They walked in. The house felt deserted, the air was stale and musty. Ed led the way upstairs to the chambers and they entered a homely but abandoned room with a bed surrounded by curtains, a chest of drawers and a washstand with a mirror over it. There were small rugs on the floor by the bed and a picture on the wall with a quotation from the Bible. A porcelain candle holder decorated with flowers stood on a small table.

So this was what Mary was hankering after, a bit of Quality. Edward would dearly love to give her these things, but he could see no way of fulfilling her dreams at present.

Ed showed him the furniture he wanted to move and they carried chairs and chests down the stairs and loaded them on the cart. There was bed linen and towels, pictures and a mirror, the candle holder, a little table from the parlour and a small number of books. Two bags full of what felt like clothes were the last to be brought out. Ed locked the door and mounted his mare, while Edward climbed up into the cart and clicked his horse into action.

They travelled back through Wadhurst and took the road towards Frant. Edward followed Waghorn to his farm. They came upon an imposing house which could have qualified as a mansion. Ed had done well for himself.

Goody Waghorn came to the door and greeted Edward. "I be hem thankful to you for fetchin' my things. Ed will show you where to put them. I want ter see you afore you go."

The two men unloaded the cart and left the housel in a wing of the house separate from the main building. Ed invited Edward to have a beer before he left and he accepted.

Ed led the way into the main parlour, where Sarah and her daughter-in-law were waiting. This room had soft furnishings in the fashion of Bathurst's parlour. Edward wondered if he would ever rise to this level of society. He wouldn't feel comfortable living like this, but he had no doubt it would please Mary. He couldn't imagine his children being allowed to run riot in these surroundings.

As Edward finished drinking his beer, Goody Waghorn said, "Now, Edward, I be minded ter give you en Mary summat ter remember we by. You have a growin' fambly en could do with some bits of furniture, surely, like cots fer the children en chests ter keep their riggin'. My house will be sold somewhen soon en I wants you ter go back there en load up yer cart with what you needs. Ed will come en help. En here's a shilling fer yer day's work." She got up with difficulty and put the money into his hand, closing his fingers over it.

Edward was entirely taken aback. "Oh Sarah!" he stuttered. "That be considerable kind. I don't know what ter say. My Mary will be wondrously pleasured."

"Not another word. You've both been good friends to Ed en me. 'Twill make me happy ter know me housel's gone to a good home." The old lady sank back into her chair with a sigh.

Edward went over to her and held her frail hand in his for a moment, before leaving the room with Ed, his head reeling.

Chapter Forty Seven   1717/8

A pony for Tom

It was nearly Christmas and John was thriving. The daily routine was back to normal. Mary counted her blessings daily, as Prudence quietly went about her work, attentive to everyone's needs almost before they knew it themselves.

"Go en get yer muvver a nice drink of milk before she feeds John,"she'd say to Tom. Or, when she could see mischief in Ted's eyes, "Ted en Mamie, come en help hang the washing in the yard."

Mary sat in the quiet parlour. She'd finished feeding the baby and was changing his clothes, ready for the night, tickling him and cuddling him, triggering a smile on his dimpled face.

Tom was by her side, handing her the clean garments and joining in the tickling. They heard a cart roll into the yard.

"Go en see if that's Farder, Tom,"said Mary. "'E be unaccountable late acomen home."

A few minutes later Tom came running back. His eyes were wide with excitement. He was breathless. "Farder's brought things but it's a secret. You mun bide in here 'til 'e be ready." He dashed out again.

There were no windows onto the yard in this room and Mary obediently stayed, bursting with curiosity. She could hear Edward's voice among creaking and banging, "Careful round that corner, John," and, "I've got it now."

Tom's voice piped up, "Where shall I put this, Farder?" A faint answer came from upstairs.

Mary wandered round the parlour in her impatience, holding the baby over her shoulder and rubbing his back.

Men's footsteps came down the stairs and she heard Prudence say, "Come, children, see what Farder's brought," then the sound of their feet climbing the stairs.

Finally, the parlour door opened and John Winder came through backwards, carrying something heavy. Edward followed with the other end of a beautiful red upholstered settee. They parked it by the door while Edward came in and moved the chairs, which looked so humble next to the newcomer.

Mary watched in astonishment.

Edward came in and kissed her. "Goodie Waghorn wanted we to have these from her house, to remember them by, like." He and John moved the settee to a place facing the fire and took two of the wooden chairs out into the hall.

"Those can go upstairs. There be a purty chair fer you, Mary, fer when you be nursen the baby." He went out into the yard.

The children came tumbling into the room. "Muvver, we've got praper cots!" said Tom. "I've got one fer meself!"

Mamie and Ted climbed up onto the settee. "Look, Tom!" they shouted. "A big chair!"

Edward carried an upholstered chair in and placed it by the fire where the other, wooden one had been. "There, Mary. Try that."

She went and sat in the new chair, sinking into the soft cushions. "Oh, my!" was all she could say.

Later, when Prudence and John had gone home and the family all sat around the table, having their meal in the hall Mary's head was still spinning with shock and excitement. They now had two beds in the children's room and a chest of drawers to keep their clothes in. Edward had hung a mirror in their chamber, over another chest full of their clothes. The rooms seemed smaller and more cramped with all this furniture but there was nothing hanging around in baskets any more.

"I be considerable grateful to Sarah Waghorn, Edward," said Mary. "I don't know what us can do to return the favour."

"They've got all they needs in that gurt house," said Edward. He thought for a moment, then said, "One of the barn cats be quick. Mebbe us could give she a kitten to raise 'er spirits."

≈≈≈

There was little to do on the farm. The wind and rain kept Edward indoors with his accounts, planning the next year's crops and playing with his children when his mind was not on other things. He rode over to Richard to tell him about his latest visit to The Slade.

The brothers sat in Richard's parlour where the fire blazed cheerfully, lighting up the brass candlesticks and warming their mugs of beer.

Edward took a mouthful of the comforting brown liquid. "I went to Slade Farm t'other day, Brudder. 'Tis in tarble disorder. Thomas jacked up a-workin' on the farm and the place be a-fallen down round un."

"You allus knew that'd 'appen," said Richard. "I don't unnerstand why you keeps a-worritten. Leave un be."

"Farder will be a-turnen in 'is grave. After all the hard work our Gaffer did ter bring it up from naught. 'Tis fambly property. 'E passed it to me in 'is will, after Thomas if un had no children." Edward took another gulp of his hot toddy and leaned forward on his elbows, shaking his head. "What a waste!"

"'Tis not your business no more, Ed. Farder's dead en it's all in the past. Turn yer mind to yer own farm en that wunnerful fambly of yourn. Thomas can lie in 'is own bed. How be that liddle nipper, John?"

Edward sat back in his chair, warming his hands on his mug. He sighed deeply and a smile crept to his lips. He gazed into the fire and said, "Bravely. 'E has the bly of his muvver. Smiling now, 'e be. Mamie can bring the purtiest chuckle out of un with 'er teasin' en ticklin'."

They talked about their children. Sam was a good worker on the farm. Meg was shaping up nicely and was nearly ready to take over the housework and cooking.

Edward's thoughts wandered back to Thomas. "Mebbe I shouldn't 'ave been so hard on un. Mebbe it would've been better if 'e hadn't had ter pay me what 'e owed."

Richard was getting impatient. He raised his voice. "'En mebbe he wouldn't have kept the farm a-going at all once Farder en Muvver had been putt in. Mebbe 'twere having ter pay his debts that kept un going. Now leave it.

"When be young Tom a-starten school?"

Edward cleared his throat. "Come spring when the weather's better. 'E be anxious ter larn. I be minded ter buy un a pony. That'll keep un busy."

"I knows a man wanten ter sell a nice pony to a good home." Richard described where the man lived. "'E be called Bassett, Abraham Bassett."

Edward drained his mug and rose to go. "Thanks, Richard," he said. They shook hands and Richard came with him to the door. Meg was in the buttery and she called out, "Goodbye, Uncle," as they passed.

It was not far to the man with the pony. Edward knocked on the door but there was no answer. He wandered round to the back of the house and found a man mucking out the stables.

"I be a-seeken Abraham Bassett," said Edward.

The man stopped shovelling and came to meet him. "I be that man," he said.

"I be avised you've a pony fer sale," Edward said. "Can I have a look?"

Abraham leaned his shovel up against a door post. "This way," he said and went to a gate in the yard which led to a pasture. Several horses stood cropping the grass, one or two of them of good breeding. Among them was a small black pony.

"I want a pony fer me son ter larn on. Be 'e gentle?" Edward asked.

Abraham approached the pony and clicked his tongue. The pony lifted his head and came trotting up to the two men. Abraham produced an apple from his pocket and gave it to the animal. "Jackanapes be 'is name," he said. "I had un fer me darter... She died." His voice broke as he said it and he coughed. "Gentle as they come."

Edward stroked Jackanapes' nose and asked how old he was. He looked at his teeth and eyes and checked his legs and feet. "How much d'you want fer un?"

"'E be two or three year," the man said. "I'll teck fifteen shillen if that be agreeable."

Edward nodded. "That be main agreeable. I'll teck un now."

They led the pony to the stables and Abraham found his bridle and saddle. "'E'll be pleased ter be ridden again," he said as he fitted them.

Edward took Jackanapes to meet Faithful. He mounted and said, "I'll bring the money termorrer."

Mistus Bassett was standing in the doorway watching them go. He waved and left the yard, leading the pony.

Part Three

Chapter Forty Eight   1718

Tom's voice.

I search for the apple in my pocket to give to Jackanapes. I'm glad to be finished with school today. It's too hot to be indoors and I long to have a cool breeze on my face. Jackanapes' eyes are covered in flies. I wave them away with my hat before I put it on my head. He is pleased to see me. He crunches the apple with his teeth and nods his head.

Stephen Bassett comes towards me. He's a big boy.

"That pony were my sister's," he says.

"Be yer sister too big fer un now?" I ask.

"Nay. She died."

I be main ernful ter hear this. "I'll tend un carefully fer un," I say.

Stephen looks down and kicks a stone. Then he looks at me. "You was larfen when I were mimicken Mr Hunt." He smiles.

I giggle. "I couldn't stop meself. He were mad at us both!"

He turns and waves goobye.

I think of him checking Mr Hunt behind his back and laugh to myself. He's good at copying people. He and some of the other big boys are always in trouble.

I jump onto my pony's back and guide him to the road home. I learned to write some more words today and Mr Hunt says I must practise them. I will if Ted leaves me alone. He's always teasing me and Mamie.

The pony's hooves clatter on the cobbled yard. I tether him and go to find a cool drink. Muvver is in the kitchen, getting the meal ready. She stops when I come in and kisses the top of my head without touching me with her sticky hands. She's my favourite person in all the world.

"How was school?" she asks.

I tell her about Stephen being naughty. "I laughed at him en Mr Hunt shouted at me," I say.

Muvver tuts.

There's a scream from the hall. I go and see Ted running away with one of Mamie's dolls. I chase after him and I get the doll and give it back to Mamie. Ted thumps me and I push him over. He grabs my feet and we fight on the floor.

Muvver comes in. "Go out into the yard and cool off, both of ye!" she shouts.

I get up and run outside. Ted follows. He grabs hold of my arm and bites me. I get hold of him to bite him back. We fight on the cobbles. Ouch! That hurts. I have him pinned down. He screams. I let go and walk away.

I don't like fighting. But Ted makes me angry when he attacks me or teases Mamie. I can't let him get away with it. But he's my brother and I don't want to hurt him. I don't like hurting anything. Even the corn when it's cut, I wonder whether it's hurting.

I take Jackanapes to the pasture. He drinks water from the trough and I caress his face and ears, laying my cheek on his muzzle. He's my friend.

I think of Stephen's sister.

Baby John is my favourite brother. He's peevish in the hot weather. I rock his crib and watch his little legs kicking. His face is bright red with crying. I go and find a wet cloth to bathe his face like I've seen Muvver do. He calms down. By the time Muvver calls us for our dinner he's asleep.

Farder comes in. His face and hair are wet from the well. His shirt's wet too. It makes me want to go and wash myself all over. Maybe I will, later.

Muvver doles out slices of roast chicken for all of us and some beans and peas from the garden. The twins eat with their fingers and a spoon. I'm learning to use a knife and fork. It's what Muvver wants me to do, but it's too slow. When she's not looking I take a handful of peas and put them in my mouth, quick.

Farder says, "We be haymaking termorrer, Tom. Be you agreeable ter come en help?"

That's good news. I like working with Farder in the fields. He's my hero. I feel safe with him. I like it when he teaches me things about husbandry. "Yus, Farder," I say and I smile at him.

'Tis the end of summer now and we're harvesting every day. Muvver and Prudence, the twins and baby John, we all go up to the field where the men are cutting the corn. John can sit up and he crawls around. Mamie stops him going too far and comes to tell us when he gets upset. We're busy collecting the corn into stooks. Ted wanders off looking for bugs and beetles and I have to go and bring him back. He doesn't like that and tries to get away. He is a naughty boy.

I don't think Muvver and Farder are happy together. They don't kiss like they did before John was born and Muvver has black rings round her eyes. Farder is short with her as if she's done something wrong. I don't understand. Prudence says they're just going through hard times.

I'm returning from another day at school. It's raining. On the way up the lane to Savages I see the man Esland, carrying a bundle on a stick over his shoulder. I get home before him. I take Jackanapes straight into the stable. I rub him down and give him a bag of hay, then I go indoors. Esland is coming round the corner.

I remember Esland from the day we visited Slade Farm. Farder said he was kind and gentle, but when I saw him he was angry. Uncle Thomas was being unkind, telling him to climb the ladder onto the roof to mend it. Esland was afraid of going up there. I wonder why he's here. I go and find Muvver and tell her.

She says, "Oh no!" as if she's frightened. Her face turns white. "Go en seek yer farder en tell un Esland's here."

I run out into the yard. The rain is pouring down. Farder has found Esland and they're standing there getting wet. Esland's pleading with Farder, his hands together as if in prayer. I go back into the house and change into dry clothes. Then I lie on my bed and think about what's happening out there in the yard and Muvver's white face.

Chapter Forty Nine   1718/9

In which Esland comes to stay

"Nay, Esland, I've no work fer you. Thomas needs you at Slade Farm." Edward looked at the dripping dwarf. He couldn't send him all the way back to The Slade in this rain.

Esland was shaking his head. "Na, na. 'E no 'ork. 'E angy." He indicated that Thomas had sent him away. He put both hands on his chest, then under his reclined head as if in sleep, pointed to the ground and said, "I here." Tears joined the rain running down his pitiful face.

Edward led the way to the barn and opened the door. "Gimme yer bundle en I'll ax Mary ter dry yer riggin'." He held out his hand.

Esland took hold of the bundle and withdrew it as he stepped into the barn. "Na, na." He indicated that he would hang things up on the rafters to dry. He struggled to enunciate clearly, "Nash Ed'rd, you goog nan." He grabbed Edward's hand and shook it vigourously.

Edward said, "Us'll talk about it in the marnen, Esland. I be making no promises. I'll ask Mary ter leave yer dinner by the door when it be ready." He left the barn door open to let in the last vestiges of light and walked slowly to the house. How was he going to break the news to her?

"E can't bide here! You don't have no work fer un en that'll be another mouth ter feed over winter. You knows I can't abide havin' un around the place. There allus be trouble when 'e be here." Mary stood across the table from Edward, wringing her hands in her apron, shouting her protests at him; something she'd never done before.

"I can't unnerstand why you be so snuffy," he said. "'Tis not as if you be with child. 'E'll keep out of yer way."

Mary scoffed, "It be hem fortunate that I beant with child. I've had enough! En I don't want un frittin' the children..." She threw up her hands in exasperation. "Oh, you'll never unnerstand!" She turned away and went upstairs.

Prudence came through the kitchen door, took in the scene knowingly and walked quietly past Edward towards the stairs.

Edward went out to the barn to talk to Esland.

Esland was adamant he would not go back to Slade Farm. He kept repeating the demonstration that he was going to stay at Savages, with or without work. He spent the next few days making himself comfortable in the abandoned shepherd's hut; cleaning it out and filling a fresh straw mattress, collecting wood and getting the fire going. He mended the leaky roof. He kept right out of the way of the family and any work that was going on. Now and then he caught a rabbit and left it by the back door, skinned and cleaned. He washed his clothes occasionally at the well and hung them over the bushes to dry. The family were aware of his presence but the children were told to keep away. Mary left a pot of food by the back door every evening. It was returned empty and clean.

One day Edward caught sight of him walking down the lane. He didn't return until evening, carrying a full bundle over his shoulder.

Edward couldn't keep the man out of his thoughts. He wondered what happened at Slade Farm to cause Esland's departure. Edward was paying his sister Ann rent for her cottage for Esland's use. He would continue paying in the hope that Esland would one day go back.

The winter rolled in, with frosty nights and wet days. Edward decided to go to The Slade and find out what was going on. He went to the shepherd's hut. Esland was chopping logs. He looked up as Edward approached.

"I be minded ter happen by The Slade 'smarnen, Esland. D'you want ter come along of me?"

Esland shook his head. "Na, na," he said.

Edward said, "I beant abouten send you back there, Esland. I thought mebbe you'd want summat from the cottage."

Esland continued shaking his head and Edward left him alone.

He went and saddled up Faithful and rode off down the lane.

He found Thomas and Eliza in their parlour, snoozing by the fire. The place smelt fusty and uncared-for. Had they lost all their self-esteem? How could they live like that?

"Be ye ailing, the two of ye?" he asked.

"No more'n usual," replied Thomas.

"I be come ter find out why Esland left so sudden."

"Oh, so 'e be come ter your place. Badgerin' fer work, I shouldn't wonder."

"Nay," said Edward. "'E beant badgerin'. 'E be bidin' in the shepherd's hut. Don't want no work. Won't come back 'ere. What happened?" He stood in the doorway, reluctant to come into the room.

Eliza spoke up. "'Twas Thomas druv un away, with his beatin', hollerin' en insults. I rackons Esland just couldn't take no more, like."

"Don't you need un here, ter fother the beasts en all?"

"Us ain't got no beasts. A cow en me mare, that's all. Us'll manage." Thomas hoisted himself out of his chair and went to put a log on the fire.

Edward felt helpless. Richard was right. Their brother had brought himself and his wife to this level of neglect through his own cussedness. There was no more to be said. He left Slade Farm feeling depressed. He wouldn't bother going there again. There was no hope of Thomas ever being able to pay his debt to Edward now. It didn't seem to matter any more.

On his way home his thoughts turned to Mary and his relationship with her. He'd tried being loving and kind and she continued to turn her back on him every night. He felt rejected and found himself speaking roughly to her. How could things be going so wrong? They had their health, a lovely family and the farm was producing enough to feed them all and put some money in the pot in case of hard times. The children were happy and Mary had help now. They had all they wanted. But the love seemed to have slipped out of their lives like a will-o-the-wisp.

She was tolerating Esland, but Edward suspected she was still angry with him for allowing the man to stay.

And what was that she said about having '*had enough*'? Enough of what?

≈≈≈

Winter released its grip and spring began to lift their spirits. Mary was acutely aware that Edward and she were leading more seperate lives. They'd fallen into a rut of cool compromise, both being careful not to tread on the other's toes. They spoke respectfully to each other and discussed family matters reasonably. But there was no intimacy, no kisses and cuddles. The longer it went on, the more difficult she would find it to reconcile the situation.

She was consumed with guilt but her instincts kept telling her, 'no more'. Every time Edward made a move towards her in their bed, she couldn't help turning away. She knew she should tell him what the problem was but she was afraid he wouldn't understand and would feel even more rejected. Time went on and they became more and more distant.

And now there was Esland. She shuddered to think of her children's reaction if they caught sight of his hideous face. She felt sorry for the poor man and he was keeping right out of their way. But the time would inevitably come when they would meet, especially now the weather had improved. The children would be going outside to play. Edward was taking Ted out with him on the farm some days, but Mamie and John were at risk.

It was time she went to help Prudence with the cheese-making. She glanced at the reflection of her care-worn face in the mirror and sighed before leaving her place of refuge in the bedroom to make her way down the stairs.

Prudence was straining the first batch of cheese through the muslin. "The sun be shining bravely," she said. "I let Mamie take Johnny ter feed the fowls. Mamie knows what ter be at en I'll go drackly ter make sure they've closed the gate." She hung the muslin bag over a basin to catch the drips and dried her hands on her apron.

Mary stood in the empty kitchen. It was quiet without the children. She went to prepare another batch of cheese for straining, enjoying the tranquillity.

Prudence came back. Her brow was wrinkled.

"The children be missin'," she said. "The gate be closed en they be nowhere to be seen."

Chapter Fifty   1719

In which Mary is in a dilemma

Prudence was never worried. Memories came back to Mary of the day Peg went missing. That time, she was the one who had to keep calm and positive. But these were <u>her</u> children. Panic rose to her throat.

The two women left the house and ran across the yard in the direction of the chicken run. They stopped and looked around them for signs of life. Then Mary remembered.

"Esland," she said.

They ran towards the field where the shepherd's hut was parked, hidden from their view by trees and bushes.

Prudence had never met Esland. She knew nothing about his history or the reason for his being here.

When they came closer the sounds of children's voices reached them. They were chatting happily. Prudence stopped Mary from going further.

"Listen," she said.

"Can you make me a doll?" Mamie's voice piped up.

"Me too," shouted John excitedly.

They heard Esland's growly voice, softly gentle and laughter from the children.

Prudence said quietly, "There be no harm in un, Mary. En the children beant frit. Come en see."

They found Esland sitting on the top step of the hut, the children on the bottom step, at his feet. Esland had a whittling knife in his hand, carving animals out of pieces of wood. He held out a horse to John, who took it and trotted it across Esland's thigh, laughing happily.

As the women approached the threesome looked up.

Mamie got to her feet and ran to her mother, "Muvver! Look what the man made. She took Mary's hand and pulled her to meet Esland, who was standing now.

The two looked into each other's eyes. Mary recognised kindness.

"Nishtush Ucke," Esland spluttered. He pointed to the two children and chuckled, hugging himself.

The last time they'd seen each other was when she'd been afraid of letting him see the baby twins.

Mary saw a different Esland now. Or was it herself who'd changed? She laughed with relief. "You be a kind man, Esland." She went and shook his hand, then gathered her children to her. "Say thank you to Esland," she said.

They responded and Mamie asked, "Can us stay en watch, Muvver?"

"Nay, Mamie," she said. "You can come en see un another time." She wanted the children close to her after the shock of their disappearance. Mamie might want to talk about Esland's face.

She was still not quite sure how she could trust Esland.

As spring turned into summer, Esland became part of their surroundings. The children accepted him as a friend and they often went to see him in his hut. He whittled more toys and showed Tom how to kill a rabbit with the catapult he made for him.

Edward found that Esland was lending a hand with small jobs without being asked and John Winder struck up a jolly relationship with him. They were often heard laughing together.

Mary's fears melted away. She began to relax in the sunshine with her happy family. Johnny was growing up and becoming quite a little character.

One day, after coager, she found herself sitting at the table with Edward. Everyone else had gone out, including Prudence.

Mary looked at her husband directly for the first time for weeks, maybe months. He looked lonely and vulnerable and her heart went out to him. She got up and went to sit next to him. Her arm crept round his waist and her other hand found one of his.

"Edward, my love," she said. "I be main ernful that we be a'most strangers these days. It be my fault.

I were anxious not to get quick again so soon after John..." She gulped. Her heart beat in her ears, not knowing what Edward's reaction would be.

He sighed deeply and turned to her. With his free hand he lifted her chin and kissed her tenderly on the lips. "I should've knowed," he said. "It beant all yer fault. I should've thought about thee instead of how I were feelin'. I've missed our embraces, surely. Can us not do that en love each other without coupling?"

Silent tears rolled down her cheeks. She said, "I dunnow. 'Tis the urge ter couple that drives a man on. 'Tis nat'ral." She paused. "I do miss the lovin' too." She allowed herself to be enfolded in his arms for the first time since she stopped feeding John. It felt good. They were both aroused.

She gently pulled away from him before his passion got the better of him. "I do love you, you know that, don't you, Ed?"

He nodded and said, "I'll wait fer you ter say the word, Mary." He got up from the table and said, "I be agwain back to the field." He took hold of her hand and kissed it before striding out into the sunshine.

Mary sat still for some time, adjusting her thoughts and feelings. Did Edward really understand? Should she stop being stubborn and submit herself to the possibility of having another child? Of course she enjoyed making love and coupling with Ed. Would it jeopardise the relationship she had with him to expect him to abstain? Should she leave it in God's hands and fulfil her wifely duty? She was well recovered from Johnny's birth and another child would not make a lot of difference. Tom and the twins were more independent and Ted would soon be starting school. That would be a relief.

The tension drained from her body. What will be, will be, she said to herself.

Before the cattle came back from the pasture for the winter, John Winder and Esland were cleaning out the barn. There was little straw left from last year's harvest and this year's had not yet been inned.

Mary stood at the back door, watching the children play in the yard. It had been a hot day but the sun was already on its way to bed and they were dispelling the last of their energy as the air cooled. Tom chased Mamie and Ted and Johnny kept jumping out at them from behind the well as they came past.

The two men emerged from the barn, covered in dust. Esland held a bat and ball. He brushed off the spiders and their cobwebs and showed them to Tom.

"Us found they hidden in a corner," said Winder. "Must 've been there fer years."

Tom's eyes lit up." Us could play stoolball, or cricket!"

Esland clapped his hands.

"Let's go to the pasture where the hay's been cut!" Tom shouted.

"What's cricket?" Ted asked.

"You'll see." Tom took the bat and ball and they all raced off to the pasture, Mamie leading Johnny by the hand.

Mary smiled.

Prudence came through from the hall. "I'll be bodgen, Mary."

"Teck one of they loaves," Mary said. "We'll do some more baking termorrer."

Prudence nodded her thanks and made her way across the yard with her bread.

Mary went to feed the fowls, feeling slightly uncomfortable with no children round her. She stopped to listen to the crooning of the hens while they picked up the grain. They'd left eggs in their nesting boxes and she thanked them.

Back in the house, she put cold meat, pies, cheese and pickle on the table ready for dinner and covered it all with a cloth. Then she strolled out to see her family playing cricket.

The pasture resounded with childrens' voices. The setting sun lit up their faces with golden light.

"Run! John, run!"

"Over here, Ted!"

Clapping and cheering as one of them was bowled out. Esland was proving to be a ferocious bowler. Tom stood at the other end of the wicket, ready to hit the ball as it flew towards him. He gave it a swipe, but missed and John, standing behind, caught it in the air to more shouts and cheers, then it was Ted's turn to bat. Esland sent a gentler ball and, much to his own surprise, Ted thwacked it hard and it went hurtling over the field.

Edward had appeared when they weren't looking. He caught the ball while Ted's legs carried him the full length of the wicket before Esland had it in his hands again. Everyone shouted and jumped up and down.

Mary had been so absorbed that she hadn't looked to see where little Johnny was. Mamie was the other side of the field, waiting for a ball to come her way and there was Johnny by her side, sitting in the grass.

Edward came over to her. "Come, hitch up yer skirts en join in," he invited and held out his hand to pull her up from her seat on the grass.

Mary had never played cricket, but she might as well have a go.

Tom saw her coming towards the wicket and called, "Muvver, come en hold the bat. I'll show thee."

Everyone had a turn, batting and bowling. There were no teams, no scoring and they played until they were exhausted. Johnny had fallen asleep on the grass. Edward picked him up and carried him indoors. Hands and faces were washed in the well bucket. John said goodbye and went off home. Esland waved and strode off to his hut. The family went indoors and tucked into their meal, chatting about the fun they'd had.

At last the children were fast asleep and Edward and Mary took a last drink of beer into the parlour and sat together on their settee. Edward's arm found its way round Mary's waist and she settled her head on his shoulder.

"Be you happy, Mary?" asked Edward.

She chuckled. "I be wondrous happy, Edward."

That night they made love.

Chapter Fifty One   1720

Tom's voice.

Now that Ted's coming to school with me, we have to walk up the road. I miss the ride into Wadhurst on Jackanapes. But we meet the other boys going to school and I'm getting to know Stephen Bassett. He has two brothers working for their father and three others; Nicholas, Thomas and William, the youngest, who come with us.

Stephen's talking to me about his father's horses. He breeds them for Quality folks.

"Come en see 'em after school one day," he says.

I'm very excited. "Yus, I'd be partial ter that," I say. "I'll take Ted home today en ask Muvver."

Ted is poking the boy sitting next to him. They whisper together. Mr Hunt has his back turned and we're all supposed to be figuring our numbers on our slates. I'm afraid Ted is planning something naughty with his friend so I put my head down and wish he wasn't my brother. I try and do my figuring.

There's a shout and a scream. We all look up and Mr Hunt turns round. William Bassett is standing on his chair. A big black beetle runs across his desk. We all wait to see what Mr Hunt will do.

He strides across the room and swipes at the beetle. It falls on the floor and he stamps on it. Ted and his friend are giggling. William climbs off his chair and Mr Hunt goes to Ted.

"Did you bring that creature in here, boy?"

Ted opens his eyes wide and shakes his head. "Who? Me? Nay, Sir."

But Nicholas, William's big brother says, "Mr Hunt, Sir, I seed Edward Lucke put the beetle on my brudder's desk."

Mr Hunt gets hold of Ted's clothes at the back of his neck. He picks him out of his seat and marches him to the front of the class. Ted squeals with fright.

Mr Hunt says, "Bend over, boy." He pulls Ted's breeches down and says, "Observe closely, boys. This is what happens to anyone who disrupts the class." He takes a long, whippy hazel rod from its place against the wall. I can't watch.

There's a noise of sharp thwacks and Ted crying. It seems to go on and on.

When it stops I open my eyes. Ted's buttocks are very red.

Mr Hunt says, "Pull up your rigging and stand there." He points to the corner of the room.

For the rest of the day, Ted stands in front of us. He is crying at first, but then just shuffles his feet and sniffs. At the end of school Mr Hunt hands a sheet of parchment to him. "You will take this home and learn all of it. I will hear you recite it in front of the class on

440

the morrow. That is punishment for bearing false witness."

Ted whines all the way home. When Muvver sees his buttocks she gasps and gets some salve to put on the wounds

I ask her if I can go and see Bassett's horses.

"Yus, Tom, but be back fer dinner. If you go on yer pony it'll be quicker coming home."

I run out to Jackanapes in the pasture and take him to his stable to be saddled. We trot down the lane and find Stephen waiting. He walks alongside to his father's farm. I leave the pony tethered in the yard and he takes me to the paddock. There are some fine horses grazing there.

"There be the sire." Stephen points to a big shiny black stallion and we walk over to him. He's twice as tall as me. I touch his coat and his skin twitches. He turns round and brings his nose close to my face. My chest thumps as I put my hand up to touch his muzzle which is soft and warm. He blows through his nostrils and my hair flies up. I laugh.

"'E be a handsome beast," I say.

"Those be 'is mares," says Stephen, pointing to two smaller horses, one black and one brown. "There be anudder in the stable. Her be in season, bidin' fer the right time ter be sired."

"Will 'er be with foal?" I ask.

"Behopes so. If her takes 'twill be about a year afore her births."

"What be 'er called?"

"Withy."

"Will you tell me when 'er's abouten birth?"

"Yus, I'll mind that."

We walk across to the mares and Stephen tells me their names; Bethwine, Blubottle and the stallion is Ash. Then we go and see the mother of my pony. She's called Sissel. I give her the apple I had in my pocket. We walk back to the yard where Jackanapes is tethered. The other boys are there, stroking and patting him. They remember him from when their sister rode him. He's enjoying the attention.

"Thank you, Stephen," I say. "Can I come en see them again?"

Stephen nods. "Us could go ridin' tergether sometime."

"Yus, I'd like that. I'll be bodgen now." I mount my pony and wave goobye to the brothers.

Ted didn't go to school for three days. He couldn't sit down and had to stand at the table to eat his meals.

"I don't ever want ter go to school again," he says.

Farder is stern. "You will go to school and you had better be quick a-larnen those Ten Commandments. Tom will hear you recite them."

Oh dear, that will be middlin' tedious.

442

It's summer now and we're all busy. When I'm not at school I'm helping Farder in the fields with Ted. Esland's helping too. We make a good team with John Winder. Esland and John are funny together. They keep checking each other and have wrestling matches. John's not a boy any more. His beard is thick and curly brown and his hair's the same. Now and again Prudence cuts it short.

The women are busy as well, making cheese and butter and a-going to market. Mamie helps them and looks after Johnny who runs around and gets into mischief. Muvver is with child. I think she'll birth before Withy. She and Farder are loving each other again.

Chapter Fifty Two 1720 September

In which Edward is devastated

Esland had been missing from their lives recently. Edward hadn't seen him for a few weeks. He was taking his meals from the back door as usual and returning the clean pot. A light flickered from the shepherd's hut in the evening. Edward wondered if he was keeping out of the way, knowing that Mary was due to deliver their child and not wanting to upset her.

Edward had never seen Esland as happy as he had been that year. The family had taken him to their hearts and his quaint personality had brightened their days. He made them laugh and he laughed with them. He refused payment for his work. John Winder said he hadn't quarrelled with his friend, so that was not the cause of his hiding himself away. He'd helped with the harvest and when all was inned, he'd deserted them. The children asked after him constantly.

They were having coager one day and Mary's birthing pains started. Tom and Ted were at school. Prudence helped Mary to the bed chamber, then came down and took Mamie and Johnny into the autumn sunshine. Edward sat at the table and savoured the quiet, expectant moment before he too left the warmth of the hall and went to join John Winder in the vegetable garden. There were pea and bean haulms to dispose of and some digging to do. They would be near enough to the house to hear any news.

He enjoyed this time of the year. The damp earth yielded to the pull of the haulms and the thrust of the spade, exhuding a rich aroma of decay. Steam rose into the cold air from the compost heap. They'd been adding horse dung to the waste from the kitchen and it was rotting fast. The winter weather would creep up on them suddenly this year. The next task would be some restoration work on the shed behind the barn before the roof collapsed. He kept the farm machinery in there and he didn't want it to get wet.

Tom and Ted came up the lane as Edward crossed the yard. They all came into the house together. Edward took his muddy boots off and poured himself a beer before following the boys into the hall. Prudence was there taking the kettle off the stove. Her face was red and her sleeves were rolled up.

"Not long now," she said as she went upstairs.

Tom put his school bag down on the bench. "Be Muvver a-birthen?" he asked.

"Yus," said Edward. "Started coager time." He went into the parlour where Mamie and Johnny were drawing pictures on a slate.

Tom went to get himself a drink of milk and followed Ted into the parlour. "Muvver's a-birthen," they said together.

They sat on the sofa. Edward took a sup of beer and said, "What did you boys larn at school today?"

Tom said, "I be larnen pounds, shillens en pence."

"Good," said Edward. "Dost know how many pence make a shillen?"

"Twelve," answered Tom.

"You'll soon be helping me with the accounts." Edward was pleased that Tom was showing promise at school. "En Ted, canst count up to twenty yet?"

Ted counted well until he reached thirteen. He shrugged his shoulders and looked at the floor.

"When you can count up to twenty, I'll give you a penny," Edward said.

A distant wail interrupted the conversation. They all looked up and Tom started for the door.

"Wait until Prudence calls," said Edward.

All was quiet. The family waited. It seemed a long time, Edward thought. Maybe there was something wrong. Fear crept into his heart.

Then another cry reached them and they heard Prudence open the door of the chamber.

"Come en see," she called.

The children raced each other for the stairs. Johnny was knocked over and Edward picked him up and carried him.

"Gently, gently," he heard Prudence say as the children clamoured to get into the room. By the time Edward went in they'd climbed onto the bed.

Mary was not smiling. She looked at Edward with sad eyes. The baby had stopped crying.

Prudence said, "It be a boy, Mas Edward."

Tom said, "'E looks like a pig," and giggled.

Ted and Mamie giggled too. There was tension in the room.

Edward said, "Tom, you get off the bed now en let Johnny en me have a look." Before looking at the baby he kissed Mary on the head. She was weeping.

He looked at the child in her arms. His eyes saw what Tom had seen. There was no hair to speak of. The face was plump and pink, but there was something wrong with its features. He couldn't recognise the creature as a child of his.

Prudence said, "Come along, children. You have ter help me meck the dinner. Muvver en Farder need ter talk." She bustled the children out of the room and closed the door.

Edward felt sick. He stood helplessly, trying to come to terms with the shock and disappointment.

Mary said through her tears, "'E beant like the others, Edward. Prudence said that 'e will allus be a child in his head. His body will grow, but 'e'll need ter be cared fer all 'is life."

"Like Peg." Edward understood perfectly. "I can't love un as my child, Mary. I can't even look at un." He turned away and left the room.

He stumbled downstairs. He had to get away. It seemed as if his whole life had ended in failure. Faithful was in the pasture and he went to her in a daze, brought her to the stable and saddled her, mounted and rode off down the lane.

≈≈≈

Mary sat in bed feeling desolate. She cuddled her new-born son and stroked his cheek. His little round eyes had a sorrowful look. She would love him as much as the others, but she needed Edward to support her.

The door opened and Tom came in quietly. He walked slowly to the side of the bed and stroked the downy head of his new brother.

"Be this un orright, Muvver? You be sad."

"Come en sit beside us, Son."

He climbed up and snuggled into her free side.

"This un'll be different, Tom. He'll grow up in his body but his head won't work like yourn. 'E won't go to school, but mayhap he'll help Farder on the farm."

"Farder be angry," said Tom. "I don't think 'e likes the baby."

"'Tis a shock fer un," Mary said. "'E'll come round. We mun leave un be fer a while."

They sat quietly together. The baby fell asleep and Mary placed him in his crib. She lay back against the pillows, holding Tom to her.

"I'll look after my liddle brudder for all of his life, Muvver. I promise."

Mary smiled and hugged her eldest son. "I knows you will, Tom. You're a good boy."

Edward went about his work as usual. He showed no interest in his new son and when Mary asked him what his name should be, he said, "You mun decide, I cannot. If you be minded ter have un baptised, you arrange it. I can take no part."

Mary gathered the children round her.

"Us have ter choose a name fer the baby. I thought as us named Johnny after my brudder John, this un should be called Richard, after Farder's brudder. What d'ye think?"

Mamie was rocking the baby in his crib. "'E don't look like Uncle Richard."

"'E don't look like none of the fambly," said Ted.

In the silence that followed, Tom came to the rescue. "I b'lieve Richard is a good name fer un. Us could call un Richy."

Mary said quickly, "That's settled then. Tom, when you get back from school 'sarternoon, will you ride over to yer Uncle Richard's house en tell un about Richy, then to yer Uncle John?"

"Yus, Muvver." Tom nodded.

Mary was grimly determined that everything should continue as usual, that Richy would be loved as the others were loved. It was not his fault that he'd been born like that. But in the back of her mind, a dreadful thought was gnawing away.

What if Esland's presence was the cause of the baby's abnormaility? He'd wheedled himself into their affections. What if he intended to put a spell on the next child she birthed all along? Was he really a son of the devil, as her mother had predicted?

She hadn't seen Esland since the harvest, though she continued to put his food out for him. She didn't want to believe he could be so wicked. She should talk to Prudence.

The baptism was a trial. Prudence came to support her and to look after the children. When people saw the baby they turned away, looking at her with pity. Richard and his family were loving and kind and Richard was angry that his brother was behaving so badly. John stood by Mary, but found it difficult to look at the creature in her arms.

There would be no celebratory tea afterwards. On the way home in the cart, Mary told Prudence about her fears concerning Esland. Prudence was quiet.

Then she said, "Esland be a good man with a big heart, but he's been treated rough all his life. I believe he has the insight, as I do. If you let un see Richy, you'll know if he's been the cause of the way the baby's turned out."

They drove up the lane and into the yard. Mary was astonished to see Esland there waiting for them. Edward stood by the stable door, embarrassed.

The children climbed from the cart, Tom helped Johnny down. They ran to Esland, shouting, "Esland, we've got a new brudder. Come en see."

Mary climbed down and Prudence handed her the baby before getting down herself. Edward took the opportunity to take charge of the horse and cart, so as not to be involved with the family.

Mary and Esland approached each other. Mary showed Esland the baby.

Esland stared and after a sharp intake of breath he looked at Mary with the saddest eyes she had ever seen. He held out his arms and she handed Richy over to him. Tears rolled down his face and he rocked the baby gently, stroking his face and head.

Mary was convinced. The man was weeping because he recognised the life this child was likely to have. He handed him back to her and shook his head sorrowfully.

Tom said, "I'll look after un, Esland"

Esland nodded, saying,"Nnnn, nnnn," and went to shake Tom's hand with both of his. He stood and watched the family go into the house.

Chapter Fifty Three

In which Esland climbs a ladder

Edward was working hard. He hardly ever rested. Esland had come back into the work routine and he found him at his side constantly. He felt the man understood the torment he was going through and was offering his support. Edward had watched the extraordinary scene in the yard after the baptism. His heart was softening. It seemed that Esland knew everything. Was this a kind of witchcraft, if there was such a thing?

The time came for Edward to climb up onto the roof of the barn and survey what needed to be done. He'd seen from below that the rafters were riddled with worm. He would need to be careful. John was checking the hedges and ditches today. Edward would need his help to do the repairs, but he could take a look to see what materials they would need. Esland helped him carry the ladder out and prop it up against the barn on the yard side.

"You stay below, Esland," he said. "Don't climb up if you be frit. I won't be long."

"Nnnn, nnn," muttered Esland. He held the ladder while Edward climbed up.

As he reached the top, a cold wind coming from the north nearly blew his hat off; a sure sign that winter was on its way.

He scrambled onto the roof. This side, over the barn, seemed to be quite sound. It was the back of the building he was concerned about. He crept carefully forward. There were some broken tiles in front of him. If he could take these off, he would be able to see the state of the beams underneath. He went down on his hands and knees to spread the load. As he approached the other side the timbers under him creaked. He stopped and reached out to pick up a loose tile.

There was another creak. Every time he moved he disturbed the wooden framework. He knew he should go back. He lay down to look underneath at the rotten wood.

There was louder creaking. He could feel the roof going. He tried wriggling backwards. The creaking increased. He lay flat, hoping that there'd be something to hold onto when the roof under him collapsed.

Then it happened.

With a deafening groan the area he was lying on disappeared, crashing to the ground. Dust surrounded him. He was now suspended on a single beam which was stronger than the rest. He looked down and saw the blades of the ploughshare directly beneath him, like the fangs of a dragon.

"I cung, I cung." Esland's cry came from below.

"Nay, Esland. Go en fetch John," he shouted back.

He looked around him. Maybe he could crawl along the beam to safety. He shifted his position, inch by inch.

He slipped. His legs were now dangling over the machinery below. He clung onto the beam with all his strength. This was not the time to die. Mary would not manage the farm without him. They would all be in the poor house…

His arms were weakening. His grip was loosening.

He felt his arm gripped by a very strong hand.

"I here," said Esland.

≈≈≈

Tom and Ted were on their way back from school.

Tom's voice: Ted's dragging his feet and stopping to pick blackberries from the hedge. I walk on. He can find his own way home now.

I walk into the yard. Muvver's standing there looking up at the roof of the barn, holding Richy in her arms. Prudence is holding Mamie and Johnny's hands and John Winder is climbing a ladder. They're all looking up.

I run to Muvver's side.

She looks down at me. "Farder en Esland be up there. The roof be c'lapsen," she says.

I look up. John is nearly at the top.

There's a tremendous crash and clouds of dust, then a long shout, "Naaaaa!"

I run round to the back of the barn. There's lots of dust and tiles and rotten wood all over the plough, the harrow and the cart. I stand watching the dust clear and I see Esland lying there. His head is split open by the blade of the ploughshare. It's a terrible sight. His body shudders for a few seconds, but I know he's dead. I look up and nearly all the roof is gone. There's no sign of Farder anywhere. I am mortal afeared.

I run round to the yard.

John is helping Farder down the ladder. Farder is shaking. He's covered in dust and he's crying.

≈≈≈

Mary strode forward to meet Edward. "Oh, Ed, my love! Thanks be that you be safe. I were afeared we'd lost you." She caught hold of Edward's head with her free hand, caressed and kissed it. She wiped the tears from his eyes and said, "Come indoors, my dear."

Edward said through his sobs, "Esland fell. 'E saved my life."

Mary heard Tom's plaintive voice, "Esland's dead!"

John Winder ran round to the back of the barn, shouting, "Esland!"

The family solemnly followed Mary and Edward indoors and sat round the table.

Mary went to put her sleeping baby into his crib and asked Prudence to find some brandy for Edward.

Mamie and Ted sat on the bottom step of the stairs, close together.

Johnny sat between Prudence and Edward at the table. He reached out to touch his father's arm.

"You be hem dirty, Farder," he said.

Mary brought a bowl of water, warmed up from the kettle and lovingly sponged Edward's face. He was still shaking and supped his brandy slowly so as not to spill a drop. She looked around the room at her family.

"Prudence, where be Tom?" she asked.

Prudence stood up from the table and went upstairs to Tom's chamber.

Edward was angry, mostly with himself for risking his life so stupidly. Esland had sacrificed his own life to save him. He'd left a gaping hole.

There were things to do before they could all get on with their lives: a coffin to make, the body to move and a funeral to arrange. He would need to clear the collapsed debris, check the machinery for damage and rebuild the barn before winter.

Having checked that Esland was indeed dead, John Winder helped to uncover the buried cart, reverently avoiding the body which they covered with sacking. Edward drove into town and called on Fred Dyne the builder.

Fred stood in his workshop among piles of wood shavings. He wore a flat cap on his balding head and a leather apron over his shirt, knee breeches and hose. His sleeves were rolled up above the elbow and he held a stick of charcoal in his mouth.

"Me barn's c'lapsed en I have ter rebuild it afore winter," Edward said. "Can you supply the materials and help me do it?"

Fred removed the charcoal with gnarled fingers. "I'll have ter come en have a look. I've got an unaccountable amount of work prensley." He put the charcoal behind his ear, leaned on his workbench and stroked his clean-shaven chin.

Edward said, "En I want some planks ter meck a coffin."

Fred looked at Edward with piercing eyes. "Be one of yer fambly deceased?"

Edward found it difficult to explain. "Er, nay. Not esackly. 'E were a labourer of mine, like."

"No fambly of his own, then?" Fred wanted to know. He was reputed to be a mite indiscreet with the information he picked up from his customers.

Edward was reticent. "Nay," he said.

Fred asked the measurement of the deceased and Edward said he was about the same size as himself.

"You'll be fixen up fer a funeral, like," Fred remarked. Edward nodded, but said nothing.

Fred went to measure up some wood and cut it up according to Edward's requirements.

"D'you think you can do the building work, Fred?" Edward persisted.

"I'll come en teck a look end of week. That'll be six shillen fer now."

Edward handed over the money and they carried the wood to the cart. He climbed up, tipped his hat to the builder and drove away.

After the next vestry meeting Edward approached the vicar, John Willett. He was a timid little man with a permanent sniffle. Edward had noticed that he was dominated by Edward Benge and the other ironmasters. He wanted to talk to the man without any interference and led him outside before he spoke.

"I be wanten to arrange a funeral, Sir,"

Mr Willett sniffed and coughed into a large handerchief. "Oh dear, which of your family has died, Edward?"

"'Tis none of me fambly, thank the Lord. 'Tis a labourer who's been abiding on me property en a-worken fer me, casual, like."

"I heard there was an accident; a fall from a roof? What was the man's name?" Mr Willett looked enquiringly at Edward.

Edward braced himself. Word had got around already. "'Is name were Esland. I didn't know another. 'E come to me farder years ago en never had a praper home of his own."

Mr Willett coughed again. "This man had the reputation of being the devil incarnate, I believe. I didn't see him in church. If there is any doubt, I could not allow his body to be buried in the churchyard."

"I don't believe, Sir, that 'e were a wicked man. 'Twere rumours that was spread on account of 'is misfortunate appearance, that were no fault of his own." As he said this, an image of his youngest son flashed through his mind. He shuddered.

"I would like to come and examine his living quarters before I can decide. I have my reputation to think of. I will bring a witness along for verification. Would tomorrow suit you?"

Edward bowed to superior authority. He had known it would be difficult. He lifted his hat to the vicar and went to mount his horse. He'd been wondering what to do with the shepherd's hut. It seemed a sacred place now. Esland was such a private person, Edward didn't want to look inside, let alone allow strangers to poke and prod. He had thought the best thing to do would be to set it alight as it stood. Now he must let the vicar do his duty. If he burnt it beforehand, it would raise suspicions.

≈≈≈

Mary woke to the sound of another of Tom's nightmare screams. She stepped out of bed and knew the route to his bedside without the need of a candle. She held him until his body relaxed and said to him, "Come, Tom," leading him back to her bed to avoid waking the others. Ted, who shared Tom's bed, turned over, groaned and went back to sleep.

Tom and his mother climbed into her bed and she folded him in her arms. He was sobbing.

"I seed Esland with his head split open in me dreams," he said through the tears. "There be snakes en giant creepy crawlies comen out of his head en his mouth." Another wave of sobbing overcame him.

"Hush, now, my treasure. What you seed beant real. Try to remember what Esland were really like; his kind eyes, twinkling with laughter when 'e were happy. Think of the gifts he gave us all; the carved animals, the catapult he made you." Mary murmered in Tom's ears until his body stopped shaking and he breathed easily. She lay with him in her arms, realising just how different it would be without Esland and how bereft they were all feeling. A funeral would comfort them in their grief.

≈≈≈

After breakfast when they were alone, Edward said to Mary, "The vicar's a-comen by 'smarnen. 'E wunt bury Esland in the churchyard bythen 'e be satisfied 'e ain't been up to devilish practises. 'E wants ter look in the shepherd's hut."

Mary looked at him with troubled eyes. "That be the final insult," she said. Tears trickled down her cheeks. She brushed them away. "Best get it over with," she said.

She cleared the empty dishes from the table and carried them into the kitchen. Edward heard her washing up, making more noise than usual.

He wandered out into the yard. The place felt empty and cold. He shivered. John Winder was attending to the beasts and Edward went to him and said, "The vicar's a-comen ter look at Esland's things in the hut. When 'e's gone we mun set about clearen the mess round the back en putten the harrow en plough under cover bythen the buildin' work be done."

John nodded and continued brushing the floor vigorously.

Two horses approached along the lane.

Edward raised his hat and held the vicar's horse while he dismounted. He took both horses and tethered them by the stables.

He led the two men into the pasture where the shepherd's hut stood quietly sheltering the coffin, which lay underneath.

Edward opened the door of the hut. The two men had to remove their hats to enter the tiny cabin. There was no room for three and Edward remained outside, leaving Willett and his accomplice to do their work.

Chapter Fifty Four

In which all is revealed

Edward perched on the step of the shepherd's hut where Esland had sat carving animals for the children. He thought of the pleasure on their faces and marvelled at their complete acceptance of the man's looks, seeming not to notice. He'd expected them to be frightened. He thought of his newborn son and his own reaction to his strange appearance. He'd seen children with those features and they were treated like the village idiot; with abuse and ridicule, as Esland had been. That's why Esland had wept when he saw the baby. Edward vowed that he would protect Richy from the treatment that Esland had suffered and teach his family to do the same.

There were noises of things being thrown around inside the hut. It was time Edward intervened. He opened the door and looked in.

"I'll thank ye to have more respect fer the dead," he blurted out before he could stop himself.

Willett raised himself from a crouched position, holding a bag filled with Esland's posessions. He held it up, his eyes sparkling.

"I think you will find that the man deserves no respect. Let us look at the contents of this bag,"

Willett said as he scrambled over the disturbed bedding and out into the sunshine. He opened the drawstring and shook out the contents.

Edward saw carved wax figures tumble out onto the grass. Esland's carving skills were extraordinarily lifelike. Edward reached out to pick one of them up. Willett and his partner crossed themselves.

"Don't touch them!" shouted Willett. "It's the devil's work! You will be tainted!"

Edward looked at him with pity. The man reminded him of Mary's mother. He proceeded to pick up one of the figures, fearing nothing.

The wax was warm and soft in his hand. He recognised the face of Robert Smith; the man who had refused to work alongside Esland and who had insulted him. There were thorns stuck into his leg; the one he had injured when laying the hedge. So this was witchcraft. Edward understood the humiliation and anger that Esland must have suffered, to be driven to this. Unable to answer back, it was his revenge for a life of abuse. Laying the figure on the ground, Edward picked up another. This one was undoubtedly Anne Paris. She had a thorn stuck right through her heart. He recognised other people in the pile of victims; his brother Thomas, with thorns in his stomach and Thomas Tapsell with one in his head.

Edward was overcome by the emotions these revelations had aroused. His hands and feet tingled and he felt light-headed. He stumbled away from the watching priest and his partner and vomited in the bushes. He sat on the ground with his head between his knees for some time before he was ready to face the judge and jury.

Willett and the other man had replaced their hats and brushed the dust off their coats. "I believe your answer is plain, Master Lucke. I will leave you to dispose of the remains in whatever way you think fit. Good day to you." They marched away from Esland and his world.

Edward watched them go, then went back to gather the wax figures and put them back in the bag, pulled the drawstring and place the incriminating evidence inside the hut. He noticed that not one of the figures was of Mary. Esland had not been the cause of harm to any of their children. He shut the door and stayed on the step until he felt fit enough to face the family. Then they would burn Esland in his hut with all his life's tragedy and bury any ashes that remained.

≈≈≈

The next evening, after they'd placed Esland in his coffin inside the hut and built a mound of rotten timber from the barn round the outside, John Winder pushed faggots underneath and set light to them.

The full moon shone brightly on the family standing in their warm clothes, holding the carved animals Esland had made, unaware of the little bag of figures inside the hut.

Mary had her hand on Tom's shoulder and held Richy on her other arm.

"We mun say goodbye to Esland and thank him for his friendship and all the good things he did," she said loudly, so that all the children could hear her.

Edward and John came and stood with the others. Mary felt her husband put his hand on her shoulder and heard him say, "And I swear that Richy will be protected from treatment such as Esland suffered. He will grow up knowing that he be loved en cared for and that he be a special child."

Mary caught her breath. The tears flowed and she had no free hand to wipe them away.

The flames took hold. Sparks flew up into the night sky. The roaring blaze drowned all other sound, recalling Esland's voice, "Nnnn, nnnn." The younger children were excited and laughed, dancing around in the light of the fire. Prudence shepherded them away from the fierce heat and they ran off into the pasture, shrieking and playing tag in the moonlight.

They sat round the table drinking hot milk before going to bed. Prudence and John had gone home and Mary and Edward were supping hot toddies.

Tom broke the hushed silence. "There be naught left of Esland now, but I feel happy, I dunnow why."

Mary said, "That's because he's left us with fond memories which will stay in our hearts for ever."

"Mmmm," said Tom.

Chapter Fifty Five   1720/1

In which Edward reckons with Thomas Lucke

Edward rode along the Lamberhurst road wondering how he would find Thomas and Eliza at Slade Farm. The last time he saw them he was shocked at the state they were in. The winter had been harsh and he could imagine the hardship they'd been through. He turned up the collar of his coat and pulled his hat down firmly to prevent the March wind pulling it off.

The geese greeted him in the yard. At least Thomas and Eliza would have had something to eat. He tethered Faithful and went through the space where the gate should have been. It was hanging limply on one hinge and rotting away. He had to wade through chicken and goose droppings to enter the back door, which had been left open. The hens were indoors helping themselves to scraps.

In the parlour, the old couple were in the same places they'd been the last time. The fire was lit, however and apart from the stench of unwashed bodies they appeared to be in reasonable health.

"Thought I'd happen by," said Edward. A candle flickered as he stirred the air around it. He sat on the end of the bench by the table.

Thomas shifted his position and sighed. "Good of you ter come," he said. "I've a few things I want ter discuss with you."

Edward was surprised at his reception and of his own feelings of benevolence towards his brother.

"'Tis mortal cold out there," Thomas continued. "Go en find yerself a drop of brandy. You knows where the glasses be. Fetch one fer me en Eliza en all."

This hospitality from Thomas was unheard of. Edward obeyed him and went through to the hall. The cold hit him after the warmth of the parlour. Cobwebs were draped over the furniture and there was a damp smell. The shutters were closed and Edward had to grope for the glasses in the familiar cupboard. He found the brandy on the side and poured it out, then managed to carry the three glasses into the parlour without spilling. He gave one each to Thomas and Eliza and left the third on the table, before going back and closing the hall door.

Thomas raised his glass, and started to talk.

"Eliza en me be considerable out of kilter just now. It's all us can do to keep alive en there be no money a-comen in. We gets wheat from the parish, but it beant much. I knows you be willed to inherit Slade Farm when I goes, but you've got Savages en this place be tarble run-down. I be ernful fer that. I be no farmer en I've been stubborn en selfish.

"But 'tis too late now ter make amends. If you be agreeable, I b'lieve t'would be best ter sell. The land will be worth summat en Eliza en me would have some money ter pay fer help en ter pay you what I owes. Then I can die with naught on me conscience, like." He took a sip of brandy and sat back in his chair.

Edward was shocked. This didn't sound like the Thomas he knew. He was aware that he himself had changed since the accident on the roof. Life was more important than property. He'd let go of his dream of owning Slade Farm. Thomas and he had been at war all their lives. It was like a childish game. Now, Thomas had given in and they had both grown up.

Edward took another sip of brandy to soften his dry mouth. "Where will ye bide?" he asked.

"Ah, well, I were a-comen ter that. I be minded ter move to Ann's cottage. It don't appear that Esland be a-comen back here, not after the way I treated un..." Thomas gazed into the past for a few moments.

Edward said, "Esland be dead, Brudder. 'E fell from a roof. Saved me life, he did."

Thomas' gaze slowly came back into the present and alighted on his brother's face. "Be that so?" he said sadly. "'E were allus afeared of agwain on the roof. Must have seed it a-comen." He looked down and continued, "'E had the gift of insight. It got on me nerves ter think 'e knowed better than me. Poor man, 'e were good in his heart."

"So 'e won't be minded ter bide in the cottage no more," said Edward, dragging Thomas back to the conversation. "I've stopped payin' his rent to Ann. You'd best fix up with she if you en Eliza be minded ter bide there. En I don't want no money off you, Thomas. The debt is cleared."

Thomas sat up. A gleam of his stubborn nature glinted in his eyes. "Nay, nay. I mun pay me debts. You racken up how much I owes en let me know. Then I can rest easy."

Edward shrugged. "Orright, but I don't need it. Savages be earning me a good livin' en I hope ter move to a bigger farm dappen the time be right. I have five children en the cottage beant big enough."

Thomas nodded. "That be good news. At least one of us has made good. Farder en Muvver would be main proud of you. I'll be making enquiries ter find a buyer fer Slade Farm, then. Be you agreeable?"

Edward nodded. "I be pleased you be getting out of this hole. Ann's cottage will be better fer ye both."

Eliza, who'd been dozing during the brothers' conversation, lifted her head, wiped away the saliva which had escaped from her mouth and said, "I'll drink ter that!"

They all raised their glasses and knocked back the remains of the brandy.

Thomas said, "Mayhap I'll grow vegetables again. The land be in good heart over there."

"I bluv yer stomach were bad," remarked Edward, recalling the wax figure with a thorn through the belly.

Nay, not no more. It got better over the winter. I be middlin' prensley. Come spring, 'twill be good ter be out in the air."

He got out of his chair and Edward went to shake hands with him. An extraordinary wave of affection for his brother flowed over him. He picked up his hat from the table and made his way out into the yard, breathing the cold fresh air into his lungs.

He mounted Faithful and rode home musing on the revelations of the morning. Thomas had time to think over his past life now. It seemed he'd come to his senses at last.

When he got home he hugged Mary and said, "There be whips of news ter tell you over coager."

He went to check on the sleeping Richy and Mary said, "'E smiled 's'marnen. I be sarten sure 'tweren't the wind. 'Twere a cheeky liddle smile."

Edward went to find his account book and sat at the table. He found the page headed *Thomas Lucke's Account* and wrote:

1720/1   March 17   Then Reckoned with
Thomas Lucke for all accounts
betwixt him and I to this day
And there is due to me twelve pounds
witness my hand   £12----0----0

Chapter Fifty Six   1721

Tom's voice

I ride Jackanapes to school. Ted walks with his friends. He says he doesn't want a horse. Soon it will be time for me to take Johnny, but Muvver says he's not ready yet. I think Mamie has over-muvvered him. He's a timid boy. He'll be frightened at school, with all the noise and rough play.

Stephen Bassett doesn't go to school any more. He helps his father on the farm with his big brothers. Nick and William are still at school. Nick is the same age as me. We'll be leaving come harvest time. Then Ted will have to look after Johnny.

When I arrive I find Nick already in the classroom. He looks up from his Bible.

"Hello, Tom," he says.

I go and sit next to him and say, "You be here early, Nick."

"Yus, I be larnen this passage Mr Hunt gave us last week. I disremembered. There's allus summat a-going on at home en I can't think straight there." He looks down at his open Bible. I move away so he can concentrate.

I get my slate out of my bag and practice copy writing from the Bible. Farder lets me practise in his account book sometimes. I write my name and copy some of his accounts. Writing on paper with a quill is harder than on a slate. I have to practise on account of Farder will pass on the farm to me when he dies. Then I'll have to do it by myself.

All the other children are at their desks now. Some of them are girls. There's a pretty one called Margaret. I like to sit behind on the other side of the room, so I can watch her. But she's come to sit directly in front of me today. I can't see her face, but I could reach out and touch her. She smells of milk.

I'm going to visit the Bassetts after school today. Nick will ride there with me. I'm excited.

There's a map of the world hanging on the wall. Mr Hunt is teaching us about the different far-away lands which are divided from each other by water. Our land is called Britain and it's an island. Here, we're not far from the ocean which surrounds Britain, but I've never seen it. People from other lands want to take possession of Britain. They come in ships that float on the water like ducks. The ships have big guns made by the ironmasters which fire heavy balls. These canon-balls make big holes in the sides of the ships, which causes them to sink. Many people die in these battles.

It's time to go. School is finished for the day. I pack my bag with books and slate, being careful to check that the catapult that Esland made for me is still there. I don't use it much but I like to have it with me as part of him. It's hard going home and finding him not there. But if he were alive, Farder would likely be dead. That would be dreadful.

Nick and I mount our horses and trot away down the hill to Bassett's farm, minding the ruts in the road. We imagine we're sailing ships, fighting each other on the ocean. We fire canon-balls and chase each other.

"Boom! You're holed!" I shout.

Nick dodges, shouting "Nay! 'twere only a scratch!"

Stephen is waiting for us on his horse in the yard. We greet each other with a wave. He says, "Shall us go over to Cogger's Mill? There be a good gallop over Best Beech Hill."

"Yus," says Nick, "There be wondrous views from there. You can see the ocean on a clear day."

We set off down the road until we come to the drove road to Mayfield, which is wet and slippery from the winter storms. In a while we reach a gate onto the down. Stephen dismounts and lets us through, leading his horse. He closes the gate after him. Now we can pick up speed on the soft turf. Galloping uphill is hard work for the horses, but Jackanapes likes the challenge. He doesn't often get this sort of exercise. I love to feel the wind in my face and the power of the horse's strength under me. Stephen gets there first. I arrive, panting, beside him.

Nick is level with me. I lean over to pat Jackanapes' neck and whisper in his ear. Then I sit up straight.

The view is wonderful, for certain sure. I look at the hills and valleys all round me. I can see the spire on Mayfield church. Stephen says it's too hazy to see the ocean. The spring birds are singing and calling to each other and there is a green tinge to the trees. My heart sings with the birds.

My attention is drawn to a house nestling in a hollow down below. It's a pretty house; plaster with timber framing. It sparkles in the sun.

"Who bides there?" I ask.

Stephen says, "That be Pennybridge Farm. 'Tis the property of Mr Edward Benge. I be well avised that he be minded ter move out to a smaller house and ter let that one."

Nick says, "Race ye to the Mill," and starts off down the hill.

He has a head start and Jackanapes has done enough galloping. I let the two brothers go ahead and think about Pennybridge Farm. I know Farder has been hankering after a bigger farm. I wonder if he knows what Mr Benge is planning.

We canter across the fields back to the road and continue towards Bassett's Farm. There are deep ruts along here. We walk slowly to prevent the horses stumbling. We pass the entrance to Pennybridge Farm and I glance down the lane, but it's such a steep hill the house is out of sight.

I say goobye to Stephen and Nick when we reach their bidance and make my way back to Savages.

When I've put Jackanapes in the stable and given him a rub down, I leave him with some hay and go indoors to see little Richy. He's growing, but he can't sit up on his own yet. He lies in his crib kicking his legs and trying to catch his toes. When he sees me he laughs and gurgles and holds out his arms to be picked up. I put my hands near his, to tempt him to get hold of my fingers. That way, he might learn to pull himself up. One day he will do it.

Chapter Fifty Seven   1721

In which Johnny starts school

It was at the next vestry meeting when Edward met Mr Willett at the door to the Grazehound Inn. He lifted his hat and said, "Good marnen, Sir."

Mr Willett didn't respond. He looked past Edward at the person behind him. Edward went in and took off his hat. He greeted the other members of the vestry. His old friend William Ashdown came and took him to one side. He was now a churchwarden with Henry Playsted. He had a worried frown as he shook Edward's hand.

"Edward, I be avised that the man Esland died while abiding on your property and that he were discovered to have been practising witchcraft. Did you know about this?"

Edward paused for a moment. He'd expected someone to make these enquiries. Praise be it was Ashdown, who knew and trusted him.

"Nay. I had no knowledge of it. 'Twere revealed by Mr Willett when he came to search Esland's bidance. When he were with us at Savages he were allus trustworthy, loyal en kind to the children. 'E saved my life afore he died. I were sick to the stomach when the evidence were discovered."

"That is what I wanted to hear," said Ashdown. "You cannot be blamed fer something you had no knowledge of. Though there were talk that he had the devil in un."

Edward felt his anger rising. "His whole life 'e were abused on account of his looks. He didn't have the power of speech ter defend hisself…"

"Orright, orright, Edward. Don't upset yerself. 'Tis eyeproof you be on his side. Whatever he might have done, I will say no more. If enquiries be made I will swear to your innocence." Ashdown squeezed Edward's shoulder re-assuringly and said, "The gossip and rumour will die down. Shall us attend the meeting?"

Evidently, the other members of the vestry had no knowledge of events at Savages, or they chose not to believe the gossip. Edward was a respected member of the community and his friends were loyal.

Henry Duplock was now chairman. Edward Benge continued to attempt to rule the roost, but was out-voted time and again. They had to appoint overseers for the coming year. Young Ed Waghorn had joined the vestry recently and he and Edward were chosen, with Edward being in charge of the money. He would pay allowances to the widows of the town until such time as they gained self sufficiency.

At the end of the meeting Ashdown handed over the money to Edward and again squeezed his arm.

Edward shook his friend's hand vigorously and said, "Thank you, William. God bless you."

He spent a few moments with Ed Waghorn, explaining the duties of overseers. He gave him the list of people in need of help, then he hurried to the door to catch John Willett.

When Edward tapped his shoulder from behind, the vicar started and turned to face him.

Edward said, "With regards to events at my farm last Fall, Sir, mebbe you b'lieve me unfit to serve on the vestry on account of sheltering…"

Willett sniffed and coughed. "Have no fear, Mas Lucke, you are too well respected. I would be in trouble from the other officers if I discharged you. Whatever my own feelings in the matter, I'm convinced that you were unaware of the activities of the man in question. I will not breathe a word of what we discovered at your farm. The matter is closed." He sniffed repeatedly through this speech and finished with a paroxysm of coughing.

Edward watched the vicar walk speedily towards his house. He took a deep sigh of relief. Ashdown must have had a word. Edward mounted Faithful and trotted down the road to his family. They were the only ones who would ever understand.

≈≈≈

Mary and Prudence went home from church in the cart with the children. Mary enjoyed Sunday mealtimes with the whole family round the table. She would make a special effort to serve them their favourite dinner. Today the children were playing outside with the bat and ball while Mary and Prudence worked in the kitchen.

It was a fine spring day and Richy was out in the sunshine in his crib where he could see the blue sky above him and hear the children. Now and again one of them ran over to talk to him and tried to get him to play with his toys. He was a placid child, but Mary worried that he'd made little progress since birth. At this age the others were all sitting up on their own, shaking their rattles and beginning to crawl.

Mary looked out of the window and saw Mamie put her hands out to her little brother. He took hold of her fingers with both hands; the first sign of progress.

"Look at Richy!" Mary shouted to Prudence.

Prudence came to the window. "Oh my!" she said.

The two women ran outside. Mamie looked up and laughed. The other children came to see.

Richy clung on to Mamie's fingers. His face was deeply concentrated, his eyes fixed on his hands, his mouth contorted. He let go and was suddenly aware of all the faces peering down at him. He squeeled with laughter and kicked his legs. Mamie put her fingers into his little hands and he held on again. She gently pulled him towards her, but he let go. Then she held out her two hands, hoping that he would reach for them, but he wasn't ready yet.

Mary picked up her special child and hugged him. "Clever boy," she said. He held his head up well and looked round at his brothers and sister. They all clapped their hands.

"Time fer coager," said Mary, as Edward rode into the yard. The children ran to tell him the news about Richy. Mary put the child back in his crib and Tom helped her carry him indoors. Prudence was already serving out the meal. Then she went home to her own family.

≈≈≈

Edward sat down at the table. The children all wanted to tell him what Richy had achieved this morning. Only Tom was quiet, letting the others have their say.

There was a hush in the conversation while they all started eating. Tom said, "Farder, I seed Mr Benge's farm when I were out riding along of Stephen en Nick Bassett. 'Twere a handsome sight."

"That would be Edward Benge, that's a member of the vestry," said Edward.

"Yus," said Tom. "Stephen said there's word that 'e be minded ter move out to a smaller place."

"Mm," said Edward. "His fambly be all growed en left home, I rackon. That place will be overlarge fer un, fer sarten sure.

"D'you know the place?" asked Mary.

"I've not been there, but I've seed it from Best Beech Hill, where Tom were, like."

"'Tis called Pennybridge Farm," said Tom. He took another mouthful, allowing the information to settle in his parents' heads and do its work.

After a while, Edward said, "'Twere all change at the vestry meeting today. 'Tis my turn to be overseer with young Ed Waghorn. 'E'll need a bit of guidance, like. I'll be attending the widows. I were surprised at the long list.

Did you know John Bellingham is dead, Mary? En Thomas Tanner?"

"Nay! That were sudden. I seed John Bellingham in town only last month. 'Is Mistus will be in need. There be a big fambly."

"There be two of 'em at school," said Tom.

That evening, Edward wrote in his account book:

> *1721   Received of the parish in money*
> *from the old officers*   2-------8-------6-------0

Nothing stood still at Savages for long. Amid the ploughing and taking stock to market Edward found time to visit the widows on his list and give them their monthly allowance. Widows Bellingham and Martin, Tanner and Longley were all dependant on the poor relief for most of the year. Then there was Will Barham whose wife died and he became sick. Edward engaged Elizabeth Pick to look after him.

He went back to Slade Farm and Thomas signed his account, though Edward had little hope of being paid.

Tom took Johnny to school with him for a week but the little boy became ill.

"Farder, I don't believe Johnny be ready fer school. 'E be so afeared that 'e beant larnen aught," said Tom to Edward.

Johnny was feverish for a few days. Mary nursed him gently back to his former self and said to Edward, "Do 'e have ter go to school yet, Ed? 'E be only five en not as stocky as Tom en Ted was when they started."

Edward regarded his son. He was small for his age and suffered from frequent coughs and colds. Until recently Mamie had always been there for him. Now, her attention was drawn towards Richy. Johnny spent a great deal of time quietly playing on his own. Edward had thought that he would be better with other children at school.

Mary said, "You took Tom to the fields along of thee at this age, Ed. Mebbe 'twould be a gentler way ter start 'is larnen."

Johnny was in a world of his own, building castles out of bricks. Edward went over and squatted down to his son's height, "Johnny, us won't make you go to school dappen you be growed a liddle more. You can come along of me en larn some husbandry instead," he said.

Johnny looked up from his bricks. His face beamed. He got to his feet and folded his arms round his father's neck and they hugged. Edward realised that he hardly knew this little boy. The others had always stolen the limelight. And now Richy had displaced him as the youngest.

"'Tis time thee en me got to know each other, Son," said Edward.

Whenever Edward was out in the fields sowing, tending the beasts or going to market he took Johnny with him. The lad began to talk more, eagerly telling the others what he and his father had been doing. When he wasn't with Edward, Mary made sure she involved him in feeding the fowls, collecting eggs and baking bread. Sometimes she would take him to John Winder when he was milking the cows or mucking out the stables. Johnny's vocabulary grew and he became more robust and self-confident.

It was a long, hot summer, as it had been the year before. The water table was going down. The wells were running dry. Edward and Tom walked out into the corn field one morning and gazed at the leaves wilting with thirst.

"'Tis a bad year fer the crops." Edward sighed and stroked his beard.

Tom said, "What'll us do, Farder, dappen the wheat don't grow?"

"Us'll have ter buy it, Son. There'll be some brought over from other countries. 'Twill cost more en us'll have less."

"Where will us get the money ter pay fer it?"

"There'll be less ter feed the beasts on come winter. Us'll sell some en behopes have enough money ter pay fer us needs." Edward was proud that Tom was taking an interest. "Thanks be there'll be two mowens of hay," he added.

The two walked round the parched fields and pastures. The sun burnt mercilessly down on them. The trees were shedding brown leaves. They noted the poor quality of the grass. The beasts were losing weight.

"Us'll have ter feed 'em on turmuts if they're to be sold. Nobody'll buy 'em in that condition," he said.

≈≈≈

One day in late September Edward was out delivering poor relief. Johnny had been helping John Winder to bring the cows in for milking. Prudence was away caring for her husband who was sick. Mary was preparing dinner. The boys would be home soon. Richy was lying on the parlour floor, reaching for toys that Mamie waved in front of him. She was trying to encourage him to roll over onto his front.

Johnny burst into the kitchen. "Muvver! There be a dog a-comen up the lane!" he said excitedly.

Mary dried her hands on her apron and tucked some wisps of hair behind her ear.

"Come en see!" urged Johnny.

"I be a-comen," said Mary, though what she would do with a stray dog she had no idea.

Johnny held his mother's hand as he led her out into the yard. A brindled brown farm dog came round the corner waving a long thin tail. He came up to Mary and she and Johnny stroked his smooth coat.

"Where've you come from?" enquired Mary. The dog sat down and pawed her hand, then looked back down the lane.

Johnny bent down and hugged the dog round his neck. The animal licked his nose and pulled away. He stood up and started to go back the way he had come, looking back to see if anyone was following. He saw that they were not and sat down again.

Tom and Ted came into the yard.

"That's Mas Ashdown's dog," said Tom.

The two boys bent down and patted the poor creature. Mary could see he was not in the mood for affection.

"Mebbe there's summat amiss at Ashdown's farm," she said. She remembered Shep and his ways of calling for help.

Tom said, "I'll get Jackanapes en go en see." He gave his satchel to Mary and went to the pasture.

The dog was still there when Tom had saddled his horse and mounted him. He said, "Come, dog." He turned towards the lane and the dog got up and ran to lead him.

Mary watched them go. Tom might not be able to deal with the crisis when he got there. She hoped Edward would be home soon. She looked down at Johnny.

"Good boy," she said.

Chapter Fifty Eight

Tom's voice.

I follow the dog to Ashdown's farm. I remember his children coming to visit when I was little. Charles and Dolly were older than me. They will be grown up bynow. I haven't seen them for a few years. Their mother was called Bella. She tended me for Muvver sometimes. This dog will be getting old. He still looks sprightly. I can't remember his name.

I ride into the yard and the dog looks round at me and goes to the back of the house. I dismount, tether Jackanapes and follow on foot. He leads me to the vegetable garden. Mas Ashdown's lying on his back on the ground. He looks dead. I don't know what to do.

I bend down to see if the man is breathing and shake his arm, hoping he will wake up.

I shout, "Mas Ashdown!"

His body is warm but he doesn't move. I take my jacket off and cover his chest and shoulders. I'd better get help.

I run up the garden to the house, wondering why the dog didn't get Mistus Ashdown. The back door is shut but not locked. I open it and go in. Everything is quiet.

I shout, "Anybody there?"

No answer.

But then I hear a noise. It's the dog. He's pushed past me and is pawing at the parlour door.

I go and open it. Mistus Ashdown's sitting in a chair by the fire, dozing. The dog goes and nudges her with his nose.

The old woman wakes up, startled and sees me. "Oh! Who be that?" she cries.

I say, "I be Tom Lucke, Mistus Ashdown. Your dog led me here."

She says, "Speak up! I be thick of hearin'." She puts her hand to her ear and leans forward.

I come nearer and shout, "Mas Ashdown be lying in the garden! I can't move un."

She struggles out of her chair, saying, "Oh my! What's ter be done? There be nobody round here who can help!" She goes to the cupboard and takes out a bottle of brandy.

She gives it to me and says, "You go en give un a sip of this. There's a blanket on the chair there. Take it en cover un over. Then you'd best go en seek help. I'll foller you out."

I take the bottle and blanket and run out and down the garden to where Mas Ashdown is lying. I take my jacket, roll it up and push it under his head. Then I cover him with the blanket. I take the stopper out of the bottle and pull his mouth open. This seems very impertinent. I don't like doing it. I pour a little of the brandy into his mouth and wait.

His mouth moves slightly.

Mistus Ashdown hobbles down the garden path on her stick, with a shawl wrapped round her shoulders. She comes up to where her husband is lying and shouts, "Come on, git up you lazy auld bumpkin!"

The old man's eyes flicker.

She pushes his leg with her foot.

I think she's being a little rough, but it seems to work. A groan escapes from his mouth.

She says to me, "Give un a drop more."

I kneel on the ground and put my hand behind his head. "Take this, Mas Ashdown," I say and I pour more brandy between his half-open lips.

He opens his mouth and coughs and splutters. Then he lifts his head and opens his eyes, saying, "Huh? Where am I?" He sits up and shakes his head, looks at his wife and shouts, "Bella! What be you a-doin' out here?"

Mistus Ashdown pokes her husband with her stick and says, "Come back from the dead, Will Ashdown, be you? I'm not rid of thee yet, then."

I'm shocked. Mas Ashdown chuckles and I realise she is joking. I stand up and he asks, "What brings you here, young Lucke?"

I tell him that his dog brought me. He chuckles again and says, "Good auld Buster! I knowed 'e'd be good fer summat after all these years."

Buster comes to him and licks his face.

Mas Ashdown's stick is stuck in the ground near to him and he holds onto it and tries to get up. I hold him under the arm, but it's no good, he's too heavy.

He says, "Well, I be bound ter bide 'ere awhile, I rackons. Give me the bottle, Boy. I needs fire in me belly."

I give him the brandy and he tips more into his mouth.

Mistus Ashdown is still standing by. She can't hear what we're saying and she doesn't want to leave her husband.

It's getting cold and dark.

I'm about to say I'll go and get help, when Buster pricks up his ears and runs off up the garden. Someone is here.

In a few moments the dog comes running back. Farder is following.

Mistus Ashdown says, "Oh my! You be an angel sent from Heaven, Edward."

Mas Ashdown shouts, "Rescued from a night under the stars!"

I go to greet my farder. "I be considerable pleased ter see you, Farder," I say. "Mas Ashdown can't get to 'is feet. 'E were lying there en I bluv 'e were dead..." I feel tears coming to my eyes and brush them away.

Farder says, "You've done well, Son. Let's see if us can lift un up atween we."

We stand on either side of Mas Ashdown. He gives the bottle to his mistus and grabs hold of his stick with both hands. We all heave together.

He slowly gets to his feet, saying, "Me legs be hem latchety, like." Farder and I hold on until he's standing.

Farder asks, "Can you walk, William?"

He says, "I'll have a go."

Mistus Ashdown picks up my jacket and the blanket. She goes ahead and we creep our way back to the house.

Mas Ashdown says to me as we start to get a little faster, "You be a stocky young man, Lucke."

I feel proud to be helping him.

We finally reach the house and sit the man down in his parlour. The fire is warm and his mistus covers him with the blanket. She gives me my jacket and I put it on.

"I didn't know who you was when you come ter wake me up, Tom," she says. "How did you come to be here?"

I go close to her and shout, "Buster come to our farm en I follered un here. 'E couldn't get in to wake you on account of the door being shut."

She says, "You be a-growen to be a brave young man. Thank you fer what you did." She takes hold of my hand and gives me a kiss on the cheek. I'm embarrassed, but I'm relieved to find she's not as fierce as she seemed.

After making Mas Ashdown comfortable on a couch in the parlour, Farder and I ride home to Savages and tell Muvver the news. I'm glad to be home in the warm and am ready for my dinner.

Chapter Fifty Nine   1701/2

A hard winter

Every week Edward continued to take the poor widows their allowances and he called on the Ashdowns on his way round.

William never fully recovered from his exposure in the garden. The doctor said he'd suffered a minor seizure. The cold went to his chest and his arthritis became worse. He put up a fight, though and was always pleased to see Edward.

One afternoon in November, when Bella was out of the room, he confided to Edward, "I be putten my house en affairs in order. I've been a-runnen the farm down fer the past year or two, like. Me sons all have their own lives to lead. Only Charles went into farmin' en 'e's managin' 'is farder-in-law's farm. William, me oldest, be willin' to care fer Bella at 'is place. She won't like it, but she can't live on 'er own..." He paused in thought.

Edward said, "Be there aught I can help you with, William? You've been a good friend en I'd like ter repay you."

"I don't know how long I've got. Betimes I be put in, meck sure she be treated as she deserves, Edward." William took hold of Edward's hand and held it. His face was gaunt. The twinkle had gone from his eyes and his strength was trickling away. His breathing was shallow and rattly.

Edward put his hand on top of William's. "Fer certain sure I'll do that, me auld friend."

They sat in silence. The fire crackled and hissed and Buster, who was lying by his master's side, shifted his position and sighed.

William drifted off to sleep. Edward put another log on the fire and went out to say goodbye to Bella before continuing his visits to the poor.

Widow Longley was ailing and not feeding herself properly. He took supplies to her as well as money and was considering hiring John Swift's wife to care for her.

He called in at the Grazehound while he was in town, hoping to meet a fellow farmer, to find out if anyone could help with supplies of wheat. He saw no-one he knew as he walked in and bought himself a beer at the bar. He took a long draught and thought about his friend William Ashdown. He missed the man's warm humour and kindly consideration.

The door opened, letting in a shaft of sunlight which lit up a shower of dust motes. John Paris entered. He took his hat off and, temporarily blinded by the contrast, he was unaware of Edward standing in the darkness of the bar.

"Good day, John," said Edward.

John looked up in surprise. "I didn't see you there," he said.

He bought a beer and they went and sat down in a corner. They exchanged greetings and news of the family, then went on to discuss the weather and the state of the crops.

"'Ow be yer store of wheat, John?" asked Edward. "Mine's a-runnen low en us'll need some fer poor relief."

"I can let you have a load. There be only me ter feed en this year's yield were better than most. I were abouten sell it in the market." John nodded his head and took a mouthful of beer, wiping the froth off on his sleeve.

Edward said, "I can pay you a good price fer it. I'll come en fetch it dappen I needs it."

John said, "There'll be many in need soon, I rackon. I be well advised that the ironworks be closen down. There beant enough water power fer the bellows to work the machinery. There'll be ironworkers out of work en agwain hungry."

Edward shook his head sadly, as he pushed a finger through the puddle of beer he'd spilt on the table, dividing it into two. "There'll be badgers on the streets come winter," he said.

John continued. "Of course there beant as much work fer the iron industry now the war with Spain be over. En I believe the iron a-comen over from Sweden en Spain be cheaper to buy."

Edward lifted his head. "Be that so?" he said. "The ironmasters will be short of money too. Thanks be us be farmers."

It was time for them to move on.

"Come by en see the fambly when you pass, John," said Edward. "They be a-growen. Liddle Richy be sitten up on his own, now."

John got up and they shook hands. "I'll do that, Edward. Good ter see you."

They went out into the bright sun shining low in the sky and pulled their hat brims down to shade their eyes.

That winter was severe. The damp and cold seeped in through badly fitting doors and windows. The sick became worse and Edward's widows needed their allowances supplementing with wood for their fires. In early January he had to find accommodation for Widow Longley as she became incapable of looking after herself.

Prudence cared for her husband, Josiah through his illness. He died in January, leaving their two eldest sons to carry on the cobbling business. Prudence declined any help with the funeral from the Luckes, preferring to grieve privately with her sons.

A month later, William Ashdown died. Edward and Mary attended the funeral with young Tom.

William's eldest son, Will, came to talk to them after the burial. It was a dark, dank day, the only comfort given by the bright snowdrops decorating the graves in the litten.

"Muvver's being ockard over a-comen ter bide with we," he said. "I said I'd leave un fer a few weeks to see how she managed. I can't keep happening by to see how she is…"

Edward interrupted. "I promised yer Farder I'd make sure she were orright. 'Er won't like it by 'erself, though she can manage the fire en the cooken en all. I b'lieve she be forgetful now en again. I'll see she has all she needs dappen she changes her mind, Will."

The two shook hands warmly. They went to Bella who was talking to some friends. Mary shouted, "Bella, we be bodgen now. Be sure en send fer we if you needs aught."

"Yus, my dear," said Bella. "Young Nick will be milken the cow en feeden the fowls. 'E be a good lad."

Edward was unsure that Bella had heard what Mary said. They waved and left.

"Behopes 'er comes to no harm," said Mary as they walked to where the cart was waiting.

"'Er's been tenden William all summer en feeden 'em both," Edward reminded her.

"Yus, but her has herself ter tend now. That be more difficult," Mary said.

Edward's stint as overseer was nearly over. Two weeks later he wrote in his account book:

February 21   then paid to John Swift's wife
            for Goodie Longley   0-------3-------10-------0
then paid Goodie Longley   0-------1--------2-------0
and to pay for her more at
Swift's for her bed   0------10-------0--------0
paid to John Paris   0------10------10-------2
paid Widow Ashdown   0-------2--------6-------0
left to me to pay for wheat   0-------0--------9-------0

                    0-------19-------1-------2

Chapter Sixty   1722

In which Ted is defeated

It was time to see what was happening at Slade Farm. Next month Edward would be busy with spring tasks; birthing, sowing and checking hedges and cleaning out ditches.

"I be agwain ter visit Thomas," he said to Mary at breakfast.

"Behopes they be still alive after that bad winter," she said, as she gave Richy another mouthful.

"Tom, you en Johnny will muck out the beasts en stables while I be gone," said Edward. "'Tis time you bodged off to school, Ted."

"Yus, Farder," his sons said in chorus.

Mamie started clearing the table. Mary wiped Richy's mouth and lifted him onto the floor. He sat looking round him. Edward got up from the table and bent down to pick him up.

"En what be you agwain ter be at this day, liddle man?" he said. He held his child under his arms and lifted him high in the air.

Richy shrieked and giggled. He got hold of Edward's beard and tugged at it, trying to put it into his mouth. "Mamamam," he said.

Edward put his hairy face close to Richy's and tickled him. More shrieks and giggles ensued and Richy was deposited on the floor once more. He sat there unsure what to do next.

Tom came and danced a wooden horse in front and Richy crawled towards it, took it and put it in his mouth.

Mamie came and replaced the horse with a crust of bread, which confused Richy. He was left to work out which to chew.

Mary said as Edward went out of the door, "Take this loaf to yer brudder, Ed. It be the least us can do fer 'em."

Edward took the bread, wrapped in a cloth and kissed her goodbye.

≈≈≈

Edward, Tom, Johnny and Ted left the house together. Mamie followed with a basket and went to feed the fowls and collect the eggs. Prudence and John arrived and Mary saw Edward giving John instructions for the day, before he trotted down the lane on Faithful.

Prudence went straight to see Richy, who'd decided that the crust was tastier than his horse. His face was covered in saliva and crumbs. He looked up at Prudence, grinned and said, "Mamamam." She picked him up and cuddled him.

Mary came and sat on the bench by the fire. She was tired today and wasn't sure why. Prudence was her staunch supporter and she'd no idea what she would do without her. She soothed Mary's worries about her children, found little jobs to do that Mary had put to one side until later; mending clothes and baking an extra batch of sweetmeats for the children. They brewed the beer, made butter and cheese and salted down the meat together.

Mary watched Prudence playing with her special child on her knee. Richy was making slow progress. She had to be patient, but it was a daunting prospect to know that he would never be independent like the others, that he would always need someone by him to tell him what to do.

She said, "Prudence, Edward be minded ter move to a bigger place 'forelong. What will us do without you?"

Prudence looked at Mary. She put Richy on the floor and gave him his horse. "I've been ponderin'. Me boys be all growed now. They be off seeking wives en now Josiah be gone they've taken over the cobblin' business. John be a-courten en will seek another labouren job if 'e can't bide here. I'll be free ter come along of ye if ye'll have room fer me ter bide." She smiled.

Mary took hold of her hand across the table. "Oh, Prudence! God bless you! I be so fortunate to have such a friend." They sat in silence for a while.

Voices outside alerted them and they looked up to see Mamie putting the basket of eggs down in the kitchen.

"Look what I found in the yard," she said, pushing her twin brother into the hall.

Ted stood before them, hatless, bloody and tearful, his coat sleeve ripped.

"Ted!" Mary cried. "What've you been at?"

"They was mockin' me!" he wailed. "Acause of me face! They be checkin' me all-on. They druv me mad en I lashed out at Bob." He sniffed and wiped his bleeding nose on his sleeve. "They set upon me. Us got into a fight en...Mr Hill sent me home." He came over to Mary. "I don't want ter go to school no more, Muvver."

Mary said, "Come, let's get you cleaned up en see where you be hurt." She peeled his jacket off. "Where be yer hat?"

"They throwed un over the hedge into Mr Scrase's garden."

Mary filled a basin with water, warmed up with hot from the kettle, sat Ted at the table and started sponging his face. His eye would be black in an hour or two. Most of the blood was from his nose which had dried up. His lip was cut. She tenderly cleaned the side of his face where the scar was, recalling the day when she tripped over him and spilled the kettle of hot water.

"I am so sorry," she said and kissed the coloured skin, not as red now as it had been, but enough to disfigure him.

She washed his hair and his hands, dried them carefully and went to get a drink of beer which she hotted up by the fire.

Prudence had taken the jacket and sponged the blood away. "Shall I collect the riggen ter wash? It be a good day fer dryen." She said to Mary.

"Yus, Prudence. I'll start on the milk churnen."

Ted sat by the fire, nursing his wounds and supping his hot toddy.

≈≈≈

Edward returned before coager. He found Ted still sitting by the fire. One of his eyes was swollen and surrounded by a purple bruise. He looked up at his father and sniffed.

"What happened to you, young man?" Edward asked sharply. "En why be you a-sitten there a-snivellen? Hast no school work ter be at?"

Ted hung his head and played with his fingers. He said, "The boys at school, they twit me about me face."

Edward, who'd already heard the story from Mary on his way in, said, "There be naught amiss with yer face. They be fools ter check you. They only want ter pick a fight en they got what they wanted. How many times have you picked a fight with them, eh?"

Ted shrugged.

Edward said, "Stand up when I be a-talken to you en look at me."

Ted stood up and looked at his father. He did look a mess. But Edward persisted. "Nobody sits idle in this house in the day time, Ted. If you've no work from school, you can sit en read the Bible. I'll find you a passage. Tomorrow you will go back to school en you'll be snickered at fer yer black eye. You mun larn ter face up to it, Son. All yer life there'll be folks a-starin'. But it don't make you a bad person ter have a mark on yer face. Show 'em you don't care about it. Show 'em you can be brave en a good friend ter have."

Ted nodded. He found his satchel, brought out his slate and some books and sat at the table with them.

Edward fetched a candle and lit it. He put it on the table by Ted. "I'll be a-comen ter see what you've been at while I be gone," he said.

He went out out into the kitchen, leaving Ted struggling with his figures.

Mary looked at her husband with a troubled brow. "Did you chastise un, Edward?"

"Mary, he'll never grow to be brave if us be soft with un. Behopes the mark on his face will fade in time, but 'e mun larn ter live with it en not let it bother un." He put his arm round her shoulder and gave her a kiss. "Stop you a-worritten."

Edward walked across the yard to see how Tom and Johnny were getting on. The stables were clean and tidy and the manure they'd collected was left in a steaming heap to be taken away by cart. The boys were now in one of the hog-pounds, shovelling the muck into a barrow. They were both covered from top to toe. They saw their father approach, looked at each other and giggled.

"I didn't tell you to bathe in the stuff," Edward said.

With that the boys collapsed in laughter. They slapped their thighs and slid around in the slurry.

Edward laughed with them. Then he said, "Ye should finish up. 'Twill be coager time anon en Muvver won't let you in the house in that condition."

The boys calmed down and set to work. It wasn't long before they were collecting buckets of water from the well to swill the remnants away. Then they stripped off all their clothes and washed themselves clean. Edward saw them run into the house naked and followed them. They dashed upstairs before Mary knew what was happening and came down wearing clean clothes.

"Jigger me!" said Tom when he saw Ted's battle scars. "You've been in a tarble set-to, Brudder! Did you outstand 'em?"

"Nay," said Ted sulkily. "There was free of 'em."

Tom said, "Would I were there, I'd soon give 'em a larrupin'. Don't you let 'em get away with it. Show 'em, Ted." He came over and put his arm round Ted's shoulders.

They all sat round the table. Mary brought the drinks and lifted Richy into his high chair. She put his food in front of him and he started eating. "Mumumum," he said.

Mary sat down next to him. "How be they at Slade Farm, Edward?" she asked.

Middlin'," said Edward. "Thomas has found a buyer fer the farm. 'Twill take a while ter complete the paperwork en legal stuff. They be minded ter move over ter bide in the cottage in the summer. 'E wants me ter help un with the housel."

Richy spluttered drops of milk all round, banged his hands on the tray in front of him and squealed with laughter.

Ted and Johnny giggled and Mamie said, "Richy! That be hem naughty!"

Tom and his father smiled.

Mary wiped Richy's face with a cloth which she had in readiness and said, "Enough! Be a good boy en eat nicely."

Tom said, "Farder, I believe the sow be quick after all. When we moved she into the clean hog pound 'er started maken a nest in the straw."

"That be good news," said Edward. "'Tis surely time she birthed. I bluv the hog hadn't done 'is job praper, like."

By now, Richy had spread soggy bread crumbs all over his tray and was hitting them with his flat hand, splashing everything around him.

Mary said, "No! Richy!" so sharply that he jumped.

He turned his face to his mother and stuck out his lower lip. "Mumumumum!" he shouted back.

She stood up, lifted him from the chair, carried him to the bottom step of the stairs and said, "You bide there betimes us be finished eaten," and waved a finger at him.

Richy kicked his heels on the step and shouted, "Na!" then looked defiantly at his mother with his little round eyes, waiting to see what she would do.

Mary glared back at him and put her finger up again, then turned to go back to the table.

Everyone sat in silence, not knowing whether to express shock or pleasure at this first display of rebellion from their special child.

Chapter Sixty One   1722

In which a Proposal is made

It was a sad day when Edward helped Thomas and Eliza move out of Slade Farm. When Edward arrived they were busy collecting the things they'd need from various parts of the house. Thomas was covered in cobwebs, having been up to the garret. He held the family clock in his hand.

"This auld thing don't work no more. But 'tis fambly. I can't leave un behind."

Edward agreed. "That were a gift to our Gaffer on 'is weddin' day. I mind it chimin' when I were a nipper. Dappen we'll get it going again, 'forelong."

The clock rattled alarmingly as they wrapped it in an old towel. Edward carried it to the wagon which was parked outside the back door and stowed the treasure safely. He went back indoors to get the old carved chair which had been made for their grandfather by Uncle Micheal.

"What were the story Farder told we about that chair?" he asked his brother.

Thomas sat down on the bench to catch his breath. "Gaffer William were nearly burned alive by a rabble from the village. They stood un on 'is auld chair that were 'is Uncle Thomas', outside the front door en built a fire under un. 'E were saved by Farder en 'is brudder Michael just in time. They made that chair fer un after, like."

"That be a fambly treasure too then," said Edward. He loved that story and wondered why anyone would want to kill Gaffer William. He must ask Thomas sometime. He carried the chair to the wagon.

When he got back to the parlour, he asked, "Be there aught else ye needs ter teck?"

Eliza was wrapping up a bundle of clothes. "Can you fetch the chest from our chamber, Edward? There be linen en towels ter take as well as riggen."

When he'd loaded all they needed and helped the old couple onto the wagon, Edward went in and searched the house for anything they might have forgotten. Dim childhood memories festooned with dusty cobwebs floated through his mind and he had to shake his head to bring himself back to practicalities.

There was furniture already in the cottage so no need to take any heavy items. He went out and said to Thomas, "What about fodder fer the beasts?"

"Yus. Load what you can en hitch the cow on the back."

"The fowls! Us fergotted the fowls," Eliza wailed.

"I'll teck this lot across en come back fer the fowls en all." Edward climbed up. "Geewoot!" he called and Thomas and Eliza held on tight as he clicked the old cart horse into stumbling traction. If he'd been looking, he would have noticed a tear run down Thomas' cheek.

After installing the couple in the cottage with all their personal possessions, Edward trundled the wagon back to the farm. He wanted to have one last look for that treasure his father had talked about. Now his brother was out of the way he could look more closely in all the likely places.

The house kept its secret and he shut the door and locked it. He cast his eye over the barn, cowstalls and stables which revealed nothing. With a sigh, he gave up all hope of finding what he sought. He didn't need it now. He'd managed without, he thought proudly.

He found a couple of chicken peds in the barn and took the hens from their coop, where Eliza had left them that morning. They'd laid three eggs which Edward put in a trug with some straw. There were sacks of corn in the corn store. He loaded all into the wagon with as many bags of hay as he could fit on. He hitched the cow and the mare on the back and drove over to the cottage, not wanting to look back.

When he entered the cottage he was reminded of Esland, who was the last person to live here. There was nothing to indicate what a strange life he'd led. He'd left no trace of his devious practices.

Thomas and Eliza appeared more cheerful. They'd already re-arranged the furniture in the parlour to their liking and Thomas was sitting in his armchair.

They'd lit the fire and Eliza was in the kitchen finding out what was there.

Edward went and installed the animals in the small pasture and the chickens in their run.

"Be there aught else ye needs?" he asked before he left.

"Nay," said Thomas. "I be minded ter teck a turn round the garden prensley. You bodge off home." He paused, then added, "I be obliged fer yer help, Edward."

Edward nodded in reply, surprised to hear this civility from the usually brusque Thomas. He was mellowing in his old age. Faithful waited for her master by the gate in the farmyard. Edward unhitched her, mounted and made his way home.

After the next vestry meeting at the Grazehound, Edward Benge approached Edward and offered to buy him another beer.

"I've a proposal to make, Lucke," he said.

Edward accepted the offer and they carried their drinks to a quiet corner of the room. On the way, two men raised their tankards to Benge in greeting. He nodded to them and indicated a seat to Edward.

"Now, I'm well avised that you be mindful of renting a greater farm," he said. "Am I correct?"

Edward's heart gave a little jump. He'd been wondering how to approach Benge on this subject. He supped his beer and nodded. "Yus, Sir," he said. "Me fambly be a-growen en I'd be partial ter farmin' more land."

"Well," said Benge, after taking a long draught from his tankard and letting it settle, "I've a mind ter let my farm at Pennybridge to a trustworthy farmer. My fambly has left home en I be getting on in years. The mistus is hankering after a smaller place en I've seen just the thing that would make her happy in Cousleywood."

Edward waited for the proposal, trying to keep calm.

Benge supped his beer, then looked at Edward.

"I believe you to be a suitable tenant. What would you say if I offered it to you?" he said.

Edward's eyes met Benge's. "That would be main agreeable," he said. He paused, gathering his thoughts together. "I'd need ter come en have a look around, like, ter see what be a-growin' en what beasts en accommodation you have. When will you be minded ter leave?"

"You could take over next Lady Day. Come along in the meantime and we'll discuss the terms."

"I be much obliged, Sir." Edward drained his tankard, stood up and shook hands with his future landlord, his mind in a whirl.

He rode slowly home, as if to stop things moving too quickly. He was just getting used to the idea that Slade Farm was no longer Lucke property. The surveyors had been to assess the value and when the time came for his brother to sign it over to Lawrence Foster, Thomas would be £160 better off. He would soon spend that on food and clothing. In a year or so he and Eliza would need to be supported by the parish.

Now, unexpectedly, Edward would be extra busy planning the move to Pennybridge Farm, deciding what to take, what to sell and what work would need to be done at Savages before they left. He wanted to leave it in a fit state to be rented out.

He came into his yard, dismounted and looked around him, seeing everything in a new light. He'd built this place up from nothing, brought a wife here and raised a family. It was now a reliable source of income and he'd put to one side enough for times such as this. It could be costly transferring to an unfamiliar place. It might take time to get to know the land and what would grow well there.

As he was standing with his thoughts he became aware of Mary approaching. She came to his side and took hold of his hand. The warmth of her body next to his gave him courage.

"Is there aught amiss, Ed?" she asked.

He looked down and kissed the top of her head. He squeezed her hand and said, "Gurt changes be a-comen, Mary. Our dreams will be fulfilled. The children maun be told just yet."

"Well?" Mary turned to face him, took both of his hands in hers and stood on tiptoes. "Don't keep me a-guessin'. What be it?"

Edward smiled into her eager face. "Mas Benge has offered me Pennybridge Farm to rent."

Mary gasped. "Oh Ed! I were hopin' that be it!" She jumped up and down like a child. "When? When will us be a-moven?"

Edward shushed her and put his hands on her shoulders. "Not yet awhile. Come Lady Day. There's much ter be done, Mary. You keep it to yerself betimes I say." He put his finger on her mouth.

They linked arms and walked into the house.

Chapter Sixty Two   1622/3

Tom's voice

The harvest is inned and the wind's getting up and blowing all the leaves off the trees. Jackanapes shuffles through them as he takes me over to Bassetts' Farm. I have to pull my hat over my eyes to stop it blowing off. Jackanapes sniffs the air and shakes his head. There might be rain a-coming.

I've more time now there's less to do on the farm. Farder's spending the longer evenings sitting at the table with his account book and using a slate to write lists of things and adding up figures. He's going round the fields looking mindful. He says he's planning what to grow next year.

Mas Bassett is larning me and Nick all about horse breeding. One day I'll be a horsebreeder. Horses are my favourite animals, especially the ones bred for racing from Arab stallions. Mas Bassett has said he'll find a little mare for Jackanapes and I can look after her before she foals. We have to wait until spring when one of them will come into season. I haven't told Farder yet. He has other things on his mind.

Muvver's excited about something and I don't know what it is. It might be that Richy is growing up at last. He runs around and gets into everything, like the others did when they were babies. But he has a terrible temper when he can't have what he wants. He likes acting the fool and makes us all laugh and he's learning some words but doesn't talk properly yet.

It's nearly Christmas now and I have a feeling this will be our last one at Savages. Farder told me that one day soon, when the rain has eased, he wants me to ride out with him. There's something in the air.

A week later, we saddle up our horses and make our way down the lane, turning right onto the road to Mark Cross.

"Can you keep a secret, Tom?" Farder asks.

I gulp and nod, hoping the secret will be what I think it is. "Yus, Farder," I say. My body is buzzing with excitement.

He says, "Us be on our way ter look round Pennybridge Farm. Mas Benge has offered to let it to we."

"Fegs! That be the best secret! But 'twill be middlin' hard to keep." I laugh and Farder laughs with me.

He says, "Us'll tell the others bythen it beant so long to Lady Day. Muvver knows."

"I've been minded you be up ter summat," I say.

"You can help me plan what ter be at when we've seen the land en what grows best there. Us'll need ter find out what beasts Mas Benge has en what 'e'll be taken with un. Then we'll decide which of our beasts to slaughter en teck to market en all," he says.

We're nearly there and my heart jumps as we turn into the lane to Pennybridge. It's a long, steep, twisty road downhill. Around every turn we expect to see the house.

"Drivin' a loaded wagon down here will not be easy," says Farder.

"Mayhap there'll be anudder way in," I suggest.

Suddenly we see it. We stop and stare. The old house is all timbers with plaster between. It nestles in a hollow, looking out across the valley. It's surrounded by buildings and an oast.

Farder says, "Bythen I be Gaffer, you'll manage this farm, Tom. That's why I wanted you ter come along of me. Us can plan it together."

"I'll be proud ter do that, Farder," I say. I feel sad-happy as I think of him getting on in years and hope I can make him proud too.

Mas Benge is a great ox of a man. He doesn't wear a frock like the other farmers I know. He wears a wig and a black jacket over his knee breeches and hose and long boots. He shakes our hands and brings us into a big kitchen where a tiny lady is washing her hands in the sink. She turns to greet us.

"This be the mistus," says Mas Benge.

She shakes our hands. "Let me show you the house," she says. "You came in through the entry hall.

There beant much happening in there save on feast days. We live in this room; cook, eat and sit of an evening." She leads us to a door. "All the work goes on out here. There's the brewhouse, buttery, milkhouse and bakehouse."

We go down a passage with all these rooms opening off and a door out to the yard where the stables and barns are. Mistus Benge leads us back into the kitchen. Her pattens tap-tap on the brick floor. Her full skirts rustle as she walks and grey curls bob below her cap and round her face.

"This leads up to the chambers," she says, opening another door. The narrow stairs go round two corners before they reach a passage with more doors off. I wonder how Mas Benge manages to move around up here. He must have to bend over to avoid banging his head.

Mistus Benge shows us the first room. "The buttery chamber," she says. "There be two beds in that room." She opens the opposite door. "The entry chamber's the one us uses. There's a view of the front from here." She leads us into the room. We go over to the window and look out into the front yard below. Then we walk along the passage and round a corner. "This be the brewhouse chamber," she says as she opens the door. There be one bed in there. Opposite this room there are more stairs, narrow and steep. "That goes up to the garret," the lady says. "There's room fer more beds up there."

Farder nods and we go down to the kitchen, where Mas Benge is waiting.

"I'll teck ye round the farm," he says. "Ye'll need yer horses."

We go outside and leave Mistus Benge indoors.

It being winter, some of the fields are fallow and Mas Benge tells us what he grew in them this year. We see cattle, sheep and a large milking herd. And sure enough, there's a track leading through the fields towards the road to Riseden, mostly level. There's grain and hay in the barns and I see two fine horses in the stables. I reckon Mas Benge will take them when he goes.

We enjoy freshly baked cakes and a mug of beer. Farder and Mas Benge write an agreement and sign it. Then they shake hands and we bodge off home. The horses struggle up the steep track. Farder is quiet with his thoughts and my mind drifts off, dreaming of our future life at Pennybridge Farm.

Chapter Sixty Three   1723

In which Thomas gives Edward his wagon

The winter storms and frost eased and spring flowers bloomed in the gardens and hedgerows. Birds sang lustily and lambs appeared in the fields. The Lucke family caught some of this energy and started packing their belongings, taking young steers to market and bagging the remains of the corn and hay.

Edward paid a visit to The Slade before the move. He found the old couple in good health and the cottage was moderately clean.

"Thomas," he said to his brother. "I've a use fer the auld wagon if you can spare un. Us be a-moven to anudder farm come Lady Day en yer wagon be justly what I need. My oxen will pull un."

Thomas sighed and nodded. "Yus, Brudder. I can let you have un in part payment of that debt I owes you. I've no need of un now. Say you writes off eight pounds fer un?"

Edward said, "I be main agreeable. Shall I teck un now?"

Thomas nodded again. "I needs the carthorse fer me cart. I wish thee good fortune in yer new place." He got out of his chair and came to stand at the door while Edward hitched up Faithful to the wagon. She'd pulled a cart occasionally and the wagon was empty so not too heavy. He would walk her back home. He waved to Thomas before leading her out into the road.

Lady Day dawned a fine, bright day. The wagon and the cart stood in the yard. The family rose early and had their breakfast while Edward gave his instructions for the move.

"Us'll get as much as possible of housel on the wagon en I'll drive un wiv Muvver, Mamie, Prudence en Richy. Uncle John's agreed ter be at Pennybridge ready ter help unload.

"Uncle Richard en Sam will come here en gather the beasts. Tom, Ted and Johnny will stay here ter help, with John Winder. The cows en other beasts will be driven with the geese. Johnny, you'll come in the cart with the fowls in their peds en the shoots. We be leaven the sow here fer now, like. Sam will drive the cart.

"'Twill need all of us ter gather the shoots into their crates. They be wondrous gantsey."

A noise in the yard alerted them to the arrival of Richard and Sam. Edward went out to greet them and the women started clearing the table. All the containers they could find were waiting to be filled with food and the equipment they needed. The Benge's would have left furniture at Pennybridge.

There was hustle and bustle in the house; the women were packing linen and clothes into baskets; Edward was carrying the heavy items to the wagon. They frequently bumped into each other on the stairs and in doorways.

"We'll teck the mirror that Mistus Waghorn gived us, Mamie. En there be books on the bedside table…" Mary was anxious that nothing important was left behind.

Tom, Johnny and Ted went to catch the hens and ducks and put them in their peds to take on the cart. Sam and John Winder were rounding up the beasts in the pastures and Richard bridled the oxen and horses ready for pulling the wagon and the cart.

Edward was loading Mary's nursing chair when he heard a squeal. A little pig ran under the wagon and out the other side. Edward turned and went towards the hog-pound. There was Richy, holding the gate open and laughing as he watched the rest of the litter escaping. The last one ran towards the stables. Richy was about to go into the hog-pound to see the sow, who was busy rooting around in thick mud.

"The shoots be out!" Edward shouted as he went to find the crates they had made to transport them.

Ten little pigs were running between legs, into corners, dodging as arms reached out to catch them.

The boys came carrying the fowls to the cart. They put the peds down out of the way and joined in the hunt. Sam and John Winder appeared. They all formed a circle around several of the pigs and moved carefully forward, ready to catch.

There was a shout from the hog-pound. Richy, covered from head to foot in mud, ran into the circle and chased the pigs, shrieking with laughter.

Two were caught. The rest escaped.

Mary came out of the house with another squealing pig in her arms. She put it in the crate, then saw Richy and shouted in horror. "Richy! Come here!" She ran to catch him but he was as elusive as the pigs. He ran into the barn.

The family watched as Mary carried a dripping Richy towards the well. She stood him on the ground, took the well bucket and before he could escape again, poured water all over him. Then she picked him up, kicking and screaming and carried him into the house.

The men and the boys resumed their efforts to catch the pigs, which by this time were scattered far and wide.

Eventually, all the piglets were encased in their crates and lay waiting on the cart, quietly snoozing after the excitement. Everyone went back to their tasks. Edward finished loading the wagon and helped Mary, Mamie and Prudence up with Richy in clean clothes and clutching a wooden horse.

The cart was also ready to move off with Sam in the driver's seat. The animals were all in pens in the pasture, waiting to be driven, with the boys and John Winder armed with sticks. Richard would ride behind, to catch any stragglers.

Edward shouted "Geewoot!" and led the procession out of the yard and down the lane. The cart trundled behind, then the beasts, followed by the geese.

On the road they met friends and acquaintances who waved and shouted good wishes. A couple of the Bassett boys were waiting by their farm entrance and came to join the drivers. The air was filled with the lowing of cattle, hissing and cackling of fowls and shouts from the drivers, accompanied by the steady sound of wagon wheels rumbling along the rutted road.

Edward's spirits soared as he turned left onto the road to Riseden. He was sure that this would be a good move for his family. In a year or two, when he'd got the measure of his new farm and the boys were old enough to form part of the workforce, he would have reached the pinnacle of his ambitions. He would be able to die happy, knowing that Tom was a fitting son to carry on the management of the farm. Mary sat beside him. She'd been a constant and loyal wife of whom he was so proud.

≈≈≈

Mary felt the energy racing through her husband's body. She caught it and held it in her heart. She needed to be confident that all would be well. She was on the threshold of a change in her life, which would be challenging. The last time she'd entered into a new phase, it turned out to be not at all as she expected.

The road went steeply downhill and wound round sharp bends. Was it a warning of what was to come? She clung onto her seat as Edward applied the brakes and she flinched as they nearly collided with a horse rider coming towards them along the narrow lane.

At last they came to a gate, held open by her brother John at the entrance to a view of green rolling fields. The road led them across land that they would be farming and her body relaxed as she gazed at the beauty around her. Soon, the farmhouse appeared and her heart jumped for joy. This was her new home and she knew she would be happy here.

They rolled into the yard and Edward climbed down, then helped her step onto the cobbles. Prudence and Richy were next and Mamie scrambled down after them. They went through the back door into the spacious kitchen. And there were Herbert and Judith Smith, greeting them with open arms. They'd come with John to help him prepare for their arrival. Mary's heart filled with affection. They'd lit the fire and the room was warmly welcoming. The kettle was bubbling steamily on the range and the table was covered in plates of coager cake and the like. Richy was put on the floor and Mamie resumed her role as childminder. Mary and Prudence went to explore the rest of the house.

Edward and John Paris started carrying in the housel with Mary supervising. She noticed he was limping; his old wound playing up. Prudence found a barrel of beer and some mugs. In a while, the rest of the company trickled into the kitchen, having deposited the young pigs in the hog-pound with the two resident sows and left the animals in the nearest pasture to explore their new surroundings.

Mugs were raised in a toast to Pennybridge Farm and everyone helped themselves to coager cake. Soon the room resounded with men's voices, recalling the journey there and all the adventures which had befallen them.

Mary looked around at the large gathering with a full heart. Richy, overcome by the noise and the booted legs surrounding his small stature, came and hugged her skirts. She bent to lift him up. He put his arms round her neck and kissed her juicily. His past misdemeanors were forgiven.

Their new life had begun.

Chapter Sixty Four 1723

Tom's voice.

We've been living here for four weeks. We haven't got the help of John Winder no more so I have to feed the beasts and Ted milks the cows. I'm busy nearly all day helping Farder sort out what we brought with us and what we need. He takes me round the fields and we plan what to grow.

"This field were ploughed last month," he says. "There be time ter sow clover here fer winter fother en more seed fer next year. We'll harrow un fust."

We spend all day harrowing. Farder larns me how to guide the oxen. Tomorrow we'll sow the seed.

We're half way sowing clover and Mamie comes to fetch Farder. Mas Bassett has come by. We're neighbours now.

Farder says, "You carry on, Tom en finish the field while I talk to Mas Bassett." He walks away and I continue sowing. Walking up and down the field in the sunshine is pleasant. The birds follow me, picking up some of the seed. I think about our life here and how much I like working alongside Farder. I've noticed he's been limping lately. He says it's from when he broke his leg a long time ago.

I'll go to Bassett's tomorrow to see Bluebell, the mare who's carrying Jackanapes' foal. She's the colour of conkers. She has a white flash on her nose. In the spring, when she's near to birthing, I'll bring her here so I can be with her when it happens.

Farder agreed to sell the sow we left at Savages to Mas Bassett. He also wanted the faggots and hay which we didn't need. We spent one and a half days carrying five loads of faggots and two loads of hay. John Winder helped us. Mas Bassett paid Farder 4/6 for the pig and 7/- for the faggots and hay and the carrying of it. Farder paid me 1/6 for my labour. That's my first wages. I put it away in the chamber which I share with Ted, in a pot under my cot.

The wheat in the corn store's getting low. We'll need some more before long. The clover I sowed is growing well and we made loads of hay in May. We should get more before September.

It's a hot summer's day and we're all sitting on bags of straw in the cart with Farder driving the cart horses. Uncle John is coming with us and I expect to see Uncle Richard, Sam and Meg. We're going to Ticehurst Fair where there'll be games to play and dancing. I hope Ted and me will be happy together for a change.

Ted doesn't go to school any more. He works on the farm. I think he's jealous of me working with

Farder most of the time. He's grumpy and won't do what I ask him to do. He won't talk to me when we go to bed at night, even when I talk to him.

It's too far for Johnny to go to school alone. Farder's told me to larn him to read and write and to work with figures. He can count up to twenty already.

The road's very bumpy and Richy is climbing all over us. He won't sit still. Muvver put a hat on his head because he hasn't much hair, but he keeps knocking it off. Mamie is trying to hang onto him but he's too strong for her. Uncle John starts singing a song about mowing hay and we all join in.

One man went to mow
Went to mow a meadow...

Richy tries to join in, but he doesn't know the words.

We drive along narrow lanes, round sharp bends, up and down hills, past Sharpes Farm, Scrag Oak and Darby to get onto the road to Ticehurst at Shovers Green. We came this way to avoid the toll at Wadhurst. There are lots of other people going the same way, on foot, horseback and in carts like us. We shout and wave to the walkers as we pass.

There are more crowds coming from other directions when we get to the Fairground. It's quite a squeeze getting through the entrance. Farder finds a place to leave the cart and horses and gives them bags of hay to keep them happy. We all climb down from the cart and stretch our legs. Johnny and Richy chase each other round in circles and Ted and I go with Mamie to the booths selling all manner of sweetmeats. Muvver and Prudence follow, shepherding Richy and Johnny. Then we all go to see the dancing. Muvver and Prudence sit on the grass.

Muvver says, "We'll look after Richy if you children want ter go abroad."

We run off together and find a place where people are rolling big wooden balls at thick wooden pegs stood on end. The one who knocks the most pegs over is the winner. Ted and I play this game and we're soon laughing together. He's better at it than I am. He wins most times. Mamie and Johnny go to another game and we find the tug of war. We join in with this until we're tired and wander round to see what else we can find. There are people making trugs, a leatherworker mending harnesses and a blacksmith. We find Farder and Uncle John there, looking at some farming tools. There are sheep and lambs for sale and didicais with their horses and caravans painted with gay patterns. A tinker's mending pots and kettles and the didicais are selling ribbons and trinkets. We watch fiddler playing for some children who are dancing.

Then I see the girl I was sweet on at school, Margaret. She's pretty. I go to talk to her and she seems pleased to see me. I tell her we've moved to Pennybridge Farm.

She says, "I bide in Riseden. Me farder does work at Pennybridge now en then."

"Oh," I say. "Behopes I'll see you again."

She nods and her face turns pink.

Ted's talking to Margaret's friend. We all walk away to find some mead to drink and we meet Mamie with Johnny. Then the girls go away together and Ted and I take Johnny to the swings.

Soon we're feeling hungry and go to find Muvver. The girls are there, but Margaret and her friend are just saying goodbye. Muvver has brought some bait with her and we all sit on the ground to eat it. Farder comes along with Uncle Richard who joins us. Sam has found a girl and they've gone off together.

It's soon time to go home and feed the animals and milk the cows. We all take something home with us from the fair. Mamie and Muvver have new ribbons for their hats, Prudence bought a trug for carrying eggs and Farder a rake for the garden. Uncle John has a new waistcoat. Ted, Johnny and I have whistles made by a didicai and Richy some new shoes. We make a lot of noise with our whistles on the way home, until Farder tells us to stop. It has been a happy day.

Chapter Sixty Five   1723/4

In which Ted is in trouble

John Paris sat at the kitchen table with Edward. It was the middle of winter and the rain and hail thrashed around the house, channelled along the passages and rattled the windows. Hanging up by the range, John's outdoor clothing glistened wet and steam rose from the side nearest the fire. The drips from his hat fell onto the hearth where they sizzled to nothing in the heat. He took a rag from his pocket to wipe his nose.

Prudence brought jugs of ale and put them down in front of the two men.

Edward said, "I have ter pay you fer that wheat I had a month or two back."

John nodded. "I'd be obliged, Ed, but that's not what I be here fer." He took a long draught of ale. "I be minded ter move to a smaller place. 'Tain't worken out where I be. Too big fer one en I've jacked up seeken a mistus. Would you be minded ter rent out Savages? 'Twould be just about my size."

Edward said, "I'd be main agreeable ter that, John. 'Twould be hem fitten as you knows the place en the land. En 'twould get it off me hands. John Winder be abidin' in the cottage next door. Mayhap 'e'll be glad of some work. Say you teck Savages over come Lady day?"

John agreed and they shook hands on it. The conversation meandered to other things as the warmth of the fire and the ale had their effects. John took his jacket off and Mary came and offered him coager.

"That would be main agreeable, Sister," said John. The two men resumed their reminiscing.

There was a kerfuffle at the back door and Tom, Ted and Johnny came bursting in, having taken off their hats, boots and coats in the passage. Their hands and faces glowed and their eyes shone.

"Is all done?" asked Edward.

Tom stood with his back to the range and said, "Yus, Farder. Beasts mucked out en fed, cows milked. Us left 'em in the barn with some hay. 'Tis considerable wild out there. Behopes the wind dies down afore we milk 'sarternoon."

Ted joined his brother at the range. He nudged Tom to move along and Tom nudged him back.This bickering continued until they were both giggling and finally tumbling around on the floor.

Mary came into the kitchen with food for the table. "Get up en go en fight in yer chamber, boys," she said, "'Tis no place fer rough en tumble where yer farder's a-talkin'. Come down fer coager when ye're sober."

The boys got to their feet and Ted chased Tom up the stairs. A door slammed and the adults heard a wail: "Let me in, Tom."

At last they were all sitting at the table eating hot potage and lashings of fresh bread and cheese. Prudence sat next to Richy to make sure he ate his food politely as they had a visitor. But when he'd finished he got down from the bench and Mary saw that he had food all down his front.

"Oh! Richy!" she scolded.

The little boy stood in front of his audience and put his hands up to his face, mimicking his mother.

"Oh! Richy!" he said.

This caused gales of laughter from the spectators. Chastisement was futile. Richy was swept away by Prudence while the family regained their composure.

"That one lifts the spirits, surely," said John.

≈≈≈

The roads around Wadhurst were notoriously impassable in the winter months. Great lakes appeared in the hollows and rivers of gushing water carved deep ruts down the slopes. Earth and stones were washed out of the high banks, forming seas of deep mud which were treacherous for horses and walkers alike. No-one travelled far.

In early spring the local population made an effort to improve the condition of their highways to enable them to travel again. Edward had been appointed to organise road repairs in the Riseden quarter. This meant being away from the farm for six days in a row. He had to engage the local farmers to supply horses and carts to carry the tools and materials they would need. The smallholders were the labourers. This would give him the opportunity to meet his neighbours.

≈≈≈

On Monday morning Mary packed his bait while Edward gave the boys their duties for the day. It was time the sheep were moved to the lambing pasture and pens were made from hurdles. This would take them all day with their other regular duties. They watched their father trundle down the lane towards Riseden with two horses pulling the cart, which was full of stones they had collected from the fields.

Johnny was already out feeding the fowls and collecting the eggs. Ted went to drive the cows to be milked and Tom took barrowloads of chopped turnips for the beasts in the meadow. Mary would take Johnny and Richy out later to sow some seeds in the vegetable garden. First, there was bread, butter and cheese to make with Prudence and Mamie.

After the family had eaten their coager together they went their separate ways to continue the activities of the morning. Mary took the hands of her two younger boys and led them to the vegetable garden. She looked forward to sinking her fingers into the soft earth again after the winter. Little had been grown here for a year or two. She'd been spending time digging over the plot and putting in stakes to mark the rows for peas and beans, leeks and carrots. She planned to sow seeds for herbs in one plot. Today they would start with a row of broad beans.

Johnny was keen to learn and was soon raking the ground and marking out the stations. Mary showed Richy how to hoe the weeds in another patch with a nidget. He was surprisingly efficient and Mary felt she could leave him to it while she prepared the ground in the herb garden. She started by pulling out the weeds and putting them in a bucket. The overgrown cabbages would be a treat for the hens.

There was a shout and Mary raised her head to see Richy hoeing up the beans Johnny had carefully planted. She went and dragged him away, leaving poor Johnny to start again. Richy sat on the ground and watched Mary for a while. She went to pick up the full bucket to take it to the compost heap.

Richy stood up. "I will help you wiv dat," he said in his husky voice. He picked up the bucket and Mary led him over to where she wanted it tipped. He turned the bucket over and shook it until it was empty, as he'd seen his mother do.

"Good boy, Richy," she said. "Shall us go en get some more?"

Richy had grown taller in the last year. He'd nearly caught up with Johnny in height and he had surprising strength for a four-year-old. He seemed to want to be helpful and Mary thought that if she could train him he would be a good labourer. The problem was making him understand what was allowable and what was not.

They were disturbed by Ted running into the garden.

"Muvver!" he shouted. "Tom's catched hurt! 'E can't walk!"

Richy mimicked, "Tom's catched hurt."

~~~

Edward brought the cart home as the light faded. The calm weather had allowed the work on the roads to progress well. As he passed the sheep, safely installed in their new pasture, he was thankful that Tom and Ted had managed to keep their differences to themselves and carry out their instructions. He knew there was an urgent need for an adult labourer on the farm, with all the spring ploughing, manuring and sowing to do. He'd met a man today, Ed Lambert, who'd worked for Benge in the past. Lambert was grateful to have the offer of employment and had an advantage as he knew the land. He would start as soon as they'd finished work on the roads.

Edward saw that the lambing pens hadn't been completed and there was no sign of the boys. He left the cart outside the yard, ready for the following day and made his way into the house, leaving his boots in the passage by the kitchen door. As he entered his eyes met a strange scene.

Tom was sitting in his mother's soft chair with Mary at his feet, one of which was propped up on a stool. She was rubbing oil into his swollen ankle.

Tom looked up. "I twisted me foot in a robbut hole," he said.

"Canst walk?" asked Edward. He could not afford to lose a labourer this week.

"'Tis considerable painful, like," replied Tom. "I'll be orright by marnen."

"Nay you will not. This be a bad sprain," Mary asserted. "You mun keep un up bythen the swellen goes down."

Richy, who was standing by, repeated, "keep un up bythen the swellen goes down."

"Where be Ted?" asked Edward.

Mary said, "I sent un ter give Johnny a hand ter finish off sowen the beans."

"Us mun finish the lambin' pens afore dark," said Edward and went to go out.

Ted and Johnny had arrived and came through the door as he opened it. "Put yer boots on again, Ted. We be agwain ter finish off in the pasture," he said.

"Oh! Nay, I be fairly beazled," protested Ted. But he knew he must obey his father.

Johnny came in and Edward closed the door behind them.

"Did you put the tools away, Johnny?" Mary asked, as she wrapped a bandage tightly round Tom's foot.

"Yus, Muvver," he said and sank down on the bench at the table, leaning his head on his hands.

Richy picked up the sombre mood and went to put his arms round Johnny. Johnny smiled and returned the hug.

Tom tried to get up. "There be the milken en the beasts..." he winced and sat down again.

Mary looked at him. "Can you tend Richy while we be gone? Meck sure 'e don't get into no mischief."

Tom nodded.

Mary called for Prudence and Mamie and they took Johnny out again to deal with all the chores.

≈≈≈

Edward and Ted struggled to construct the pens in semi-darkness. Ted's work was sloppy and slow. Edward's temper was already up. It wouldn't take much to cause him to snap.

"Where d'you think you be agwain with that hurdle?" he shouted, as Ted started off in the wrong direction. He turned back and flung it down in front of his father.

"I can't do nuffin' right," he said. "Where does you want un, then?"

Edward bit his lip in an effort to keep calm. This was not the way to get Ted to work. He picked up the hurdle and gave it back to Ted.

"Fix un there," he said, indicating where he wanted it.

They finished the job. Ted was moody and stormed off to the house ahead of his father. When Edward came into the kitchen the family was waiting for dinner to be put on the table. They were all tired and the atmosphere was tense. They knew they were now under pressure to share the extra work between them until Edward had finished the road repairs and Tom's foot was healed.

≈≈≈

Mary saw that Edward was exasperated with his second son. Now the overseer duties were finished and they had Ed Lambert labouring for them, work on the farm was settling into a pattern. But there was lambing to attend as well as the rest and she didn't want Tom damaging his foot before it was healed. Ted was going out every day with Edward and the two of them were not getting along.

"That boy be lazy en careless," Edward said to Mary one evening. "'E'll not make as good a farmer as Tom."

"'E be but a child, Edward," said Mary. "Mayhap you be drivin' un too hard."

"'E be eleven year, Mary. I were a-labouren on the farm when I were seven." He paused, then added. "En 'e be stubborn with it."

The next morning Tom bumped himself down the stairs and said to Mary, "Ted be gone from 'is bed, Muvver. 'Is riggen be gone. I didn't hear un go."

Johnny had come down earlier with Mamie.

"You two go en see if Ted be out there milken or anywhere else you can think of," Mary urged them.

Edward came in from checking on the sheep.

Mary asked him, "Did you see Ted out there?"

Edward looked surprised. "Nay, What's 'e done now?"

Tom sat on the bottom step in his nightshirt. "I reckon 'e's gone away" he said.

Mary gasped. "Nay, 'e wouldn't do that surely?"

Chapter Sixty Six   1724

Tom's voice.

Ted's been gone three days and nights. Farder went out on his horse but came back with no news. He'd called at all the neighbours along the way and they're searching for him in their barns en all.

I looked in my money pot and there's nothing in it. Ted must have taken it for food. Muvver said there was a loaf of bread and some cheese missing from the milkhouse.

I'm in the stable with Bluebell, talking to her and telling her to hurry up with her foal. She's listening by waggling her ears around and nodding her head. I'm upset that Ted took my money. I was saving it to buy a stallion when I'm a man, so I can start breeding horses. They cost a lot of money and it will take me a long time to save enough.

Today is Lady Day. We've been here a whole year. Uncle John is moving to Savages and Farder has gone to help him load the cart. He'll be away all day.

Suddenly I realise that Ted might be hiding in the barn at Savages. That's where I'd go if I didn't want to be found. He doesn't know that Uncle John's moving in today. Farder will be very angry when he finds him. I must warn him somehow.

I grab my stick and limp out to the pasture where Jackanapes is grazing. I'll have to manage without the saddle. I lead him out of the pasture, shut the gate and scramble onto his back. We go round the front of the house where there's less chance of someone seeing us and make our way up the steep, rough lane and out onto the Wadhurst road. It won't take long to get to Savages. I hope we make it before Farder and John arrive.

There's a flock of sheep on the road. I have to wait until they pass. The lad who's shepherding them is making a mess of it and I can't help him with my foot strapped up. It seems a long time before I can squeeze past the last of them and be on my way. Then I go as fast as Jackanapes can go with the road still rough after the winter. From the end of Savages lane I can see no sign of a cart full of housel.

I hurry up to the yard. All is quiet. It seems strange being here with no-one else around and no animals. There are weeds growing in between the cobbles.

I dismount and hobble to the barn, shouting, "Ted! It's me, Tom!"

I open the barn door. There's no-one there. But there are signs that someone has been. There's a cloth that Muvver uses to wrap cheeses. Where can he be?

Now I hear the sound of a cart coming up the lane. I can't get away without being seen. I leap back onto Jackanapes and turn to meet them.

Farder rides in on his horse. He asks, "What be you a-doin' here, Tom?"

I'd better tell the truth. "I thought Ted might be hiding here, but I've not found un."

Farder shakes his head. "'E'll come back when 'e be hungry," he said. "You'd best bodge off home afore Muvver thinks you be run off en all."

I start off down the lane. I know Farder's more worried than he's making out.

I get to the end of the lane. I see Ted walking down the road from Wadhurst. He looks unhappy, shuffling his feet, his head bent over. He lifts his head and sees me.

He stops.

"Ted!" I call. "Come here en I'll give thee a ride home."

He walks slowly, then starts running. He reaches me out of breath, but grinning, with tears running down his face. He clings to my leg.

"Farder will beat me!" he protests.

I give him a lift up. "Farder's helping Uncle John move into Savages," I say. "You can't go back there. I'll get you home afore 'e gets in. Muvver won't let un give you a laruppin'."

We put Jackanapes back in his pasture and I go with Ted to the house. Muvver's putting food on the table for coager. She nearly drops it in surprise when we walk in.

"Ted!" she cries. "Where have you bin?" She hugs Ted and wipes his tears away. "Look at you!" she says. "You need a good wash en clean riggin'." She hugs him again.

Then she holds his face between her hands. "You gave we a terrible fright, Ted. I bluv I'd lost thee. Just be minded, however hard Farder is on you, it don't mean he don't love you. 'E only wants you to become a good farmer. Now go en wash en change yer riggen afore you eat."

We spend the afternoon helping with the lambing. Muvver's good with the sheep and she don't get flustered when the lamb gets stuck. She teaches us what to do and how to know when to help the sheep. Even Ted's enjoying himself. He's glad to be back with the family.

In between lambing we go to the top of the pasture and watch for rabbits. I have my catapult ready and when they come out to play I take a shot. Sometimes I miss, but we've killed three so far. Ted's retrieving them for me. We'll have rabbit for dinner tonight.

We're all sitting round the table and Farder comes in.

There's a hush while everyone waits to see what he'll do when he sees Ted.

Ted stands up and goes to Farder. "Farder," he says. "I be hem ernful fer agwain away. Please don't be mad at me."

Farder's face turns from surprise to happy. He doesn't have time to be angry. He hugs Ted and says, "Welcome home, son. Us mun have a talk after dinner."

They both sit at the table and we all breathe again.

Johnny says, "'Tis robbut pie fer dinner."

"My favourite," says Farder.

We all start talking and the room is filled with happiness.

I'm getting up early this morning. I want to go and see Bluebell. I believe she's near to birthing. I can't get my breeches on quick enough. I bump down the stairs and grab my stick, open the door and slip my good foot into a boot. It's the wrong one. I kick it off and search for the other. Standing on the bad foot is not so painful, though it's still swollen. I think I can manage without the stick soon.

I limp as fast as I can to the stable door, open the top half and peer in.

I'm amazed! Bluebell has just dropped a foal, covered in stickiness. She turns round and sees me, then starts licking her baby clean. It's just like Jackanapes; black with a white flash on its forehead. I think it's a colt, though I can't see clearly.

I don't move. Bluebell knows what to do. The foal is soon clean and looking at its new surroundings. Bluebell gives a gruff whinny. As I watch, my heart beating fast, the foal tries to stand up. It totters to its feet, standing on long legs splayed out to get its balance. He seeks his mother's milk and starts suckling.

I realise there are tears are running down my face. I am so happy I want to shout and dance. I leave the mother and baby in peace and limp back into the house. The family are coming down for their porridge.

"Bluebell has a foal!" I shout.

They all say, "Ooh!" and "Aah!" and laugh with pleasure.

"Can us go en see un?" asks Johnny.

"'E be feeden now," I say. "Leave un bythen you've had yer breakfast en you can go two at a time."

Muvver gives me a hug and Farder slaps me on the back and laughs with me.

Chapter Sixty Seven   1725/6

In which Edward cares for Thomas in his need

It was a couple of years later. Edward was in Wadhurst, delivering goods to George Klifon and James Apps, both regular customers. Then he went to call on John Wachas the cordwainer to settle up with him. Winter was a period when Edward sold wheat, oats and meat. As people used up their own stocks and, as long as the roads remained open, it was a lucrative time.

He'd left a harrow with Ed Chapman the blacksmith to be sharpened, who was also checking his horse's hooves. Edward went to the Grazehound for a jar and a gossip in the meantime. The Inn was crowded with farmers and the air was stale and hummed with conversation. Edward pushed his way to the bar and found himself standing next to an old friend from Lamberhurst. They shook hands and Stephen bought Edward a beer.

"Did you know yer brudder Thomas be ailing, Edward?" said Stephen.

"Nay, I've been minded ter go en see un afore long. What state be the roads?" Edward enquired.

"I got through today with me cart, but 'tis easier on horseback," his friend replied.

"What be up with Thomas, then?" asked Edward, not sure how seriously to treat this piece of news.

"They've been on poor relief fer a couple of months, but when the overseer delivered the last goods, he were middlin' concerned that they'd soon need nursing, like"

"Mm, sounds like I'd best be visiten," said Edward. "What other news from Lamb'rurst?"

They talked for a while about this and that until their jars were drained, then pushed through the crowds into the clean air. They said goodbye and went their separate ways.

When Edward reached home the family were out doing their various work. Tom and Ted were in the copse cutting cordwood with Johnny tying up bundles of faggots. Mary and Mamie were in the vegetable garden and Prudence had taken Richy for a walk.

Edward went to the high shelf above the range where he kept the money pot and counted what was in there. He was satisfied that he could afford to pay for help for his brother if he needed it. He spent the rest of the aftenoon walking round the farm. Soon, when the ground had dried out, he'd need to employ another labourer. He'd signed off Ed Lambert early in the winter as there wasn't enough work for him. Tom and Ted were strong enough now to do men's work.

John Cornford had said he was willing and would accept being paid with goods. Edward knew that he himself was slowing down. His eyesight was deteriorating and his strength failing him.

That evening he said to Mary, "I be well avised that me brudder en 'is wife be ailing. They be dependent on the parish en might need nursen."

Mary said, "You mun go en attend to their needs, Edward. There beant much work on the farm afore the weather improves en Tom seems ter know what ter be at. You've trained un well." She put her mending to one side. One candle's light was not enough to see by and she kept pricking her fingers.

Edward said, "I'll visit them termorrer. 'Twill teck me all day. The roads beant fit fer fast travellin'. I'll do what I can, but I don't want ter bide there if I can help it."

"You do what be necessary, Edward," said Mary. "'Tis justabout time I be agwain to me bed. Me eyes won't stay open. She pushed herself out of her comfortable chair, rubbed her back and bent to give her husband a kiss, before making her way up the stairs.

Edward arrived in Lamberhurst and rode into the entrance of the cottage. The place looked neglected. He had to step over weeds to get to the front door. He knocked loudly and heard a faint voice.

"Come in."

The door resisted his efforts to open it. A smell which he couldn't identify met him and the room was dark and cold. There were papers and clothes and dirty plates strewn on the floor. He made out two shapes in chairs and as he approached he heard Thomas' feeble voice.

"Who be it?"

"'Tis Edward, Thomas. You be in a hem ernful condition, Brudder."

Thomas held out his hand and when Edward took it he was pulled close to his brother. The smell intensified.

"It be 'er, Ed. She won't do aught ter help a poor old man. I ain't ett in days en I can't get up to do aught meself."

Edward glanced over to where Eliza sat in her chair, snoring loudly.

"She beant fit, Thomas," he said. "I be come ter get help fer ye."

Thomas clung onto his hand with an icy vice-like grip. "Don't leave me, Brudder. There be no knowing what she be at. She's stolen all me money." He exploded into a rattling fit of coughing, which caused him to lift his head and clutch his chest. His breath was foul.

"I be agwain ter fetch help," Edward said when the paroxysm was over.

He left the house and mounted Faithful. On the way down to the village he passed Widow Bocher walking up. He stopped and called to her.

"Widow Bocher, can you avise me?"

The lady stopped and turned. "My! If it ain't Edward Lucke!" she said.

Edward said, "Me brudder Thomas be mortal sick en 'is mistus be ailing. I mun find a nurse en a maid who'll attend to their needs."

Widow Bocher said, "It be a long time since we've seed you around these parts. Goodie Button be the woman ter ax. You knows where she bides?"

"Yus, I knows. I be much obliged, Ma'am." Edward searched in his money purse and gave the lady four pence. He clicked Faithful on.

He called at the Buttons' house in the village. Martha opened the door and smiled in surprise when she saw who it was.

She showed Edward into the parlour and exclaimed, "Oh! Mas Lucke! I ain't seed you in years!"

Edward explained the situation and asked, "Would you be willin' to nurse 'em? I'll find a maid to provide food en keep the fire lit."

Martha said, "I'd heard tell they was on the parish books, but I weren't aware it were that bad. I'll come en see what's ter be done." She nodded and went to get her cape.

Edward called at Foster's village store and asked if they knew of a girl who could attend his brother and his wife. They knew just the one and would send her as soon as they'd tracked her down. On the way up the hill, Edward passed Goodie Button and waved.

He reached the cottage a few minutes ahead of her and announced to Thomas that help was on its way. Thomas was confused and it took him time to realise who Edward was. By the time Martha arrived, he was fully aware and Eliza had woken.

"Edward!" she cried. "What a blessin' ter see you. We be in a tarble hike. Thomas be losen 'is wits en I can't do aught ter help un. The parish officers call now en agin, but I can't cook nor ..."

"Don't fret yerself, Eliza," interrupted Edward. I be getting' help fer ye. Here's Goodie Button ter nurse ye en there's a maid on her way."

"But we ain't got no money," wailed Eliza and started sobbing.

"I'll pay fer yer needs, Eliza." Edward went and patted her shoulder, not wanting to get too close to the stench.

Martha spoke. "Us'll have ter get 'em out of these chairs, Mas Lucke. They'll need clean riggen en a good wash. 'Twould be better fer 'em ter be in cots. Be there any up aloft?"

Martha Button and Edward spent the rest of the day cleaning up the old couple and putting them into cots, propped up on pillows. The maid, Mary May, arrived and set to cleaning the floor and lighting the fire. The chairs they'd been sitting in were left outside to be burnt, along with the clothes they'd been wearing. Mary May found some food which had been delivered by the poor relief and she cooked a meal for Thomas and Eliza.

"I'll bide 'ere," she said. "I can sleep upstairs, then I can see to the fire en all."

Edward thanked her and said, "I'll call again in a couple of days. You buy what's needed." He gave her a few shillings.

Martha said, "I can call every day en give them the care they need. Will you get some strong waters when you go through Wad'urst?"

Edward nodded and shook her hand. "Thank you Mistus Button."

She put her cloak round her shoulders and left.

The candles were lit and the room was warm. Thomas and Eliza sat in their cots, looking more comfortable. Edward said, "I be bodgen now, Brudder. The maid be biden here, she'll tend you. I'll be back afore long."

He went and held Thomas' hand. It was now warm and relaxed. Thomas said, "I be failen, Edward. I beant long fer this life. Thank you fer what you're a-doin'. I want you ter have the heifer. Will you knock three pounds off what I owes?"

Edward was astonished that Thomas was still keen to pay off his debts after all this time. He'd lived with this burden for thirty-four years. Edward squeezed his brother's hand.

"That will be hem agreeable, Thomas."

Eliza was snoring again and Edward popped his head round the kitchen door to bid Mary May goodbye.

He plodded home on Faithful in the gathering dusk.

For the rest of February Edward travelled to Lamberhurst every few days. The maid didn't stay every night but the old couple were well cared for. Edward entered all that he spent into his account book:

1726 February ye 12
What I have Laid out for Thomas Lucke in his Need

13	*Then I had the heifer away*	
	for what he owed me in part	*3 --- 0 --- 0*
14	*Paid to Henry Plaster for meat*	*0 --- 1 --- 5*
	& Edward Burgess for strong waters	*0 --- 0 --- 10*
18	*Paid Widow Tiast for linen*	
	Three pairs of sheets	*0 --- 4 --- 0*
19	*more for some small things*	
	At Mr Fosters	*0 --- 0 --- 6*
	Paid Widow Bocher	*0 --- 0 --- 4*
	And so on…	

Thomas Lucke's health deteriorated. He became more confused but in his more lucid moments he was still worrying about repaying his debt to Edward.

March 1   More to pay the maid   0 --- 0 --- 6
*   7   then I had the mare*
*   from my brother's order to keep   2 --- 0 --- 5*
*   13   then I had the clock*

Thomas said, "I've naught more to give you, Edward. I knows this was a treasure to you. See if you can get un working en remember me when it chimes."

On March 30th Edward called in the afternoon and found that his brother had died in the night. He paid Martha Button for the laying forth and for an affidavit to prove that he was buried in wool. On April 4th they buried him. Richard, Ann and Martha declined to attend the funeral. There were few there, mostly Edward's friends. They went to Kemp's afterwards and Edward bought them all beer.

Eliza hung on two more weeks. She kept asking where Thomas was. "There be no purpose fer me to live without un!" she cried. Mary May and Goodie Button stayed with her until the end. She was buried on 17th April.

By the end of April Edward had paid all debts for the caring of the old couple and outstanding rent. He could return to his home, content in the knowledge that he had done his best for his brother.

Epilogue

The clock rattled as Edward put it down on the clocksmith's counter. John Upton looked at Edward and said, "This be a clock me gaffer made years ago. I'd know one of 'is clocks anywheres. Best look inside en see what's ter be done. It don't sound good to me." He tried to open the little door at the back, but the catch and hinges had corroded. He worked on them with some oils and a cloth and tried the door again. It opened stiffly.

There was a clatter as the contents fell out onto the counter. Tom gave a little gasp.

John Upton looked at his customers in astonishement.

Edward and Tom couldn't see what it was from where they were standing. The clock was between them and the cause of the rattle, its face smiling at them benevolently. The hands stood at twelve o'clock, as they had for many years.

Beautiful chimes filled the room. The three stood still and listened. Edward felt weak at the knees. He was hearing a ghost. This could not be happening.

As the clock struck twelve, John came to his senses first.

"Well, there be naught amiss with the clock. A good clean wouldn't hurt. You be a deal better off than you thought, Mas Lucke. He scooped up the items which had spent so long hidden away and held his cupped hands out to his customers.

Edward and Tom stared at eight gold sovereigns, lying in a bed of moth-eaten pieces of hessian.

'The treasure,' breathed Edward.

The End

Historical Notes

The characters in this book were inspired by my Lucke ancestors from the 18th century, derived from my family history research. Some of the names have been changed for ease of identification. Slade Farm remains in Lamberhurst in the area called The Slade, but the Luckes would hardly recognise it now. Savages was a Lucke property for many years, but no longer exists. Pennybridge Farm has survived and is massively restored with extensive landscaping. Some of the interior is recognisable as the original Tudor house and the traditional timber and plaster exterior has been maintained.

I have, as far as possible, kept to the dates of baptisms, marriages and burials found in the archives, and have used original documents such as wills. Edward did keep an account book which was passed down the family. With the help of Christopher Whittick, archivist at the East Sussex Record Office, I spent many months transcribing it and have used Edward's entries as the skeleton of my story. Many of the supporting characters are mentioned in the account book and I have quoted some of the entries. Esland is briefly mentioned by Edward but I have built up an entirely fictitious character round his quaint name. The account book is now held at ESRO, Ref. Acc.8413.

Glossary

abide	live, put up with
abode, bidance	place to live
abouten	about to
abroad	away, outside
adone	leave off
afeared	fearful
afore	before
aggy	peevish, out of sorts
agin	against, near to
agreeable	would like to
ague	plague, high fever
ailing	unwell
all manner of things	all sorts
all-in	tired out
all of	as much as
all-on	all the time, incessantly
allow	admit, give an opinion
along of	together with
anon	at once
appleterre	apple orchard
applety	loft for storing apples
at two	quarrelsome
avised	to know for a certainty
badger	beggar
bait	refreshment on a journey, or in the harvest field
bannicking	beating
barrer	barrow
bat	stick
be	am, is
beant	am not, is not
be at	to do

beazled	tired out
be bound	be sure
befit	to be suitable
behopes	hopefully
betimes	by the time
bidance, abode	dwelling place
bide	live
bine	stem of hop plant which binds round the pole
bliv, b'lieve	believe
bluv	believed
bly	resemblance
bodging	going away, home
boffle	confusion, mistake
brave, bravely	in good health, well
breech	break through (animals through a hedge)
bre'ncheese friend	true friend
broody	ill tempered
brudder	brother
bunt	push, shove
buttery	place where beer barrels are stored
bythen	by the time that
call	cause, reason
call cousins	on intimate terms, usually used in the negative.
cantankerous	bad tempered
catch hot	take a fever
catched hurt	had an accident
check	taunt, tease
chipper	lively, cheerful
cledgy	sticky (Wadhurst clay)
close	farmyard, any walled enclosure

coager (pron. cojer)	lunch
come	when such time arrives
cord, cordwood	wood cut up for making charcoal
cordwainer	shoemaker
costrel	leather or wooden bottle
coulter	plough share
course	rough, as in weather
croft	pasture for horses
cushti	nice
dang	bother, damn
dappen	if it happens
darter	daughter
dearly	extremely
dick	ditch
didicais	true gypsies
doddle	walk infirmly
dracly-minute	immediately, at once
druv	drove, driven
dunnow long	don't know how long
dunnow the time when	don't know when
dunover	worn out
e'en amost	nearly
en	and
ernful	sad, lamentable
ett	eaten
eye proof	evident
fagging hook	blade used for hedge trimming
faggot	bundle of twigs to start a fire
fail	fall ill, catch a disease
fairing	getting on
fair to middling	not too bad

fall	autumn
fall	to fell (a tree)
fambly	family
Farder	Father
Fegs	exclamation
fet'n anon	fetch him quickly, at once
fitting	appropriate
footing it	walking
forelong	as soon as possible
fother	fodder
fower	four
frit	frightened
frock, round frock	loose over garment worn by country people
fust	first
Gaffer	Grandfather
Gantsey	lively, frolicksome horse
geewoot	call to the horse to get on
getting in years	becoming elderly
gimme	give me
git	go on/ away
Goodman	respectable member of the parish
Goody	widow
Gowd'rst	Goudhurst
Grammer	Grandmother
Gridiron	fire grate
groat	small coin of unknown value
gummut	lout, stupid fellow
gurt	great
happened along	called in when passing
harness	tools and equipment
have	lead or take
hem	very, a lot

hike	a mess
hoe	fuss, temper
hog-pound	pig stye
hop bin	sack into which the hops are collected
houghy	posh
House of Correction	local goal
housel	household belongings (when moving house)
hoving	sheep bursting with eating over-rich plants
husbandry	farming
ill-conditioned	ill-tempered
jack-up	give up, give in, retire
jackut	jacket
jigger me	a mild oath
just now	recently, at this present moment
justabout	certainly, extremely
justly	really, exactly, rightly
kine	cows
knowledgeable	well educated
Lamb'rst	Lamberhurst
lamentable	very
lapsy	lazy, slow, indifferent
larn	teach
larruping	beating
latchety	not working properly
lay up	hide away
liddle	little
litten	churchyard
like	adds to force of meaning

lope- off	go away in a secretive manner
Lunnon	London
maid	young girl
main	very
manner	manure
mardy	cross patch
marling	spreading marl as a manure
Mas	title of married master of the house
masterful	self-willed
maun	must not
Mayfild	Mayfield
mayhap	perhaps
me	my
Medston	Maidstone
midden	dung heap
middling	can mean anything from all right to very bad
mind, minded	remember, have a mind or intend to
Mistus	Mrs, mistress, wife
moil	trouble
moithered	bothered, perplexed
mortacious	very, mortally
mortal	very, mortally
mucked-up	in confusion
mun	must
Mus	title of master of a workforce
Muvver	Mother
muvver	take care of
nabble	gossip
nabble traps	gossips
nay	no

nexty	the day after tomorrow
nigh	near to
nipper	youngest in the family
no'but	nothing but
non-plush	completely bewildered
no-ways	in no way
now-en-again	sometimes
ockard	awkward
on account of	because, the reason being
ornary	unwell
orright	all right
otherwheres	somewhere else
otherwhiles	sometimes, occasionally
outstand	stand up to, get the better of
partial to	like very much
ped	willow box or crate for taking live chickens to market
personable	comely
pet	a stack of wood covered with turf to make a clamp for charcoal burning
pesky	troublesome
poached	trodden by cattle
poke	long sack
powdering tub	for salting meat
praper	proper, unusually good
prensley	presently, now
purty	pretty
put in	bury
Quality	gentlefolk and nobility
quern	small hand mill
quick with child	pregnant

rackon reckon,	suspect, count
Ratherfild	Rotherfield
rigging	clothes
ringle	wed/ put a ring in a hog's or bull's nose
ripier	men carrying fish in baskets from the coast to towns
robbut	rabbit
rod	straight stems cut from a hazel stool
sarten sure	certainly
scratch along	pull through hard times
seed	saw
sen	since
sheet	a one-year-old pig
shoot	a piglet
shruck	shocked
sidy	surly, moody
skillon	shed or outhouse
skits	plenty, a great many
skrow	ill-tempered, surly
somewhen	at some time
spry	vivacious
standing	market stall
stan' fast	hold on, to riders on the waggon before moving off
start /start-up	a fuss, excitement
steddle	temporary table made with trestles
stocky	strong, well-grown
stotter	stagger
summat	something
swish	smart
Teec'rst	Ticehurst

terrify	tease, taunt
to be at	attend to
toddy	warmed up ale
turmuts	turnips
twit	taunt, tease
un	him, her or it
unaccountable	unusual, unexplainable (used often)
upstanding	upright, honourable
varmint	vermin, rascal
vittels	food
Wad'rst	Wadhurst
whapple way	a bridle way through fields or woods
windrows	line of grass left by the mowers, to let it dry
worritted	worried
wunnerful	wonderful
wunt be druv	typical Sussex characteristic, obstinate
yer	your
yet	still
yourn	yours
yoystering	playing around roughly
yus	yes

Reversals of she/her and we/us are common

Acknowledgements

First of all I have to thank my fellow writers and my tutor Chris Sparkes for their support and encouragement. The book would not have been such fun to write without them. Secondly, my granddaughter Bryony Pillath who read the draft and gave a detailed critique. I am so grateful for her excellent constructive comments which helped me edit the manuscript drastically. I must no forget the encouragement my family and friends have given me, especially my daughter, Sarah Jane Toleman who designed the cover of the final book. The picture of the house is of one of the cottages at the Weald and Downland Living Museum in Singleton, West Sussex. I am grateful for their permission to use it.

My researches have led me to many places on the internet and a number of books as follows;

A dictionary of the Sussex Dialect by the Rev. W.D.Parish 1875, augmented and expanded by Helena Hall 1957.

Wadhurst, a town of the High Weald by Alan Savage and Oliver Mason

The Diary of Thomas Turner 1754-1765. Edited by David Vaisey

English Costume by Dion Clayton Calthrop. 1907

Among many others.